I0650832

Tales of Hardooth 3

THE LIES WE TELL
TO SURVIVE

Dara J. Carr

Tales of Hardooth 3

THE LIES WE TELL TO SURVIVE

Dara J. Carr

Harrison House Publishing

Tales of Hardooth 3: The Lies We Tell To Survive
All Rights Reserved
Copyright © 2016 Dara J. Carr
Edited by Betty Powell and Linda S. Carr
Artwork by Eric A. Carr

Harrison House Publishing
www.theharrisonhousepublishing.com
info@theharrisonhousepublising.com
ISBN: 978-0-9974935-4-2
Library of Congress Control Number: 2016962993
Harrison House Publishing and the "HH" logo are trademarks belonging to Harrison House Publishing.

PRINTED IN THE UNITED STATES OF AMERICA

TXu 1-919-970

OTHER BOOKS BY

DARA J. CARR

The Semi-Dragon Tale

Revenge Cometh Forth

Here Are My Shorts (a collection of short stories)

Volunteer…Spy?

The Original Owlam

What New Things We Can Learn?

THE LIES WE TELL TO SURVIVE

1

Shortly before the fourteenth year of the tenure of Supreme Officer, Nakalak, disaster struck. The different peoples of the continent were starting to get a little complacent about the Algothon, because they no longer seemed to be a threat. Twenty-two years since the firestorm attacks and not a hint of another attack since (mainly because the Owlamites kept fouling up all of the guidance and launch systems). The Algothon were content to destroy and/or enslave everyone on their continent of Neopaure until they fixed all of the problems that were plaguing them. All of the news from overseas said that they were having a difficult time controlling their own continent, what kind of a nightmare would it be, attempting to control everyone on a second…or third continent?

Nakalak was sitting in the conference room with *most* of the Staff. Holla and Wilfadge were late because of something personal that they wanted to take care of. Since their Vice Commanders were already in attendance, Nakalak decided to go on with the meeting and those two could be briefed later.

Two of Nakalak's Aides, Nayna and Akantini were trying to get some work done, however, there was too much noise and distraction going on as some much needed repairs to the Command building were being accomplished. The two hopped into Observation dimension (with their computers) in order to get some peace and quiet. They both smiled at each other regarding this clever thought and started working on the task that had been put in front of them.

Suddenly the two women were surrounded by flames. They both sat there frozen in shock, with their hands poised over the keyboards on their computers. The flames burned brightly for several moments and then quickly died out and they saw the building collapsing around them. Then it turned mostly dark. They sat there staring at each other (what they could see of each other) in fear for a few moments more.

Akantini tried to speak, however nothing but a strange gargling noise came out. She cleared her throat three times before she could finally speak. "What...should we do?"

Nayna shook her head. "I...don't know. I...hope that that wasn't another firestorm...attack."

"What...happened to the people...inside?"

Nayna gritted her teeth. "Have you tried to contact anyone?"

"Uh...no."

"Before you ask me what happened to them, why don't you try to contact them?"

Akantini closed her eyes and concentrated for several moments. She opened her eyes and looked at Nayna terrified. "I...can't find Nakalak or Teetya."

Nayna clenched her jaws even tighter. "Neither can I." She closed her eyes and did some concentration of her own. She opened her eyes. "Let's Jump outside...to the parking lot."

Akantini cleared her throat loudly, trying to keep from crying. "Okay I'll...uh...all right."

The two of them did the Jump. They saw both Holla and Wilfadge standing in the parking lot staring in horror at the destroyed conference building. Nayna slowly walked over to the two remaining Staff members.

"Excuse me, Sirs," said Nayna. "I don't think that anyone who was in there...survived. If...Supreme Officer, Nakalak is dead...who...is the new *Voice of Power*?"

Holla and Wilfadge looked at each other. Wilfadge dropped to his knees, went to all fours and started kissing the ground.

Holla looked at Nayna and sighed. "I guess I am." She looked back down at Wilfadge. "You can stop."

Wilfadge got up looking rather embarrassed. He cleared his throat a few times as he dusted his pants off and tried to look as if nothing had happened. He turned his head to the side and spat a small pebble out of his mouth. "So, you're the new *Voice*. Where're you going to establish your new headquarters?" He turned his head and spat out another pebble.

At that moment they heard another explosion off to their

left. Holla clenched her eyes shut and started sending out a mental command. "This is the new Supreme Officer, Holla. Nakalak has been killed in a new attack...from source...unknown. At this time, all Owlamites, who are in the home city, hop to Spy dimension and take your houses and any vehicles that you're responsible for with you. If you're out spying on some other city, such as Algothon...come back and protect your home – from any more bombings. Spy Team Algothon...I want to know...did this attack originate from Algothon?"

A response came back almost immediately: "This is Officer Leader, Nachichi. I'm the one in command of Team Algothon. I don't know where the attack came from. I can assure you that absolutely nothing was launched from the city of Algothon. For once, these *chokwads* are innocent."

Holla opened her eyes. She turned to what was left of Nakalak's Team. "Officers, Nayna and Akantini, we're going to need your help. It appears that there have been some fatalities...to your Team...and mine. I've received a mental message from my Team that Officer, Yoyana...was killed by...one of those blasts."

Wilfadge interrupted with his teeth clenched: "I just received word that Officer, Noyabi, one of my Team members, was killed as well."

Holla closed her eyes and shook her head trying to think. "Officer, Nayna, do you think that...anyone could have survived... inside there." She pointed at the wrecked building.

Nayna scoffed. "LOOK AT THAT PLACE...Sir! It's a mess. No one could have possibly survived inside there. Have you been doing any mental calls…to other members of the Staff?" She wiped tears off her cheeks.

Holla nodded. "Yes, I have. I haven't received any response - other than Officer, Wilfadge."

"Same here," said Wilfadge.

Holla looked up, fighting back tears. "All right, so all three of our Teams have been hurt. From this day forth, Officer Nayna, you are a member of my Team. Officer, Akantini, you are now a member of Officer, Wilfadge's Team…any questions?" She looked at Nayna, Akantini and Wilfadge. They all stared back solemnly. "Okay, that's settled. Now, I know that there was a safe inside that had a list of who the next *Voice of Power* is supposed to be in order of birth and a listing of all the people in the chain of command. Is there any way that any of that information survived…so we can reestablish our High Command…and all that?"

Nayna sniffed. "Neenatha had all of that hidden in that safe. Nakalak thought that that was ridiculous. He had it put in the mainframes of all of the computers of the High Command Staff. If any of the offices of any of the Staff are still in one piece, then they have that information on their computer. We should be able to access it from any of the computers…and get…some form of…normalcy back."

"We'll never get normalcy back, but we can get some order," muttered Wilfadge angrily.

Much to their chagrin, they found out that every single one of the offices of the Staff had been hit. Everything was in shambles. Now they found themselves in a bit of a dilemma -

until they found out that it was still in the computers of the former Supreme Officers Team 5. Amakili, Yantoy and Meemiy still had it in their computers, so they were able to obtain the lists and establish a new High Command Staff. They then entered the birth order information into all Owlam computers.

Holla was now the Supreme Officer of the Owlam forces. The only thing that did not change was Master Officer, Wilfadge who was still the Commander of the Southern Forces.

The newly promoted Master Officer, Ahandi, of Team 20, was now the new Northern Commander with, newly promoted, Senior Officer, Dwalooa as the Northern Vice Commander. Newly promoted Master Officer, Teelila was now the Eastern Commander, with, newly promoted, Senior Officer, Hadathoo was the Eastern Vice Commander. The newly promoted Senior Officer, Hoynama, was the Southern Vice Commander. The newly promoted Master Officer, Chaza became the Western Commander, with the newly promoted Senior Officer, Shyshee was the Western Vice Commander.

Holla gave a new order: All personnel were to, permanently, have a list of the Owlamites and the order in which they could become the *Voice of Power*. This way no one would have to guess where the information was and they would be able to establish an uninterrupted chain of command, no matter how badly they were hurt in any attack.

Once again the Owlam found themselves in a quandary, wondering where this new attack had come from. They also found out, from all of their allies, that all of them had been attacked as well. Seeing as how no one had any form of radar that looked to the sky, no one knew where this attack had come from.

The one strange thing about the allies being attacked was that while several of the bombs hit near the Turgon Wall, none of them actually hit the wall. Numerous T'Mor were killed in the attack, however, no one on or in the wall was hurt. The wall was still intact as far as keeping the Turgons isolated to the peninsula. Whoever was responsible for the attack did not want to hurt the Turgon Wall or the purpose for its existence.

The Owlam spies in Algothon turned out to be the ones who came up with the answer. The Algothon did have a network of radar that looked to the sky, the main purpose of which was to follow their intercontinental missiles. They had seen these foreign missiles coming in (too late to stop them) and from the trajectory of their flight, the Algothon were able to determine that the missiles had come from a city on the continent of South Chilamte - the city of Neksheth-Or was the closest city to their estimated site of origin. Missile silos spotted in the city confirmed the origin of the attack.

The primary difference between what the Algothon launched and what the Neksheth-Or launched - conventional weapons. There were no nuclear bombs in the warheads of the Neksheth-Or missiles. There were high explosives and incendiaries, which did do a lot of damage, however, nothing compared to the mass devastation (and genetic manipulation) accomplished by Algothon.

Holla sat in her office, brooding over the information about these Neksheth-Or people. There was information coming in from Owlamites spying on Algothon that gave location, however, no one, still alive, in Owlam was that familiar with the South Chilamte continent. While they had done some initial exploring, once they found out about Spy and Jump dimensions, most of the attention had been placed on any city that they knew was hostile. This hostility from Neksheth-Or had come twenty-two years after the firestorm attack, so those people had never been looked at closely…until now.

Holla gave an order for there to be some personnel sent to the city of Neksheth-Or immediately. She wanted any and all information on them that could possibly be gathered. The problem, again, was that no one (who was still alive) in Owlam was precisely sure where Neksheth-Or was - or how to properly arrive there through Jump.

In Algothon, Officer Grade 6, Kronom, of Team 5333 watched one of the Algothon technicians as the man was doing what he could to determine the location of the silos from which the new flying bombs had been launched. The Algothon had been hit as well and they were a little upset over this fact, especially since they had not been able to launch any of their weapons again, due to all kinds of problems that appeared to be from sabotage. They were having a terrible time trying to figure out who was sabotaging, and it was driving them crazy. Now that they had been attacked, they were now looking, very suspiciously, at Neksheth-Or as the originators of the sabotage problems.

Kronom had been watching the Algothon technician and had finally figured out what was being done. He needed the technician to get out of the way, in order to facilitate the Owlamites getting to Neksheth-Or, for a full investigation of what needed to be done. Kronom sighed, picked up a pair of scissors and gave the Algothon citizen a reason to leave. The Algothon technician had a sudden *stabbing* pain in his right side. He fell out of his chair and crawled to an intercom in order to call for medical help.

Kronom now took the seat and telepathically called to Holla. "Sir, this is Officer Grade 6, Kronom. I'm sitting at an Algothon monitor and I can help lead···someone···to this city of Neksheth-Or. Who do I need to contact?"

Holla sent back: "Officer Leader, Natsa, of Team 82 used to be the Commander of the Team that was spying on Galsino. Contact her and see if you can get her steered in the right direction."

Kronom nodded. "Thank you, Sir. I'll contact her immediately. This is Officer Grade 6, Kronom, calling Officer Leader, Natsa. Can you hear me? I'm here at Algothon and I'm going to use their system to lead you directly to Neksheth-Or."

"This is Officer Leader, Natsa. I hear you. How're you going to get me there?"

"First of all, I need to know exactly where you are."

Natsa sighed. "I am at···probably the most northern point of the South Chilamte continent."

Kronom made a few adjustments on the computer. "Okay, I've found that area. Is there some sort of place there that really stands out as identifiable and it couldn't be mistaken for anywhere else?"

Natsa scoffed and looked around. "Just a moment." She did a quick Jump to a nearby location. "Okay, I'm still at the most northern part of the continent. I'm standing on the edge of a very large cliff."

Kronom growled to himself. "That doesn't help at all. That entire area is a high cliff. There's no way to get on land from there, except a few large beaches that are all at the base of high cliffs."

Natsa sighed. "This spot, in particular has a cut in the cliff. There's a long arm of the sea going into the land. It appears, from where I'm standing, that this cut goes···oh at least nine or ten kilotaja, before it ends··· rather abruptly."

Kronom made a few more adjustments on the monitor. "Okay, I think I've found your cut. I can't see you though. Are you in Spy dimension?"

Natsa scoffed. "Of course I'm in Spy dimension – where else would I be?"

"I don't see anyone else in the area, so why don't you hop to Home dimension?"

Natsa scoffed again. "Okay, I've hopped to Home···now what?" She was getting a little upset over what was going on.

Kronom smiled. "I see you now. Let me expand this thing a little and see where I can get you."

Natsa's jaw dropped. "How could you possibly see

me? I'm here on one continent, you're on another. How the *chokwad* could you see me at all?"

Kronom cleared his throat nervously. "I···uh···don't know. All I know is, I'm looking down at you···from way up."

Natsa looked up at the sky. She saw absolutely nothing but sky. "I don't see a thing. So, again, how could you possibly see me?"

Kronom shook his head. "I don't know, except that I can see you. I can see that you're looking up right now."

Natsa was feeling very vulnerable and a rather concerned. She cleared her throat nervously. "Okay···so you···can see me from···way above. This conversation is sounding weird. So···what kind of instructions can you give me···in order to get me···to that *chogo* city···of Neksheth−Or?"

"First of all, Jump to the very southern tip of that cut in the cliff."

She shook her head. She took a deep breath, took a good look at the area he had pointed out. She made the Jump. "Okay, I'm here."

"I know, I can see you."

She looked up again, feeling even more exposed and irritated. 'What kind of technology could there possibly be that could allow him to see exactly where she was?' "Okay, what next?"

He sighed. "I don't know if you can see it – probably

not – but there's a huge gorge, about thirty kilotaja, probably more, from your location. The thing is due south of you."

She shook her head. "All that I can see, due south is a large forest of dead trees. I can see a walled city in the distance. That city is southwest of me."

"That's a good spot. Get to the city and get up on their wall. You might be able to see the gorge from up there."

Natsa Jumped to the top of the wall. She gasped and grimaced as she realized that she was not alone. She quickly hopped to Spy and looked around at all of the people that were on top of the wall. "I'm not alone here. There's a bunch of Heyyah up here." She looked as a little girl came walking over to where she was standing. The girl had seen her and was not sure what to make of it. The little girl looked around rather confused. After seeing that no one was there, the girl went back to her parents shaking her head. Natsa sighed in relief.

"Can you avoid them?"

"Yes, in Spy dimension."

"Good. So look to···the southeast now and···"

"Hold it, they have a very tall lookout tower here on the wall. I'm going to Jump up there and take a look. I should be able to see for quite a ways up there."

"I can't see any tower."

"If you're looking at it from directly above, it's a

little difficult to see it. I'm looking at it from the side and it's huge." She did the Jump. "Wow! This is great. It gives you a real sight to look at. I can see that gorge that you were talking about." She scoffed. "Thirty kilotaja, my foot! It's at least forty–five from where I'm at now."

"If you can see that far, can you see a bridge that goes across the gorge?"

Natsa strained her eyes looking. "No, I can't see any bridge. There does seem to be a little mist way off in the distance. I don't know what it's covering···or hiding."

"I found the mist. It's about two kilotaja north of the bridge. Look for a good place to Jump to, on either side of the gorge. We'll follow the gorge for a good five hundred kilotaja and that'll get us quite a ways closer to the target city."

Natsa sighed. "Okay, here we go." She saw a tree that was just on this side of the mist. She Jumped to a spot next to the tree, looked around, saw no one so she hopped back to Home. She looked up. "I'm standing near a dead tree···on the west side of the gorge. Can you see me here?"

"Yes, I found you. Look south. Can you see through that mist at ground level?"

She turned south. "Yes I can. I can see···I guess it's a bridge."

"What do you mean···guess?"

"Hold on a moment, I'll Jump over to it." She did the Jump and was shocked at what she saw. "This, and I use the word jokingly, bridge! It's a mess. I wouldn't even want to try to cross it. It's in such a state of disrepair. It's a total mess. I'm surprised that it's still standing."

"Fortunately it's not the destination. It's just a vantage point. There's another bridge about twenty-five kilotaja south of you. Can you see that one?"

She sighed. "Yes, I see it. It looks like someone is there. I'm going back to Spy." She made the hop and then a Jump to the next bridge. "Would you believe that there's a bunch of Heyyah here? They're charging a toll for people to go across?"

"This bridge must be in much better shape."

"It is. Is there another bridge, further south?"

"According to what I'm seeing here, not for at least another one hundred kilotaja. Use some trees or boulders···or some other piece of landscape."

She made four Jumps before she was able to see the next bridge. "Looks like another bunch making a fortune charging tolls for crossing the bridge."

"Why don't you go ahead and get on the east side of the gorge? Pretty soon you'll be leaving the gorge and using some rather rugged landscape as landmarks to get you most of the way out of this area."

He directed her for several more Jumps before she arrived at a lower elevation of land. "How much further?"

"Why, are you getting tired?"

"No, I'm just getting a little impatient. And I'm still confused as to how you can see me."

He sighed and took a look at the monitor. "It's about⋯ oh maybe four or five more Jumps. Can you see a large plume of smoke off in the distance?"

"Yes, I can. What is it?"

"Someone who lives close by the Neksheth−Or and seems to have irritated them. It's not even a walled city, it's just a farming community."

"Conquerors don't care who they kill. They just attack and ask questions later." She made a Jump that brought her much closer to the burning village. "Uh⋯is there anyone left alive?"

"Can't tell from my vantage point. All I can see is smoke."

"There's not much else to see."

"Okay, look to the southeast. Can you see the walls of Neksheth−Or yet?"

"No."

"Pick an object somewhere southeast of you and Jump there. Then look for the walls⋯to the southeast."

She made two more Jumps southeast before she finally saw the walls of the city in the distance. "Finally! I'm getting a little more tired than I thought I was. I may have to rest before I do anything else."

"That's all right. At least you're there and we can get someone else there, soon."

"No! It's not all right! I'm going to get this done now. Once I have someone else here, then I can rest." She made two more Jumps before she was at the wall. It really did not look much different than any of the other city walls that she had seen. She stood there a few moments breathing deep, trying to gather some more strength. She looked up to the top of the wall. 'About fifteen floors high,' she thought. She shook her head. 'What's new?' She did one more Jump to the top of the wall. "I'm here! I'll get some bearings and a good place for us to Jump to. Then I'll be back at the big parking lot to pick some people up and bring them back here."

"What do these *Doovofts* look like?"

"Would you believe that they look like another bunch···with an exoskeleton? Their skin is···well it looks metallic and···the color···the closest thing I can think of···is bronze. They're about···oh say a little more than seven taja in height. They look mean and nasty too."

"Can you see their eyes?"

"Can't you? They don't have eyes like the Sodle, if that's what you mean. They have dark little beady eyes. They just look···mean."

"Have you chosen a landmark yet?"

"Yes."

"Who do you want standing at the ready in the big parking lot?"

She moved to a staircase and sat down to rest. "I guess I'll start with my Team. There's Officer Grade 3, Osskood, Officer Grade 6, Siy and Officer Grade 6, Eesteesee."

"Do you want me to call them?"

"No, I'll contact them when I'm ready. What I'd really like to know something about, and I think that Supreme Officer, Holla would want to know about it as well — how were you tracking me?"

"That's an extremely good question. I'm going to have to study this a little further and see just exactly how the Algothons got some crazy camera way up there in the sky that we can't see···but it can see us···or anything else on the planet."

He did a few manipulations with the computer, zooming in and out. The long distance pictures were incredible. He pulled back with the camera and was amazed that he could see almost the entire continent on the monitor. He telepathically called the rest of his Team to this room so that they could all try to figure out what was going on with this crazy camera.

The rest of Team 5333 showed up. Officer Grade 4, Siski, Officer Grade 6, Eehoy and Officer Grade 7, Binda. They watched him as he did a few more of the zooming in and out with the computer. They all got on a keyboard, in the room, and started studying this new phenomenon.

They were not getting very much as far as satisfaction so they called in one of the specialty computer Teams. Team 254 showed up and they all started working on finding out what they could in regards to this new Algothon toy they had just found and had not investigated before.

Natsa had finished studying the area. She had a decent landmark memorized that she could Jump back to. She Jumped to the big parking lot. She saw the devastation that had been done to the Headquarters building. She turned away from the horrid site and sniffled a little. Standing in front of her was her Team. She took a deep breath and let it out. "Osskood, Siy, are you ready?" They both nodded. She took hold of their hands. "First we go to Spy." As soon as all three were in Spy, she Jumped them back to Neksheth-Or. "Okay, you two…get your bearings. I'm going to have to get some rest. I've done a lot of hopping and Jumping today and I'm exhausted."

Osskood nodded. "No problem, Sir. We'll take care of the rest of the people."

Siy looked around at the city of Neksheth-Or. She turned back to Natsa. "I don't know if you were told or not, but, we have Teams 110, 254, 330 and 5333 to assist us in finding out what's going on here and sabotaging the place."

Natsa nodded. "Five Teams to start fooling with the enemy, most of whom are at Algothon right now." She shook her head. "I hope that this foolishness doesn't persist. I'm getting tired of war and killing." She looked around. "Wasn't there someone who mapped out this area…and could have come directly here?"

Siy shook her head. "From what I understand…in the roll call…the Team that had this place mapped in their heads…all killed in the attack…by these people. It's a rather scary coincidence."

Osskood shook his head. "If I remember correctly, Jahong

and Nakalak felt the same way about war and killing. They were both getting very tired of it all."

"They did," said Natsa. She sighed. "Go ahead and let's get this…battle started. The sooner we get it started, the sooner we can get it over and done with and go home." She sat down on a bench that was on top of the Neksheth-Or wall.

Osskood and Siy looked around a little longer. They picked their landmarks and Jumped back to Owlam to pick up the next group of Owlamite saboteurs that would be causing no end of grief to the people of Neksheth-Or.

Holla and Wilfadge were sitting in Holla's new Supreme Officer's location. They were both reading about this toy that the Algothon had come up with. A camera that was somewhere up there in the sky and could look down on any place, anywhere at any time on the entire planet and no one could see it. It could zoom in and out. It could go out and see almost half of the entire planet. It could zoom in and see a single object. They were both fascinated and frightened by this thing.

Wilfadge got a little bored reading because they knew something existed that was doing this, however, no Owlamite was able to figure out how it was being done. He looked up at Holla. "How old are you?"

Holla looked at him somewhat surprised. "Where did that come from?"

He sighed. "I was just thinking." He shook his head.

"That firestorm hit. Six days later, I turned sixty-one years old. Now, I'm eighty-three. When I look in a mirror, I don't look a day over thirty. Neither do you. Since you have that *Power* and I don't, you're the elder. I was just curious, how much older you are."

Holla snorted. "Of all the things to think about at a time like this." She sighed. "I turned sixty-one years old three days before the firestorm hit. So...nine days. Does that help or change anything?"

"No, it just helps me accept a few things. We can't procreate - possibly because we don't need to. I talked to Doctor Shurmook a while back and I found out that no Owlamite has suffered from any disease since the firestorm attack. We've had many who've died from battle and we've had several who have suffered some broken bones. We've not had anyone die from old age problems or disease. No one is suffering from any form of old age problems, even though the youngest of us, since all children were killed in the firestorm, is at least forty-one years old."

"You say that we don't need replacements? I think we might. We haven't been able to replace any of the people that were killed in any of the battles. That'd mean that we do need replacements, from battle fatalities, in the form of children." She looked off to the side sadly. "We just haven't figured out how to have children, seeing as how no one has had the desire or capability of having sex. All of the men are impotent and all of the women are sterile. How're we supposed to reproduce...with no abilities of that kind?"

Wilfadge sniffed. "Then let's try to concentrate on surviving, in spite of people like the Beetsik and Sodle and this new bunch in Neksheth-Or. Do we have any full count on the dead yet?"

Holla looked up sadly. "The count is, forty-three men dead. One hundred fifteen women dead. According to Doctor Shurmook, of the broken bones or shrapnel damage - none of them are life threatening, so they're not really counted among the casualties. One hundred fifty-eight are dead. That leaves 6,756 men and 20,277 women. Two hundred forty Teams have been completely wiped out, including all of those back to Nagasoom's folly. Forty Teams are shorthanded." She hung her head. "I didn't want this job. But it looks like I don't have a choice."

"So let's quit feeling sorry for ourselves and try to do something about it. I think that crazy new technology that our people discovered in Algothon, maybe we can put it to good use, against both Neksheth-Or and Algothon. We just need to figure out a way to use it to our advantage and smack both of them down hard."

"Let's wait for some reports from both Neksheth-Or and Algothon before we start smacking anything or anybody down."

The missiles that they found in Neksheth-Or were not as sophisticated as the ones in Algothon. They were, however, still a highly technological system and as a result, the Owlam spies had very little trouble in sabotaging numerous systems in each missile, thus making them incapable of flight or being programmed to fly a certain route and bomb a specific target. Now the people of Neksheth-Or were having the same unexplained problems with their systems, that they had never experienced before or even dreamed about. The Owlamites, on the other hand, were having lots of fun screwing things up and inventing new ways to screw things up.

One new thing that the Owlam spies in Neksheth-Or found out was that these conventional weapon warheads did not need to be timed or follow any pattern in order to detonate. The Algothon warheads required specific timing in order to reach critical mass (whatever that is). The Neksheth-Or warheads simply required a hard jolt (such as a hard impact into the ground) to detonate. Now all the Owlam spies had to figure out was how to give the warheads a jolt and not be in the same area at the time. It was found that the easiest way to do it, was to be in Observation dimension with a rock. Drop the rock into Home dimension directly on top of the warhead. You may have to drop several rocks in order to get the proper jolt, however, eventually they were getting all the positive results that they needed and there were numerous members of the Neksheth-Or race that were blown to pieces trying to figure out why their warheads were detonating before any launch took place.

The Algothon were using their spy satellites to watch the fiasco in Neksheth-Or. They had been originally planning on launching another nuclear bomb at Neksheth-Or until they saw that those people seemed to be doing some sort of accidental cataclysmic self-destruction. They decided to hold off any launch, until either the accidents stopped or they could figure out why none of their systems were working either.

While Holla and the rest of the new Staff were pleased with the results of the sabotage going on against Algothon and Neksheth-Or, they were all getting a little disturbed at how their resources were getting spread somewhat thin on different continents and they still did not seem any closer to any kind of permanent peace anywhere in the world because some ambitious bunch of monsters were constantly deciding to try and conquer everybody else.

2

Back in Algothon, one of the Owlam spies, Officer Grade 7, Onggot, of Team 256, was sitting in one of the most secure offices in Algothon. He had been assigned here to see if he could pick up any useful information from these security types. Most of the spying that had been done was on the weapons systems. This office had been ignored for the most part because they did not deal with the weapons. They dealt with security for the weapons, however, they did nothing in the daily upkeeps. Only *very special* people were allowed beyond this massive iron door. Most of what they did was check up on their own people, seeing if anybody had become a traitor. So far he had heard nothing about Owlam - until now.

He had been wandering beyond the iron door in the hallway where there were three doors to the left, three to the right and one that was straight ahead. He checked each one and found that most of the people in these offices were busy looking at computer monitors that covered many things. In one room they were monitoring their own city. The next room, they were monitoring different areas of their continent. One was an overall command center. Another office was where the great exalted high muckity-muck had his office and made his decisions.

The third door on the right was more like a conference room than an office. There was a bit of a conference that was about to be started between six people. They had different uniforms than the military. These were some kind of special police that kept eyes on everything. These police were feared wherever they went. They seemed to have some kind of purpose and power. Whenever or where ever they showed up, just about everyone in those areas would stop talking and look at them with fear, trepidation and horror. Onggot stood off to the side waiting for the conference to begin, hoping that he was in the correct room in regards to Owlam.

A seventh Algothon man came into the room. The other six stopped conversing with each other and looked up at him, some with disdain, some with curiosity. The seventh man walked up to a podium and plugged something into it. A large monitor behind the podium activated and started warming up.

"Thank you for coming. I am Investigator, Shon Toivok. I've found something that goes beyond strange. I'm sure that all of you have been rather curious about this city called Owlam. Our spy satellites have been passing over the city for some time and have picked up some rather unusual things. Seventeen months ago, because of some of these strange phenomenon, we parked a satellite, in a fixed orbit, in order to keep the city of Owlam under constant surveillance. We've seen many very strange things going on there and it should not and cannot be ignored any longer."

One of the men scoffed. "Ever since we launched that mass attack, we've seen several very strange things going on in each and every city we hit…at least the ones that had survivors, of course. Why should we listen to you and pay so much attention to just one insignificant city?"

"Because, Sir, we've seen some things that are manifestations of some kind of technology that…so far, it has baffled everyone who has looked at it. We need to keep more than just one satellite on them. We need to keep a full team watching their every move and try to…"

Another man stood up. "Stop talking about the satellites and get to the point about these…Owlams. You said strange - what's strange?" He sat back down scoffing. "It certainly isn't the satellites that are strange!"

Shon cleared his throat nervously. "Yes, Sir, of course. These people have shown…some kind of…teleportation technology. They can move people, vehicles…and in a few cases…it seems…an entire building. We've also seen that they have some kind of…device for…rendering themselves…totally invisible."

Two of the men seated started laughing.

A third man scoffed at Shon. "What you're talking about borders on some kind of tale that you use to scare naughty children into obedience. How and why should we believe this nonsense?"

Shon looked a little aggravated. "SIR! I can show you some recorded examples. Unfortunately, they're incomplete because the satellite was passing overhead at the time and only got a portion of the sequence of events. Since we established that one directly over Owlam, some of the sequences are complete… and *very* puzzling."

The third man chuckled and leaned back in his chair. "Oh by all means, entertain us."

Shon hit a few buttons on a keyboard. "This first one, Sirs, is from several years back." He looked up at the monitor, where it was showing several different new icons. He picked one and hit the switch to open. "This one is sadly incomplete, because of the moving satellite, however, it does raise some very bewildering… or intriguing questions."

The monitor was now showing the gorge that was just northwest of Owlam. No Owlamites could be seen, however, there were thousands of Axswain soldiers making their way along the north face, inside the gorge.

Onggot nearly lost his lunch. "Officer, Toytay, Officer, Toytay, this is Onggot. I need you⋯and probably several others in this Algothon high security conference room⋯ immediately!"

Officer Grade 3, Toytay was startled as she was trying to eat some lunch. She looked around and at first was trying to finish chewing her food before responding. Then she realized that it was a mental communication and she did not need to worry about what her jaws were doing. "This is Toytay⋯who is this again⋯ and what's so flaming important?"

"Sir, this is Officer, Onggot. I'm in a conference room in that high security area."

Toytay nearly spat her food out. "What's so important in there? We're supposed to be trying to find a way to permanently sabotage their firestorm weapons. Not listen to a bunch of high security *h'oolyach* bellyaching about precautions."

"Sir, the precautions that they're bellyaching about are US! They're talking about us and our home city. They have films. A film of that final battle with the Axswain! A film that was taken from directly above with one of their high flying hidden cameras."

Toytay sat there for a moment in shock. 'Why should these people have something like that?' She shook her head. "Which conference room, in which hallway?"

"I'm in that special hall, fourth floor, room 79. It's the third door on the right! You need to see this! I'm just not sure that you'd believe me unless you see it for yourself."

Toytay finally swallowed what food was still in her mouth. "Team 256, this is Toytay. Get to that special hall, that fourth floor room number 79, now!" She Jumped to the hall just outside of that special door. She waited until the other two members showed up.

Officer Grade 6, Wasee Jumped into the hallway. She walked up to Toytay. "What's the emergency, Sir?"

Toytay shook her head. "Let's wait until…"

At that moment, Officer Grade 5, Ini Jumped into the hall. "Here, Sir, what's going on?"

Toytay looked at the other two women on her Team. "Follow me." Since they were all in Spy dimension, the iron door was no barrier at all. She led them to the third door on the right and they walked through that door.

It was a lot darker in this room and they had to stop and let their eyes adjust to the difference.

"Over here," said Onggot. "This is a pretty good vantage point."

Toytay scoffed. "I prefer the middle of the conference table. We're not going to block anyone and we get a pretty good look at what's going on."

Onggot sighed. "Yes, Sir." He joined the three women.

Ini shook her head. "What's that…on the screen?"

Onggot took a deep breath. "THAT is the final battle that the Owlam had with the Axswain."

The jaws of all three women dropped.

Shon started orating again. "Now, this is not the unusual part. The Axswain were attempting some…offensive against Owlam and they were trying to sneak up on the enemy…going through this gorge. If you'll look at the other side of the gorge… uh…in just a moment…it will…"

At that time, a row of the big 161 Assault vehicles appeared on the south side and started blasting the helpless Axswain on the north face. Everyone in the room watched silently as the massacre unfolded. The satellite was moving, so they could not focus on any one spot. The battle raged on for several moments until the satellites spy camera was no longer looking at the battle area.

The third man spoke up again. "So the Owlams demolished

the surprise attack by Axswain. SO? You act as if there's never been a surprise counterattack to a surprise attack."

Shon scoffed. "NOT the point, Sir. The point is: Where did those trucks, with the power weapons, come from? One moment there's nothing - the next - an entire row of them." He started hitting the keyboard again. "Let me show you again." He looked up at the monitor and watched as the film was being played backwards. He took it back before the appearance of the trucks. "Now, if you'll watch, and I'll play it in slow motion, we see no trucks...we see no anomalies...we see no distortions of any type. We see nothing that indicates that there's anything there at all. We can't even see the tire tracks of all of those trucks driving up to the positions where they were parked...nothing!" He slowed it down to one frame at a time and did a magnification on the south side of the gorge. "Again, I see no tire tracks in the dirt. I see nothing indicating that there is anything there at all." A 161 appeared on the screen. "As you can see, one frame the truck is not there, the next frame, it is. This...invisibility device does not take very long to...go on or off. There's no waiting time...it just...does its job of rendering the item invisible - *immediately*, or visible - *immediately*! No waiting time, no warm up...just there...or not."

The second man snarled. "This tells us something...but it's an incomplete picture. We need more information...of some kind."

"We do," said Shon. "Uh...have some more information."

The third man sighed. "Okay, you've punched my curiosity button. What other pertinent information have you got to share with us?"

Shon smiled. "Thank you, Sir. This next one…took place at a time…uh before that Axswain massacre…you can see the date/time stamp marked at the bottom of the screen."

The second man scoffed. "A picture of…a desolate area? Because of that continual radiating energy, there are, unfortunately, a lot of areas like that…all over the world…what's so special about this one?"

Shon cleared his throat. "If you'll be patient…Sir…you'll see." He hit a few keys and the zoom went back, showing a larger area. "Ah! There it is! Down at the bottom of the picture… unfortunately mingled with the date/time stamp. Wait a moment… let me see…if I can adjust…there!"

The second man scoffed again. "So there's a vehicle, of some kind, driving along, kicking up some dust…big deal."

Shon was getting irritated. "What…vehicle…Sir?" He zoomed in near the lead part of the dust cloud. "I can see…tire tracks, forming rapidly in the dirt and kicking up a dust cloud… but what vehicle?"

All six of the other men were now frowning at the screen with open mouths.

Shon saw that he had their attention. "Here, Sirs, it seems that they did leave tracks in the dirt. At the battle site…later…they had somehow fixed this dilemma and thus rendered their vehicles even more invisible and very untraceable." He switched this film to slow motion. "Now, for some reason this vehicle stops. As you can see…when I zoom in…we CAN see tire tracks." He zoomed in even closer. "Now…here…you can even see…the appearance of…at least three sets of footprints…with no sign of any person walking around there." He looked at the other men. Their jaws were open even wider. "Now…here come those non-mechanized gliders that those Teltermak people developed." He speeded the film up to normal time. "We can see the Teltermak scouts landing and starting an investigation…and then the satellite continued on the orbital path and this area was out of range. The next time that it came across this area, the Teltermak scouts had been massacred. Their gliders were still there and there was absolutely no sign that a vehicle had been driven through…at all. Our conclusion: At this time, the Owlam vehicles were invisible but leaving a trail. At the site of the gorge, they had remedied this situation - again… rendering their vehicles invisible *and* untraceable."

The first man spoke up. "How can you be sure that this… invisible vehicle was…without any reservation of being wrong… Owlam?"

Shon smiled. "The direction that the vehicle came from… Owlam. The direction that it was headed…Teltermak. Plus, the wheel base, it is consistent with one of the types of truck that the Owlams use. At no time have the Teltermak ever shown any form of invisibility. They've attempted some tunneling in their attacks, but never invisibility. The only Elf group that has shown any form of invisibility…the Owlams."

A fourth man spoke up. "What about that bunch…the Roistee?"

Shon shook his head feeling a little disgusted. "That's camouflage, Sir, we can still track them...even through the camouflage. The Owlams show invisibility...that makes them untraceable."

The third man cleared his throat. "Is this your final point or is there something...more important?"

Shon nodded smiling. "Oh, yes, Sir...there is something... much more intriguing...and...sinister, Sir."

The third man leaned back, looking up at the monitor still frowning. "Please continue."

Shon smiled. "Yes, Sir." He hit another icon. "This one... again you can see the date/time stamp. We see...the aftermath of an attack on an Owlam patrol, by a Teltermak patrol. The Owlams were taken by complete surprise...plus there was only four of the Owlams. The Teltermak are now...for some insidious reason... harvesting organs from the Owlam bodies."

The second man huffed. "We're well aware of the fact that the Teltermak, among others, were openly practicing cannibalism. So what?"

Shon closed his eyes and fought the urge to scream at these people. "Yes, Sir, they were cannibals...at least at that time. The puzzle here...why are they only harvesting...certain organs? Normally a cannibal would go for muscle tissue. Muscle is the most abundant meat in any body. Here, again, they're only taking a small portion and leaving the rest to rot. It appears that they're taking the brain, the heart...and...for some strange reason...it appears that they're taking the liver."

The second man looked thoroughly confused. "Since when...is a cannibal picky about...what portion of the body... they take?"

Shon shrugged. "It is a conundrum, Sir. All four bodies... they did the same thing - the brain, the heart and the liver."

"Okay," said the first man. "So what's next?"

Shon shook his head. "Believe it or not, it's the same site, however, it's several months later...if you will look at the date/ time stamp. As you can see, the corpses are all dried up and show no signs of any scavenger or insect eating the bodies. An Owlam patrol has discovered the scene...and...now, we see all kinds of personnel and vehicles...just appearing...with no sign of how they got there. They just appear and start their investigation... they clean up...and then they disappear...without leaving a trail... again."

The first man let his breath out slowly. "So...it's either... total invisibility, or teleportation. Either way...we need to get someone in there and steal this technology. It's awesome. Thank you for the briefing, Investigator Toivok." He started getting up.

"I'm not finished, Sir," said Shon.

The first man stood there at half crouch. "Are you telling me that there's a bigger point?"

"Oh, yes, Sir," said Shon gravely. "MUCH bigger."

He sat back down looking at Shon suspiciously. "Continue." He looked back at the big screen.

Shon sniffed and cleared his throat. "First, a preface… before I show the next clip. This bunch on South Chilamte, the Neksheth-Or, who also figured out how to launch intercontinental missiles in groups. They weren't having any difficulty in launching and directing their missiles, much like us. It's been over twenty years since we launched the mass attack…and we've been having nothing but grief ever since. None of our systems are working correctly and the only possible reason…sabotage. Someone is getting in here…past all of our security measures…and there *kussking* up the works completely…faster than we can fix the problems."

"We know that," said the second man. "We just don't know who is doing it."

"I think this might give us an important clue, Sir," said Shon with a diabolical grin.

All six men glued their eyes to the screen.

"Again a preface: Neksheth-Or launched an attack… like ours, but with conventional weapons. I don't know what they were hoping to accomplish, because all they did was make everyone mad…at them. They didn't show that they're capable of demolishing an entire city with one bomb…like us. Shortly after that attack, *we* discovered that it was Neksheth-Or and set a satellite in a fixed position over that city. Now, we had an incident where one of our satellite watch technicians had a very unusual injury…"

The second man snarled in anger. "I don't care about the clumsiness of some *fonsosk*! I need you to get to the point!"

"That's *part* of the point," said Shon through clenched teeth. "He was injured and called for medical attention. He was the only one in that room at the time. Yet someone else got on his monitor and...used it extensively...while he was at the infirmary. The times recorded by the physicians confirm this. The computer was being used...under his password...while he was out cold on the surgeon's table."

The second man now looked confused. "Is this...extensive use part of your point?"

"It is the point, Sir."

He nodded. "All right." He turned back to the screen.

"Here is a recording of what happened, while the technician was under sedation." He hit another icon. "Here we see the, new and improved, world watching satellite array being used. As you know, they work together and form a complete picture... depending on where the technician is attempting to get a closer look. Since we got this into play, we don't really need that many roving satellites. Anyway, it starts here on the northern cliffs of South Chilamte. We see this Owlam woman standing there alone. Suddenly, she disappears and reappears...several *hyzink* to the south."

The first man scoffed. "Couldn't possibly be the same woman."

Shon cleared his throat and backed the film up. He zoomed in, to the point where Natsa's left shoulder took up the entire screen. "If you'll notice here, Sir, there is a small stain on the shoulder and a frayed section where the sleeve is hemmed to the shoulder of the uniform. Also..." He pulled it back slightly. "When she's looking up you can see that she has a very small birthmark, next to the left eye." He pulled back and forwarded the clip to where she was at the south end of the cut in the cliff. He zoomed in on the left shoulder again. "Same stain, same fray... and..." She looked up. "...I see the exact same, tiny birthmark." He looked around triumphantly. "It most certainly IS the same woman."

The first man leaned forward. "You have my undivided attention," he said gravely.

"All right, now, I'm not controlling anything. I'm watching what the spy did, to somehow, lead that woman to Neksheth-Or. We watch...in very short time segments...as she moves, in some cases, over fifty *hyzink*. Each time, he finds her...and depending on whether or not there are any Heyyah in the area, she is either visible or invisible. When she's visible, we don't see her moving her mouth, so...there are those who think that these Owlam...are capable of some form of mental telepathy."

The second man squawked. "Mental telepathy...above and beyond the teleportation and invisibility?" His shoulders sagged. "We either have to get this technology...by getting them on our side...or exterminate these *Hongoths*."

"Yes," said Shon. "Now...the point! Shortly after this Owlam woman found her way to Neksheth-Or, they started having all kinds of problems with missile systems, that they hadn't had any problems with before. The problems are recurring, constant and no matter what they fix, something else breaks. It is the conclusion, of the personnel that I've been working with…the Owlams are the ones who are sabotaging the Neksheth-Or systems…and it has to be the Owlams who are sabotaging OUR systems. No one else has shown any such capability…other than the Owlams."

Toytay stood there stunned. "We…have to…do something about this these *Doovofts*."

Ini looked at Toytay with quivering lips. "I suggest… Jahong's Death. That's a good place to send this whole bunch."

Wasee reached over to the closest one and hopped him into Jahong's Death. Toytay and Ini did the same. Before the other four Algothon personnel in the room could react to the disappearances, three more vanished. Shon was the last one.

Onggot tried to stop the women. "DON'T…DON'T DO THIS!"

Too late. Shon Toivok was now in Jahong's Death as well.

Onggot sat down and hung his head. "That was stupid… so completely stupid."

Toytay was ready to slap Onggot. "What was stupid? We had to stop them before this conversation got any further than this room."

Onggot looked up disgusted. He rolled his eyes. "You weren't listening at all. That guy – Shon - he said that he AND HIS TEAM had come to that conclusion. Where's the rest of his team? How many of them are there? Have they discussed this with anyone else?" He glared at Toytay in a patronizing manner. "Well…what do we do now? This'll only trigger a further investigation. It'll start them looking closer at Owlam and they may decide to attack us. They may also start telling the rest of the world what they've seen, just to get everyone else to turn against us."

Toytay cleared her throat and stammered a little. "You were supposed...uh...to know...and find out...uh..." She closed her eyes and tried to think. "Which office did he work in?"

Onggot shook his head. "I don't know. I've never seen him until today."

Ini looked sick. "So...how do we find his office?"

Onggot rolled his eyes. "Why don't you ask someone who's a little higher in rank than you? Maybe they can give you a decent thought on that subject."

Toytay snarled at him. She stood there brooding for a few moments." "Officer, Holla, this is Officer, Toytay. I have···er···I seem to have made a bit of a mistake···in my tactics. I need a little guidance on how to remedy the situation."

Holla came back. "A mistake? What kind of a mistake are we talking about?"

"I···uh···found out···that the Algothon know a few things about us. They seem to have some crazy camera that's···so far up there···that we can't see it. It can see us···but···well···they've been watching us···and···they figured out···that we're the ones who are···sabotaging their missile."

Holla was ready to scream." "How···did they find out?"

"It seems that they recorded that···guidance that was given to Natsa···when she went to Neksheth−Or. Right after Natsa got to···Neksheth−Or, the systems there started going *chokwad*. They figured out that since, right after we showed up, things went wrong, they figure that we're the ones who are causing all of the trouble···in the systems at Algothon."

Holla sat back thinking. "What really makes you think that they could do something to us···about that situation?"

"We heard the briefing···and we took all of the personnel···at that briefing···and threw them into Jahong's Death. It wasn't until after we tossed all of them···one of my Team···realized that···we didn't get···all of them."

"So···get the rest of them!"

"We don't···know who they are."

"Why not?"

"We···got rid of the ones···at the briefing. We didn't get the rest of the Team···that figured it out."

"And···?"

"We don't know who the rest of the Team is."

"You said that his Team is watching us···right?"

"Yes."

"So···go through the offices, where they're watching everybody and find out who it is that's concentrating on US!"

Toytay sat there and turned a little red. "That···sounds like a good···idea. I'll get the rest of my Team working on it, immediately."

"Thank you."

Toytay turned to the Team. "Okay, we have our orders. We have to start looking for the others…where *ever* they are."

Onggot rolled his eyes again and shook his head. "Wonderful suggestion," he muttered. "Where do we start?"

Toytay looked at him angrily. "We start in this hall. If we can't find anyone in this hall, we go to the ones to either side. We expand our search until we find them…then we eradicate them."

Onggot shook his head. "Yes, Sir."

The Team started checking each one of the rooms in this hallway. They found several people looking intently at their monitors. They were looking at different cities. None of them, in this hall, were looking down at Owlam. They all stood there looking a little despondent.

"Okay, Sir," said Onggot. "Which way do we go and what are we looking for?"

Toytay scowled at him. "You know *what* we're looking for. It's the *where* that we have to determine." She sighed. "Let's start looking in the hall to the left.

They proceeded to another iron door and walked through in Spy. They discovered numerous Algothon personnel who seemed to be doing rather redundant activities. They found some thirty different monitors, in at least five halls, where the focus was on the Turgon Wall. They found several personnel who were looking intently at Neksheth-Or. They found a few personnel who were reviewing the kite training done by Bonarain on the Teltermak wall. It took almost six days, however, they finally found a hall, four floors up, where there were fifty-two different personnel, all looking down and studying the city of Owlam.

Ini was the one who stated the obvious. "This is no minor procedure. When he said that his Team was looking at Owlam…I thought he meant…a Team like ours…just four people."

"I didn't see this much scrutiny for Neksheth-Or," said Wasee. "We can't take out an entire room like this without their High Command noticing it. They'll launch an attack against us… now."

Onggot shook his head. "Even if we did take out everyone in this room they still have those *chokwad* archives and we still don't know where those archives are kept."

Ini scoffed. "Once we find the archives, if we find the archives, we have the problem of trying to figure out which mainframe holds all of the information on us."

"No," said Toytay. "If we find the archives…or should I say…WHEN we find the archives, we take out the whole mess. Deprive these *Doovofts* of all of their precious information and they'll be just as blind as the rest of the world."

Another Owlam Team walked into the room with Team 256.

A woman walked up to Toytay. "Hello, I'm Officer Grade 3, Choynda, Team Leader of Team 910. The rest of my Team: Officer Grade 5, Zanzee, Officer Grade 6, Stog and Officer Grade 7, Tway. I just heard what you said. Do we have any clue where to start looking for these…archives?"

"Our first clue…," said Onggot. "…we know that they're not kept in this building. We may have to get another fifteen or more Teams in here, searching the entire city."

Choynda scoffed. "*That* we know. We got a briefing from Gagan when we first got here. He said that his Team has been looking for the archives for some time now. So far…nothing."

Zanzee was looking around in shock. "I thought someone said that these *chogo* were looking at us through…some crazy flying camera."

"They are," said Toytay.

"I've got news for you," said Zanzee. "I've been looking at these monitors. No one has the same thing on their monitor. Each one is looking through a different camera…or that camera can look at many different things…all at the same time."

Choynda sighed. "It's not *A* camera…it must be an entire array of the things." She hung her head. "One thing we might have to do is take out that array…then do something drastic… about Algothon…before they can get another one in place."

"Meanwhile," said Stog, "We still have to keep the saboteurs in place. If we ever let these *Chokwads* pull off another successful launch of those firestorm weapons…Owlam will be *the* primary target."

Ini was looking around the room at all of the personnel. She looked up at one side of the room and grimaced in pain.

Toytay thought she was being dramatic and sarcastically responded. "Okay, what's the problem? You've seen Algothon Heyyah before."

Ini looked at Toytay with deep concern on her face. "Yes, I've seen them…many of them. But now I realize that the situation is much more critical than we thought." She pointed at a group of five men. "The two up there…with the gold shoulder boards… they're…Prominent Investigators."

Choynda looked confused. "Is that…significant?"

Toytay's shoulders sagged. She looked at Choynda in a dull manner. "Have you been briefed on Algothon ranks?"

Choynda noticed some of the concern on the faces of Team 256. "Apparently not thoroughly…why?"

Toytay sighed. "In this city…of almost twenty million people…there are only four people who…stand out a lot. These four people have achieved the rank of Prominent Investigator. They answer to no one. They make up their own rules as they go along. When they do an investigation…the only one who is allowed to question a Prominent Investigator…is another Prominent Investigator…and that doesn't happen very often. Here we are and we've just found out…that Owlam has the full attention of…two of these…self-appointed-gods."

Choynda now looked more concerned herself. "Before you

continue, could you…give me a briefing…on this rank structure?"

The rest of Team 256 looked at Ini.

Ini sighed. "The Algothon Security Forces have seven ranks. At the bottom of the group is the Investigator Trainee. One up from that is the Investigator. Next is the Second Investigator, then Senior Investigator, then Chief Investigator, High Investigator, then the Prominent Investigator. In watching the people of Algothon, any time a Chief Investigator shows up in your section, most people wet their pants. A High Investigator makes them fill their pants with other debris. A Prominent can cause heart attacks…and suicides." She looked at Choynda. "Here…watching over Owlam…we have a double whammy heart attack."

Choynda scoffed. "How many of those Prominent Uppity *Doovofts* did they have watching over Neksheth-Or? Those people attacked Algothon, so I'm sure that it had to draw the attention of somebody."

Toytay sighed. "From what we can gather, from what we've found so far, there was only one of them that looked at Neksheth-Or. All four of these…demigods…act completely independent of each other. We have the attention of two…united. We've got trouble."

Officer Leader, Nachichi came into the room. "Do I understand that we've got a dilemma on our hands?"

Toytay was a little startled. "Who called you?"

"I did," said Onggot. "We need less talking and more

action. So far, all you've done is talk."

Nachichi stomped her foot. "So…what's the crisis?"

Onggot pointed to the Investigators. "Can you see what's in here?"

Nachichi looked where he was pointing. Her jaw dropped. "Two…of the…Prominent…on us?"

Onggot nodded in an over-exaggerated manner while smiling.

Nachichi growled. "Have you discovered anything else… that I may need to know about?"

Toytay swallowed. "Yes, Sir. We've found that this… flying camera, is not just one camera. It appears to be an entire array. Each one of the monitors…in this room…is focusing on a different part of Owlam. The only way that that is happening - more than one camera."

Nachichi clenched her teeth. "Is there any way…that we can shoot that thing down?" She looked at the other Team Leaders. "Does anyone know how high up these headaches are? Does anyone know the full range of a 459?"

Toytay shrugged. "Call Supreme Officer, Holla…ask her."

Nachichi closed her eyes and shook her head. "Supreme Officer, Holla, this is Officer Leader, Nachichi. I need to talk to you."

Holla came back. "This had better be important."

"It is, Sir."

"Okay, what is it?"

Nachichi, Toytay and Choynda all briefed Holla on what they had found and the significance of two Prominent Investigators being involved.

Holla considered it for a few moments. "You say that we need to destroy this flying camera. How? We can't even see it. From what you're telling me, the wretched thing can see any part of Owlam, so it has to be quite a ways up there. What do you suggest?"

Nachichi felt fearful of asking the next question, however, she could not think of anything better. "Sir, do we know what the actual destructive range of the 459 is…yet?"

Holla's response was more curious than angry. "I don't know. It'll be an interesting way to find out if it can reach this mystery camera that we haven't been able to see. The problem now…since we can't see it – how and where do we aim?"

Nachichi thought for a few moments. "That Officer… who lead Natsa to Neksheth—Or…who was it?"

Toytay huffed. "It was Officer, Kronom…why?"

Holla broke in: "Bring him in on this one. He figured out how to use it to guide her. Maybe he can guide the aim of a 459…or two."

A few mental messages and Jumps later, Officer, Kronom was in the room. He looked around at all that was going on and after he was briefed, he seemed a little skeptical. "How do you know…if it'll work?"

"We don't," said Nachichi. "We really won't know… unless we try. If we don't try something we might as well print up banners and let these *Chokwads* know exactly what each one of us is doing…all the time."

Kronom sighed. "Anybody got any suggestions as to how we start this…grand experiment?"

Nachichi pondered for a few moments. "Why don't we try a four corner approach?"

Kronom had a dull look on his face. "Which means exactly…what?"

Nachichi closed her eyes and let out her breath slowly. "First, Officer, Kronom, pick a monitor and start watching it."

Kronom shrugged. He walked up to the closest monitor and started staring at it.

Nachichi tilted her head back. "Master Officer, Wilfadge, this is Officer Leader, Nachichi. I need to talk to you."

Wilfadge came back. "This is Wilfadge, what do you need?"

"Thank you, Sir. I need to know…do you have a 195 Assault Truck?"

"Of course."

"Good…who is your primary gunner?"

"Officer Grade 4, Oolooa, why?"

"I need her to go to the truck, set up the 459 cannon and stand by for orders···from me or Officer, Kronom."

Wilfadge sighed. "Done!"

Nachichi looked around the room a little fearful. "Uh... who is the Northern Commander?"

Toytay giggled. "That would be Master Officer, Ahandi."

Nachichi turned a little red. "Thank you." She cleared her throat. "Master Officer, Ahandi, this is Officer Leader, Nachichi. I need to talk to you."

Nachichi got one gunner, each one sitting at the headquarters of the North, South, East and West, all standing by.

Nachichi went to Kronom. "They're all ready."

He looked at Nachichi slack jawed. "For what?"

Nachichi clenched her teeth. "For directions on where to shoot!"

Kronom clicked his tongue. "Who am I talking to?"

"In the North, you have..."

"Please write them down, Sir!"

Nachichi grimaced in anger. She bit her lower lip. She licked her lips. "All right, we'll write them down."

"I got them," said Ini as she handed Kronom a piece of paper.

Kronom sighed as he read it. 'Start with the north,' he

thought. "Officer, Nashisi, aim your cannon straight up and pull the trigger. Please hold the trigger down." He waited a few moments. "Are you firing and holding the trigger?"

"Yes."

"I know that you're trying to aim directly up, but⋯ what direction are you facing?"

"North."

Kronom grunted in exasperation. "Swivel around in your turret. Face south and then fire." He waited again. "Are you doing it?"

"Yes, I am."

Kronom sighed. "Okay, start lowering your cannon, still aiming it due south." He watched the screen waiting to see a familiar red beam. Nothing happened…at first.

One of the Algothon personnel called a senior officer in the room. Some foolish Owlamite was aiming one of those power rifles skyward for an unknown reason.

Kronom hurried to that monitor and saw that the beam was on the right side of the screen. "Okay, I see your beam now. You can stop, but don't move the cannon."

"I have to," said Nashisi. "This power pack is faulty. It's overheating badly. I need to replace it."

Nachichi sat there muttering. "It had to happen sooner or later. The equipment hasn't been replaced, upgraded or repaired in twenty-two years. We just don't have anyone who knows how to manufacture or repair any new weaponry."

"Okay, replace the power pack, but try to not move the cannon." He checked his list. "Officer, Sorn, in the east. What direction are you facing?"

"I'm facing north."

Kronom took a deep breath. "Officer, Sorn, please face west, towards the city. Officer, Oolooa, in the south, please face north. Officer, Tathba, in the west, please face east."

All three of them responded accordingly.

Kronom smiled. "Officer, Sorn, please aim skyward, pull the trigger and hold it down."

"Here's another *Fonsosk*, shooting at the sky," said another man watching the monitors.

Kronom tried to think for a moment. "Sorn, move your aim, slowly···a little to the west." He continued watching the monitor he was on. He glanced over at the other monitor, attempting to get some bearings. "Now, move it slightly to the north." He watched as the beam came into view on his monitor.

Several of the Algothon personnel chorused the question: "What are they doing?"

Kronom hoped that he could get the mission accomplished before any of them figured it out. "Officer, Nashisi, have you replaced the power pack yet?"

An exasperated response came back. "Yes, but we

figured out that it's not the power pack, it's the cannon that's faulty. Don't worry, we've already got the other cannon in place. Officer, Kiykay is at the trigger."

Kronom closed his eyes, took a breath and gritted his teeth. "Officer, Kiykay, have you attempted to position the cannon···in a comparable position to the other one?"

She came back. "It's as close as I can get it···from just looking at it."

"Pull your trigger and hold it down."

He maneuvered her aim until the beam was well within the view of the monitor. He then called on and adjusted the aim of Oolooa in the south and Tathba in the west. Now all four beams could be seen in the monitor. He talked to each one, making final adjustments on their aim.

One of the technicians in the Algothon computer room figured it out. "I think that they're trying to shoot the array down."

Another one scoffed. "From that distance? Our array is fifty-two *hyzinks* above the surface of the planet. Even if they do zero in on the array, there's no way that they could be dangerous or damaging at that distance."

The first one gave the second one a nasty look. "So why are they trying?"

A third technician snarled at the first two. "You two are missing the point completely. The fact that they're trying to get four laser guns aimed at the array...yes they're trying to destroy it. The primary question though is: How can they possibly see it...

especially from that distance?"

Several other technicians got a good laugh at the comment. The two Prominent Investigators did not laugh. They did realize that there was something very strange about the fact that these four cannons, all coming from different parts of the Owlam city, were all getting their beams dangerously closer to the array.

One of the Investigators got on an intercom and called for someone to find the frequency of whoever was guiding the beams and get it shut down.

The other Investigator went to the Chief Technician in the room. "Can they hit it?"

"I didn't think so…before, but now that I can't see the end of the beam. They appear to have the range. I still don't know if they have the destructive capability…at that range."

"Is there any…defensive shield…that can be activated?"

"There isn't any in it! No one…could possibly have foreseen this."

"Can we readjust it?"

The Technician shook his head. "Any adjustment that we try at this time…would be futile. We have to plan it in advance… and it takes almost half an *askitch* to warm up the engine…and the batteries."

The Investigator snarled. "Well, let's just hope that they can't…"

At that moment, one of the beams went directly across the

lens of one of the monitors and within four heartbeats, only one monitor had something other than snow and static on the screen. What that last monitor had was a brilliant view of a constellation off in the eastern sky…just before it changed to snow.

Kronom laughed out loud. "We did it! How…I…it…we did it!" He looked triumphantly at Nachichi and laughed again.

Nachichi had a big smile on her face. "Yes, we did it. Now let's see what these *H'oolyachs* do."

One of the Prominent Investigators shouted at them. "We've got to get another array up there…immediately!"

The supervisor of the technicians just stood there shaking his head. "How? They've sabotaged everything that anyone has tried to launch for…I don't know how many years."

"I'm going over there to oversee a new launch myself," said the other Prominent.

The supervisor just threw his arms out in exasperation. "Like that's gonna do any good!"

The one Prominent left the room, the other got on the intercom and started informing someone that a new launch must be accomplished. He was calm and business like at first. He began to get a little aggravated, stopped being nice and was giving orders instead of suggesting. Next he was shouting at whoever was on the other end of the line.

They were in the section of the city where the missile silos were located, so it did not take the other Prominent very long to get to a launch site. He had every single technician out there, looking and double-checking all of the systems. He was going to make sure that all systems were working and ready to go and would not allow any outsider a chance at performing any sabotage any time before the launch.

A call came in from the launch pad. "Officer, Nachichi, this is Officer, Quinkka of Team 5449. We can't get in there to sabotage this thing without them knowing it··· immediately. How should my Team and I even attempt it?"

"Let me think···" Nachichi started pacing around the room as all of the technicians were staring at the Prominent and their supervisor. "Officer, Quinkka, was there a missile already set up with a new array?"

"Yes, they've had it set up for quite some time. They just haven't been able to launch anything because we always *chogo* the thing up before it can be launched."

"So, what's stopping you now?"

"They have an entire army of technicians on the missile, checking all of the systems. If we foul something now, they'll notice it now. If we mess it up, while they're watching, I'm sure that they'll notice our full capabilities. All of the people who have been the *Voice of Power*, have all told us to keep it a secret."

Nachichi gritted her teeth. "Does anyone have a suggestion···that might help us here?"

"This is Officer Grade 6, Ulokom. I'm on Officer, Quinkka's Team. May I make a suggestion?"

He made a suggestion and everyone listening began

snickering and laughing. Nachichi gave her blessing and Quinkka's Team 5449 went to work.

The Algothon technicians kept working feverishly in order to make the attempt at a successful launch. It was nearly half the day before the Algothon personnel were satisfied that they had thwarted any sabotage that could have possibly taken place on this missile.

The call was made that the missile was ready and how long it was until they were going to ignite the engines and liftoff would occur. All of the technicians scattered, in order to keep from being charred to a crisp by the searing flames coming from the exhaust cones. Most of them got into vehicles that sped off as rapidly as possible. There were a few that jumped into special blast shielded bunkers near the launch pad.

The ignition sequence started and the missile started up, slowly. It quickly gained speed and continued up, leaving the giant plume of smoke behind.

While many technicians were cheering in the launch room, there were several others who were still apprehensive and kept checking the telemetry information, over and over, just waiting to see if they actually had avoided any sabotage. Everything was going totally according to the plan of a successful launch. It was the first successful launch in over twenty years.

They continued to watch all of the monitors. No problems, no glitches. Everything was going perfect...or so they thought.

The missile achieved final altitude and the array was deployed. The adjustment rockets on the array were working perfectly. It was a very short time before the array was placed in a synchronized orbit, where it could keep a permanent watch on the city of Owlam. It would be able to spy on any part of the city of Owlam.

Once the array was in place, the launch crew informed the spy technicians that they could activate the array and begin doing their job again. The supervising technician fed the proper code in and started the coordination of synchronizing each monitor in the room with a camera on the array. After several minutes of looking things over, the supervisor hung his head and sighed. He shut the system down, got up and headed for the exit.

The Prominent frowned at the Supervisor. "Where do you think you're going?"

The Supervisor stopped. He sighed again and turned around. "I think I'm going to go to a tavern and get raging drunk… for the next…oh, I don't know…for the rest of my life."

The Prominent started getting angry. "You have some work here to do…right now!"

The Supervisor snickered. "With what?"

The Prominent started advancing towards the Supervisor with a menacing look on his face. "With that new array that we went through all the trouble to launch!"

"Oh," said the Supervisor sarcastically. "You mean that array…that is totally BLIND?!"

The Prominent froze in his tracks and his expression changed to fear, terror and confusion.

The Supervisor snickered. "The saboteurs allowed us to launch that rocket. They didn't sabotage the rocket - they sabotaged the ARRAY!"

The Prominent swallowed hard several times. "Uh…" He cleared his throat. "…what…uh…happened?"

"Whoever the *Hongoths* are that did this, they let the array go up there…without one single *shybeelan* LENS! The array is totally blind. I got the same error message on all sixty cameras. There is not one single lens up there. Nothing but a blind array… that we cannot recover and/or fix."

The Prominent went back to his desk and flopped limp in his chair. The Supervisor departed. The rest of the technicians started gathering up their possessions and departing with a total overall melancholy attitude.

Quinkka and her Team were sitting near the launch pad, in Spy, playing with the sixty lenses that they had removed from the array. They were peering through them and trying to use them as telescopic glasses.

"That was a pretty good idea, Ulokom," said Quinkka.

Ulokom smiled, bowed and said: "Thank you," in a very congenial manner.

Nenny snickered. "It actually gave those *Bimyocks* a little bit of hope…and then crushed it completely when they realized that they spent all of that time, effort and money…for nothing."

Weetaka looked at one of the lenses in her hand. "What should we do with these things?"

Quinkka smiled. "Let's take them back to Owlam. Maybe someone there…can make good use of them."

3

The four Prominent Investigators of Algothon decided that it was time to have a meeting. A very important meeting in regards to the biggest headache that had arisen from the ashes of the nuclear bombs, in the form of the city of Owlam. Something had to be done. It was obvious to them that the Owlams had been the main saboteurs in everything that had gone wrong for the last twenty-two years. No one could determine how, however, there was nothing else that made any sense. There was no one else that seemed to be doing anything at all. Now, the top echelon of the security personnel of Algothon could not afford any more procrastination or even methodical investigation. The Owlams had to be dealt with - at all costs. Again that nagging primary question: How? No one could find anyone in Algothon who was not born in Algothon (all slaves that they had dragged in as slaves were accounted for). No one had seen any of the sabotage being performed, in spite of over 8,000,000 security cameras that were constantly sweeping the city of Algothon looking for anything out of the ordinary. How do you fight an enemy that can hide from the most sophisticated surveillance on the planet? How do you stop them from communicating when they have a communication system that defeated the Sodle jamming systems?

The Teams that were spying on the city of Algothon knew

now that their mission was going to become either more critical or more difficult…or both. They got all twenty Teams together and had a meeting of their own.

Officer Leader, Ota looked at all of the personnel that were currently under her command. "As you've all heard, the four Prominent Investigators in the Algothon Security, have decided that the city of Owlam and all of the citizens thereof must be destroyed. How do you think we should stop them?"

Officer Leader, Blana stood up. "Why don't we just continue making some of these *Bimyocks* having fatal accidents?"

Ota sighed. "Do you really think that that is going to help?"

Officer Leader, Natsa scoffed. "The more of their leaders we destroy, the more we decay their leadership capabilities. If it takes a few thousand fatal accidents, then so be it! After a while, they're going to have to admit that they're defeated. If they can't, we just keep on eliminating any of the thinkers that can come up with some strategy to stop us…or even slow us down."

Ota sighed. "You've heard that they've got all of this computer stuff on some *h'oolyach* central archives. It's some mainframe that we still haven't located. How are we going to stop them from referencing what these others have decided?"

Officer Grade 2, Kloob stood up smiling. "I have all of my Team in the secret conference room with those holier-than-thou four high-ups. According to my Team, they haven't fed anything into any computer…yet. They're having a big discussion, but no one is taking notes. If we get rid of those four - NOW, then no one will know what they said."

Ota looked around. "I don't think that killing them and leaving their bodies in that room is going to accomplish that much."

Kloob snickered. "Then send them to Atsi's Death. We know the same thing that happened to the Beetsik in Jahong's Death, happens in Atsi's Death. Send them there while the meeting is going on and no one will know for quite some time that they're missing."

Ota looked around the room at all of the faces. She turned back to Kloob. She sighed. "Do it."

Kloob closed his eyes and sent a mental message to the members of his Team. A few moments later he opened his eyes. "Done!"

Ota nodded. "All right people, what else do we need to get done?"

Officer Leader, Nachichi frowned. "Why don't we send the people, who aren't watching the missiles, and have them start looking through the entire city and find this *chokwad* mainframe that has all of the archives?"

Officer Grade 2, Ko shook his head. "We've found at least five buildings that have a large amount of computer banks. We still don't know if any of these are the one we're talking about."

Nachichi scoffed. "Then let's start pulling some plugs and *h'oolyaching* some hard drives and see what they do or don't cry over. Sitting here talking about it isn't going to accomplish anything. Wrecking some hard drives will."

Half a day went by before the Algothon Security realized that something was amiss in the Top Four meeting. No one had sent for any lunch, no one had asked for any new news, no one had sent out any messages…nothing. After one High Investigator finally conjured up the intestinal fortitude to knock on the door and attempt an inquiry did they realize that something had gone dreadfully wrong. The door was forced open and all that was found in the room was the conference table and ten chairs that surrounded the table. All computers, pads, pens and personnel, everything else was gone.

Step 1: Assign four of the thirty High Investigators to the Prominent Investigator position. Step 2: Attempt to find out what was discussed and get that discussion going again…recorded this time. Step 3: Act.

Holla was getting regular updates from Algothon and passing them on to the Staff. She was getting rather frustrated at the tenacity of the Algothon people and their tunnel-vision attitude towards Owlam. It seemed that just as soon as you put out one fire, another one springs up that is just as, if not more, deadly than the last one.

The Staff was called to a meeting.

Holla sat there looking rather glum as each one of them filed in. Once they were all there and seated, she still stared at the table for several moments. "I hate to say it…but we just might have to come up with a plan…for a retreat."

Teelila was aghast. "Where do we have that we could use as a collection point…for any retreat?"

Chaza gritted her teeth. "You sound as if we're defeated already. We haven't lost this or any war lately."

"I know," said Holla flatly. "But when you consider…we didn't see the attack coming from either Algothon or Neksheth-Or. They both hit us by complete surprise. Did any of us see any of that coming?"

"Doesn't mean that we have to run," said Wilfadge angrily.

"I agree," said Ahandi. "Why should we run…anywhere… at all?"

Holla huffed. "I didn't say that we must. I am simply saying, that with everything that we've seen so far, we should consider some place that we could retreat too…at a moment's notice."

Teelila shook her head. "Do you have a place in mind?"

"Yes," said Holla. "If you take a look at the map of South Chilamte, you'll notice, in the northern part of the continent there's a huge gorge. It divides almost the entire northern part of the continent."

Ahandi scoffed. "What good would that do us? We'd probably have to fight for the property and then all that'd accomplish is we'd make a new enemy."

"No." Holla shook her head slowly. "Not *in* the gorge itself."

Wilfadge looked a little skeptical. "What? There's nothing…or nobody down in the gorge…everything is…up top…so…what?"

"Yes," said Holla flatly. "Both the east and west face of the gorge, for its entire length is just a sheer cliff. Down in the bottom, there's nothing that the people who live there can use. Mainly there's nothing that they can use, because they'd have to come up with some kind of tremendous elevator system or they'd have to come up with a very, very long pathway that leads up the face of the cliffs. The gorge is over five hundred kilotaja in length, it is five kilotaja wide - at the widest point and the whole thing, from north to south, is just over nine kilotaja deep."

Chaza leaned back in her chair. "So if there's nothing down there, what makes you think that we could make a refuge there?"

Holla smiled. "No one else can use it. No one else, in all of the centuries of this planet's history, has ever used it."

"So…" said Wilfadge with apprehension in his eyes. "…what are you suggesting?"

Holla closed her eyes and let out a long breath. She opened her eyes and smiled. "We choose a place in the cliff and we start moving a lot of earth and stone. We make rooms and halls and whatever else we need, in order to make the place livable."

Teelila shook her head again. "But…there's no power or

water there. What do we do for water and electricity? All of that will take time to build and install."

Holla nodded. "That's why we start now. In all of the time that we've been spying on Algothon and some of our other neighbors, we're finding out that we still haven't figured out how to spy on them…in a totally professional manner. We're still fledglings. We had an intelligence network and it was destroyed by the firestorm. We also had some counterintelligence measures and they were destroyed by the firestorm. We still haven't got the hang of all of it and…I'm scared. Almost all of the personnel, we still have here were all trained to watch for any enemy on a computer monitor. We're having to learn how to repair electrical conduits, plumbing systems, weapons systems, vehicles…and everything else…from scratch. Building a community in the east or west face of that gorge will help us get people trained in that sort of thing. It'll also give us a place to retreat too…if the need arises."

Wilfadge looked at his fingernails for a moment. "Are you really scared, or are you just wanting something where we don't get caught with our pants down again?"

Holla looked at him with no expression at all. "Yes."

Teelila scratched her chin. "The electrical part won't be anything where we start from scratch. There were a lot of personnel who rebuilt that eastern section of the tram after the Galsino attack. I'm sure that they won't have to completely start over, in order to wire up a new community, in the face of the cliff."

"The main problem," said Chaza, "will be the building of

a big enough power plant for all of it."

Holla smiled. "We can use the solar panels for that."

Teelila huffed. "That's ridiculous! If we're supposed to go there and hide…any solar panels would be seen every time the sun comes up and reflects all of that glare."

Holla smiled again. "Not if we hide them in Spy."

Teelila's jaw dropped. "What good would they do us if they're hidden in Spy?"

Holla chuckled. "I thought of this idea several months ago. I moved all of the solar panels, for this building, into Spy at that time. The power in this building has gone on uninterrupted in all that time. The only ones who would see the panels…us."

"Okay," said Wilfadge, "so you've solved that problem, how about the plumbing?"

Holla looked around at all of the faces. "That…is where you need to pick some of your people, who have some capabilities of being trained in that area, and get them trained in plumbing."

Chaza sighed. "So…where in the gorge do you want us to start?"

Holla smiled. "At the widest point. There are several bridges that've been built across the gorge. All of them were built at some of the narrowest parts of the gorge. If we go to the widest, that'll be the area where we have the least amount of any foreign population getting in the way of our endeavor."

Wilfadge snickered. "And even if Algothon finds a new

way to watch us, we can always Jump to that area, with everything of value and they'll then have to find us…all over again."

Chaza looked around the table. "Do we have any architects?"

Teelila snickered. "That may be where we have to start… in order to get this project going."

Wilfadge snarled. "Meanwhile…what do we do about Algothon and Neksheth-Or?"

Holla shook her head and sighed. "Just keep on screwing up their missiles to make sure that they don't get any of them launched…especially at us."

Four High Investigators were promoted to be the new Prominent Investigators. Now they got together for a meeting. They chose a different room, where numerous Security personnel could look through thick glass and see the four top investigators. If these men disappeared, it would be known immediately and they would see how it happened.

Officer Leader, Ota and Officer Leader, Nachichi went into the glass room, in Spy, to listen, feeling a little frustrated as to how they were going to take care of these new appointees. There were several other Owlamites in the room who were there to take notes and mentally relay the meeting to the rest of the Owlam Spy Team as well.

"All right," said Janekt. "It has been determined that I am the ranking one of the elite four. I remember the others…before their strange disappearance, saying that among us four, rank was not that important, unless there has to be a final decision. I'll treat it the same way. I have an idea of what needs to be done, but I'll accept suggestions as a precursor to any…new way of trying to figure out how those Owlams are doing it…and what we should do to stop them."

"Very generous of you," snickered Trown. "I remember the complete and utter frustration that our previous four were going through. I'm of the mind that we should just launch an all-out invasion of that wretched city with whatever we have… and see how many of them we can take alive for torturing and questioning."

Zykorm pounded his fist on the table. "An attack would accomplish nothing positive at this juncture. First, we have to find their spies - capture, turn or kill them and then we'll be able to launch an offensive, without them knowing in advance. The problem is finding these *Fonsosk* spies."

Hallang shook his head. "The only way that I can think of, to find the spies, dope our entire water system with that drug…I can't even pronounce the name of it. It's the one that you can completely control someone with it and get everyone compliant. Then, we put out a verbal order, broadcast it to the entire city, the Owlam spies are to turn themselves in."

Janekt scoffed. "Drug the…entire city? Doesn't that seem a little drastic?"

Hallang snarled at him. "Think! For over twenty years, those Owlams have been laughing at us. They've fouled up every launch we've attempted for *over twenty years*. Yes, I think that it's time for something drastic...*very* drastic!"

Zykorm shook his head. "So...how do we drug the entire city and keep ourselves from being drugged as well?"

Hallang shrugged. "We drink only bottled water. We each get a supply of bottled water and we touch nothing else. That drug takes a very short time to make one compliant. Once we flood the entire water system - it won't take long."

Zykorm nodded. "So...once we have enough of the drug... we go ahead and get used to bottled water...and keep a secret... even from our security personnel."

Janekt looked grim. "Are you sure that we want to drug them, our security forces I mean?"

Hallang clenched his teeth. "How deep have these Owlams infiltrated us? How many of our personnel are possibly Owlams? We have no idea. Once we've drugged them all...we'll find out... everything."

Janekt shook his head. "If we decide to do this, how long will it take to manufacture enough of the drug and then deploy it? Beyond that...do you have any idea how much that'll cost? That drug...it's so horribly expensive and...the deployment would be another tremendous expenditure. We'd have to come up with some kind of justification for something that expensive."

Hallang snickered. "One of the previous Prominent Investigators, my good friend and boss, Vathent. He thought of this plan...about two years ago. It took fourteen months to get all of the necessary amount of the drug manufactured. Yes, it was costly. It took six months to containerize and distribute the containers…to the most advantageous locations. Yes, that was costly. He was accumulating a large enough supply of bottled water, so he and a few trusted colleagues could remain free of the effects of the drug when, he suddenly disappeared. The canisters containing the drug…are in still in position. The drug can be deployed…in the next few *kadzinks*. It'll take…probably three days for the maximum effect to take place on everyone in the city. Then we make the call over the main broadcasting system and we also tell everyone, who is not an Owlam, to forget what was said. This way, we get the Owlams and none of our people are aware that they were drugged."

Janekt was sitting there with his eyes wide in shock. "Uh… where is the…clean…bottled water?"

Hallang smiled. "I think that the four of us, should spend the next few days, in the house where Vathent used to live. It'll definitely be to our advantage to do so."

"So…" said Janekt, "…before we do the deployment… let's go!"

The four of them got up, opened the locked door and walked out. They silently headed for their private vehicles and followed Hallang to Vathent's home.

"Oh my," said Nachichi. "Should we stop them?"

Ota stood there thinking. She closed her eyes. "Okay people of the Spy Team Algothon, does anyone have any suggestions?"

A thought came back: "I do."

Ota frowned. "Who is this?"

"Officer Grade 2, Gagan. I suggest that we do nothing. Let them deploy their drug. Let them dope up the entire citizenry. Let them go through the frustration of finding no one who is one of us, because we're going to be drinking our own supply of bottled water···not from the Algothon wells."

Nachichi scowled. "What good'll that do? All that I see happening there···is···yes they get frustrated, but it leads to some other more drastic measure."

Gagan mentally chuckled. "It might. It also gives us a chance to ask some questions of our own."

Another thought broke in: "This is Officer Grade 5, Ini. Do you think that maybe we should dope their bottled water as well?"

"No," thought Gagan. "Leave them out of the stupor. That'll add to their disappointment. They'll be able to prove nothing! They, so far, haven't found any Owlamites and they won't find any Owlamites. If they're clear headed, that still leaves them at square one. Meanwhile, we can get a few answers for some of our questions···from some very compliant···Algothons."

Ota looked at Nachichi. "Officer, Gagan…that man has a very devious mind."

"Thank the Makers for that," said Nachichi.

Ota closed her eyes again. "Everyone, start now! Go

get a good supply of bottled water. For the next month, or until we hear that the Algothon water is clear, we drink nothing but bottled water!"

Holla and the Staff made a mental call out to all of the citizens of Owlam. The request was for anyone who had any experience in, or training as an architect. There were two Teams who responded to the summons and showed up at Holla's headquarters.

"I am Officer Grade 3, Assa-Ee. Two of my Team 915, informed me that before the firestorm, they were studying architecture. Officer Grade 7, Nimizi and Officer Grade 7, Queefa."

Holla smiled. She looked at the two women that had been pointed out. "How far did you get in your studies?"

Nimizi looked down. "I'd finished, but the final test was never completed. I had designed a small building and it was built...and that..." She looked off to the side angrily. "...the firestorm knocked it down and burned it up before I was graded."

Queefa shook her head sadly. "I designed one...but the firestorm hit before I could even get all of the equipment together."

Holla nodded. "Do both of you *feel* competent?"

Both women nodded.

Holla sat there looking around at the other faces of the Staff. She turned to the other Team Leader. "Who, on your Team, has some experience?"

"Officer Grade 4, Roosook, Team 3784. I have a bit of experience in this field. I helped redesign and rebuild the Tram area that was destroyed in the Galsino attack." He turned to one of his Team. This is Officer Grade 6, Yaytee and she was a very good student of architecture…before the firestorm. Because of the fact that she knew that I had experience as an architect before the firestorm, she requested being on my Team when the Teams were being assigned."

Holla again nodded. "What we have is eight people. Two different Teams where half of each Team has some experience in architecture. Do any of you have any problems…of any sort…if I reassign some people here? I'd like to have a Team of architects… for some future planning. If there are no major problems, we can do the reassignment right now."

Nobody voiced any problems.

Wilfadge smiled. "It appears that you have what you needed and wanted."

Holla smiled back. She turned to the Teams. "If the four architects would get in one group, and the other Team over here, we'll change the Team roll call in the books." She turned to one of her Team members. "Officer, Niyniy, please enter the changes."

Niyniy was pulling the roll call up. "Yes, Sir, right away." She hit a few more keys and watched her monitor. She looked up. "Ready."

Holla sighed. "Just give your names to Niyniy and the

changes will be made…starting with Team 915."

"Officer Grade 3, Assa-Ee, Team Leader for Team 915."

"Officer Grade 6, Taniba. I was on 3784...now on 915."

"Officer Grade 6, Jototoom…no changes on 915 for me."

"Officer Grade 7, Sisskay. I was on 3784, now on 915."

"Got all of that," said Niyniy.

"Officer Grade 4, Roosook, Team Leader for Team 3784... the new full Team of architects," he said proudly.

"Officer Grade 6, Yaytee, Team 3784, no changes."

"Officer Grade 7, Nimizi, formerly of 915, now on 3784."

"Officer Grade 7, Queefa, formerly of 915, now on 3784."

Niyniy looked around the room. "Okay. All of the changes are officially made in the computer. Teams 915 and 3784 are rearranged, according to orders."

"Thank you, Niyniy," said Holla. "Team 915, you are dismissed. Team 3784, I have some new orders for you… once everyone finishes saying their good-byes to each other and everyone has moved their personal items to the proper place. Please try to get the moves done in under three days."

All eight of the personnel on 915 and 3784 saluted and then vanished.

Chaza cleared her throat. "They'll probably need a *lot* of help. Shall we get the personnel who helped rebuild the Tram area and the wall area from the Galsino attack?"

Holla nodded. "That'll be a great help. I don't want this project to be delayed at all."

Chaza nodded. "If you'll have Niyniy pull up the roll call, I'm sure that there's some annotation as to which Teams were a part of the rebuilding of the destroyed Tram system."

Everyone turned to Niyniy. She smiled wide-eyed with trepidation, turned her gaze to the monitor and then started her fingers rapidly going over the keyboard.

Holla shook her head. "All of the people of Owlam who survived and we only have four architects. No wonder we all seem like lost children. It seems like every time we want to do something new…we find out more about what we lost in that firestorm."

The four Officer Leaders of Spy Team Algothon were sitting at a table eating lunch when the city wide loudspeakers made the announcement about all spies reporting to the main Security Headquarters. All Owlamites immediately turned a recorder on, so that no one could get the orders wrong. They were very interested in the disclaimer that would follow for all Algothon people to forget this order and forget that they were drugged.

After the orders were completed, Ota sent the message out. "People, to your assigned marks. Start asking the questions of them quickly. If they don't know, then go to your secondary marks. We don't know how long this drug is going to last, so we need to act quickly."

The "marks" that they had chosen were the highest ranking computer repair personnel, who also appeared to be the most competent.

Ota Jumped to her first mark. He was getting ready to leave his home and go to work. She hopped to Home dimension. "Stop what you're doing!" She looked around the room and saw that his wife was caught in the trap of the compliancy. Both people stood there with a glazed look in their eyes. Ota shook her head. The thing with the wife could not be helped at this time. "Sir, you are one of the primary computer repair personnel in this section of the city, are you not?"

"Yes," he replied in a dull manner.

"Do you know where the main computer banks are kept, that house and record all of the city archives?"

"No."

She let out a grunt of disgust. "Do you know anyone who is one of the primary maintenance personnel for the archives?"

"No."

Again a grunt of disgust. She huffed. She glanced back and forth between the husband and wife. "Both of you will forget that this conversation ever took place. You will not remember me…at all. You will go about your normal business as if nothing, out of the ordinary, has happened. Do you understand?"

Both responded with a dull yes.

Ota hopped back to Spy and Jumped to her secondary. The results there were just as frustrating. She wanted to call out to all of the other seventy-nine Owlamite spies in Algothon and see if anyone had achieved any positive results. She decided to wait, just in case someone had and they were now obtaining the information. She Jumped back to her normal hiding place to wait. She sat there nervously fidgeting waiting for someone to mentally call out.

"This is Officer, Oymana. I got one! He's telling me that there are five archive spots. One main and four redundant backups. He only knows the location of backup number two."

'That's better than nothing,' thought Ota.

"This is Officer, Yosko. I found the one that can lead us to backup number four."

Ota sat there giggling. Gagan's plan was working. Two down, three to go.

"This is Officer, Sankiki. I got the location of backup number one."

Ota had a tear run down her cheek. 'Please continue, please continue, please…continue.' The thought kept repeating through her head.

"This is Officer, Apa⋯I got backup three!"

Ota was feeling even better now. All four backups were now within their reach. If they could not find the main, the four backups should have what they need…hopefully.

"This is Officer, Sangtee···I got the main big boy *chokwad*. The *Doovofts* hid it in a hospital, in the northeastern sector of the city."

Ota let out a huge sigh of relief for the overwhelming success of the mission. They had used the doping weapon, of the Algothon Security, against them and had found the locations of the archives that had been eluding them for years.

"This is Officer, Teeba···something funny going on here."

Ota's jubilation came to an abrupt halt. "Officer, Teeba, what are you talking about?"

"I'm at Security Headquarters. There's a bunch of Heyyah···who are coming here and confessing that they're···spies."

Ota sat there stunned. She shook her head to clear some cobwebs. "Are they···uh···do you recognize any of them··· from Owlam?"

"None of them are from Owlam. They're all confessing to being spies···for different areas···on this continent."

Ota was again shocked. "How did that happen? He wanted Owlam spies!"

Blana broke in. "He didn't specify! He made a generic call out. He didn't call-out JUST Owlam spies, he made a general call-out for ALL foreign spies. He just cleaned out the spy personnel for all the areas of this continent. Owlam is safe."

Ota sat there giggling uncontrollably. The security forces were now going to be kept busy, questioning spies that had nothing to do with Owlam. The plan had been a huge success and at the same time it had backfired on them. She took several deep breaths to get herself under control. "All right now, we do have the location of all of the different archives are…correct?"

Oymana answered first. "Of course. Backup number two is hidden under a security gate that keeps track of people going from one section of the city to another. It has the appearance of a small office area, but if anyone was to count the number of people who go in the building, that is above ground, couldn't possibly hold that many people. It seems that there are other things hidden down there as well."

"Officer, Oymana, did you get some specific instructions…as to the exact location in the building?"

"Of course."

"Good, we'll use that information wisely…later. How about the main archives? Who found that?"

"This is Officer, Sangtee…remember, I told you that it's hidden under a hospital in the northeastern section of the city."

"Oh…right…sorry…thanks. How about backup number one? Who got that and where is it?"

"Officer, Sankiki. The number one backup is in the underground maze. It's in Bay number 4n121."

"Does that 4n121 mean anything?"

"Yes! It's on sublevel 4, north section, room 121."

"Can you find it from that information?"

"Eventually, yes."

Ota sighed. "How about backup number three?"

"Officer, Apa here. Backup number three is located in the maze as well. 6e229."

"Can you find it?"

"I'm already on sublevel 6 and···oh *h'oolyach*! I'm in the south sector. I've got to get to the east sector. Don't worry, I'll find it."

Ota bit her lip to keep from giggling again. "How about backup number four?"

"Officer, Yosko here. Believe it or not, that backup, it's not even inside the city walls. It's located under a tavern that's about two kilotaja south of the city complex."

Ota had to think about that one for a few moments. "Are you on your way there?"

"Absolutely!"

Ota sat there shaking her head. She hoped that no Owlamite was forgetting anything. Each individual, who had obtained the information, was to tell their "mark" to forget the conversation, once the exact location was divulged. Then, get the rest of your Team and find it. Once they were all found, the decision would be made as to exactly what to do with all of the archives. "Officer,

Teeba, I believe you said that there were a bunch of foreign spies that are going in and confessing to being spies. What were you doing in the security headquarters?"

"My "mark" was there at the time. When he couldn't help me, I went to my secondary, and he was in the headquarters building as well. By the time I found him, the enemy spies were crowding their way up to the front desk."

Ota had been ready to admonish Teeba for not being where she was supposed to be, however, she was exactly where she had been assigned. She shrugged. "Do they have a head count of the spies?"

Teeba mentally giggled. "Ninety-two and counting."

Ota sat there in shock for a few moments. If the Owlamites had exposed that many foreign agents…if anyone ever found out, they would be making more enemies than they had ever had before. It was now imperative that no one found out who uncovered all of the agents. "Let me know when they have a final tally."

"It's gonna be a while. They're still coming in the door. We're well over one hundred now."

Janekt stood there glaring with clenched fists and teeth. "ONE HUNDRED FIFTY-FOUR SPIES!" He turned and looked at the other three Prominents. "Not one of them has been in place for more than ten years and not one of them is from North Chilamte." He paced back and forth with his arms stiff at his sides. "We have a very expensive and very successful sweep of the city, get all of the spies out in the open and we still don't have a clue how the Owlams are doing it. This is totally unacceptable!"

Trown looked at his colleagues bewildered. "Is it possible...that we were wrong? Is it possible that there are no Owlam spies here?"

Zykorm nodded. "Misdirection! That's one of the most powerful tactics in any conflict. Keep the enemy looking here, while you're *shvoking* everything up, over there. Make it look like it's the Owlams that're doing it...while you're doing some... hidden thing...over there. Could it be a misdirection on that grand a scale?"

Janekt snarled. "NO! We've got several different personnel doing the questioning and so far, none of them have anything to do with Owlam."

Hallang picked up the list and gave it the once over. "Are we sure that they're telling the truth? Are they being asked about this misdirection?"

Janekt pounded a fist on the table. "We're still injecting those spies with that expensive compliance drug...that no one can pronounce. They're complying and answering questions... whether they want to or not. No one has yet admitted that they work for Owlam and yes, I do have them being asked about any misdirection."

"Then there's only one other possibility," said Zykorm. He looked around the room grimly. "The Owlams did have a spy here. He or she sneaked...into the Security forces...and obtained a high level of security...and helped destroy the array...then sabotaged the new array. Then exposed…by the Prominents… who were then murdered in order to hide the identity. The Owlam spy…was one of the four previous Prominents. When he was exposed…he killed the other three Prominents and fled. I can't think of anything that…explains the situation…other than that."

Hallang looked at Zykorm in horror. "That thought is so appalling! Do you actually think that a spy could've been here that long working so covertly? Our four predecessors - the longest that any of them had been in the office…was nine years…prior to the disappearance of all four. Yes, there were a few assassinations… but…they were all solved. Could there have been that much misdirection…and…nasty moves…and killing…in a game of espionage?"

Zykorm huffed. "Well…you come up with a more feasible theory. That's my best guess. I know that I can't substantiate it but why else would all four Prominents disappear all at the same time?"

Janekt sat down and sighed. "Theories are nice. What we need is some proof. Otherwise we can't really justify an all-out attack on anyone, let alone Owlam…on a different continent… when we have all of these spies…all of which came from our own continent."

Trown looked disgusted. "Plus, we still don't have any good working theory…on that woman that kept…teleporting all over South Chilamte. She was being guided…by someone here. Someone here was guiding the laser fire of those Owlams…on our array. Someone allowed us to launch a rocket…with a new array that had been sabotaged. Theories about misdirection are fine...but it still doesn't answer the questions about the Owlams... teleporting and turning invisible."

Janekt sighed again. "If you're serious about the possibility that one of the four previous Prominents *was* an Owlam spy... then it's prudent that...one at a time, each one of us undergoes a dosing with that drug. We each get questioned and...our loyalty to Algothon is proven beyond the slightest shadow of a doubt."

Trown scoffed. "Do you know how long it takes to clear that *thwod* out of your system?"

"It takes between nine and fifteen days...depending on your metabolism," said Hallang.

"That's going to take some time," said Zykorm.

Janekt glanced around at his colleagues. "Then we take the time."

"Agreed," said Zykorm grimly.

"Agreed," said Trown.

Hallang sat there thinking. "I think that we should instill this test at a lower level as well. Let's say that we make it a prerequisite of being promoted to...oh...Chief Investigator."

"This whole thing is expensive enough," said Trown. "If we go to that level...it will..."

Janekt interrupted and snarled it. "BE WORTH IT! If we can stop any other spy from...possibly obtaining the rank of Prominent...it's absolutely worth it." He sighed. "Besides that, we've already dosed all of them anyway."

The four architects of Team 3784 stood in the center of the gorge looking up at the face of the cliff.

"This is a tall order," said Roosook. "How in the world are we going to dig out…that many dwelling places?"

Yaytee scoffed. "Digging out isn't the primary problem. We're going to have to figure out a way to supply power and water to all of the apartments."

Nimizi shook her head. "Not to mention an acceptable sewage system…that we somehow have to hide…in order to hide that fact that there's an entire population here living in this… usually unpopulated area."

Queefa snickered. "We're going to be spending a tremendous amount of time dimension hopping in order to get this done."

Yaytee looked around. "So, where do we start? Will it be the sewage system, a way to hook up electrical and water or designing apartments?"

Roosook looked to the south. "I think that the best thing to start with is wait for a rainy day."

The three women looked at him bewildered.

He pointed up at the cliff face. "Look at the lines on the face of the cliff. Those are water lines. How heavy is the rainfall here? How often and how much? How many times does the water reach the upper lines? That'll determine how low the lowest apartments will be. We don't want to see any of the apartments getting submerged…in a light rain. We also want to prepare for the worst possible flooding. We can experiment with electrical, water and sewage…but until we see a good hard rain…we don't start examining the rock in order to find out where the lowest apartments will be."

4

Janekt was thinking through the situation. "First of all, we have to decide what questions will be asked. How deep are we going to delve into the life of the individual being interrogated… under the influence of the drug."

"No limits," said Trown adamantly. "We're talking the top Investigators in the Security system. Make sure that everything is known and that way, no one will be able to make them do anything…untoward. It'll already be known to the Security forces. No one will be able to extort them, because we already know what they've done."

"Film the questioning," said Zykorm. "Film it, so that the one who has been questioned…once it's over, can watch the film and know that they've hidden nothing. We know what they've done, they know we know it and thus…any extortion is smashed before anyone can even attempt it."

"I wish that this had been done to our predecessors," said Hallang sadly. "Can you imagine…having one of the Owlams here…being completely open about that teleporting and invisibility? What we could've done to increase our technology… that would've been awesome."

Janekt growled. "Yes, everything is always wonderful in hindsight. We can't go back and change things, let's just look to the future. We need to get this stuff written, the 'will do', the 'will not', the procedures, and...I like that idea about filming the questioning. It protects everybody." He sighed. "Let's start writing."

Zykorm cleared his throat. "Uh...should we include the High Investigators in this writing? If we get a few more minds thinking about it, it might get some of the things that we've overlooked in there faster."

Hallang shook his head. "Write what we think of now. Let them all read our ideas and then ask for ideas from them."

"Good idea," said Janekt. "Let's start."

The rainfall that Roosook wanted to see came nineteen days later - in the form of a torrential downpour. Team 3784 had hopped to Observation dimension and they were standing on a ledge half way up on the east face of the gorge. They watched as the entire bottom of the gorge started filling up with water and eventually turned into a raging river flowing north.

"That is a *lot* of water," said Roosook. "It gives me an idea about how we can supply the community with plenty of water."

"But it's all flowing away," said Yaytee. "How do we stop it?"

"We make a bunch of tunnels or shafts in the bottom of the gorge...on our side. We then position some pumps to raise the water up to a reservoir – location to be determined later. If we have to make several reservoirs…so be it. Either way, we get plenty, or all that we can get, of water from any rainstorm and utilize it."

Nimizi nodded. "The external part of those tunnels and shafts will have to look like normal rock. That way, no one up top will be able to tell that they're here."

Queefa chuckled. "If we have any windows looking out into the gorge, they'll have to be some kind of big awning that can withstand a lot of rain fall and erosion. Otherwise, we won't have to have any pumps that bring the water into the apartments. They'll also have to be disguised to look like normal rock as well."

"Now," said Roosook, "We have to come up with a way to get rid of the sewage. It would be nice if we could dump it into that river to wash it away…but we don't know where the river goes and if it goes directly to some community from here…they'll know that something is amiss…because of the smell."

"I've got an idea about that," said Nimizi. "I just need to do some scouting…and I'll get back with you on that."

Queefa looked up. "How low should we start the lowest level for the apartments?"

Roosook looked up the face of the cliff. "I think that we should start no less…than fifteen taja above the highest water line. That way…we should be protected from just about any amount of water that fills the gorge."

Yaytee looked north. "Another thing, we need to find out

how the water is departing the gorge. I didn't see any opening...
anywhere up north of here. The gorge just...ends. There's a
cliff face there. There has to be some kind of drain hole that's...
somewhere north of here."

"Water supplied, utilized and drained." Roosook nodded.
"Good place to start with the planning."

Queefa stood there thinking. "Water...for how many
people?"

"Just over twenty-seven thousand," said Yaytee.

"I'd say...at least six reservoirs for drinking and two in
reserve...just in case it doesn't rain enough," said Queefa.

Nimizi checked her pad. "According to what we've got
here, it usually rains, during the dry season, at least once every
fifteen days. During the wet season, it rains almost every day."

Yaytee chuckled. "An equatorial area is certainly different
than what we've been used to all of our lives. It could be a bit of
a shock for most of us."

Roosook nodded. "The good thing is that we won't have
to worry about heating any of the apartments. It never gets cold
here."

Queefa sighed. "So, how much more scouting do we
have to accomplish before deciding where to start digging the
apartments?"

Roosook smiled at his colleagues. "We start right here.
We start by juggling a few things with dimension hopping and see

what comes of it."

Janekt was the first to be drugged. He was kept in an office, with a cot and a camera. He was questioned on his loyalty to Algothon and his determination to keep the city growing into an empire. He passed.

Trown had his turn, then Zykorm, then Hallang. All of them passed.

Janekt was pacing around the room while thinking. "I don't like the idea of going to all of the High Investigators and informing them of the need to make them go through this. It must be done."

Zykorm frowned. "Why? Didn't we just go through a major doping of the entire city? Of the one hundred fifty-four spies that came forward, I don't recall any of them being in the ranks of the Security Forces. Why should we need to…dope them again?"

Janekt stopped and grunted. He licked his lips. "Good point. If any of them had been a spy…"

Trown interrupted. "Yes we do need to do it. They don't know what was done to them. They didn't know about the doping, so they'll think that this is the first time. Once we've done it to the High Investigators…all of them, and established it as standard operating procedure, then no one can question it from then on."

Janekt flopped down in a chair. "Another good point. Sometimes I get very tired of intrigue and subterfuge."

"So," said Hallang. "When do we start doping them and how do we decide which one to dope first?"

"We start tomorrow," said Janekt. "They'll be brought in alphabetically. That way, no one can say that we're showing any favoritism."

Ota brought the three other Officer Leaders and followed Officer, Sangtee to the specific main archives room. The hospital that the computer bank was hidden under did not stand out in any way. The comings and goings of several different computer technicians would not be noticed or looked upon as unusual. Very good place to store and hide the main archives.

If it were ever to get out that this was the storage facility for a military target like the main archives, it would make a hospital a primary target for a strike. Very bad place to store and hide the main archives.

Ota shook her head. 'Either a very bad decision or total arrogance,' she thought. 'What a conundrum?'

They walked down three sublevels. Sangtee led them through a hallway to a set of huge doors. In Spy dimension, she walked right through the wall. Ota and the other Leaders all snickered and followed her lead. On the other side of the doors was a set of hydraulic mechanisms that controlled the entire area. All of the hydraulics on the inside kept any snoops from seeing any form of a hinge or swinging mechanism or what was in here.

There was a desk with two security personnel sitting there

looking rather bored while they were reading the latest updates from headquarters. Sangtee walked past them to a large iron security door where she walked straight through that door.

On the other side was the computer banks that made up the main archives. It had the mundane appearance of a row of wide lockers with metal doors.

Sangtee stood in front of one of the doors. "If I open this, it'll set off a bunch of alarms. We're going to have to just walk in…while we're in Spy."

Ota looked at the other Leaders and shrugged. "What's new?"

Sangtee smiled. "If you'll follow me." She walked through the door.

The Leaders followed.

Once inside, Sangtee turned a flashlight on. In the middle of this "locker" was a pole that went from floor to ceiling. At spaced intervals there were ten round plates, each about the size of a large dinner platter, that were centrally mounted on the pole. There were armatures that came out of the wall and had one part above, the other part below each plate. Every few moments the pole would spin rapidly and there were small lights on each armature that would randomly blink. Each time the pole stopped spinning there was a bank of lights in the back of the locker that would start blinking randomly.

Sangtee smiled. "Sirs, welcome to the largest computer memory bank that any one of us has ever seen. Each one of the plates is capable of holding five hundred trillion bytes of information on the top of the plate and five hundred trillion bytes on the bottom of each plate. So each plate can hold one quadrillion bytes of information times ten plates. This set of plates is capable of ten quadrillion bytes of information. That's a one followed by sixteen zeroes. This specific computer bank, in this array is number eight...of forty-five computer banks...in this main archive."

Blana's jaw dropped. "There are...forty-five of these... and each one is capable of...ten...what?"

Sangtee snickered. "Quadrillion."

Nachichi shook her head. "That's a lot of memory. Do they actually need that much?"

Ota scoffed. "With that capability, they never have to worry about overloading their system. I remember, back before the firestorm, one of the techno-freaks told me that all of the collected memory and history of Owlam had just over sixty-seven trillion bytes of information." She shook her head. "That'd barely make a dent in...this."

"Yup," said Natsa. "Four hundred and fifty quadrillion bytes. They could probably store all of the information of all the world...with room to spare."

"They also have room for expansion," said Sangtee. "I couldn't believe it when I saw it, but, the forty-five sets of memory poles...only take up about one third of the room."

Blana grimaced. "You don't think...the backups...the other four...I wonder if they're just as big as this one."

Ota shrugged. "There's only one way to tell. We'll visit them and see what we see."

"So we go to backup number one," said Nachichi. "Officer, Sankiki found that one."

"Yeah," said Natsa. "It's in the sublevel maze under the main city."

"Sublevel," said Blana. "How unusual," she said sarcastically as she rolled her eyes. "These people have more underground facilities than anyone could have ever expected."

Ota scoffed. "All that digging…where'd they put…all of that dirt?"

Nachichi gave her a dull look. "They have three massive walls surrounding each section of the city. Where the *chokwad* do you think they put it?"

Ota closed her eyes and flushed. She opened her eyes gave them a helpless smile and sniffed. "Let's go take a look at backup number one."

The four Leaders visited each and every one of the four backups. All five archives were designed exactly the same. All had forty-five poles with the same capacity. Each archive was in a room that allowed for plenty of expansion.

Then they had a meeting with all of the Team Leaders.

Blana looked at Ota. "What's the plan? Are we going to blast…or burn…or erase?"

Ota gave Blana a big grin and an evil chuckle. "Steal!

We're going to get enough personnel here, each one grabs a container…and when the order is given…we hop all of them into Observation."

"They'll still be hooked up to the city, though," said Kloob. He looked around at the other Team Leaders. "If we don't cut the cable, then the Algothon will still be able to add or extract information…without being interrupted at all."

"Then we cut the silly cables," said Gagan. "What's the problem there?"

"Each one of the primary cables is as big around as your neck," said Natsa. "You don't just give one little snip to cut that thing."

Ota groaned. "Okay people…what's a good suggestion in cutting off the Algothon from their computer memory bank supply?"

"Acid," said Yotonjo. "Concentrated acid being poured on the cable…at a certain point."

Ota looked at him as if he were crazy. "Just exactly what is supposed to protect us and what we're stealing from the acid?"

Yotonjo smiled. "Hop the computer stuff into Observation. Pick a spot on that cable and hop about…oh…one or two taja into Spy. Pour the acid onto the cable and as soon as it burns through, hop the burned section back to Home. Once we've burned through, we pour the neutralizing agent onto our end of the cable. Now we've got the other end of the cable and the memory banks, with all of that beautiful information…and the Algothon have a big mess and a massive mystery."

"I've got a better idea," said Ko. "Instead of cutting the cables with acid, let's use a pulse rifle. It'll take just about the same amount of time and make *our* end a lot less messy. We can then, douse their end with acid, to make it look like that's what happened…and let them have to clean up the mess and put up with the fumes. Besides, if we use acid to cut the cable, there's always the possibility of causing some electrical arcing, while the acid is eroding the connection."

Ota stood there with her eyes wide open and a big smile. "I'll run it past Supreme Officer, Holla. We'll need some extra personnel, in order to do a mass hop like that. Let's see what Holla and the Staff say."

"We're going to need a whole group of people," said Blana. "This is a major operation that will set Algothon back…at least two centuries. It'll be well worth it when we've finished and sent them into a complete panic."

Holla called back to Ota. "What is going on with these things?"

Ota sighed. "Sir, the archive array is huge. They have all of these things that look like lockers. Inside each locker, it looks like someone took a spear and rammed it through the center of ten plates. Each one of those plates is a hard drive for storing memory. They can put an incredible amount of memory on each side of the plates and considering the fact that there are forty-five of these memory poles in each archive, it is gonna take at least two hundred thirty–five people in order to steal the poles and cut the cables."

Holla shrugged. "How long is it going to take, once you have everyone in there? I hate to think that we're going to have that many people there for several days."

"Oh, no, Sir. Once we have everyone here, it'll be a short briefing. We'll get everyone in place, which shouldn't take long. Then we give the order of execution···poof···it's done. We'll get it all done···in less than half a day."

"Okay, send enough people back here in Jump, so that they can Jump the necessary personnel over there. Let me know when you're ready to execute! I'm sitting here just waiting for Algothon to suffer a major setback like this."

Ota giggled. "Yes, Sir." She turned to the people under her command in Algothon. "Everybody who's been set up to Jump to Owlam and bring the people back...it's a go. Do it!"

The people were back in Algothon very quickly after getting to Owlam and holding hands with the assigned personnel Jumping back.

Ota had decided to get her hands dirty as well. She was going to be one of the people who grabbed one of the computers and hopped it to Observation dimension.

Nachichi was the one who was assigned to give the command of execution as soon as everyone was ready. She sat there in the conference room of the Prominent Investigators. They were not here now so it was rather boring just listening to all of the Owlamites as they each got briefed, got over their awe of the size of the computer banks and readied themselves to assist in the theft. There was a lot of mental chatter going back and forth as they all got into position.

Suddenly the chatter all but ended. Nachichi sat up with a start. She listened for any more sendings - any at all. She sensed none. 'Could we be ready?' She shrugged. "This is Officer Leader, Nachichi. Is everyone in position in the main archive?"

"This is Officer Leader, Ota. We're ready."

Nachichi nodded to herself. "Backup number one···is everybody in position?"

"This is Officer Leader, Natsa, we're all ready."

Nachichi smiled. "Backup number two···are you ready?"

"This is Officer Leader, Blana. We're ready."

Nachichi's smile got bigger. "Backup number three··· are you ready?"

"This is Officer Grade 2, Kloob. We're just waiting for the word."

Nachichi licked her lips in anticipation. "Backup number four···are you ready?"

"This is Officer Grade 2, Gagan. We're ready as we'll ever be."

Nachichi sucked in a deep breath and let it out slowly. "All personnel···on my mark! Three, two, one, EXECUTE!" The computer screen that she was watching in the conference room did not react in any way at all. She was a little confused at first until she realized that this computer was simply tuned in to one of the many cameras around Algothon that was set up to try to catch people in the act of a crime. This one was recording what was currently going on and would not be affected by the loss of any history. She grunted. "Are there any problems in any of the areas?"

"Yes." said Ota. "We had all kinds of lights start going off as soon as we cut the cables. I did a quick hop to Spy and heard a bunch of alarms that are making a horrible amount of noise. I think the security forces will be here···very quickly. To all of you, who're pouring that acid on their end of the connection, dump your empty canisters into Stink. That way we don't have to worry about cleaning anything else up. I don't think that we'll be needing those things anymore."

Nachichi giggled. She could just imagine what was going on there. She decided to take a walk around some of the offices here in Security Headquarters and find out what was going on here as a result of the theft. As soon as she walked out of the closed door to the conference room, she witnessed utter mayhem. She had forgotten that she was in Observation as well and could not hear anything in Home. She moved to Spy and her ears were assaulted with a cacophony of noises from alarms and people yelling. They were all attempting to get something organized in order find the breach in security and get it fixed. It seems that all of the proper protocols on breaches was kept in a file…in the archives…that no one seemed to be able to access…at all…for some inexplicable reason.

Nachichi went back to Observation. "Officer, Ota, I think that we have the attention of the Algothon Security personnel. They're going absolutely *chogo* trying to find anything on their computers."

Ota came back sounding sarcastic. "Really? I wonder what they're trying to find…and why they can't find it…at all."

There was some more chatter as others were responding mentally in some sarcastic, condescending or jubilantly victorious manner.

Ota made a mental call out for everyone to stop. She had a few questions of her own. "Where are the Officers who are our computer experts?"

"Officer Grade 3, Sankiki. I and my Team 254 are in the main archive vault."

"Officer Grade 3, Yotonjo. I and my Team 255 are in the backup one facility."

"Officer Grade 3, Toytay. I and my Team 256 are in the backup four area."

Ota nodded. "Will we be able to get some of our computers hooked up to all of this stuff and start getting information out of them?"

Yotonjo scoffed. "I think that it'd be better if we purloin some of the Algothon computers. Their computers are already compatible with this system. It won't take any special setup to get them hooked up and running."

Ota gritted her teeth. She looked up at nothing in particular. "Why didn't I think of that?" "Go ahead and start getting what you need. The more the merrier and as soon as you've got all of that on line···you can teach some of the rest of us how to use it." She heard all three of the Team Leaders call out to their Teams to start finding some suitable computers to snatch and hook up.

"Officer Leader, Ota, calling Supreme Officer, Holla, do you hear me?"

"This is Holla. I hear you. How'd it go?"

"Perfect! We have ALL of the memory banks and the Algothon have all of the chaos."

"Have you obtained some good passwords, in order to be able to access all of the information?"

Ota sat there in shock. Passwords! Not once had she thought of that. "I'll have to get back to you on that. I was trusting our computer experts with that one."

"Okay, keep me informed."

"Yes, Sir." She sat there almost in panic herself. Was it possible that they had all of this information and no way to access it? She closed her eyes and took several deep breaths trying to calm herself. "This is Officer, Ota, calling my computer Team Leaders···did you obtain the necessary passwords··· for us to be able to get into this system?"

Toytay came back. "We only need four."

Ota's jaw dropped. She pondered that statement for a few moments. "Why do we only need four different passwords? Are you telling me that there's some rule⋯that limits the passwords that the Algothon people were allowed to use? Millions of documents and there are only four passwords?"

"Oh, my no. There's a set program in the system. The passwords of the four Prominent Investigators will open ANY document or program. All we needed was their passwords and we're in all of it without limitation. Seeing as how they no longer have access to these, we won't have to worry about them changing their passwords on us."

Ota had to get over her laughing fit before she could get back to Holla on that information. Only four passwords. The passwords of the four nosiest *bimyocks* in all of Algothon. "Supreme Officer, Holla, this is Ota. I've been informed that we have all of the passwords that we need. Everything is under control."

Holla smiled. "Thank you, Officer, Ota. Good work!"

"Do you have some place in mind⋯where you want us to move these memory banks?"

"Yes I have a place⋯but not yet. It's being worked on at this time. It may be some time before it is completed and ready for moving in."

Ota chuckled. "Fine. They're not going anywhere – at this time⋯yet."

Janekt was livid. He was trying to get hold of anyone in Security Headquarters and no one was answering his hail on the intercoms. He finally gave up, got in his vehicle and drove to Headquarters…at full throttle. He arrived in a very short time… and saw numerous personnel standing around looking at different regulations, arguing and trying to figure out what to do and where to go.

He walked to the middle of the room. "WHAT'S GOING ON HERE? DON'T ANY OF YOU HAVE A CLUE AS TO WHAT TO DO?"

A Senior Investigator looked up from a regulation. "Sir, we've never had a complete and total shutdown of the computer system. Most of the instructions are in the computer mainframes. Since we can't access them, we have to look it up…to do things manually."

An Investigator Trainee looked up rather confused. "What do you mean…manually?"

Janekt walked up to the Trainee and sucker punched him, knocking the young man sprawling on the floor - out cold. He looked around at the *now* silent room. "First thing you do…go to the vaults…and check on them to make sure that they haven't been sabotaged at the source."

No one moved.

"WHAT ARE YOU *FONSOSKS* WAITING FOR - AN ENGRAVED INVITATION?"

The Senior Investigator swallowed nervously. "Uh… Sir…where are they…uh…the vaults…I mean?"

Janekt's shoulders sagged. "You don't know where they are…or how to find them?"

The Senior looked sick. "I…do…on the computer…Sir."

At that moment Zykorm came running into the building. "Is anybody trying to figure anything out…oh…Janekt…you're here."

Janekt turned his dull gaze to Zykorm. "Yes. I'm here. And I just found out that none of these…" He looked around the room. "…Security people…know a thing about looking up the location of the facilities…in the regulations."

Zykorm looked at the shelves where all of the seventy-five regulations, fifty-one manuals and over two hundred codes, statutes and ordinances were kept. He slowly walked up to one of the three binders that was still on the shelves. He set it down on a counter, opened the binder, took hold of the third tab and opened it up to that page. He spoke quietly. "What do you *Fliggits* need to know?"

Trown and Hallang walked in at that time.

"I need to know what's being done about this total collapse of the computer system," said Trown.

"Very good question," said Hallang.

Janekt gave both of them a very dirty look. "That's what we're trying to do, but we just found out that no one here can function without relying totally on the computer. Since the computer is completely down, they've all been running around like a bunch of *Shybeelan Hongoths*. We now know that...once we get that thing back up and running, we're going to have to have at least one day, per month, where we do everything manually." He walked over and kicked the Trainee that lay unconscious. "We're also going to have to teach some of them...what the word 'manual' means."

Trown huffed impatiently. "So, where are we in this investigation?"

Janekt sighed. "We're just beginning. I'll head for the main archive and check to see what happened there. Trown, you go to Backup Number 1, Zykorm, you go to Backup Number 2, Hallang, Backup Number 3...and...is there a High Investigator anywhere in the building...at this time?"

The Senior Investigator cleared his throat. "Sir, until you arrived, I, Senior Investigator Zasoosk, was the ranking man, currently in the building."

Janekt rolled his eyes. "SOMEONE GET OUT THERE AND FIND ME A HIGH INVESTIGATOR...NOW!!!"

Zasoosk stood there with his fists clenched tightly at his side.

A few of the lower ranking personnel started using intercoms in an attempt at finding a High Investigator.

Janekt shook his head. "Forty High Investigators and three times that in Chief Investigators and no one can find a single one," he muttered.

One of the men on the intercom held his intercom piece up. "Sir, I've got High Investigator, Choyskot on the line."

Janekt slowly walked over to the man and took the intercom. "Where are you Choyskot?"

An angry response came back: *"Who is this and who do you think you are interrupting me?"*

"THIS IS PROMINENT INVESTIGATOR, JANEKT! I'M INTERRUPTING YOU AND COMMANDING YOU TO GET YOUR *K'FATH* OVER TO COMPUTER BACKUP NUMBER 4 AND FIND OUT WHY IT'S NOT FUNCTIONING! ANY MORE STUPID QUESTIONS?"

He cleared his throat. *"Yes, Sir…right away…Sir…Sir… I'll get…uh…where in the…uh…city…is…uh…Backup Number 4?"*

Janekt stood there with his teeth clenched. "Get over here to Security Headquarters, check the book for its location and then go."

"Yes, Sir…right away…Sir."

Janekt threw the mouthpiece back to the man he had received it from. He turned to the other Prominents. "Let's get out of here and try to find out…anything."

Each one of the Prominents picked a team of four Investigators to go with them to the scene of the crime. The team that went with Janekt piled into his vehicle and off he went to the hospital. Being one of the Prominent Investigators, he could park anywhere he wanted to and no one dared say anything. He parked directly in front of the hospital. The team entered and went to the elevators. Down to the sublevel where the computer room was.

At the computer room door a maintenance man stood there looking a little nervous.

Janekt walked up and checked the number on the door. He looked at the maintenance man. "What does it take to open it?"

"It takes your code and two others. The problem is… that the codes are kept on file…in the archives themselves. Since the archives are not accessible right now…it can't confirm and authorize the opening of the door."

"Can you open it?"

"Only if you authorize it, Sir. If I try opening it without your approval, I could end up in a lot of trouble."

Janekt snarled. "I am standing right here and I am ordering you, in front of four other Investigators, to open that *fonsosk* door," he growled with a glaring look in his eyes.

The maintenance man smiled weakly and cleared his throat. He went to a control panel next to the door and plugged a carry-all computer into the panel. After making three entries on the keyboard, the door panel beeped, changed colors from blue to orange and the door opened. Fumes came out of the door and all of the men in the hall started gagging and coughing. The maintenance man quickly hit another entry on his keyboard. The panel beeped again and the door closed. He then hit a large orange button on the wall near the door and a huge exhaust fan turned on, sucking all of the fumes out of the hallway.

It took a few moments before any of the men could breathe normally.

Janekt looked at one of his team. "I think that we're going to need some special suits to get in there. Go get some…now!" He turned to another member of the team. "Get on the com. Call the other teams and tell them what happened here. Let them know that they may come across the same thing."

After waiting impatiently for an inordinate amount of time, several hospital personnel came to the door wearing protective suits. They brought suits for the Investigators and the maintenance man to wear as well.

After everybody was dressed, the door was opened again. More fumes came out of the room. One of the hospital personnel held a sensor up, in an attempt at analyzing the fumes. He looked at the monitor that the sensor was connected to.

"Concentrated acid…that's been used to dissolve something. It lost some of its punch when it dissolved…something, so I don't think that any of you will have any prolonged ill effects. I still think that you should be examined by the medical staff though…just to be sure."

Janekt huffed. "Can we get in there…yet?"

"I'm going to hit the exhaust fan in the room. Let it do its job for a few moments and then it should be relatively safe." He opened a small panel near the door and hit the only button behind the panel. The sound of the exhaust fans became almost deafening. He held the sensor just inside the partially open door and kept an eye on his monitor. When he was satisfied, he shut his sensor off, shut the exhaust fans down and opened the big iron door.

The maintenance man walked in and froze in shock. "THIS IS IMPOSSIBLE!"

Janekt grabbed his arm and spun him. "What's impossible?"

"The…cabinets…containing the memory banks…are all… gone! That can't be! It took three of us to move each one of the cabinets. They're so heavy…they left some marks in the original floor. We had to repair the floor…and…now the cabinets…all forty-five of them are gone…and there are no marks on the floor. I…don't see how that…could be done."

Janekt looked down at the floor. "Those…metal studs…in the floor. Is that where the cabinets were…?"

"…bolted to the floor, yes! They've been…cut! They've been completely…sheared off…right at the floor level. What could do that?"

"I see that they used acid to cut the cable connections to the memory banks. Could they have used that same acid to break the cabinets from the floor?"

"No, Sir. You'd see a puddle of the acid on each one of the studs. The only puddle of acid is…on the primary cable connection."

"Are there any security cameras…that could have filmed…

whoever did this?"

The maintenance man hung his head. "Yes…and the filming would have been stored…in the archive memory banks."

Janekt growled in frustration. "So we have…absolutely no evidence of…who did this."

"Not without the memory banks."

"You said that…you couldn't get in…without my authorization. Is there something on the door…that records each time it was opened?"

The maintenance man looked up at the door. "Yes! It has one chip in it…that keeps track of that." He quickly went to the back side of the door. There was a place to plug his hand-held into the door itself. He plugged it in and started furiously punching keys on the pad. He watched the monitor and then hung his head again. "The entries…it shows…the two times that I just opened the door…today. Other than that…it hasn't been opened for over three months. That was when we installed cabinet number forty-five, just over three months ago. Other than that…the door hasn't been opened…at all."

Janekt walked out of the room. He went to the Investigator that was holding onto the com. "Anything from the others?"

"Sir…" He sighed. "…they're reporting…that the exact same thing happened at all four backups. All of our…computer recorded memory history has…*all of it*…been stolen."

One of the Investigators walked around the empty room. "Don't those…Owlams…have some kind of technology that…

makes things invisible?"

Janekt wanted to slap the man. He wandered through the area where the cabinets had once stood. "Don't you think… even if the cabinets were invisible…we'd be bumping into… SOMETHING? The things aren't in here. Yes, they showed us that they can make things invisible. They've also showed us that they can teleport things as well. Somehow…they teleported all of the cabinets. Where and how…we're going to have to conquer those *Hongoths* in order to get our memory banks back."

The maintenance man scoffed. "It may be too late to retrieve the hard drives…already."

Janekt walked over to him. "Now why is that?"

"If those things have been taken somewhere…other than a strictly controlled environment…the hard drives are already trashed."

"Please elaborate."

"This room and the rooms where the backups are kept are all highly controlled. The reason behind this is because of how the information is entered on the plates themselves. We can put information on both the top and bottom of the plate. The armatures that are near the plates…they're so close…that if anything gets in between the armature and the plate…you get irreparable damage… to both."

"Just how close are these armatures?"

"Lint…is too thick. A finger smudge…too thick. The only thing that's not too thick is air…pure air. If they moved the cabinets to a place where the air is not totally purified…well, we don't have to worry about the enemy being able to access any information from the hard drives. Once the plate is damaged… even though it may be a small place on the plate, the whole thing is worthless and you can't get any information from that plate, no matter what."

"Do you think that they knew this…before the theft?"

"Highly doubtful. We haven't told anyone this information…in regards to the design of the hard drives. It is still our secret."

Janekt shook his head. "That's a small comfort. We don't have it any more, but they can't get anything off of them either."

Ota was relaying this information back to Holla as they spoke. The new information came as a shock, however, since the cabinets had not been removed from the pure air, they now knew that they were going to have to come up with their own pure-air room before Jumping the cabinets out of Algothon…or they could just leave them where they were.

Holla called Team 3784 for a meeting. They Jumped back to her headquarters to find out what was so important.

Holla smiled at them. "We've found out that we're going to need a special room…that might need to be rather large. We have to remove any form of contaminant…in the air…from that room in order to prepare it for the introduction of some special computer memory banks."

Roosook smiled weakly. "Contaminants?"

"Yes, we found out that there is a special quirk in the design of these things. There is this hard drive and an armature that is used to record the information on the hard drive. The armature never touches the hard drive. However...it is so close to the hard drive...that even a finger smudge is too thick...to allow the thing to operate properly."

"It may be some time before we're ready for that kind of a setup," said Yaytee. "I don't...even know how to attempt...to clean the air...like that. How do you purify...air?"

"It'd take some very special filters," said Nimizi. "It can be done, but, we just don't have anything in our...designs...that're nearly good enough to extract ALL contaminants...yet."

Queefa shook her head. "Just think of how you have to make sure that there are absolutely no leaks...anywhere in the room...that allows anything in or out."

Holla nodded. "So it's going to be quite some time before this can be accomplished."

Roosook nodded. "You've given us a task for setting up a living community. We can do that...with a few sacrifices... at first. Once everyone has moved in then we can get everyone cooperating and worry about...special circumstances or special rooms."

5

The Owlam Staff was sitting in the conference room considering things they heard about the archives of the Algothon. They all agreed completely that the archives had to stay where they were until the architects were able to come up with a "clean" room for this new acquisition. They considered the fact that they were extremely lucky because none of the acid fumes had gone to Observation with the hard drives.

"That was a short meeting," said Ahandi. "It wasn't even a briefing, it was a statement."

Chaza grunted. "When do you think the architects can have one of those special rooms ready for us?"

"Unknown," said Holla. "We don't even know how the Algothon did it. We'd have to get into their architectural archives in order to figure it out."

Hadathoo grimaced. "Can we do that…get into their archives, that is, and find all of the information we need?"

Holla nodded. "Sankiki and Yotonjo said that it'd be about fifteen days before they have a hookup completed. Then we can get anything we want out of the Algothon archives."

Teelila looked a little melancholy. "You mean that we're actually doing something positive, without killing anyone? It seems that...ever since the firestorm, all we've done is figure out some new way to kill...this enemy or that."

"Don't forget," said Wilfadge, "Other than the Axswain, all of these others attacked or tried to abuse and misuse us. We've every right to survive and live free. It's just like the Kalash said: We're not going to attack anyone, but we won't back down from defending ourselves...or something like that."

Holla scoffed. "That does seem to be the one thing that we're becoming more proficient at...faster than anything else... killing that is. I wish we could do some building for once."

Ota watched as the maintenance personnel started preparing the clean room. They were setting it up to replace the cabinets and they needed to get all of the caustic gasses from the acid out of the room before they could start rebuilding.

"Officer, Ota calling Supreme Officer, Holla. Do you hear me?"

Holla responded. "This is Officer, Holla. What did you need?"

"I think that you need to get the architects here to Algothon. It seems that there are some special requirements that are needed···and the computer people don't understand what it is that's needed. Can you send the architects···as soon as possible?"

"We've already sent the architects. They said that they won't be able to do anything for some time, as far as creating a room for the archives."

"Sir, there's more to it than that. Our computer people don't seem to understand what their computer people are doing. I think···there's a big difference between computer programming and computer repair···or building. They're doing something and···if the computer programmers and the architects don't understand it, we need some computer repair technicians."

Holla sat there with her hands over her face. 'What next,' she thought. "I'll have to get back with you on that."

"Yes, Sir, I'll be waiting···uh···please hurry."

Holla went limp in her chair. She sat there drawing a complete blank as far as what she needed to do. She sighed. "This is Supreme Officer, Holla. We need to have a full Staff meeting at my headquarters···NOW!"

Moments later the Staff personnel started entering the room and taking their seats.

Wilfadge checked to make sure everyone was there. He smiled at Holla. "Okay, what's on the agenda?"

Holla smiled and informed them of the problem that Ota had sent to Owlam. She looked around at them. "Any suggestions?"

Teelila looked a little nervous. She cleared her throat. "I…uh…heard of something…that…either Jahong…or Nakalak did."

Holla noticed the consternation. "If you think it'll help… what in the name of progress is it?"

Teelila smiled. "When he couldn't find…anybody to… send to Algothon to…do computer work…he picked some Teams…at random. He ordered them, using the *Voice of Power*, and made them become…I guess you could call it enthusiastic… about computer programming. Since given that order, they've been doing a wonderful job of programming and whatever else it is that they need to do. If this repair work is so different than what the programmers…or operators have been doing then maybe you should pick some Teams at random and make them become enthusiastic about…repair."

Holla sat there with a blank stare. "Any suggestions…on whom I should choose?"

"She did say random," said Ahandi flatly.

Holla sighed. "Team 1000, report to the Supreme Officer's Headquarters, immediately!"

Moments later Team 1000 walked into the conference room looking somewhat apprehensive.

Holla looked up again. "Team 1001, report to the Supreme Officer's Headquarters, immediately!"

Team 1001 entered looking just as confused as 1000.

Holla looked around at the staff and shrugged. "Team 1002 report to the Supreme Officer's Headquarters, immediately!"

Now Team 1002 came in and stood with the other two

Teams.

Holla was staring at the ceiling. "One more." "Team 1003, report to the Supreme Officer's Headquarters, immediately!"

All four Teams were now in attendance.

Holla smiled. "Team 1000, introduce yourselves."

A woman stepped forward. "Sir, I am Officer Grade 3, Tula, Team Leader of Team 1000. My Team consists of Officer Grade 5, Zozz, Officer Grade 5, Nowma and Officer Grade 7, Seennka."

Holla nodded. "Thank you. Team 1001, introductions please."

A man took one step forward. "Sir, I am Officer Grade 3, Sunggosh, Team Leader 1001. My Team consists of Officer Grade 6, Hiyshee, Officer Grade 6, Quistie and Officer Grade 7, Toopa.

Holla smiled. "Thank you. Team 1002, introductions please."

Another woman stepped forward. "I am Officer Grade 3, Shanah. My Team members are Officer Grade 6, Loskani, Officer Grade 6, Brong and Officer Grade 7, Yuyana."

Holla smiled. "Thank you, and finally, Team 1003, Introductions."

"Sir, I am Office Grade 3, Atsuska. My Team members are Officer Grade 6, Jeeshee, Officer Grade 7, Toonjom and Officer Grade 7, Wahamee."

Holla smiled and then looked at the Staff. She sighed again. She closed her eyes. "Teams 1000, 1001, 1002 and 1003. From this day forth, you're assigned to become computer repair technicians. You'll go to Algothon where you'll watch the computer repair technicians there, as they build the new archives. You will learn their procedures and you will be drawn to excel passionately in this field of work. I need you to report to Officer Leader, Ota at the earliest possible opportunity in order to begin your new career. You may go and take care of anything that you need to clean up or finish up here, before departing." She looked at the Staff and shrugged. "Teams 1000, 1001, 1002, 1003, you are dismissed."

The sixteen "newly assigned personnel" all vanished.

Holla looked at Teelila. "Is that what you had in mind?"

Teelila nodded. "I think that'll work."

Holla looked around the room. "Does anyone have anything else?"

Everyone shook their heads.

She sighed. "Mission accomplished. Meeting adjourned."

Holla went back to her office. Nayna and Niyniy were waiting for her with strange looks on their faces.

Holla smiled. "May I help you?"

Nayna tried to say something. She had to clear her throat twice before she could speak. "Did you...do anything...like that...to us?"

"No. You were already dedicated to what you're doing. I didn't need any special circumstances. I accept you for what you do and I haven't tried to alter any of you."

Nayna simply smiled while Niyniy let out a long sigh of relief.

Three days later, after taking care of some affairs at home, all sixteen of the new computer technicians were in Algothon watching closely as the Algothon technicians performed their duties.

Janekt was sitting in the clean room, under the hospital, watching the technicians as they installed a new cabinet with a brand new blank quadrillion byte hard drive.

There was a Chief Investigator who was in the room as well. "Sir, I just don't understand. Someone came in here and stole forty-five of these cabinets…right under our noses. Why are we putting more of these…very expensive mainframes in here… again?"

Janekt snickered. "Shallwon, there are two reasons why we're still using this room. One: It is way too expensive to set up another clean room. This one is already here. Two: From this day forward, there will always be at least three armed guards standing outside the door. They'll be there and they'll have an axe hanging over their heads. If anyone steals any of the cabinets, while they're on guard…if they don't stop them or if they say that they didn't see anything…they will be immediately taken from here to a place of execution."

"So you feel that the threat of death will stop any further thefts?"

Janekt gave Shallwon an evil glare. "Wouldn't that give you some extra motivation?"

Shallwon sighed. "I suppose it would, Sir." He cleared his throat. "How...are we going to replace all of the information... that was lost?"

Janekt grunted in disgust. "We can't! We can replace a lot of it...from school textbooks or from some of the written manuals...in certain areas. We'll never be able to replace all of it, but we can certainly try to get as much information in there as we can find in any and all written books that are within our borders."

Shallwon hung his head. "THAT is going to take quite a bit of time."

"Do we really have a choice?"

"No, Sir, we don't. We either try to get all of the information amassed that we can...or just give up. I don't like the idea of ever giving up."

Janekt smiled. "Neither do I, Chief."

"Sir, are we going to put more of these cabinets...in the other four backups?"

"Of course. Those rooms are set up for this and we need to have our computer system and the backups...in spite of any enemy and anything that the enemy is capable of doing."

Shallwon sat there nodding approval. "If you don't mind

my asking, Sir…how is the questioning of all of those spies… uh…how is it going?"

Janekt grunted. "We found out most of the information, which those *Hongoths* knew, in the first two days…including the fact that those wretched monsters in Neksheth-Or learned all that they know about rockets…from information that they stole from us. That's flaming embarrassing, getting bombed by an enemy, with your own technology. Now, we're just using those spies to teach some of our younger security personnel the finer, more painful and the most effective ways of torturing the enemy."

"Did we learn anything more about those Owlams?"

"We learned that their spies are…very possibly immune to certain types of coercion…when it comes to attempts at exposing them. We may have to try something…a lot more drastic before this thing is over."

"Would that include attacking Owlam?"

Janekt nodded. "Attack…and conquer…or eradicate…if necessary."

Ota, all sixteen of the new computer technicians and the architect Nimizi, were standing there listening to the conversation. Ota was ready to dump Janekt into one of the nastier dimensions right now. She held her temper, for the moment. She was waiting for an order from Holla and then she would have some fun of her own with this monster.

Roosook was doing a little mapping of the area in order

to determine just how they were going to fit all of the citizenry of Owlam into this area. There was more than enough room. The only problem was designing something that everybody could approve of and appreciate.

Yaytee looked at his design. "Which one of the current homes has caused the most envy?"

He turned to her. "What do you mean?"

She scoffed. "Are there a few places that most of our citizenry is envious of? That might be the best to choose from... as far as a final design...for everyone."

"So, which one or ones are you the most envious of?"

"I heard a bunch of things about that Team *Bimyock*. That's the only place that I know of, where different Teams were going to and challenging that Team for ownership...of their quarters."

He sighed. "I heard about that as well." He looked around at their first experiments. "Queefa, have you heard about any... place...other than the living quarters of Team *Bimyock*...that anyone was fighting for"

Queefa looked up from her designs. She pondered for a few moments. "No. No one ever fought over any other place."

"Okay," he said. "Let's Jump to Team *Bimyocks* headquarters and see what everyone was fighting over. That might be the best design overall for all of us, here in the gorge."

The three of them Jumped to a place on the south central portion of the great wall. They looked down at the street.

"It's supposed to be somewhere in this area," said Queefa.

Roosook scoffed. "Okay, but where? I don't see anything, in this area that'd be worth fighting over."

"Wait," said Yaytee. "Look at that empty lot. If I remember correctly, when those *Doovofts* from Beetsik came here, Team *Bimyock* hopped their home into Spy dimension. Is it possible that they…just left it there?"

Roosook shrugged. "Let's hop to Spy…and take a look."

The three of them performed the hop and immediately saw a four story building standing where the vacant lot had been. Over the front double doors, they saw the number "7016" proudly displayed.

Yaytee snickered. "That's it."

Roosook nodded. "Let's go inside and measure the place. See what all is in there and we'll go from there."

"I wonder if we should go in…if Team 7016 is not at home," said Queefa.

Roosook shook his head. "We're going in to get measurements. We're not going in to steal anything. We just find out how the place is laid out, measure and map it…and then back to the gorge to check for any feasibility."

Queefa had a bit of a guilty look. "I still think that we should knock first. Find out if anyone's home and get their permission…first."

Roosook laughed. "Don't worry…we'll knock."

They Jumped down to the front door of 7016 headquarters. Roosook walked up to the door and knocked. He looked back at the two women and smiled. He knocked again.

"It doesn't sound like anyone's home at this time," he said with a smile.

Kiyalee appeared right next to Roosook. "Guess again, *Bimyock*."

All three of the architects jumped in surprise.

Roosook snickered nervously. "Uh...the Supreme Officer told us to design homes, in a completely different area, just in case we had to...flee from Owlam. We...heard so much...about your home...and how so many people were...highly envious of it. We were wondering if we could come in and look at the layout...and use that as a guideline for the homes...in the new area."

Kiyalee stood there with her head cocked to the side, listening to him. "What else did you want?"

"We just...want to see the design...and get some measurements," said Roosook with a smile.

Kiyalee looked skeptical. She rolled her eyes, scoffed and vanished. A moment later she was unlocking the front door. She opened the door for them. "Right now, Bonarain and Chyning are each in the bathtub, washing the back of their necks. Don't disturb them!"

Queefa grunted. "Yeah. Washing the neck! I'm beginning to really hate that...twice daily ritual."

Roosook smiled. "We'll do the bathrooms after we've finished the rest of the place and they're finished…cleaning."

Kiyalee sighed. "Okay, here, we have the main dining room, coupled with gaming room. Over there, by the gaming room, there's two bathrooms…for guests. On the other side of the big long bar, there's a kitchen and a storeroom. In the back of that hallway, there's the garage for our big 161, a freight elevator and the back door."

Queefa looked towards the bar. "That double door there. Is the kitchen on the other side of the double doors?"

Kiyalee nodded. "Yeah."

Yaytee frowned. "Where's your personal space? Where's your area for…personal entertainment?"

Kiyalee pointed up. "That's all on the second floor."

Queefa's jaw dropped. "You have…two floors…to your Team home?"

Kiyalee frowned at Queefa. "No, we have all four floors of this building. This, the first floor, is where we eat and entertain guests, like my lunch, that's sitting on that table and getting cold. The second floor is our personal areas. The third floor is our gymnasium. The fourth floor, we use for storing whatever we want to store up there."

Roosook closed his eyes and shook his head. "No wonder there were other Teams coveting this place." He opened his eyes. "I'd have almost been ready to kill…in order to get a Team home where the personal area and storage space…are in the same building."

Queefa looked at the food on the table. "I...don't recognize...that stuff."

Kiyalee shrugged and sighed. "When we found that bombed out city called Hashkay, on the other side of the Turgon Wall, we checked it for any subterranean storage vaults. We found six levels. We found all kinds of food in them. We brought some of that food here...for us. Didn't you get the message on that?"

Roosook chuckled nervously. "I...guess I need to get up to date on reading my messages."

Queefa looked around. "You said that two of your Team members are taking a bath. Are they on the second floor?"

Kiyalee nodded.

Yaytee looked around merrily. "Looks like we're going to be doing a great deal more of measuring than we originally thought."

"So," said Roosook, "Let's get to it."

Ota was watching as the Algothon technicians were installing another cabinet in the main archive area. "Should we really wait until they've finished? How are you going to move all of the cabinets to Owlam after they have all of them bolted to the floor?"

Nimizi had an evil grin on her face. "Once they've done all of the installation, troubleshooting tests and programming, we're going to Jump the whole *chokwad* room to Owlam. They said that it's an expensive undertaking, making a room like this. So, we wait until they've finished all of it…and then we steal…*all* of it."

Ota looked at Nimizi with concern. "Can we get away with that?"

"Of course," snickered Nimizi. "How're they gonna stop us?"

Tula came back over to Ota. "All that they're doing right now is some of the redundant testing of the new hard drives. I already got that, so all we really have to do is wait until they're finished doing all of the installation…and then we can proceed with our purloining, at our leisure."

Ota grunted. "Why don't we do all of that now?"

"For one thing," said Tula, "We don't have any specific place to put all five of those archive rooms. Second, if we swipe the stuff now, they still have several more of those memory bank poles that they can use to build a new set of archives."

Ota was shocked. "Are they able to make those…poles… that quickly?"

"No, they had forty-five of the things that were sitting in reserve until they needed them. They didn't need them until we disconnected the ones they were using. They've already started manufacturing new ones…while they're installing these."

Ota nodded. "So we'll be able to Jump them to Owlam and then hop them back to Home and then use them."

"No," said Tula. "As long as the city of Algothon exists and their tracking technology exists, we'll have to leave them in Spy. Or we can put them into Observation. Each one of those poles has a chip in it...that sends out a signal. They can triangulate on that signal and know exactly where the things are. They'd then be able to go and get them. If we leave them in Spy - they'll never know where we put the silly things."

In Neksheth-Or, Officer, Boneech was having a meeting with the nine Team Leaders that had been assigned to harassing this city.

She was doing a little pacing as she pondered. "We've got to do something more than just harass these people. We've got to disarm them. These *chogo* rockets that keep on getting launched at us are beyond being a nuisance. While the Supreme Staff argue about how to handle these Neksheths...we're still stuck here... doing a bunch of minor sabotage. I'd like to get rid of all of these rockets and go home. Does anyone have an idea of how to get rid of all of the rockets...here?"

Hadeetz huffed. "We've been stealing a bunch of their microchips that they put in the rockets. We make sure that we steal the same one, off of each, so that they can't replace parts from one to another."

Boneech shook her head. "That doesn't stop them, it just slows them down. What we need is a permanent solution."

"We've been blowing the warheads up on the ground," said Lolathiy. "That'll keep them from launching because they don't have a warhead anymore…or the top portion of the rocket."

Boneech stomped her foot. "Again, that's only temporary. Have you seen how fast they can get another rocket put together in those silos? Taking out the warheads is not permanent."

"I've got a thought," said Azhgon. "We get some of those computer types to come here. We have them reprogram the chips that control where the things go. We have them reprogram these chips that steer the things and have them go straight up…without any turns…north, south, east or west."

Boneech huffed. "So they fly straight up…so what."

"So," said Azhgon, "Whatever goes up…has to come back down. If the things go straight up, they'll come straight down, when they run out of fuel. The Neksheth-Or get bombed by their own weaponry."

"That's no good," said Miskanasa. "The amount of fuel that those things have, by the time they run out of fuel…they'll be so high that…well, according to what we've read about this… outer space…they won't be coming back down."

Azhgon chuckled. "So, we fill the fuel tanks full of rocks."

Waha squawked. "What good's that gonna do?"

Azhgon smiled. "Every rock that's placed in a fuel tank will displace a certain amount of fuel. For every drop of fuel that the rocket does *not* have, that's a shorter distance that the rocket will fly. The more rocks we put in there, the more fuel we displace. Plus the added benefit - the rocket is not getting much lighter as it burns fuel, so it has to burn fuel faster, and thus it does not fly up very far and comes back down…sooner."

"We need to be careful on that," said Hizee. "If we put too many rocks…with too much dirt on them into the tanks…they won't even be able to get off of the ground. Any dirt that's in there could foul the rocket engine so badly - it can't lift off. It just burns up all of the fuel in the silo and doesn't go anywhere."

Quall chuckled. "We put some kind of filter, of our own, in the tank. This way, the engine gets only pure fuel. We could even make the filter somewhat fragile. That way, as the fuel is fed through the pump, the first batch is pure, then it gets contaminated fuel, it chokes the engine off…and down it comes."

Boneech listened to the plan. "Sounds good." She took in a deep breath and let it out. "Let's start making those filters and start filling tanks. I'll talk to Holla and see if we can get one of the computer people here…to realign the steering program."

Babeena scratched her chin. "How badly do you think this city will be damaged by that kind of a disaster?"

Quall shrugged. "We won't know until we do it."

Three of the computer operators showed up in Neksheth-Or: Officer Grade 5, Tay, Officer Grade 5, Ini and Officer Grade 6, Nolila. After being briefed on what needed to be done they took some of the computer chips that were designed to steer the rockets and wasted no time getting into the program and seeing how they could completely rewrite it without the Neksheth-Or knowing about it.

After all the time that they had been working with the Algothon programs they were, at first, surprised to find that the Neksheth-Or computer language was almost identical. Once they found out that this computer information had been stolen from Algothon, it was almost comical in regards to how the Neksheth-Or did not have enough imagination to change any of the programs at all.

Finally, after twenty-nine days, one of the control chips had been reprogrammed. The trio sat back congratulating themselves.

"Officer Leader, Boneech, this is Officer, Tay. Can you hear me?"

"Officer, Tay, this is Boneech, what is it that you need?"

"Sir, we're reporting that we have finally figured out how to totally reprogram the rocket steering system. We've got what you need. We have a chip that's ready whenever you need it."

"Outstanding! Now, Officer, Tay, we need only four hundred fifty-five more of them, reprogrammed and ready to go."

Tay went slack-jawed. "Sir⋯you⋯need⋯WHAT?"

"The Neksheth-Or have a total of four hundred fifty-six silos. Each one has a rocket in it, right now, that's ready for launch. The only reason that they haven't launched them is because we keep fouling the mechanisms. Once you get enough chips to plant in each rocket, we'll do it and let them launch. Any questions?"

"Uh···yes, Sir···uh···why are you going to allow them to launch···their rockets?"

"Because once you've made all of the changed chips and we've replaced them, we control where the rockets go."

Tay hung her head. "Yes, Sir. We'll get them done as quickly as possible."

Ini looked sick. "Oh, my," she said sarcastically. "Only four hundred fifty-five more to go. I wish they'd told us that information sooner."

Nolila looked at the pile of computer chips that were sitting in the room. "Should we tell them how many chips we totally messed up, trying to get the program that they wanted?"

Ini sighed. "No. I'm sure that they can find plenty of replacements."

Tay snickered. "I think you're right. Let's get to work."

Eighty-two days later, all of the needed chips were ready, with the new program, to be placed in the rockets. The ten Teams assigned to spy on Neksheth-Or had been practicing, during that entire time, on doing some quick switch-out replacing of the necessary chips.

Boneech called out. "Is everybody ready?"

After getting the affirmatives from everyone in the roll call (including the three computer operators), the execution command was given. Twenty-four of the saboteurs had to redo eleven rockets each. Sixteen saboteurs had to redo twelve. The three computer operators Jumped immediately to the Rocket Launch Control Office (RLCO) and started creating a few diversions in order to keep the personnel in there from noticing some warning lights on their monitors. Once the Twenty-four were finished, they were to Jump to the RLCO and get everything ready for launch.

Boneech finished the eleven switch-overs that she was responsible for and Jumped to the RLCO. Eight other Owlamites had arrived there ahead of her.

As each new member of the Owlam spy Team arrived in the RLCO, the more of the Neksheth-Or computer operators there were that got tossed into Jahong's Death (when they were out of the room). It did not take very long to toss all of the Neksheths out of the Home dimension.

Boneech looked out a peephole in the door to the Main Launch Center to see if there was anything going on out there. They had been able to pull the entire thing off without any of the Neksheths (outside of this room) aware that anything was amiss.

Boneech sat down in the back of the room. "All personnel… to Home dimension, NOW!" She hopped and watched the room, again, fill up with Owlamites. "Remember, since there are only thirty launch monitors and forty-three of us, that leaves plenty of personnel who WILL stop anyone from coming through that door."

Thirty Owlamites sat down at the monitors and started feeding the launch codes into the rockets. The timers were set so that all of the rockets were scheduled to launch at the same time, thus giving no one outside of the room any warning.

Boneech went back to the peephole and watched. Still, they were successful in keeping their surprise attack unnoticed by the Neksheths. She breathed a sigh of relief and went back to watching the people at the computers, while Officer, Zhosh went to the peephole.

The launch codes were fed in and any and all changes to the launch sequence were locked out. They knew that someone who was in a silo trying to figure out what sabotage had been done to that rocket might be able to hit some keypad out there and prevent the launch. The no-change order, coming from Launch Control would prevent them from stopping the launch.

Finally everyone was done feeding in the information.

Izzanto looked up at Boneech. "What do we do now, Sir?"

She looked back at Zhosh. "Is there any activity out there?"

"Nothing yet," said Zhosh.

Boneech nodded. She looked around at all of the personnel staring back at her. "Take their keyboards and monitors and put them all safely in Spy dimension. That way if something bad happens there's not a *wathoot fovok* thing that they can do about it."

All of the computers disappeared from the desks.

"Now, we can think about resting for a few heartbeats," said Boneech.

It turned out to be very few. Part of the 'preparation for launch' included the top-side doors to the silos opening up. An alarm sounded at each silo as each of them started opening up at the same time.

Zhosh pulled out his pulse pistol. "We've got activity! Only one of them is headed for the door, but, that usually don't mean anything."

Boneech stood up. "All personnel, hop to Spy…NOW!"

Zhosh (in Spy) was still looking through the peephole. "He's picking up the intercom."

A voice came through a speaker on the wall. "*What's going on in there? Nobody said anything about a launch…especially an all-out launch.*"

"It looks like he's getting mad," said Zhosh.

"I don't care," said Boneech.

Everyone in the room snickered.

A Neksheth officer started pounding on the door.

While the first Neksheth hailed the people in the room again. "*Is everyone in there deaf? What's going on? Open the door.*"

"Looks like somebody is coming up to the door with some keys," said Zhosh.

"Let them come," scoffed Boneech.

Zhosh put a brace against the door and walked away

chuckling.

After unlocking the door it took three hard bashes against the door in order for the Neksheths to get through.

The officer that had been on the intercom was one of the first to come through. "WHAT ARE YOU DOING IN…here?" He stood there dumbfounded as he saw no one in the room and all of the monitors missing as well.

Several more Neksheths piled into the room and were, very quickly, all standing like statues, absolutely bewildered.

A Neksheth looked at the ranking officer in the room. "Sir…what happened?"

He threw his arms out is exasperation. "HOW SHOULD I KNOW? Check the bathrooms, see if they're all piled in there, with their computers."

There was a mad dash by four Neksheths to follow his order.

Boneech looked at Tay. "How soon are those *chokwad* things supposed to take off?"

"Look up at their clock," said Tay. "When the last two digits show 22, we'll have a mass launch."

Boneech looked up at the clock and groaned. The last two numbers were currently showing 16. She shrugged. "Make yourselves comfortable, it's gonna be a little while. Officer, Tay, why does it take so long?"

Tay shrugged. "Each rocket has to do its own pre-launch

trouble shoot before taking off. Once it's done with that - off we go!"

The Neksheths that searched the bathrooms came back out.

"No one in the male bathroom."

"No one in the female bathroom."

The one in charge put his hands on top of his head. "What's going on here? How…when…why…" He let loose with a long, loud growl. He looked out of the launch room. "Birkbool, have you been able to do anything about this?"

The response from outside the room came back. "No, Sir. Some kind of lockout has been executed. All of them are going to launch and there isn't a thing we can do about it. Five and a half *toonsok* till launch."

Another Neksheth looked frantically at the ranking officer. "Sir…what're we going to do?"

He shrugged. "We're going to watch all of our killer rockets…launch." He shook his head. "And there's nuthin' that we can do about it….except…watch."

In Algothon, a technician was watching through one of the spy satellites over Neksheth-Or. "Commander, from what I'm seeing, those *Fliggits* in Neksheth-Or are getting ready for another one of their mass launches."

The Commander stood up. "Put your monitor on the big

screen. Is there any way that we can tell where those things are headed?"

"Not until they're airborne, Sir."

The Commander growled. "Let's just hope that they're not headed for us. There isn't much we can do about that...right now."

All eyes were on the big screen (including the Owlam spies that were in the room).

The Commander watched the screen fill up with smoke. "What's all that interference?"

"That, Sir, is the smoke from the rockets. Four hundred fifty-six of them, all taking off at the same time, filling that entire area with smoke...as they launch."

The Commander snarled. "I can't see a thing! Pull back on the magnification, maybe that'll help."

The magnification was adjusted and now they could see the noses of the rockets coming up out of the smoke.

"Okay," said the Commander. "Have you got a direction yet?"

The technician shook his head. "This...is ridiculous!"

"WHAT?"

He turned to the Commander. "Not a one of them, according to the telemetry that I'm getting...has altered their flight pattern... by more than two degrees. Sir, they're all flying...straight up."

The Commander sat there with his mouth wide open. "That's stupid! Unless…maybe since…they all launched at the same time…they've got to get more altitude before altering their flight plan otherwise…they'd all be banging into each other."

The technician sat there shaking his head. "Some of them have altered three degrees…one of them altered four degrees… otherwise, still no changes."

Four other technicians called out a confirmation on the direction.

Back in the RLCO, Izzanto snickered. "Once those things run out of fuel and fall back it's gonna be utter devastation around here."

Boneech gasped. "Yes, and it's gonna get awful loud! All personnel, hop to Observation dimension…NOW!"

The Algothon technicians all were looking up at the screen in shock.

The Commander looked confused as well. "What…are those things running…out of fuel…and just…falling?"

One by one, each of the technicians in the room confirmed that the rockets were just running out of fuel and falling.

There was nothing but silence in the room as all of the Algothon personnel were sitting limp in their chairs as they watched a disastrous scenario unfold in Neksheth-Or.

The Neksheth Commander was screaming at everyone, telling them to get to the bomb shelters. It was total panic in the other section of the RLCO as they ran for safety. In the rest of the city, people were gagging and coughing from all of the smoke, totally unaware that all of the rockets were now falling back down.

Zhosh had gone back to the door to watch.

Boneech huffed. "Are they all gone?"

"Yes, Sir," said Zhosh. "All of them cleared out of there in record time."

"Do you think that some of them will make it to the bomb shelter?"

Zhosh shook his head. "That, is a very good question, Sir."

One by one the rockets hit and did their job of exploding and causing maximum damage in the area where they hit. The Owlamites did not hear anything while sitting in Observation. They saw huge flaming explosions and saw debris flying everywhere. One of the rockets came down and scored a direct hit on the RCLO and now they could see nothing but smoke.

"Don't panic," said Boneech calmly. "We'll just wait it out."

The Algothon technician shook his head. "The bombs... are landing back...all over the place...in Neksheth-Or. I...don't think that there's going to be…very much…if anything…left of that city."

The Commander just shook his head. "We have just witnessed an entire city committing suicide. I don't know what to think of that."

One of the technicians shrugged. "Is it possible that…it was a malfunction…of some type?"

The Commander wanted to throw something at the man. "All of them? All four hundred fifty-six rockets? All experiencing the exact same malfunction? Are you crazy? Who'd believe that?"

Another technician looked up. "Is it possible…that it was some kind of…mass sabotage?"

The Commander looked at him wide-eyed. "Call Security Headquarters. A mass sabotage is…the best thing…I can't think of anything that…is more feasible. I think that the top security personnel will definitely want to know about this."

Forty days later, the Owlam spies gave up looking for any survivors. They found no one, not even in the subterranean areas that had survived the mass blasting of the city. None of the Neksheth who saw what was coming made it to the bomb shelters in time. No one had been in the subterranean levels at the time. No one that was out in the open survived. The devastation was complete and the Neksheth-Or no longer existed.

6

Boneech stood in the conference room with all of the Staff. She looked very despondent and shaken. "Supreme Officer, Holla, Sir, I came here to report that we…uh…have…accomplished the goal…of stopping the Neksheth-Or from any more damage to us…uh…Owlam that is. We looked all over the city after the smoke cleared. It seems that many of the…citizens…were killed by blast. There were others who died as a result of…the massive concussion…that happens…when one of those bombs went off. The rest of the…" She swallowed hard. "…fatalities were…a result of suffocation from smoke inhalation." She sniffed. "Once again, Sir…we've completed the job…that the Algothon started."

Holla carefully watched all of the actions of the Officer Leader. She saw the wringing of the hands, not being able to make eye contact with anyone, constantly looking around at anything else, the shadows under the eyes and several more things that were going on. "Thank you, Officer Leader, Boneech," she said quietly. "Your Team has done its job very well. Owlam is no longer threatened by Neksheth-Or. It's a shame that…all of them died, but, if that's the only way to stop an enemy from destroying you and your kind…so be it." She looked around the conference table at all of the Staff members. "Does anyone have anything to add?"

No one said anything.

Holla smiled at Boneech. "Again, thank you. You're dismissed."

Boneech turned and walked slowly out of the room.

Holla sighed. "I hate to do this...but it has to be done." She closed her eyes and took in a deep breath. "To all Owlam citizens everywhere. This is Holla speaking. It seems that we've done it again. We've wiped out another species...that were created by the firestorm weapons. I notice that some people feel very bad about all of that killing. I do as well. From this day forth, no one will feel bad about taking a life of any enemy. It doesn't matter what the age or gender is. Killing the enemy is not a crime. Killing an enemy, even to the point of genocide...from this day forth no Owlamite will feel any remorse for destroying any enemy, no matter how you kill them or how many you kill. This order is given for the mental health of all Owlamites. We cannot feel any despondency for killing any enemy whose goal was to kill all of us." She sat down. "Does anyone else have any more business at this time?" She looked at all of their faces. No one said anything. She sighed. "Then this meeting is officially adjourned." She watched them all vanish and then went limp in her chair. "Now, if I could only do something about my own despondency." She hung her head. "I just hope that I haven't turned everyone into some kind of a sociopath."

Team 3784 took a walk around the newly created home in the cliff. A home that was, for the most part, an exact duplicate of the home of Team 7016.

"I think we did a pretty good job," said Roosook. "It's spacious, has a private room for each member of a Team, several bathrooms, plenty of living space and plenty of storage space. It's very nice."

Yaytee scoffed. "It would be even nicer if there was running water and electricity."

"I don't like these…poles…that infest each room," said Queefa.

Nimizi shrugged. "We gotta have those poles…or the roof caves in."

Roosook grunted. "I'm sure that you and a bunch of other women will always find some way to decorate those…" He glared at Queefa. "…*COLUMNS.*"

Queefa grunted right back. "How is it possible to decorate something like that?"

Roosook shook his head. "How can you be an architect when you have no imagination?"

Yaytee scoffed again. "Here you are talking about decorating the columns…and we still don't have any running water or electricity. What's going to be done about that…and when?"

Roosook clenched his teeth. "When we get those people who rebuilt that Tram on the west side, we'll have the *chokwad* electricity."

Yaytee clenched her teeth right back at him. "That was wiring the electricity. Now…how about running water? They didn't have to do any plumbing in order to redo the rails."

Roosook sighed. "They did when they rebuilt that watch station that was destroyed."

Yaytee looked at him surprised. "They…a watch station? Oh…then they…could…or might know how to set up the plumbing."

"It's not so much the water coming in," said Queefa, "It's getting rid of the waste afterwards that bothers me."

"I've been working on an idea on that," said Nimizi.

Yaytee was skeptical. "Yeah? When are you going to share this wonderful idea with us?"

Nimizi crossed her arms and tried to act smug. "As soon as I finish scouting out some areas."

Roosook shook his head. "If you're finished with all of your scouting and nit-picking and bickering, why don't we invite Holla here and let her take a look at our rough draft?"

"Good idea," said Nimizi.

The other two women just nodded their approval.

Roosook closed his eyes. "Supreme Officer, Holla, this is Roosook, the Team Leader of the architects, can you hear me?"

"This is Holla, what have you got for me?"

"Sir, I have an invitation for you and all of the Staff. Come here to the gorge and look at what we've done so far."

"Do you think I'll be impressed?"

"I don't know. I just wonder what you'll think of our progress."

"I'll call the Staff and then you can Jump all of us there to take a look."

"Glad to. Be right there, Sir."

Team 3784 made the Jump to headquarters. They waited until all of the Staff was there and then Jumped all of them to the construction site in the gorge.

Since they had no electricity in the structure yet, everyone was handed a flashlight. The big room was very dark and smelled like plowed earth.

Holla and Wilfadge were wandering around the first floor snickering. "I wonder where they got this design," said Holla sarcastically.

Wilfadge laughed harder.

Hoynama shook her head. "You know full well where this design came from."

Roosook shrugged. "Can you show me any other building in Owlam where people fought over it? It has more than what most of us have been used to over the past twenty-some-odd years. Plus it has plenty of space…for whatever you want to use it for."

Holla snickered again. "I didn't say that I didn't like it, I just never thought of copying…yes, the one and only place in Owlam…that we had people fighting over. Good choice."

"We have two very large problems, Sir," said Roosook. "First, it's going to take several thousand kilotaja of wiring in order to set up all of these places…which we don't have. Second, we're going to need help from the people who helped rebuild the Tram, in order to get all of the wiring laid out."

Hadathoo snickered. "Do you have a place…to store several thousand kilotaja of wire…if you were to get it?"

Yaytee shrugged. "We can store most of it on the third and fourth floor of this home…until we use it."

"No problem then," said Hadathoo with a devious grin.

A military construction worker, in Algothon, went running up to the desk of his section officer. "Sir," he shouted panting. "It…they're gone!"

The officer glared at him. "What's the matter with you? Don't you know how to properly report to your superior?"

The enlisted man snarled, snapped to attention and saluted. "Sir! Second Worker Vorbyzz here to give a report!"

"That's a very sloppy salute," snarled the officer.

Vorbyzz glared back at him. "Just in case you're interested, Sir, someone has stolen twenty-eight of the giant spools of electrical wire."

The officer opened his mouth to admonish the enlisted man again. His mouth suddenly closed and his eyes were wide with shock. "What…it would…TWENTY-EIGHT?" His shoulders sagged. "It'd take at least six trucks to move that many spools!"

Vorbyzz sighed. "Seven, Sir. You can only fit four of them on one truck."

The officer thought for a moment. "Yes…seven…but… there haven't been any…spools moved out today…or yesterday."

"No, Sir, there haven't."

The officer tried to think. He looked up at Vorbyzz. "Thank you for the report…you can go."

"Thank you, Sir!" Vorbyzz spun around and departed. Once outside he muttered. "Stupid *Fliggit*!"

The officer picked up his intercom and punched in a code. "Hello, Security force, this is Officer Tanjoost. I need to report the theft of…an incredible amount of wire."

Hadathoo came back to the group to continue the tour of the new home design. "Did I miss anything?"

"No, we just got to this spot," said Holla.

Hadathoo nodded. "Officer, Roosook, you have fourteen spools of wire on the third floor and fourteen spools of wire on the fourth floor."

Roosook's expression changed from a smile to confusion.

"Fourteen of…on each floor…uh…why couldn't you…all on the same floor?"

Hadathoo shrugged. "They wouldn't all fit on the same floor and I stopped at twenty-eight, because…I can't get any more in there."

Dwalooa stood there akimbo. "Where did you get…all of that wire?"

Hadathoo tried to look innocent. "The Algothons aren't using it. I just brought it here for when we need it…because we need it…more than they do."

The room was filled with laughter, for quite a while.

Holla wiped some tears from her eyes. "Are you going to steal all of the supplies that we need from Algothon?"

Hadathoo looked up as if lost in thought. He looked back at Holla with a huge grin. "Good idea…why not?"

Another long laugh filled the room.

When she finally regained control of herself, Teelila scoffed at Hadathoo. "Are you going to get the workers from Algothon as well?"

Hadathoo shook his head sadly. "Wish I could. If I did though…I think those *Bimyocks* would probably give this position away."

Holla flapped her hands at everyone. "Enough of the jokes! Let's get back to business." She sniffed and did some gyrations with her mouth to try to stop herself from more laughing. "I'll get with Officer, Niyniy and find out who the personnel were that helped rebuild the Tram. I think that we can spare eight Teams to assist you in getting some of this wire laid out."

Nimizi held her hands up. "Whoa! We won't need them until we have at least fifty of these units set up. If we bring them in here for each one, as we finish it, they'll spend most of their time Jumping back and forth. Let's make it worth their time."

Holla nodded. "That sounds like a good use of time." She looked around the room. "I notice that you have these...ugly columns...all over the place. Is there a reason for them?"

Roosook smiled. "The reason for them is that they're *absolutely* essential. If we didn't have the columns...the roof would cave-in."

Holla walked around one of the columns eyeing it with disdain. "I suppose...I could put some shelves...or a coat of paint...or some planters on it...hang some pictures on it...to make it look presentable."

Roosook gave Queefa a big sideways grin. Queefa stuck her tongue out at Roosook.

Wilfadge stroked his chin. "How soon do you think you'll get fifty of them done?"

"It's going to take a while," said Roosook sadly. "It's a lot of work and...we do have to get some sleep...between construction times."

Chaza dropped her chin. "Huh! Sleep! Why?"

"It's a lot of work," said Yaytee. "It's a lot of hop work."

Holla got very curious. "Please…show me."

Roosook shrugged. "Why not? We have the first room started, on the next unit. We can show you how that's done. If you'll follow me…"

Ahandi got a little upset. "Hey, aren't we going to finish the tour? Isn't there a third and fourth floor here?"

Hadathoo scoffed. "Yes, and I filled them with giant spools of wire."

Ahandi closed her eyes and clapped her hands over her mouth. She dropped her hands opened her eyes and smiled.

Roosook led the group back down to the first floor, through the main room, through an exit that they had added in the gaming area, into a hallway and into the next unit. "As you can see, there's a lot of work to be done here. We've barely started on this one."

Shyshee looked around confused. "Are you excavating that much dirt and rock out of the side of this cliff?"

Roosook turned to Yaytee. "I'll let you describe this, seeing as how it was your idea."

Yaytee smiled. She walked over to a wall. "What we do is…we use the hopping capability. We pick a certain part of the wall…" She placed her hands on the wall. "…we hop it into Spy… and then Jump the hopped piece…into another portion…of the wall." She pulled her hands back after doing the demonstration. "Now, what you have is that piece that was moved is now joined with the area that I pushed it into. The rock is twice as strong now and therefore, can withstand...quite a bit more punishment than before."

Teelila looked unconvinced. "Do you do this...joining... up, down and sideways?"

"Oh, yes," said Yaytee merrily.

"If you're making the rock stronger - why do you need those ugly columns?"

Yaytee licked her lips and smiled again. "Yes, it makes the rock twice as strong but it also makes it twice as heavy. If we have to move a portion of the rock...oh say...five times...think of how heavy it'll get."

Teelila grimaced. "I don't want to think about that. I'll accept the ugly columns."

Holla sighed. "So you end up doing a lot of sleeping, because you're doing an incredible amount of hopping."

Wilfadge nodded a little. "If you're making the walls, floors and ceilings stronger...are you also making the columns stronger?"

"Oh, yes! Absolutely," said Yaytee. "It'd be foolish not to."

Dwalooa shook her head. "I'm seeing all of this and I'm wondering how you were able to get all of that first unit put together...without any mistakes? I mean...usually something that's experimental...like this, aren't there some failures...in the process?"

Roosook smiled sheepishly. "Yes, we had several failures…until we got the process down."

Holla's eyes darted around. "So…where are the failures?"

"On the other side of the gorge," said Yaytee with a sigh. "We tore up a few places over there before we came back here and put one together properly."

Wilfadge ran his hand along the wall. "Maybe we should try this process…just for giggles."

Roosook cringed. "If you do, Sir, please do it on the other side of the gorge. We had a hard enough time mastering it for ourselves and I'd hate to mess anything up on this side."

Hadathoo scoffed. "Why do you want to do it?"

Wilfadge sighed. "Just to see if I can…or others can as well. If we can get more people here doing this same thing, I think we could get this place built a lot sooner."

Holla crossed her arms. "What's the rush?"

Wilfadge looked around sadly. "We've lost a lot of people since the firestorm attack. Initially we had 7,016 Teams. We've lost about 240. That still leaves almost 6,800 of these units that we need…if we have to evacuate Owlam and hide here. You have one unit…where you've completed the walls. That only leaves… just under 6,800 to go. How long is that gonna take?"

Holla shook her head. "Let me make a quick inquiry." She closed her eyes. "Officer, Niyniy, this is Supreme Officer,

Holla, do you hear me?"

It took a few moments before there was a response. "Yes, Sir, I hear you. What can I do for you, Sir?"

"I need for you to get into the computer and find the Teams that were the primary workers on rebuilding the Tram after the Galsino attack. I'll stand by while you're looking."

"Yes, Sir, checking now."

Holla opened her eyes and smiled at the group. "Niyniy is checking. She can find someone who can help. She needs to check in the computer."

"Supreme Officer, this is Niyniy."

"Yes, Niyniy, what'd you find?"

"There were originally nine Teams that worked on it from beginning to end. One of those Teams was wiped out in the Neksheth attack. I've got a list of the other eight Teams."

"Hold on a moment, I'm going to write this down." She pulled out a pad. "Go ahead."

"Teams 2656, 2790, 2998, 3169, 4005, 6782, 6850 and 7010. Did you get all of them?"

"Yes, I did. Contact all of those Teams and if they're not busy right now, have them standing by at my Headquarters for a briefing."

"Yes, Sir. Anything else?"

"Yes, find that Officer, Bonarain. If we need someone to do some supplemental teaching, she always seems to get the job done better than anyone else."

"Yes, Sir."

Holla smiled at Roosook. "Do you think that eight Teams, who are experienced in construction will speed things up?"

Roosook smiled. "You don't *know* how much that'd be appreciated. We still have a few more problems to work out and I have no idea how long each one of those will take."

Holla frowned at Wilfadge. "You need to do some of your math a little more specifically. The exact amount of Teams left… even incomplete ones…6,776."

Wilfadge wrinkled his nose at her. "Picky, picky, picky."

Hadathoo shook his head. "I've looked out that little peephole you have in that one wall. From what I see, we are *way* up from the floor of the gorge. Why are you starting so high…or is this going to be the highest elevation you put the units on?"

Roosook smiled. "This unit is on the bottom floor. The reason that this one is as high as it is and is on the bottom, the first time you're here and you see one of those torrential downpours, I don't think that you'll ever question why we're so high. The water flowing through the gorge can get awfully high."

Holla placed her hands against the wall. "If I wanted to do that…big joining of rock…in order to build like that…could I do the entire wall?"

"I wouldn't advise it, Sir," said Roosook. "The bigger the block of rock, the more energy you use. When I'm talking about more energy, I'm not talking about just a little. It seems that energy use increases exponentially."

Holla stood there thinking. "Be ready...to train a lot of Teams. I may give you...those eight construction experienced Teams permanently...and get several others here temporarily. I hate to sound paranoid, but I want this project finished and ready for us...just in case."

Hadathoo narrowed his eyes. "In case of...what?"

"The worst possible scenario," said Holla grimly.

The Staff arrived back at Owlam. They all went to the conference room, however, there was not that much to discuss. The eight Teams and Bonarain were waiting outside of Holla's office when she got back there.

"We're going to have our meeting out here," said Holla. "My office is too small for this many people, so get comfortable where you are."

Everyone sat down in chairs that lined the big hallway.

"You eight Teams were the primary workers in rebuilding the damaged part of the Tram after the Galsino attack. I'm going to be asking you to do some more building. This is going to be a situation where we're setting up a place of retreat...if we have to. I hope we don't, but, if we do, it'll be there."

Bonarain grimaced. "Uh…Sir…I'm not…I've never done any construction work. Why am I here? I never went near the reconstruction project…on the Tram."

"No, you're not in construction. You're a teacher. For some reason, every time there's a problem for anyone in learning something, you've figured out a way to get the point across. That's where I need you. Watch what they're doing, learn it yourself, and if I need some more people taught how to do it…you already have been able to grasp the concept."

Bonarain smiled sheepishly. "Thank you…for your faith…in me." She sat down and swallowed hard as a feeling of desperation hit her. 'I don't know *h'oolyach* about construction,' she thought.

The next day, all eight Teams were in the gorge, along with Bonarain.   Two months later, Roosook called Holla. "Officer, Roosook calling Supreme Officer, Holla. Do you hear me?"

Holla grunted in disgust. She was in the bathtub, cleaning the mucus off of the back of her neck. "This is Holla, what did you need?"

"More people, Sir. Now that we have those eight Teams and they're proficient, we could use a few more hands and really get this project going."

"Are you saying that those eight Teams are not enough, or⋯what're you saying?"

"That Officer, Bonarain figured out a way for us to do every aspect of the job in a simpler more efficient way. We're getting the whole job done, not just the walls, in about thirteen days. When you came to visit, that unit that you saw was incomplete. It took us almost three months, just to get the walls in place. Now with the wiring, the plumbing fixtures, the kitchen fixtures and all of that···she figured out a way to get all of that done and we can get an entire unit completed in thirteen days···by working smarter···not harder."

"Where're you getting all of these kitchen and bathroom fixtures?"

"We were stealing a lot of them from Algothon. Now, we're sending people to Axswain, Galsino, Teltermak and Zee–Altha. We're doing some scavenging of everything we can find from those places. We're also doing some scavenging from some of the unoccupied homes in Owlam. We decided to leave Algothon alone for a while, because that might've made them a little suspicious and if they're putting chips, they can chase, in hard drives···they just might start putting those chips in some of the fixtures and furniture···if they were to start show up missing."

"Are you saying that there are a bunch of units that···someone can move into···now?"

"Oh, no, Sir. We have all of the fixtures and electric. We're still trying to figure out the plumbing."

"Why don't you have Officer, Bonarain help you there?"

"She's already reading up on it right now."

"I'll see what I can do···for more personnel."

"Thank you, Sir."

She finished scrubbing her neck and sat there contemplating. "Well, whattaya know?"

"Supreme Officer, Holla, this is Officer Grade 6, Bonarain. I need to talk to you."

Holla looked up disgusted. 'Why do they always call when I'm in the tub?' she thought. She sighed. "Officer, Bonarain, this Holla, how can I help you?"

"I need to have a classroom in Owlam itself. I need it there, because there's no facility at the gorge. The electricity is sparse and I need a room with a big monitor in order to give proper illustrations."

"Can we use your 7016 Headquarters?"

"Sir, you want me to teach AND host them?"

"You don't have to host them, just teach them."

"Then if you want me to use my Headquarters, you need to supply the monitor and have the students bring their own food."

Holla snickered as she continued washing the back of her neck." Done! Anything else?"

"How soon can I get the monitor?"

"Call one of my Aides···Officer, Niyniy. She'll be

able to set things up."

"Thank you, Sir." Bonarain picked up the wet washcloth and continued cleaning the back of her neck. 'Seems like the only time I can call anybody is when I'm in the tub,' she thought.

Roosook glared at Nimizi. "You've been promising, for months, about some kind of way to get rid of the waste. We've been leaving you alone on it. When are we going to see any positive results…or even ideas?"

Nimizi smiled. "Are you ready?"

"For what?"

"I've already completed it."

"You…uh…what is…where is it?"

She snickered. "Grab your flashlight. There wasn't any reason for lighting in a sewer pipe."

He stood up and closed his eyes.

"What are you doing?"

He held his hand up to quiet her.

A few moments later, Yaytee and Queefa walked into the room.

Yaytee held up her flashlight. "Why do I need this?"

Queefa stood there with her arms crossed and had a questioning look on her face.

Roosook smiled. "According to our colleague, the sewer problem has been taken care of."

Yaytee and Queefa now turned surprised faces to Nimizi.

"Yes, I did," said Nimizi proudly. "I'm going to show you what I've done and how I set it up."

Yaytee smiled back. "Let's go!"

Nimizi proudly led the way.

They followed one of their long connecting corridors that had been "dug out" in order to have all kinds of access to any portion of their underground hideaway city. They came to an area that, once the city was finished, would be very near the exact center of the city. Nimizi opened a door that led to a circular staircase - that had only one way to go from there current location - down.

"I don't remember *this*," said Queefa

"I've been doing it in my spare time," giggled Nimizi. She led them down.

As they walked down, Queefa was counting the steps in her head. When they reached the bottom, she realized that they were thirty-three taja below, what was supposed to be, the lowest level of homes. "Isn't this breaching the limit? The hallway was at the lowest agreed level…we've gone down…three floors below that. What's the reason behind that?"

Nimizi folded her arms. "You know the saying about *that which rolls downhill*! Well, if you want the sewage out of the homes…give it someplace to go…downhill."

Roosook shrugged. "Point taken! Now what?"

Nimizi shined her light to an area just ahead of them. The light showed that there was nothing in this lower room except a giant circular shaft that stretched off into the darkness. "That is our drainage pipe."

Roosook looked it over. "It's…what diameter…is it?"

"Twelve taja," said Nimizi.

Queefa snickered. "That thing'll hold a lot of *h'oolyach*," she said sardonically.

Nimizi gave her a precocious smile. "That's the whole idea, sweet cheeks."

"Okay," said Roosook. "We see this end of it…where's the other end?"

Nimizi shined her flashlight down the shaft. "It empties out at the coastline of this area, directly into the ocean."

Roosook nearly dropped his flashlight. "That…that's… nearly, OVER several hundred kilotaja!"

"Yes, it's somewhere around there," snickered Nimizi. "But remember, it rolls downhill. The shaft goes down one degree, per kilotaja, for the entire length. By the time it gets to the ocean, it's at sea level."

Yaytee scoffed. "So…what's to prevent someone from climbing up the shaft…to invade us?"

Nimizi huffed and folded her arms. "You wanna see the

other end?"

Queefa grunted in disgust. "You think that'll help?"

Nimizi smiled peevishly. "Don't gripe until you've seen it."

Roosook sighed. "Okay, let's see the other end."

"Let's Jump up top...all the way up top," said Nimizi.

The four of them Jumped to the top of the eastern side of the gorge. Each one had their own landmark so they ended up being separated by quite a distance.

Nimizi sighed in disgust and signaled the rest of them to come to her. Once all four were together, she pulled them close in a group hug and Jumped all four of them to the eastern coast of the continent.

"Now," said Nimizi, "Here is the area where the shaft empties out."

Queefa looked around. "Here? Up here?"

Nimizi clenched her teeth and eyes. "NO! It empties at the base of the cliff." She opened her eyes and glared at Queefa. "If you'll follow me to the edge!" She walked over towards the edge of the cliff with her arms held tightly against her side.

Yaytee snickered. "I think you're irritating her, Dearies."

Queefa snickered.

Roosook just grunted in disgust.

Queefa stopped and looked around in fear. "The…ground is shaking!"

"It…is," said Yaytee.

"That's normal in this location," said Nimizi. "Get over here and you'll find out why." She got down on all fours and crawled to the edge of the cliff, where she laid down.

The rest of Team 3784 copied the actions of Nimizi. Once all four of them were at the edge and looking down they could see why this part of the land was suffering from a few tremors.

Nimizi rested her chin on her hands. "At this point right here, the cliff height is just over two kilotaja. Those waves that are currently slamming into the cliff face are…oh…between thirty and forty taja in height. Normally, they're higher than that. Rarely are they much smaller. Now, if you look into Spy dimension, you'll see a little red flag that I put on the face of the cliff. That flag is directly over the exit end of that sewer pipe."

Roosook chuckled. "So the exit end…is in a location where…it would be extremely difficult for anyone to enter in and climb up the…" He chuckled. "…poop chute."

Nimizi smiled. "Even if someone does figure out how to get in there, they'll have to do a march, of over seven hundred kilotaja, through some of the nastiest muck, slipping and sliding the whole way, sniffing up nothing but stench. Because of the width of the pipe, they wouldn't be able to get more than four abreast as they're doing it. Plus when they get to the other end, you have that staircase. It's only wide enough for one person. If one person is going up and another is going down…someone is going to have to change direction."

Queefa scoffed. "Are you telling me that we'll be dumping raw sewage…out into the ocean?"

Nimizi huffed right back. "As long as those big swimming mammals can take a crap in the ocean, how can you say that our…droppings…are more nasty or filthy than theirs?" Those creatures have lived and been dumping in the ocean for…untold millennia. Do they have some sewage treatment plant down in the bottom of the ocean for them? I don't think so. Until someone can explain how my excretions are filthier or nastier or can poison the whole ocean…I'm gonna take a *dump* in the ocean."

Yaytee looked queasy. "Fortunately, I'm not an expert on…feces." She swallowed hard. "Can we change the subject?"

"Not yet," said Roosook. "I understand how, because that shaft, goes downhill the entire way, you're setting it up for an easy…flow. I think that we need to…have some sort of flushing system that'll guarantee that nothing…stops…and solidifies."

Nimizi frowned. "How do you suggest we do that?"

Roosook looked out over the ocean while he contemplated. "I suggest that we make another reservoir…just for the flushing system. It doesn't have to be anywhere near as big as any of the ones for our drinking water and it must be absolutely independent of the drinking water reservoirs. Then…maybe…once a day or… every three days, we flush the pipe out. That'll make sure that nothing backs up on us."

"You want to make this one totally independent," said

Queefa. "Just to make sure that it never drains into the drinking water system, I suggest that it is also lower than the others."

"Good idea," said Nimizi.

Roosook watched a few more waves hit the cliff. "Are you sure that all of the bad stuff gets washed away? I mean look how the waves are slamming up against the cliff…is it possible…that they might force something…back *up*?"

"No," said Nimizi. "I tested it with a bunch of pieces of rotten fruit. When the wave hits, the water then recedes back for the next wave. I dropped about twenty pieces of fruit in the water, just before a wave hit. The wave caught all of them and out they went. Only one piece came back in the next wave, and that one only came back once."

"Must be a powerful undertow," said Yaytee.

"Okay," said Roosook. "I've seen enough here. We'll head back, utilize this in our waste management and get some of the other things built and hooked up."

In Algothon, Ota was in her little hiding place eating her dinner. The other three Officer Leaders, Nachichi, Natsa and Blana came wandering in and sat down.

Nachichi looked at what Ota was eating and then looked at her fingernails. "Has that architect…Roosook…put in any more orders for anything for us to swipe…here?"

Ota simply shook her head while chewing.

"I'm getting bored. I'd like to steal something," said Blana. "It just drives those security people absolutely crazy whenever we grab something. They haven't yet figured out how the stuff is disappearing or who's doing it or where it's going."

Ota swallowed and grunted. "I'm sure that they're still trying to blame it on us."

Nachichi chuckled. "As long as they're concentrating on these strange thefts and still trying to safeguard their new archives...they don't have much time to think about us."

There was a knock on the open door.

Ota looked up. "Yes?"

A man and a women walked in.

"Officer Grade 4, Roosook, reporting as ordered."

"Officer Grade 6, Bonarain, reporting as ordered."

Ota looked at the other three Officer Leaders. "I...didn't call either of you."

The other three women shook their heads in bewilderment.

Another woman knocked on the door. "Hello, Sirs, I'm Officer Grade 3, Nayna, one of Supreme Officer, Holla's Aides. I think I can clear up the situation for all of you."

Ota looked around. "By all means...come on in and clear it up," she said mockingly.

Nayna walked in smiling. "Thank you, Sir."

Natsa looked around in apprehension. "Maybe it's some new orders."

Nayna snickered. "Partly. Officer, Roosook is here to take measurements. Officer, Bonarain is here to assist in training…if anyone needs any."

Ota rolled her eyes. "Measure what…train what?"

Nayna cocked her head to one side. "Supreme Officer, Holla has decided that since we might have a tough time building our own clean rooms for those special Algothon archives…we're going to steal the whole room."

Ota had been taking a drink while Nayna was talking and now ended up spitting the liquid out…most of it through her nose. She got up gagging and coughing, walked over to a sink and attempted to clear any foreign liquid out of her nose. She looked up with red eyes and coughed again. "You could warn someone… before they take a drink!"

Nayna was sitting there with her fists over her mouth looking almost terrified. "Sorry," she said in a small voice.

Ota shook her head as she came back to the table, repeatedly clearing her throat in a very loud manner. She sniffed and looked at Nayna. "Okay, what's the reason? Why are we going to steal all five of the rooms?"

Nayna still looked a little concerned. "After talking to some of those computer people, Holla decided that it's too much to try to figure out how to build one of those clean rooms. So, we take the entire clean room and move it…to either Owlam…

or the gorge. Roosook is here to…attempt to take some…outer measurements of the clean rooms…and then go back and set up a place to put them."

Ota glanced away from Nayna to Bonarain and then back. "And that one is here…to assist in…any training that…might… what?"

Nayna shrugged. "Just in case someone needs it?"

"I still don't understand why we have to take all five arrays…AND THEIR ROOMS! Why can't we just take…a few pieces…at a time?"

Bonarain smiled. "Because of what we learned from the computer people. There's a program in there that places the information randomly on the different hard drive plates."

Ota shrugged. "So they put the information…wherever there's room, what's the big deal?"

"No, Sir," said Bonarain. "It's not quite that simple."

Ota looked aggravated now. "Okay, teacher - teach me." She leaned back with her arms folded across her chest looking rather defiant.

Bonarain smiled. "As you know, each cabinet contains ten plates, where it can use either the top or bottom. That makes twenty hard drives per cabinet. Multiply that times the forty-five cabinets and that makes nine hundred different hard drives that it can choose from. Now, say someone wants to put a five page document into the archives. The way it's set up, it doesn't really look for an open area and put all of the information there. It scatters the stuff randomly…anywhere in the nine hundred drives. It could put page one on drive number 70. The second page is put on drive 170. The third page is put on drive 870. The fourth page is put on drive 570. The last page is put on drive 7. If you stole just one of those cabinets - all you'd get is one page. Now consider if you had an eight hundred page document. Scatter that…everywhere with no real numerical sequence, as far as where they're…"

"I get it," said Ota with her hands raised and her eyes closed. "You take all of it or…you got nothing but meaningless partials." She shook her head. "That's a big order!" She sniffed. She looked around at everyone in the room. "I'm trying to think of who to call. I can't remember any of the names of those computer people."

Nachichi snickered. "I was talking to one of the men today. His name is Zozz."

"Thanks," said Ota. "Officer, Zozz, this is Officer Leader, Ota. I need to see you, or your Team Leader in my office···as soon as possible."

After several moments a response finally came in. "This is Officer Grade 3, Tula. I'm the Team Leader for Zozz. He's kinda busy right now. Can I help you?"

"Yes, you'll do. Please come to my office."

"Right away, Sir."

Ota sighed. "Okay, Officer, Roosook, your tour guide is on the way."

"Thank you, Sir," said Roosook.

Ota gave Nayna a nasty look. "Can I take a drink now or are you gonna spring another surprise on me?"

Nayna flushed as she snickered. "No, Sir, no more surprises...and never again while your drinking something."

"Thank you," said Ota acerbically. She picked up her mug and took a long full swig of her beverage.

7

There were several Teams that had been practicing. It had been mainly the construction Teams who had been getting ready, however, other Teams got into it, just in case someone else had a better twist. They were getting ready for the final theft of the Algothon computer archives. Take the entire room, all five, at the same time. Currently there were four areas at the gorge and one at Owlam where the archives would be moved to a new underground area far away from Algothon.

At the same time they were preparing to appropriate the archives there was another group of Owlam spies who were keeping a close watch on the Algothon scientists who were vainly trying to get the rockets back in good working order. The spies had marked the most intelligent and most dedicated ones. They kept track of any entries that these people were reentering into the "new" archives. Several computers and several manuals were marked for pilfering, once the command was given.

The computer technicians had been able to hook up to the main archives and were now obtaining a wealth of information. They found out how the rockets were built and able to fly so high that they could not be seen. They found out about the nuclear warhead and learned about things like - splitting the atom and critical mass. They learned all kinds of new things about the satellites that were flying overhead and spying on everyone on the planet and how they would be able to reprogram them and use them instead of the Algothons using them. They found that these flying cameras could also show them weather patterns and how they could take advantage of this information. They found out numerous things about the atmosphere. They found out numerous things about creatures that lived underwater, mammal, fish, mollusk, crustacean and a few that had not been categorized. All this and they had just barely scratched the surface and the archives were still in Algothon.

Holla sat there impatiently drumming her fingers on the conference table. "I wish those *Doovofts* would hurry up. We planned this…for months and now we're just waiting on…what… four lousy Heyyah?"

Wilfadge chuckled. "Don't worry. They're doing the final installation of the last one of those computer poles that they have. When that one is installed, we make the mass Jump and we have all of it and the Algothon are starting from scratch."

Teelila yawned and stretched. "Yes, and then it'll all have been worth it. We defeat the Algothon without ever destroying their city and leave them with a bunch of missiles that they can't and don't know how to use." She sat there chuckling.

Hadathoo sat there with a smug grin. "How many, did you say, of the units at the gorge are finished?"

Holla looked up. "Do you mean…ready to move in?"

"Yes," said Hadathoo.

"632," said Dwalooa.

Hadathoo frowned. "I thought that they said it would only take thirteen days to get one done."

Holla shook her head. "We misunderstood. That was thirteen days, to get all of the walls, floors and ceilings in place. Once they've done that, it seems to take forever to get all of the small stuff done. You have to set up a kitchen with all of the refrigerators, stoves, sinks with plumbing, electrical terminals along with outlets and intercom hookups. Then there's the living area and the bathrooms. It just goes on and on. The big stuff gets done quickly. The small stuff...a seemingly endless list."

Ahandi looked at her fingernails. "They were also slowed... when this plan was talked about." She scoffed. "They had to set up all of the places to put these rooms, along with electricity and air filter exhausts and air filters."

"Having to set up all of the water reservoirs didn't help the timing any," said Hoynama. "Along with all of those air filters, they have to maintain a certain amount of...what was that called?"

"Humidity," said Shyshee.

"Right," said Hoynama. "Humidity has to be maintained at a certain level inside that room, otherwise...the whole thing gets messed up."

Holla shook her head. "I'm sure glad that we waited and found out all of the special information about those rooms before moving them."

Chaza huffed. "Yeah, we found out a lot of the information

by accident." She huffed again. "Stupid luck!"

Teelila cocked her head and turned to Wilfadge. "What was that about the passwords?"

Wilfadge chuckled. "Their high up, holy exalted security types have these special passwords that can get them into anything. All we needed was those four passwords and we can get into anything in the old archives. Once they started setting up the new archives, the holy exalted ones changed their passwords. It took one spy, less than half a day, to get all four of the new passwords. We can get into anything…and so far we have."

Holla blew air through her teeth. "Officer, Tula this is Holla, what's the holdup?"

Tula groaned. "Sir, this is Tula. They're still doing the final trouble-shooting before they put the thing on line. They're still following all of the proper protocols and checklists. You should be grateful, Sir. They're making sure that it works properly…for us…once we steal it."

Holla put her head down on the table. "I wish they'd hurry up. I'd like to get this done. We've got over a thousand Owlamites just…twiddling their thumbs waiting for those four *Doovofts* to finish…trouble-shooting."

Wilfadge chuckled again. "Relax. Think nice thoughts. Think of how frustrated the Algothon will be…once they have no computer archives at all."

Holla could not stop herself from giggling at that thought. "All of that beautiful information at our fingertips. They set all of it up and now they won't be able to use a single bit of it."

Hoynama leaned forward. "What would happen if we went ahead and Jumped the rooms…with those four…still in there?"

Holla waved her hand to shun that idea. "They'd know the very moment it happens. They'd know instantly and…probably try to destroy all of the cabinets in that room. If anyone knows how to destroy one of those things, it's the person whose been trained to put it together."

Hoynama shrugged. "Why can't we move four of them… and then the fifth…after the trouble-shooting is done?"

Hadathoo snarled at her. "Because they'd notice it and then fill that fifth room with soldiers. We'd have to put the whole lot into Stink and that would probably befoul the air in the room… and we've lost that entire array."

"I was just wondering," said Hoynama defensively.

Holla snarled at her. "If you're going to do any thinking… think intelligently." "Officer, Tula, how close are they to being finished?"

Tula hung her head. "They're on step 4 of 22 steps."

Holla smacked her fists on the table. "Somebody get me a drink."

Niyniy was standing there. "A drink of…what, Sir?"

Holla looked at her with clenched teeth. "Something that burns going down."

Niyniy sighed. "I'll see what I can find."

Tula called back. "They're on step 5."

Wilfadge hollered at Niyniy as she left the room. "Get me something to drink as well!"

Niyniy stopped and turned around with a smile. "Anybody else?"

Everyone else at the table raised their hands.

Niyniy grunted. "I thought so." She turned and headed for the liquor cabinet.

Several people at the table were on their second drink when Tula called back again.

"They're on step 6."

Ahandi put her glass down. "I don't know which is worse. Not knowing or getting a step by step update."

The Staff sat at the table watching the numbers on the chronometer changing (and killing two more bottles of wine).

Tula called in again. "They're on step 21, Sir. Step 22 is one of the shortest. Hopefully, it won't be long now."

Shyshee raised her arms. "Hallelujah!" She scoffed. "I need it to get done quickly. I'm getting drunk."

Holla looked over at Niyniy through bleary eyes. "Put all of the booze away and lock the cabinet."

Niyniy giggled. "Yes, Sir...right away, Sir."

Holla looked up with a bit of surprise on her face. "Officer, Tula···do we have a copy of that trouble-shooting manual?"

Tula grunted in exasperation. "Yes, Sir, that's how I know what the steps are and how long they take."

Holla sighed in relief. "I should have more faith in my experts."

"They're on step 22, Sir."

Holla clenched her eyes and teeth. "It's about *chogo* time!"

"Officer, Holla, this is Officer, Brong, at the door of the backup archive number 2. It looks like···I think someone is wanting to get in there and···do some kind of work."

Holla now had clenched teeth and eyes wide with anger. "Officer, Brong, can you tell me what kind of work?"

"He wants to change the air filters in there."

Tula broke in. "There's a trouble-shooting protocol after they do that as well. It's horribly time consuming."

Now Holla was even madder. "Officer, Brong, if they try to open that door···prevent it···even if you have to kill everyone in that hallway."

"Yes, Sir, standby."

Several heart pounding moments went by as they waited for a report from Brong.

Holla could not wait. "Officer, Brong, what the *fovok*

is happening?"

"The situation is taken care of, Sir."

"So···they're not going in the room?"

"No, Sir, not with those air filters."

"What did you do···mass murder?"

"I grabbed one of the guards and hopped his nose and mouth into Stink. I waited until I felt his stomach convulse and then I hopped his face back into Home. I aimed his face at the filters and he hurled all over them. They have to go back and get a new batch of air filters from the storeroom···where there aren't any more filters, because we already stole all of them."

Holla looked around in a panic. "How long will it take for them to find out about that···theft?"

"Officer, Holla, this is Officer, Loskani. It's going to take quite a while. He was at backup number 2. The filters are stored···uh···were stored in 9w45."

Shyshee closed her eyes and looked as if she were going to hurl as well. "He made that man…" Her entire body shuddered and she let out a noise of some kind as she stuck out her tongue in disgust.

Hadathoo scoffed at Shyshee. "Hey, it was effective."

"It's still disgusting," said Shyshee.

Holla looked confused. "Uh…9w45?"

Niyniy smiled. "That's sublevel 9, west sector, room 45."

Holla looked a little relieved. "So…does that mean it's gonna take him a while to get there."

Shyshee smiled. "He has to go up the elevator from the sublevel at the gate. He then has to get transportation to the entry point for the west area sublevel storage vaults. Elevator to sublevel 9 and then find room 45. It should take him quite a while."

Holla let out a very loud groan of relief.

Wilfadge could not help himself. "The guy who puked⋯ is he getting chewed out?"

"He's catching all kinds of unholy⋯you-know-what."

Wilfadge leaned back in his chair chortling.

Shyshee growled. "Will you shut up about that…?" She did another entire body shudder from disgust while some strange noises escaped her lips.

"Sir, they've finished step 22. Now all they have to do is close it and get out."

They watched a few more numbers change on the chronometer.

"Officer, Tula⋯what are they doing?"

"They're standing around going yak, yak, yak."

Holla looked up at the ceiling. "I don't believe this!"

"Will you *Melafathan Fovoks* shut up and get out of here!"

Holla looked a little shocked. "Officer, Tula, did you
know that you thought that…in sending?"

"I…did? Uh…sorry."

Wilfadge could not stop laughing. Holla glared at him
which only made him laugh harder.

"Finally! They're leaving."

"Officer, Tula tell us when."

"Yes, Sir."

Ahandi scoffed. "Well, we might actually get this done
today."

"They're out the door! They're closing the door!
They're sealing the door! They're walking away!"

Holla took in a deep breath and let it out with a big smile on
her face. "All personnel who are involved in the mission…
get ready to execute the theft." She looked around the table
and wiggled her eyebrows at the Staff with a smile. "This is
Supreme Officer, Holla…on my mark! Three, two, one…
EXECUTE!"

Nayna, Aktool and Niyniy were standing by status boards,
waiting for each one of the personnel to report in. As each one
called in "mission complete", check marks were being annotated
all over the boards. The five archives were Jumped to Owlam and
the gorge. Certain computer hard drives that were mainly used by
the physicists were stolen. 620 manuals of which there were 35
copies of each were all stolen. Four special computers, belonging

to the four Prominent Investigators were stolen. Fifteen guards at the doors of the five archives disappeared into Jahong's Death. Eighteen top nuclear physicists all disappeared into Jahong's Death. A large machine (that no one in Owlam understood what it was for. They only knew that it had something to do with splitting an atom.) was stolen.

Once all of the reports stopped coming in, Holla's three Aides stepped back and looked over the status boards to see if there was anything that was not checked off. When they saw that all tasks had been accomplished and checked off, all three smiled and put their markers down.

Niyniy leaned over to Aktool. "How does one person steal 620 manuals all at the same time?"

Aktool rolled his eyes and grunted. "You take the whole *chokwad* bookcase."

Niyniy smiled sheepishly. "Oh…okay." Her expression changed to confusion. "What if someone is reading one of the manuals…at that time?"

Aktool grunted again. "Then you bounce some other heavy book off of his head, take the manual, put it on the shelf… and Jump."

Niyniy nodded. "Sounds good."

All nine of the Staff were looking over the status boards with nervous hope. As each one finally saw, for themselves, that all boxes were checked off they sat down, each releasing a sigh of relief.

Now the Aides went to the status board on the other side of the room. They now had to wait for the call-ins that confirmed that all of the thefts were successful. All computers were hooked up and running in Owlam or in the gorge. All of the manual libraries were complete. That crazy atom splitting machine was safely out of the hands of Algothon. These call-ins took a lot longer. There was nowhere near as much trepidation as they waited for each one of these call-ins.

Holla sat there grinning. "I'll bet its total chaos over there in Algothon."

Tula came back. "You don't know the half of it. All of the personnel, who're still here in Algothon, have all switched to Observation. The noise was so···intensive and incredible. Every single alarm that was anywhere in the city seems to have gone off."

Holla looked around the table. "Tonight, I may get even drunker…to celebrate…what has to be the greatest theft, ever accomplished, in the history of our planet."

Shyshee clicked her tongue. "Is this another secret that we keep from our allies?"

Hadathoo scoffed. "What do you think?"

In Algothon, the calls coming into Security Headquarters were jamming every single line they had. No sooner did someone end a call the buzzer went off again and another report was being taken.

The main lobby of the security building was jammed with people as well. Many of them had given up on any attempt at getting through on the intercom and had come to the building itself, to make their report.

Prominent Investigator, Janekt rushed back to Security Headquarters. He had to shove his way through numerous bodies as he went through the front door. He tried several times to out-shout all of the pandemonium that was going on in the lobby. He finally gave up and continued pushing his way through in order to get to his office and find out what was going on.

Prominent Investigator, Zykorm was not far behind Janekt, however, because of all the noise he could not get Janekt's attention. He had to push and shove as well in order to make any headway.

Prominent Investigator, Hallang was standing outside of the Security Headquarters watching as the throng continued to push itself into the building. He was wondering if there was some way to climb the outside of the building in order to get to his office that way.

Prominent Investigator, Trown was unconscious (and bleeding) on the floor of his office in the Security building. He had been reading a report from one of the other Investigators on, yet another, theft of some giant spools of electric cables. When the "execute" order was given for his computer to be commandeered, Officer Grade 6, Quistie was standing behind him (in Spy dimension). She could not wait for him to finish reading the report. She had to take the computer. She picked up a large paperweight off of his desk and clobbered him, leaving a large dent in the back of his skull. She threw the evidence of the weapon into Stink, grabbed the computer and Jumped back to Owlam.

Janekt finally got through the lobby into the main hallway. He stood there for a few moments panting and wiping the sweat off of his brow. He heard a noise like someone else was attempting to open the door in the hallway. He was ready to shove the door shut until he saw Zykorm trying to push his way through and then Janekt assisted.

Zykorm stood there panting and wiping off sweat, using his sleeve. "What's going on? Have you been able to figure anything out yet?"

Janekt had finally caught his breath. "I haven't gotten to my computer yet. I'll bet that there's a whole truckload of messages on there. Maybe we can figure out what all of this is about from that."

Zykorm nodded. "Right! Let's check some messages and then compare notes."

"Hey, have you seen Trown or Hallang?"

Zykorm scoffed and pointed towards the main lobby. "Maybe they're somewhere in that mess. Maybe they'll be able to make their way in here…later."

Janekt nodded. "To the computers," he said flatly.

They walked to the elevator, still wiping away sweat from their faces. Zykorm hit the elevator call button and the door came open immediately.

"Well…at least something is cooperating!"

Janekt just huffed.

They entered the elevator and Janekt entered his code for the top floor. The elevator door closed and up they went. At the top floor, the door slid open. The top floor hallway was very simple. One door that was opposite the elevator was the latrine. To the left there were two offices and to the right there were two offices. There was nothing else on this floor. Janekt went right, Zykorm went left.

Janekt walked up to the door to his office and started to enter his code on the pad. He had not finished when he glanced off to his left and noticed that Zykorm was standing, with his mouth open, staring into the "open" door to Trown's office. He froze. "What?"

Zykorm slowly turned his head and met Janekt's gaze. He lifted his right arm slightly and gave a halfhearted beckoning with two fingers without saying a thing. His attention went back to the inside of Trown's office.

Janekt walked rigidly to where Zykorm was standing, expecting the worst possible scenario. He was not disappointed. The body of Trown was on the floor, with a badly dented head and in the middle of a large pool of blood. "Oh, marvelous," he said flatly.

Zykorm let out a sigh. "The body is only part of it."

Janekt closed his eyes. "What could possibly be worse?"

Zykorm sniffed. "His computer is missing."

Both of them were hit with realization simultaneously.

Janekt could only whisper. "Computer? Missing computer?"

They looked at each other wide eyed. They both went to their office doors and entered their codes. Janekt got an error reading on his first attempt. The second attempt got the green light. Before he could open his door, he heard Zykorm scream. He looked back at Zykorm as he pushed his door open. Zykorm was standing there in a mid-crouch, fists clenched at his side and he was staring into his office in horror. He pushed his office door open slowly. He looked at the desk where the computer *should* have been sitting.

Janekt and Zykorm, once again, looked at each other. Janekt slowly turned his gaze to the door of Hallang's office. He looked back at Zykorm and sighed. Zykorm slowly walked up to Hallang's door. Janekt fed his code in and hit the override button on the pad. Zykorm entered his code and pressed the override button. The door clicked open. Janekt pushed the door open and saw another empty desk where a computer should be sitting. Both men stood there shaking their heads.

Janekt sniffed. "The most secure building...in all of this city...possibly the world. Nowhere else...has more. Yet... someone...got in here, murdered Trown and made off...with four computers."

Zykorm looked up helplessly. "You missed it again."

"What?"

"Where are the book shelves with our manuals?"

Janekt looked in the office and saw an open place on the floor where the book cases were supposed to be. He went back to his office and saw the same blank spot.

Zykorm just stood there shaking his head. "How?"

Janekt clenched his teeth. "THOSE…*SHYBEELAN FLIGGIT* OWLAMS!!!"

Officer Grade 7, Wahamee had been standing there in Spy. She had watched while they had entered their codes and made the annotation, on her pad, of the office entry codes of the two Prominent Investigators. She was confused as to why the Owlam High Command wanted these codes, however, she obeyed the order. There was no real reason why they needed the codes. If an Owlamite wanted into a room, all they had to do was hop to Spy or Observation…or even Ghost…and walk right through the door. She looked at the two despondent Algothon men with scorn. "I'll show you…*shybeelan fliggit*…you…Algothon *h'oolyach*!"

Hallang was sitting on the floor in the hallway on the ground floor panting. He shook his head. "What a mess!" He finally regained a little strength, stood up and went to the elevator. He pressed the button and leaned against the wall to wait for the elevator. He heard the doors slide open and staggered into the elevator. He entered his code on the pad, the door closed and up he went. The elevator stopped, the door slid open. He walked out and froze in horror. He crouched down, reached down, pulled his pistol out and pulled the hammer back. He quickly looked back and forth in the hallway, listening intently for any sound. The only door that was closed was the door to the bathroom. He went to Zykorm's office and peered in. No perpetrator, no computer and no manuals. 'Oh no,' he thought. He turned and looked in Trown's office. A skull-crushed body, no perpetrator, no computer and no manuals. He walked to the bathroom and slowly pushed the door open. There was nothing amiss in there. He slowly walked to Janekt's office door. Same results as before. He looked in his office and saw that he had been cleaned out as well.

He looked down at the two dead bodies and scoffed. The scorch mark, that each one had on their foreheads, told him that they had been killed with one of the power weapons...at very close range.

He listened again. The only sound that he could hear was his own breathing. He sank to the floor, holstered his gun and hung his head.

"This is *not* my best day," he grumbled despondently.

Hallang sat there for a long time just staring at the wall. Suddenly he was the ranking Investigator of all the citizenry of Algothon. He was the ranking Investigator and he did not have a clue how the crime that had been committed, right here in this hallway had been accomplished. He had seen Janekt and Zykorm pushing their way through the crowd. He had finally conjured up some intestinal fortitude and pushed his way through as well. Once up here, he found that not even this hallowed hall was exempt from being penetrated by...sources unknown...to commit unlawful acts.

He shook his head and got up. He straightened his uniform

and headed for the elevator. No time like the present to attempt to find out just exactly what it was that had committed the crime up here and had brought the entire city to a panic. He slowly walked to the elevator and pressed the call button. The wait for the elevator took far less time than he wished it would. The door opened, he walked in and pressed the button for the next floor down. That floor was where all thirty of the High Investigators had their offices.

The elevator door slid open and Hallang found himself in another area that was currently filled with confusion. He walked in the hall and saw several people, all wearing the rank of High Investigator, with looks of panic on their faces. Several of them were babbling at each other and no one seemed to be listening to anyone. He also saw several dead bodies laying in the hallway.

Hallang shook his head in disgust. "WHAT'S GOING ON HERE?" He looked both ways up and down the hallway.

Everyone became silent. Most of the people in the hallway started heading to where Hallang was standing. Four of them reached his location at the same time and two of them started babbling again.

"QUIET!" He looked at them angrily. "You're wearing the rank of High Investigator. You do *not* panic. You might cause panic, but you do NOT panic."

Three of them stood tall and their expressions were now calm and business like.

The fourth was looking around, still with that fear in his eyes. Hallang slapped the man as hard as he could. The look changed from fear to shock and anger.

"That's better," said Hallang in a commanding way. "Now…whoever is the ranking one…if you have any knowledge of that concept…report!"

A woman pushed through the men. She appeared to have some fire in her eyes. "I'm High Investigator, Steenda. You know that I'm the ranking one right now, because you're the only one that stood between me and the rank of Prominent Investigator… when you were promoted…after those disappearances."

"Correct," said Hallang quietly. "So…report."

She elbowed both of the men on each side of her in order to get some room. She gave each one of them a nasty look and then turned to Hallang. "Sir, it appears that someone has infiltrated this headquarters. They've breached this secure hallway and committed several acts of murder, theft and vandalism." She glared at some of the other personnel who were still standing. "I've attempted to ascertain just exactly what happened…but considering the actions of some of my…colleagues…we're having a difficult time determining any form of…who and how."

A man growled at them and hollered. "YOU WANT SOME SILLY REPORT…WHILE WE'RE IN THE MIDST OF THIS MAJOR PROBLEM?"

Hallang looked around angrily. "Who said that?"

The man pushed forward. "High Investigator, Koosk!"

Hallang stood there nodding. "You said…major problem. Excuse me, you *Fonsosk*, but we went beyond mind-boggling cataclysm before you had a clue as to what's going on." He glanced around at all of the faces. "Do any of you know…how many High Investigators are dead…or just injured?"

Steenda licked her lips. "Yes, Sir, I've counted eight dead."

"Where are the rest of the High Investigators?"

Steenda took a deep breath. "The other twenty-two are all here, uninjured and accounted for."

"How…and when did you get here?"

"Sir, we all…had to push our way through that…crowd. When all of those alarms went off, we came here…uh…reported for duty. We each went to our office…to try to find out what the emergencies are…and where we're needed."

Hallang smiled. "Do you see…how calm she is in reporting the information to me…INVESTIGATOR KOOSK?" He sniffed. "That is how you're supposed to act…as a High Investigator." He glanced around again. "Does anyone know which eight are dead?"

"Sir, we can do a quick roll call…check on the board…see who's standing…and who…" She pushed her way to the board that had all of the names and which office was theirs. The names were listed by rank. She placed her finger by her name. "Obviously, I'm still alive." She pointed to the next name. "Molheedrow!"

A man responded.

"Pasket!"

Another response.

"Bramiks!"

Another response.

Hallang had heard enough at this point. "STOP!"

Everyone looked at him confused.

Steenda looked almost furious. "Sir, you wanted…"

"The roll call can continue…after I've told you something… very important." He closed his eyes and collected his thoughts. He opened his eyes and smiled. "This hallway wasn't the only one that was infiltrated. Whoever these criminals are, they were upstairs as well."

There were several gasps heard.

"The first three names…that were called…in your roll call…you three are now…promoted to the rank of Prominent Investigator." He looked at the board. "Steenda, Molheedrow and Pasket…you're the promoted ones. Bramiks…you'll be the one to continue the roll call…then report."

"Yes, Sir," said Bramiks as he moved to the board. He checked the next name. "Agabon!" No one responded. "AGABON!"

A man pointed. "Agabon is over there…dead."

Bramiks pulled a marker out and ran a line through the name. He continued the roll call. When he was finished he turned to Hallang. "Sir, the dead are: Agabon, Zeedzer, Biybimin,

Jajimit, Fondonisk, Izikitan, Hox and Yotahant."

Hallang knew that he was wasting valuable time, however, he had to show them all that he was in complete control and that that was the only way to maintain control and possibly end the pandemonium that was currently happening on the ground floor. "All of you will now move up on the board...with one exception." He got directly in the face of Koosk and tried to sound as sinister as possible. "You...Investigator Koosk will move to the bottom of the list...of the survivors. You are being put there and you might drop to number thirty, until you learn how to ACT like a High Investigator. Do you have any questions, Koosk?"

"No, Sir," spat Koosk through clenched teeth.

Hallang looked at the board. "Where does that put Koosk?"

Bramiks did some quick counting. "That would be number nineteen, Sir."

"Who is number eighteen?"

"Sir, that would be Vetgithok."

Hallang had no idea which one of these personnel was Vetgithok. He stared forward and gave the command. "Vetgithok, you will take Koosk. You will go downstairs. You will inform the Chief Investigators that the top eleven of them are now promoted to High Investigator, in order to get our numbers back to where they're supposed to be."

Vetgithok moved forward. "Yes, Sir."

Hallang again got in the face of Koosk. "Once he's made

that determination, you'd better get…whoever is left down there and get them organized. If you don't…you'll be joining them down *there* and we'll bring another Chief up *here*. Any questions?"

Koosk tried to maintain a blank face. "No, Sir."

Hallang nodded. "Good. The two of you…move!"

Vetgithok and Koosk wasted no time getting to the elevator.

"Investigator, Steenda!"

She walked up to him. "Yes, Sir?"

"I can see what you were talking about with the murder of eight High Investigators." He took a deep breath. "What were you referring to, when you said…theft and vandalism?"

"Sir, all of our computers…have been stolen. All of the manuals have been stolen. There's also a lot of damage to some of the desks, chairs, charts and other office supplies…that we haven't finished a full inventory of…yet."

Hallang shook his head. "High Investigators…your attention…the hall upstairs…looks exactly the same. Whoever did this…stole the computers and manuals…and killed…Janekt… Zykorm…and Trown." He cleared his throat. "Someone…get forensics up here and start gathering evidence. The rest of you… start inventory on everything that's missing or damaged. New Prominent Investigators…with me." He turned and headed for the elevator.

Steenda stayed by his side. "Sir, what's on the agenda?"

He pressed the call button for the elevator. "Wait until

we're out of ear shot."

The four of them stood there silently until the elevator door opened. They entered, the door closed and Hallang hit the "stop" switch.

"First…the three of you can forget the Sir nonsense. We are the four Prominent Investigators and we don't *Sir* each other… regardless of the fact that I outrank all three of you. Second…we're going to go down one floor and see…if it's as big a disaster…as the top two floors. Third…I'm going to set your codes…for the top floor. Fourth…we're going to the top floor and the three of you…can fight over which office you want. Number three is mine and I intend on keeping it. You three can have either one, two or four. Fifth…the three of you will start the investigation and get some forensics on the top floor. Any questions?"

There were three responses of: "No, Sir!"

He grimaced. "All three of you already forgot number one."

Steenda shrugged. "Old habits, Sir…uh…yes…uh…old habits. Uh…what do I call you?"

"Hallang!" He hit the button for the next floor down.

Vetgithok had eleven of the Chief Investigators off to the side, while Koosk was calling the roll.

Hallang shook his head. "Investigator, Vetgithok, are there any computers on this floor?"

Vetgithok shook his head. "Cleaned out on this floor, Sir.

The ones on the next floor down are still there."

Hallang sighed. "Thank you." He shook his head again. "That makes at least...one hundred thirty-four computers stolen."

"Sir," said Vetgithok. "These new High Investigators... who's going to give them access to the next floor up?"

"You're a High Investigator...you have the authority to authorize it."

"Sir, I...don't know how...no one has..."

"Get in here! Bring the top two with you."

Vetgithok turned to the eleven people. "Shahalask, Hashasee, with me."

A man and a woman followed him into the elevator.

Hallang opened a panel in the elevator. "Vetgithok, enter your code on the pad." He watched as it was done. "Now, we push *new promotion* and...the two new people enter their codes."

Shahalask and Hashasee made their entries.

"Now, you two are allowed up to the High Investigator floor."

Both of them acknowledged.

"Vetgithok, do you have any questions on how to set the other nine up?"

"No, Sir."

"Good, you may exit the elevator. We have other business

to attend to."

The three High Investigators departed, the door closed and Hallang punched in the codes to allow the three new Prominents access to the top floor. When he finished, he smiled at the other three. "You're in, okay?"

"Thank you," said Steenda.

"Thank you," said Molheedrow.

"Thank you," said Pasket.

"Thank you," said Officer Grade 7, Wahamee as she finished making the annotations on her pad. She gave Hallang a sour look. "*Bimyock!*"

Holla was sitting in a tub of hot soapy water cleaning the back of her neck. She sat there feeling rather proud of herself and all of the personnel that took part in what had occurred today. They had successfully stolen several quadrillion bytes of information from Algothon. All of the people who were experts or even dabbled in computer technology were checking and rechecking everything to make sure that it was all hooked up properly. She knew it was hooked up correctly because there were several others who were already calling up all kinds of information off of these archives. They were calling up information that they were accustomed to. They were also pulling up information that no one in Owlam had ever even dreamed about.

Officer Leader, Till, the Team Leader of Team 31 found some interesting items on astronomy and astrophysics in the archives that piqued his curiosity. He spent two days gathering all of the information that he could find on the subjects. After amassing quite a bit of information, he was soon obsessed with this new found treasure chest of information and could not get enough of it.

Doctor Shurmook and the other medical personnel were going through it trying to find anything where they could help their people get over their sterility. They found nothing that could help them.

Hallang and the other Prominent Investigators went into the offices of the Senior Investigators. There, they finally found some computers that had not been stolen…yet. In these computers they were finally able to get some of the reports, from around the city that told them why so many people were in such a panic. Computers were stolen - this they knew. Manuals, regulations and tutorial books were stolen - this they knew. Many key personnel in several different industries were murdered - this they knew. They could not gain any access to the archives - Hallang nearly had a heart attack.

Hallang went to a military computer technician. "I need you to get a look at the archives…the front doors to each one, I mean."

The tech looked at him fearfully. "I…don't have the clearance…for that kind of search, Prominent, Sir."

"You're not looking into the vaults, you're just looking at the front doors of the archives to make sure that the guards are still on duty."

The tech looked up surprised. "Oh…you mean…a guard duty schedule…is that what you're talking about…Sir?"

"Yes, that'll do. Check on it."

The tech started keying in the search. "Okay, guard duty schedules…and I need…schedules for…archives facilities…and I need to see…uh…" He looked up at Hallang. "Sir…what am I looking for?"

"You're looking to see if the guards are on duty."

He went back to his keyboard. "Okay, current duties… guarding the archives…security check…observation of current personnel on duty…and AHA! There it is…" He looked closer at what was on his monitor. "I think."

"What do you mean…*you think*?"

"Sir, I have…a picture…current according to the time/date stamp on the bottom of the picture…as a matter of fact…live… but…there's no one there."

Hallang felt a cold chill. "There's no one on duty?" He went to the monitor and looked for himself. He almost felt like panicking like the High Investigators had done earlier. He could not afford to drop his guard though. He clenched his teeth "There's…no one…on duty!" He glared at the tech. "Can you look at all of them?"

"Yes, Sir. Look up top at the icons. You can choose which ever one you want to look at. Just highlight the icon. Right now, the one for the main is highlighted."

"So you can check any of the others?"

"Yes, Sir."

"Do it!"

"Okay, Sir, here's Backup Number 1...and there are no guards there. Here's Backup Number 2...uh...no guards." He nervously cleared his throat. "Here...is Backup Number...3... oh *thwod*, there's no one there either. Uh...Backup Number 4... again...no one is there."

Hallang turned and was heading for the door, ready to find some guards and feed them to any wild animal that was out there if they could find any.

The tech suddenly blurted out a statement that stopped Hallang cold in his tracks. "Hold on! Forget the guards...where're the *fliggit* doors?"

Hallang slowly turned around. He smiled nervously. "Uh...doors?"

The tech looked up. "Yeah, I can't see any doors...to any of those vaults...in any of what the camera is picking up...live."

Hallang swallowed hard. He slowly walked back to look at the monitor. The tech kept hitting different icons, however, each camera was picking up the same thing. There were no guards on duty and where the doors to each of the vaults should be, there was nothing but a gaping dark hole. He was now heading for his truck - at a dead run.

The other three Prominents were waiting in Hallang's truck. They were getting a crash course in what it was like to be a Prominent. When they saw him come running out of the Main Electronic Surveillance center, they were not quite sure what to do...other than just go along for the ride. Hallang jumped in his truck started it and was heading out at full throttle before any of his students could even think of a question to ask. He turned on the siren, lights and the trucks klaxon. No one was going to get in his way.

He screeched to a halt in front of the hospital and jumped out without turning any of the noisemakers off. He went to the back to grab some of the emergency flashlights that were located in his mobile supplies.

While Hallang was getting his supplies, Steenda was shutting the ear-shattering siren and klaxon down. The three students were rubbing their ears when each one got a flashlight thrown at them. They did not ask why, they just followed Hallang into the hospital, having a hard time keeping up with him.

Hallang got to the security door and entered his code...he thought. He hit the door and it did not open. He looked at the pad and saw an error message. He growled and entered his number again. Another error message.

Molheedrow took hold of his arm. "Slow down! You're in such a rush, you're not thinking. One digit at a time...and you'll get it."

Hallang had been ready to punch the man. Instead he heeded the warning. He closed his eyes and took several deep breaths, trying to calm himself before entering the code again.

What he did not know was that a certain mischievous Officer Grade 7, Wahamee was with him at the keypad. While he was entering his code - rapidly - she was hitting a few random buttons to screw things up. Now she watched closely as he slowly entered the seven characters, one at a time. Since she was in Spy, she did not have to worry about blocking his vision or standing to the side. She had her nose very close and watched carefully where he placed his fingers. Now she had full confirmation of his entry code and would be able to use it anywhere she wanted to use it… even though she still did not know why anyone in Owlam needed it.

The door clicked open and if was off to the races again.

Pasket was following feeling very confused. "Where are we going?"

"I don't know," said Molheedrow. "Wherever it is…it must be important to him."

Hallang finally arrived at his destination. He ran through the empty hole where the door was supposed to be and…fell down… flat on his face. He looked up rather surprised. His flashlight was sitting close by, still lit. He crawled over to it, picked it up and started looking around the…room (?).

When the archive vault was stolen, it had been determined that they needed to take all of it…completely. They needed the entire foundation of the vault, they needed all of the walls of the vault, they needed all of the ceiling area of the vault…they needed all of the door area and the front wall that led into the hallway. They also needed the back wall. They had taken the vault, including every part that made up the vault - interior and exterior.

If the vault had still been there, the floor of the vault was level with the floor of the hallway. Since the foundation was gone, Hallang was now standing in an empty hollow hole in the subterranean area below the hospital. The bottom part was well below the floor of the hallway and when he stood up in the hollow hole, the floor of the hallway was level with his waist.

He shined his light around the empty space looking for anything that would give him some form of evidence of how... His mind was completely blank. He had absolutely no idea how this had happened.

Steenda was shining her light inside the hole, even more confused because she had no idea why they were here. "Excuse me...Hallang...uh what is this...hole...here for? Why's it so important that you...nearly killed us...several times...driving over here...to see a hole?"

He looked up helplessly. "This...*hole*...used to be where the main computer archives was located."

"So...somebody moved it out?"

He wanted to slap her. He walked back to where she was standing. "Okay, explain to me how they did it. The height of the vault...taller than the hallway is wide. The width of the vault... eight times the width of the hallway. The length of the vault... thirty-two times the width of the hallway. How did somebody get the vault out...in less than one day...and not leave any pieces...of anything…behind?" He put his flashlight down and climbed up out of the hole. "Explain that conundrum to me."

Molheedrow cleared his throat. "What…about the backups? Is it possible that…someone…got those as well?"

Hallang gave him a disgusted look. "I don't know," he said sarcastically. "Let's go look."

They took a grand tour of the backup locations and found the same empty, hollow hole at all the backup sites.

At Backup Number 4, Hallang just sat there for a long time totally bewildered, frustrated and despondent. The amount of concrete and metal plus all of the fixtures in the vaults made the weight of all of it absolutely staggering. "I think we need to talk to the military," he said quietly. "Maybe." He hung his head in despair. "I don't know. I'm seriously beginning to believe in this…teleport…technology."

8

High Commander, Krondon was giving Hallang a patronizing look. "Finally, you decide to come to the military. We have all of the organization, tactics, personnel and equipment already set up. They were in place even before that massive world strike, where you push-button soldiers launched an attack and you had no idea what the aftermath would be like. Finally you come to us for assistance. You've managed to do the impossible and… somehow…*lose*…over six billion in equipment, archives and rooms. Rooms? How someone loses a room…that's unique."

"All right," said Hallang angrily. "Yes, you have your tactics and strategy…and equipment. We were trying to…end all of the wars and…win the whole thing…in one massive blow."

"Yes, you wanted to win a military victory without the military. Do you know what that is? That's normally called a political victory and the proper term for a political victory in a military situation is called an oxymoron."

"To put the attack plan and all of the equipment for it, under civilian control was the decision of the Algothon Supreme Leader. I didn't make that decision he did. I'm here because the Supreme Leader is too embarrassed to come to you…and beg. I think that he finally realizes that you…and the military forces are the only ones who can bring this catastrophe back to victory."

Krondon looked at his Aide. "What do you think of that Commander, Bajahon? They turned the world into a radioactive wasteland and now he wants the military to clean up the mess. Isn't that just like a megalomaniac? They dirty their pants and now they want the military to change their diapers. And then afterward they'll take the credit for the cleanup."

Bajahon scoffed. "That's typical of someone who suffers from that form of delusion Sir."

Hallang sighed. "If it makes you feel any better, I agree with you. That attack was a military action and should've been executed by the military. The scientists didn't even know that there would be this…horrible residual effect and now…the whole world suffers. The difference now…is that it's not just a call for the military to clean it up…it's…no one else has anything that they *can* do. We've lost most of the upper echelon of the Security forces. We've lost most of the upper intelligence of the scientists. The military has lost nothing…but a little pride. This is your opportunity to show who is supposed to have control of the military and get the job done. The High Councilmembers have done nothing but argue. They won't get anything positive accomplished."

"Thank you for your faith, Investigator Hallang. I don't really see a problem because of something that we…the military… kept a secret from the High Councilmembers and the Supreme Leader and from…even the High Security forces of Algothon…"

Officer Grade 7, Wahamee, Jumped back to Owlam. She decided that she did not want to talk long distance about this situation with the new information. She also wanted some kind of reinforcement that what she was doing was useful. She went directly to Holla's Headquarters. She went to the office of Nayna and requested to be able to speak to Holla as soon as possible.

Nayna sat there at her desk with her arms folded. "What's so important about this information? If you want me to get you in to see Holla personally, you'd better impress me first. If you don't, you don't get anywhere by me. Any questions?"

Wahamee sighed. "No, Sir, no questions."

Nayna smiled. "Good. Now...as I said...impress me."

"First of all...I don't understand why I'm collecting all of these passwords...from the personnel in the Algothon upper echelon. We don't need them. We can walk through any of their doors that we want to and...I don't see how they can stop us or why we need to know this."

Nayna closed her eyes and huffed. She leaned forward giving Wahamee the evil eye (x2). "If you had gone to your Team Leader, you'd have your answer to that one. Of course, we can go through any door and leave them wondering what happened. What we're going to do with those passwords...we're going to open the doors *with* those passwords, we're going to purloin a bunch of goodies, from wherever we open the door and leave them wondering, how and why, some thief got hold of the password of the number one investigative *bimyock*. We expect that once they find that it is his password that's being used to assist all of these thefts, they'll change his password. Then…you get us the new password and the thefts continue. Pretty soon, everyone will be questioning just how secure they are, when petty thieves can obtain…freely…the password of the number one *doovoft* in the security force. This creates chaos. NOW, do you understand why we want the passwords?"

Wahamee stood there with a red and anguished face. She swallowed hard and cleared her throat. "Yes…Sir…I understand… now. I guess…I should've asked Officer, Atsuska…before I… wasted your time on that one."

"I agree," said Nayna smugly. "Is there anything else?"

She bit her lip. "Yes, Sir…and this one…is a lot more important."

Nayna rushed into Holla's office. "Sir…I've just received some new information. I think, Sir…you need to call a full Staff meeting…uh…now!"

Holla noticed the concern on Nayna's face. She closed a yellow binder and put it off to the side. "You really think that it's that important?"

"Oh, absolutely, Sir. Very, very important…Sir."

Holla sniffed. "All right, I'll call them." She closed her eyes and sent the messages to all of the Staff. She opened her eyes chuckling. "There are three of them who are in the tub right now, cleaning their necks."

"Sir, I don't like being interrupted...cleaning my neck either...but...I think that in this case...they...need to throw on a robe and get here...now."

Holla got up and walked around the desk. She got face-to-face with Nayna. "This had better be *VERY* important!"

Nayna did not back down at all. "It...is...*VERY*...important, Sir."

The two women stood there staring at each other for several moments. Finally Holla nodded. "All right," she said quietly. "I'll call them." She closed her eyes and sent out the telepathic messages. She opened her eyes. "To the conference room."

"I'll meet you there, Sir." She spun around and went back to collect Wahamee.

Holla went down the hall to the conference room. She made sure that she stayed to the extreme left in the hall. There were eight spots in the hall that were set up as Jump landmarks for each one of the Staff members. This way, when you use your landmark, no one Jumps in on you and vice versa.

She saw Ahandi Jump in from her home. Ahandi was wearing a bathrobe and had a towel wrapped around her head. Chaza Jumped in moments later, dressed exactly the same. Both had mean looking frowns on their faces.

They walked into the conference room. They all went to their seats and looked to see if anyone was missing. One person - Teelila - was not there yet.

Wilfadge cleared his throat. "Should we wait?"

At that moment, Teelila came walking in, dripping wet. She had on a robe and a very nasty scowl. "This had better be something earth shattering," she fumed.

Holla smiled. "I'm assured by my Aide that it is. Please, everyone be seated and we'll get the briefing accomplished."

Teelila stomped over to her seat, trailing drops of water with each step. She sat down and stared angrily at Holla.

Holla cleared her throat and chuckled. "Officer, Nayna, report!"

Nayna walked in with Wahamee right behind her. "Sir, it'll be Officer Grade 7, Wahamee, who gives you the report."

Holla sighed. "Officer, Wahamee…report."

Wahamee smiled nervously. "Yes, Sir." She stood tall and cleared her throat. "I was performing my duties, following the number one Prominent Investigator in Algothon. After those acquisitions that we did, he…uh…the Prominent…he went to a meeting with the High Commander of the Algothon military."

Holla interrupted. "You're babbling, get to the point."

Wahamee cleared her throat again. "Yes, Sir. Uh…the Algothon military is planning a decisive military strike…against Owlam…at the earliest possible moment."

Ahandi, Chaza and Teelila had all been glaring at Wahamee…at first. Now all of the Staff were staring at Wahamee in astonishment.

Holla leaned forward. "Are you absolutely certain of this,

Officer?"

"Oh, yes, Sir. I sat there and listened to a lot of what they were saying."

Holla shook her head. "How much of their plan are you aware of?"

"Sir, they have a harbor…on the west coast of that continent - Neopaure. They're getting ready to load their army onto thirty-four troop transport ships. According to what I heard, each ship can hold up to 2,900 troops…with all of their equipment."

Wilfadge sank back in his chair in shock. "2,900 times 34…that's over 98,000 troops."

"Yes, Sir, it's 98,600. They also have four ships that are supposed to be bringing some…special equipment. I don't know what it is because…all they said…was…special equipment. No one ever said exactly what it was, they just…" She cleared her throat. "Anyway, they estimate that their forces will be arriving on the eastern shores of our continent…twenty-two days after they leave that harbor. They estimate that once they've landed here, a forced march will get their army within striking distance…in another eight days."

Holla looked around the table. "Is there any way…we can stop these ships…from getting here?"

Wilfadge scoffed. "The first time, in ages, that any Owlamite was on any kind of ship…on any sea…was when we started exploring the world…and Nakalak rescued the T'Mor from the other side of the Turgon Wall. Other than that…I don't even know what the difference is…between a ship, a yacht and a boat."

Wahamee blurted it out without thinking. "A yacht is a luxury boat and can be of varying sizes, and the difference between a ship and a boat is the size." When she saw the reactions of the Staff members she covered her mouth with her hands and her face turned very red.

"Oh," said Chaza. "Thank you *so much* for that explanation," she said acerbically.

Holla grunted. "Okay, so we've got to get a Team educated quickly on…what a ship is and how to stop it. From what she said, we've got about twenty days to accomplish this." She stood up. "Officer, Wahamee, thank you for your report, but now, we have some planning to do, so…"

"I'm not finished…Sir," said Wahamee nervously.

Wilfadge looked at her in shock. "There's…MORE?"

Wahamee smiled. "Yes, Sir, there's more."

Holla leaned forward a little. "Is it important…as well?"

"I…think so…Sir."

All of the Staff had started to get up and were all standing at a half crouch. Holla signaled, with waves of her hands, for them to sit back down. Holla sank back into her chair as well. Wahamee was now looking at nine open mouths and nine sets of dull eyes.

Holla sighed. "Officer…report!"

"It's…the archives, Sir. We didn't get all of them." She waited for a reaction from somebody…anybody on the Staff. There was nothing. "When we acquired those archives…and the four backups…all we got was the…civilian…archives. The military…has their own archives. They have a main…and at least two backups…that I heard about." She stood there apprehensively waiting for a reaction of some kind.

Holla covered her face with her hands and sniffed. She lowered her hands so that her eyes were uncovered. She dropped her hands to her lap and sighed. "These new archives can wait. Right now…the main goal is to stop the Algothon military before they can reach the shores of this continent…if we can. If we can't…we may have to prematurely move…to the gorge."

Dwalooa scoffed. "There's still just under a thousand units that're not completely ready. That's not an option."

Holla closed her eyes and held her hands up for silence. She opened her eyes and smiled at Wahamee. "Officer…is there anything else…to report?"

Wahamee smiled back. "No, Sir. There's nothing else… at this time. I can go back to Algothon…and try to find out… something else."

"You do that," said Holla. "Dismissed."

"Yes, Sir." Wahamee spun around and exited the room.

Holla sighed. She stood up and drew in a deep breath. "Team 2000, report to the Supreme Officer's Headquarters immediately! Team 2001, report to the Supreme Officer's

Headquarters immediately! Team 2002 report to the Supreme Officer's Headquarters immediately!"

Shyshee looked up at Holla. "Are you doing…what I think you're doing?"

Holla shook her head. "We don't have much of a choice."

Moments later Teams 2000, 2001 and 2002 walked into the conference room looking somewhat surprised.

Holla smiled and closed her eyes. "Teams 2000, 2001 and 2002…from this day forth, you are assigned to become knowledgeable about ships. We need to know about ships and how we can stop them from bringing enemy troops to our shores. Go to Algothon where you will watch for a large military movement. Find a large group of Algothon military, boarding several ships. You will learn what you can about ships that will keep them from arriving here on our continent. If you have a problem finding these ships, find Officer Grade 7, Wahamee in Algothon and find out from her where these ships are. Usually I would allow you some time to take care of anything you need to here…before departing. Unfortunately, we don't have that kind of time. You must stop these ships at all costs. **Do you have any questions?"**

They all shook their heads.

"Teams 2001, 2001, 2002, you are dismissed."

After the new shipwrights departed, Holla sank back down into her chair.

Wilfadge cleared her throat. "I wonder if this…Officer,

Wahamee contacted Officer Leader, Ota…before making her report here. We didn't hear it from Ota…so…"

Holla shook her head. "Go ahead and contact Ota. Let her know about these other archives." She huffed. "Does anyone have anything else?" She looked around. "No? Okay, dismissed." After everyone was gone, Holla sat there contemplating. "Nayna! Where are you?"

Nayna came running in. "Yes, Sir!"

"Did you get all of that…conversation?"

"Yes, Sir."

"Good. Right now…I think I'll take a bath. My neck feels nasty."

Using the flying cameras (now that the Owlam had control of them). They were able to steer the three Teams to a port city on the western coast of Neopaure. The Teams did not have a hard time finding the ships that were being loaded with military troops.

Team 2000 walked aboard the nearest ship (in Spy dimension).

Officer Grade 4, Dinshee, the Team Leader of Team 2000 was trying to assess the situation on this ship. "How are we supposed to learn enough about this floating city in time to do anything about it?"

Officer Grade 6, Yobdool shook his head. "Even if we start throwing them all into Jahong's Death…I don't know if we could complete the population of one ship, let alone thirty-four."

Officer Grade 6, Bekani scoffed. "I think that they'd notice something…if suddenly they all had more room. Look at this… giant sleeping room. The bunk beds are stacked five high. The job is daunting. I don't see how we're going to do it."

Officer Grade 7, Winmit looked at the rest of her Team. "We have to do something."

Dinshee clicked her tongue. "Let's see if we can find… something that tells us…something about the maintenance of the ship. If there's a weakness in the ship…maybe we can exploit it."

Winmit snickered. "Is that the best that you can think of right now?"

Dinshee shrugged. "No, I just got a mental message from Officer Grade 4, Eebahee, the Team Leader of Team 2001. She suggested it. Officer Grade 4, Voldom, the Team Leader of Team 2002...he agreed."

Winmit scoffed. "Where are we going to find that?"

Bekani scoffed right back. "We're not going to find any of that information while we just stand here flapping our jaws."

Yobdool growled. "They should've allowed us a little bit of time looking in the Algothon computers…on anything that they have on ships."

Dinshee stood there for a moment with her eyes closed. She opened her eyes and smiled. "Voldom just ordered one of his Team members, Officer, Moonta, to Jump back to Owlam and do just that. Maybe she can find something that we can use. Meanwhile, let's go ahead and explore this monstrosity. Get used to what is where…so once she does find something, we can use… in our favor…we'll have a clue as to where it is."

Bekani sighed. "Do you think that…maybe all of the ships are identical?"

"I hope so," said Dinshee.

They started exploring.

The first day out was rather uneventful - as far as finding out any useful way to sabotage the ship. The second day, they did discover that most of the personnel were not used to traveling on ships.

Yobdool shook his head. "I can't take much more of this. I think that we should be in Observation instead of Spy. That way we don't have to listen to all of these people…puking all over the place."

Dinshee looked somewhat queasy herself. "No… unfortunately we can't…go to Observation. We have to listen to any…orders being given by the ships Officers. See if the ship is in any trouble…and utilize that to our advantage."

Winmit scoffed. "If we're gonna listen to those Officers, we should get up to that Command Center up top. I don't think that there's very many of the ships Officers, sitting down here… hurling."

Yobdool snarled. "Has that...Moonta...learned anything yet?"

Dinshee sighed. "Let me check." She closed her eyes. "Officer, Moonta, this is Officer, Dinshee. Can you hear me?"

"Yes, Sir, this is Moonta. I can hear you, what did you need?"

"Have you found anything that we can use yet···to do something···anything?"

"Sir, it's not that easy. You have to learn a whole new language when you're dealing with these big floating buckets. They don't have floors, they have decks. They don't have a command center, they have a bridge. They don't have windows, they have portholes. Right is starboard and left is port."

"Enough with the language lesson! Is there anything that we can do···like foul an engine···or some other part of the ship?"

"I'm still looking! Oh, fouling an engine won't help much. They have several redundant systems that can take over so fast it's ridiculous. Patience, it's only been two days."

Dinshee scoffed and shook her head. "Patience? *H'oolyach*! We came out here to kill something!"

Eight days later, Moonta called out to her Team Leader.

"Officer, Moonta to Officer, Voldom, can you hear me?"

"This is Voldom! Please tell me that you found something. I can hardly wait to get off of this···rocking tin can."

"Yes, Sir, I found something. Landmark something on your ship and help me Jump out there. I'll show you when I get there."

"Uh···where will I meet you···in Owlam?"

"Why not our home?"

"See you there in a heartbeat."

Voldom made the Jump to Owlam, grabbed Moonta and was back out with the armada in a very short time. Moonta immediately found out that she did not have any sea legs (or stomach) at all. While the other two members of Team 2002, Yista and Vingami tried to help, the already seasick Moonta, Voldom called out to the other two Team Leaders.

"Officers, Dinshee and Eebahee, this is Officer, Voldom. Can you hear me?"

"This is Dinshee, yes I can hear you."

"This is Eebahee. I can hear you as well."

"Officer, Moonta has come aboard the ship. She's got a way that we can sabotage the ships···but right now, she's···getting a little seasick."

Eebahee shook her head. "What···is she turning green?"

"Very."

Dinshee snarled. "What's the word? We can worry about her getting sick later. How do we mess these things up?"

"We need to all get on the same ship," sent Voldom. "You need to Jump over here."

Dinshee stood there with her fists clenched. "JUMP WHERE? All these *chokwad* ships look the same."

Voldom groaned and slapped himself in the forehead. "I'll get up top···and see if I can find a ship···that has something unique. We can all go to that ship."

Eebahee shook her head in disgust. "Good idea···hurry up! We've only got fourteen more days before we get to North Chilamte."

Voldom Jumped to the bridge of the ship that he was on. He looked to see if there was a way that he could get even higher. He noticed that there was a ladder that went up. He grinned. There were two men that were way up on the top of this pole (with the ladder) and they were using binoculars to look around. He figured that he should be able to get a good look from up there. He Jumped up and was amazed (and a little queasy) at how high up he was. He looked around and grinned. He found a difference. The one and only difference of one ship versus all of the others.

"Voldom calling Dinshee and Eebahee."

"This is Dinshee, I hear you."

"This is Eebahee, still waiting for info."

He snickered. "Look to the middle of the front of this bunch of ships. There's one ship that has a huge white and green banner that has some kind of gold fringe on it. That's the only ship that has that banner. Do you see it?"

"This is Eebahee, I see it."

"Where is it? I don't···oh, there it is. I see it now."

"Good! Let's all meet on that ship."

In a very short time, all twelve Owlamites were on the bridge of the flagship of the task force.

Dinshee was standing there with her arms crossed. "Okay, now what?"

Moonta was trying to get control of herself. "We…have to…go down."

Eebahee gave her a side glance. "Down where?"

Moonta closed her eyes. "DOWN!"

They started the journey "down". No matter when they asked where they should go next, all that Moonta would say: "DOWN!" They continued.

Finally one of the members of Team 2001, Quoolz got tired of hearing just one word. "Excuse me, Moonta, but are we going all the way to the bottom of the ship?"

Moonta nodded.

"Okay," he said. "I can show you a lot faster way. I've

been doing some exploring in the bottom of the ship and I think that I can get us there a lot quicker than just guessing."

Quoolz led the way while the others took turns dragging the weakened, dizzy and nauseous Moonta.

On arriving, Moonta shook her head. "I'm gonna be sick!"

Dinshee scoffed. "If you're gonna be sick, hop your face into another dimension, so that we don't have to slip in it or smell it."

Moonta was listening to Dinshee, when she suddenly convulsed and lost her lunch. An Algothon seaman was walking in the area at the time and got a very unpleasant baptism. At first he shouted a few curses and then looked around totally baffled, trying to figure out the origin of the mess that was dripping down his front.

Yista tried to comfort Moonta. "Do you feel any better now?"

Moonta sadly shook her head.

Dinshee huffed. "Look…just try…something to brief us!"

Moonta nodded. "Okay, okay! These ships have a lot of weaknesses. Now, in the rear of the ship they got these big plugs. If we pull the plugs out…we can sink the ship."

Yobdool snickered. "So, let's start pulling plugs."

"Not that simple," said Moonta.

"You're right, it's not that simple," huffed Eebahee. "What

kind of a *bimyock* puts plugs in the bottom of a ship? Anyone could just come along and sink it. That makes no sense. Those… plugs…have to have a different purpose."

Moonta groaned. "That's what the plugs are for. If you want to sink the ship *on purpose!*"

Eebahee shook her head. "Dumb!"

"No," said Moonta. "Let's say that you're the one in charge of this ship. You've been told that there's a special cargo on your ship. You have to get that cargo to your allies. You're told that 'under no circumstances whatsoever', do you allow the enemy to obtain the cargo. Then you find yourself surrounded by enemy ships and cannot get out of there and know that they'll obtain the cargo. What do you do…you pull the plugs and make sure that the enemy never gets it."

Eebahee had been staring at her with a mocking skeptical smirk. Now she turned a little red as she glanced around. "Okay… that does make a little sense."

Voldom shook his head and huffed. "You said that we could pull plugs and sink the ship and then you say it's not that simple. Okay, what's the not-so-simple part?"

Moonta pointed at the opening between compartments. "There's a big, strong door that slides shut in that archway. It's capable of holding the water back. It's designed to prevent the water from flowing from one compartment into another. The entire bottom of the ship is filled with them from fore to aft."

Winmit looked puzzled. "Four of what?"

Moonta grimaced. "In order to understand the ship, you have to use ship words. I'll have to translate all of them. When I say from fore to aft, I mean from the front to the rear."

Winmit snarled. "Then why didn't you just say that?"

Dinshee held up her hands for everybody to be silent. "Obviously we have a problem here. We're not understanding things and we're all getting confused. Maybe we should bring that...Officer from Team *Bimyock*, who has that knack for teaching. Maybe she can get us all on the same page."

Eebahee shook her head snickering. "It's worth a try."

After some mental communication and some fancy Jumping was accomplished, Team 7016 was on board the flagship in one of the lower sections of the ship, receiving a full briefing on what had been learned and accomplished so far.

Bonarain listened to the information on the ship. She chuckled nervously. "So, what's the problem?"

Eebahee grunted. "How do we pull those plugs and at the same time keep the flood doors from closing?"

Soolchakan laughed. "You don't!"

Bonarain turned to Soolchakan to admonish him for interrupting. Soolchakan gave her a "shut up" glare and held his hand up.

"What I'm trying to say," said Soolchakan, "they might be set up for a situation where somebody accidentally pulls the plugs. The flood doors might be just a backup. If I was in charge of building the ship, I'd have a setup where…if you can pull the plugs out…you can also put them back…by some kind of switch or mechanism…or fail-safe. Now, Officer Moonta, did you see anything like that in the stuff that you were reading up on…about the ship?"

Moonta looked confused. "I…don't know. I don't remember seeing anything about a…backup…or fail-safe."

"Okay," said Soolchakan with a smile. "In order to bypass any of their *possible* fail-safes, we do something completely out of the range of what they're prepared for…we don't pull the plugs. We make a hole…or two, somewhere in the bottom of the ship… but before we do that…we hop all of those flood doors into another dimension."

Dinshee snickered. "Got any suggestions as to which one…just to make sure that we're all on the same page?"

Bonarain shrugged. "Why not Desert? We've been trying to conserve a lot of equipment in order to reuse it. Those doors are made up from a LOT of steel. We hop them to Desert and… there they sit, waiting for us to pick them up when we need them. They're in the desert, where it's nice and dry, so they won't rust on us."

Voldom looked at the hull. "So, how do we make these holes in the side of the ship here…without a pulse cannon?"

Soolchakan gave him a sideways look. "Have…any of you…been to the gorge…to lend some temporary help…yet? Have any of you received any of the training on how to move… portions of rock?"

All the members of 2000, 2001 and 2002 shook their heads, no.

"I guess I'll have to teach them," said Bonarain with a smile.

"No," said Soolchakan. "We can do the portioned moving. The rest of you people…you do know how to…hop a door…albeit an extremely heavy steel door?"

This time all of them nodded a smiling yes.

"Okay, good," said Soolchakan. "We'll do the portioned hopping and you people will hop the doors. Now, before we begin making all of these big floating buckets to glug, glug, glug, what's this stuff about…four ships with…*special cargo?*"

Dinshee stormed up to Soolchakan. "WHY SHOULD WE CARE ABOUT THAT? WE WANT TO STOP THIS BUNCH OF SHIPS!"

Soolchakan did not flinch. "Maybe we might want to keep some of that special cargo," he said calmly.

Dinshee opened her mouth and sucked in a lung full of air in order to yell at him again. She stopped herself and froze with her mouth still opened and holding her breath. She backed up a step, let the air out of her lungs, closed her mouth and contemplated. She looked at the other two Team Leaders. "That might be a good idea. Have either of your Teams been on any of the…special cargo ships?"

Eebahee and Voldom both looked thoughtful. They both gave a 'no' shake of the head.

Soolchakan shrugged. "That means that since we've still got a little over thirteen days before these buckets hit North Chilamte to do a quick exploration of all the ships. Who knows, we may be sending a *lot* of things into Desert dimension."

Dinshee snickered. "All right people...back up to the top and let's see if we can distinguish the difference between ships... and search them all."

Back up on the bridge, they looked at the ship that was starboard of the ship that they were on.

Bonarain took a close look at it then walked across the bridge and looked at the ship that was immediately port of her current position. She groaned in disgust. She tried to say something to the rest of the saboteurs, however, the personnel on the bridge were making too much noise. She grunted in disgust this time. "EVERYBODY HOP TO OBSERVATION SO WE DON'T HAVE TO LISTEN TO THE ALGOTHON NOISE!"

Nobody argued. Once in Observation, the silence was incredible.

"We should have done that a long time ago," said Fyning.

Dinshee snarled at her. "It was suggested...a long time ago...but we had to stay in Spy so that we could hear the Algothon conversations."

Bonarain crossed her arms. "Are all of you...telling me that you can't see any difference in the ships on either side of the one we're on?" She saw a group of puzzled faces. "GO LOOK AT THE *CHOGO* THINGS!"

Everyone stared at the starboard ship.

Bonarain stood there dismayed and appalled. "Okay, everybody, go look at the one on the other side."

They all walked across the bridge, some giving Bonarain some dirty or confused looks. They all stood there staring at the ship on the port side.

Soolchakan turned around a little red faced. He walked over to where she was standing. He let out a guilty chuckle. "Numbers?"

"Thank you," she said with extreme accentuation!

Voldom looked back. "What'd he say?"

Bonarain slapped her arms down to her sides. "NUMBERS YOU *BIMYOCKS!*"

Everyone looked back at the port side ship and then there were quite a few red faces.

"The ship you're looking at has the number 88 on its rear. The ship on the other side has the number 229 on its rear. All of these ships probably have different numbers. That's how *these* people tell the difference at a distance...ANY QUESTIONS?"

All the red faces shook their heads, no.

Bonarain cleared her throat, trying not to show her revulsion at their stupidity. "Okay, here's my suggestion on how to do it: Everyone get their pad out. They've got seven ships in the front row, with four rows of seven and one row of six in the rear. Two people go to each ship in this front row. We do a quick inventory of each ship, if it's all troops who are either puking, sleeping or gambling, it's not the special cargo. We keep track of all the numbers that have troops on them and we scratch them off the list. We then do the same with each row."

The four Team Leaders were the ones who stayed on the flagship while the other twelve started Jumping to the other ships.

Dinshee had her pad out. "What's the ship on the far right?"

"This is Yobdool with Bekani. It's number 90 and there's nothing but troops on this ship."

Dinshee made the annotation. "What's the next ship in?"

"This is Quoolz with Am—Eesa. Ship number 183 is nothing but troops."

Another annotation. "Who is on 229?"

"This is Winmit with Fyning. 229 is another troop ship."

Dinshee looked up from her pad and grimaced. They had been taking inventory and forgot to get the number of the flag ship. Several had looked over the side, however, they could not see the number because of the curvature of the hull. "Winmit, could you take a quick look and see what the number is on the ship that I'm on?"

"You're on ship number 17," came a giggling response.

Dinshee cleared her throat. "Ship number 88···who is on

that one?"

"This is Yista with Moonta. Number 88 is a troop ship."

"What's the next ship on the other side of 88?"

"This is Bonarain with Kiyalee. This ship is number 64. Just another troop ship."

Dinshee sighed. She looked at the other Team Leaders. "What do you wanna bet the *special cargo* is either in the middle or in the rear?"

"I don't know," said Soolchakan. "Did anyone check this ship?"

Dinshee grimaced and turned red faced...again. "No, they didn't", she said through tight lips.

Eebahee and Voldom immediately started down into the lower portions of the ship to find out.

Dinshee scowled at herself for forgetting this one. "Okay, the ship on the far left···what have you got?"

"This is Vingami with Chyning. It's ship number 206 and it's nothing but troops."

Dinshee shook her head. "Okay, people···let's all Jump one ship back and do those."

The second row consisted of ships 67, 313, 102, 55, 79, 100 and 145. All of them were troop ships. The third row was 74, 151, 93, 299, 44, 113 and 62. Again all of them were troop ships.

Dinshee sighed. 'Only two more rows to go,' she thought.

The fourth row was 80, 306, 56, 28, 39, 127 and 122. Seven more troop ships.

Dinshee stood on the stern of ship number 28, looking back at the last row. "We better find something different back there. We got nuthin' else left." She shook her head. "Who is on the far left?"

"Yobdool on ship 101. Still nothing but troops."

Dinshee looked at the other Team Leaders. "We still haven't found any of the four special cargo ships…and we only got five left. We better find something!" She went back to her pad. "The next ship in from 101···who's there?"

"This is Quoolz. We got one! This is ship number 18 and there's only about 300 people on this one···upper area. The cargo compartments are full of trucks that have some very big crates lashed down on their beds."

Dinshee smiled. "Start checking those crates. See if there's anything interesting in them. What's the next ship in line and what's on it?"

"This is Winmit. We're on ship number 19. Just like his···there's probably about 300 people. Down below, there's trucks, trucks, trucks and more trucks. They're full of boxes, but all these boxes are marked as field rations."

"Makes sense," said Eebahee. "You gotta bring a lot of food for all those troops."

Dinshee nodded. "The ship next to 19, what do you have?"

"Yista reporting from ship number 20. We got a few···trucks that are full of field rations···but we also got these two long flatbed trucks. They got these···cone shaped things on them – four on each – and covered with tarps. I don't know what's on those trucks yet."

Dinshee made the annotations. "Who is on the next ship?"

"Bonarain. This one is another ship full of trucks··· full of field rations···nothing else special."

Dinshee smiled. "We're finally down to the last one. "What's on the last ship?"

"This is Chyning. This is ship number 173 and it's just another troop ship."

Dinshee puffed out her cheeks as she blew air out. "Do you think that we should check those...unmarked crates...and the cone-shaped tarps...before we start punching holes in the ships?"

Eebahee scoffed. "What possible reason should we have for checking them? Let's just send this whole bunch to the bottom and go home."

Soolchakan scoffed back at her. "There might be something there that we can use. Plus...consider how long it's been since we've had any new vehicles. The ones we've got are all over twenty-five years old. They're falling apart and being held together with *h'oolyach*, spit and prayers. These trucks that they have here are all relatively new…and full of FOOD! I say… we get some other people in here to Jump the things to Owlam and then find out what's in them."

Dinshee nodded. "I agree…to a point. We'll Jump the food trucks to Owlam. The ones with the unmarked crates and those…cones…we check them out here…before we take them to Owlam."

After several mental communications to Owlam and Algothon, and several more Jumps to get extra personnel on board the ships, the food trucks were all being Jumped to Owlam and the gorge. Ota and Nachichi were brought in from Algothon to see if they could read anything - if there was any writing inside all of those unmarked crates. Ota went to the crates and Nachichi went to the cones.

Ota waited while Yobdool and Bekani pried one of the crates open. As soon as the lid was off Yobdool and Bekani stood there wide eyes.

"They're Algothon pulse cannons…of some type," said Yobdool.

Ota looked around in the box for some kind of tutorial manual. "Yes, it appears that they are. I don't know whether or not they're stronger than our 459's though."

"Who cares," said Bekani. "They're newer…just like those trucks."

Soolchakan looked in the crate. "I can tell you one thing… they're bigger. Our 459's are just under seven taja in length. These things are…at least eight and a half…if not more."

"I can see that," said Ota. "Doesn't mean that they're stronger."

Bekani stood there almost pouting. "They're still newer."

Ota shrugged. "I don't see any reason to leave them here. Go ahead and Jump them to Owlam. We'll have more time to look at them closely there."

Dinshee scratched her head. "Uh…didn't you see anything like this…in Algothon…before this?"

Ota sighed. "There's only forty of us and there's three sections to Algothon and we have to constantly keep track of certain key personnel. We haven't had time to really do a full inventory of what's in the city and their seventeen subterranean levels."

Soolchakan shook his head. "Somebody may have to rethink the amount of personnel in Algothon and what they're doing. If the task is that daunting…needs more people."

Yobdool scoffed. "Why don't we just…get rid of all of them? Here we sit, waiting for them to attack us again and it could all be solved by just…well, just get rid of them."

Ota sighed and hung her head. She looked up. "There are currently, just over 20,000,000 of them. They're city is spread out over three sections. They're building a fourth section. There is all kinds of things that we haven't discovered yet. If we just get rid of them, how many other cities will come in and start scavenging the whole area. Who knows…who will get hold of what? We can't just get rid of them until we have full knowledge of what all is there and what we can do to make sure that we're not attacked… with any of that stuff again."

Yobdool sat down and grunted in exasperation.

Ota looked around. "I'm going to contact Holla. I'll tell her that as soon as all of those people are finished Jumping the food trucks…we'll take these cannons as well."

Dinshee nodded in approval. "Shall we go over to that other ship and see what Nachichi found?"

Ota snickered. "Why not?"

Several of the personnel on the "ship" Teams Jumped to ship number 20. There they saw Nachichi standing there on one of the flatbeds, just staring in horror.

Ota climbed up on the flatbed. "Nachichi, what's wrong?"

Nachichi just shook her head. "Those…Algothons… they're serious about killing us off."

The ones with Nachichi had pulled the tarp off of one of the cones and Ota now looked at the exposed cone, seeing what Nachichi was so horrified by.

Now Ota's jaw dropped. "Is…that…what I think…it is?"

Nachichi just nodded.

Dinshee stomped her foot. "Well…what is it?"

Nachichi slowly turned to Dinshee. "It's a firestorm warhead. Those *Chokwads* are taking…EIGHT of the things…

to Owlam. They can't launch them...so they're just planning on taking eight of them to Owlam...plant them around the city...and blast the *h'oolyach* out of Owlam...eight times over."

Dinshee looked around at all of the other faces. "Can't we...take them...with us and...hide them?"

Nachichi grabbed Dinshee by her collar. "Those *Chogos* can detonate them...remotely! Where do you suggest we hide them?"

Ota put her hand on Nachichi's shoulder. "Wait...can't we...deactivate them?"

Nachichi let go of Dinshee. She looked back at the nuclear warhead. "Call...Kloob...and Gagan. They were working on..." She trailed off and shook her head. "The Algothons, they hate our complete existence."

After a few more mental communications, Kloob and Gagan were on board cargo ship number 20. They were briefed on what was found.

Kloob shook his head. "I really don't want to try hiding them. If we have them in Home...those *Doovofts* can detonate them. It wouldn't matter where we put them, they'd be detonated... just to make sure that no one else has them. If we hide them in another dimension...I don't know."

Gagan smiled. "So, let's just deactivate them."

Nachichi snarled at him. "Are you absolutely sure that you can?"

Gagan snickered. "They're very sophisticated pieces of equipment. Usually, with something like that, one thing can completely foul it up." He rubbed his hands together. "However, now that I found out what makes this nasty little thing operate, I can pull its heart out and kill it completely." He hopped to Ghost dimension. He leaned down into the cone and reached for something inside. He stood up straight and held a fist-sized ball in his hand. He hopped back to Home. "That's it," he said triumphantly.

Dinshee was horrified as well now. "You mean…that little ball…is the guts of this thing…and…that little ball…is what wiped out…most of the city of Owlam?"

Gagan nodded as he looked the ball over. "This thing is squeezed by several different explosives, from all directions simultaneously. The result is, what those physicists call, critical mass. Once they've achieved this critical mass…you have a firestorm." He weighed it in his hand. "Without this ball…no critical mass…no firestorm…just a little boom…and very little destruction."

Dinshee nodded. "So…we steal all of the balls…out of all of the cones…and make sure that they can never find them again…and use them."

Gagan snickered. "Like I said, a highly sophisticated piece of machinery can be messed up with just a slight difference. All we have to do is take these balls…hit it with a hammer…and it's useless. The ball has to be *perfectly* round. If it's not round…no good…and they can't be repaired. If we send the damaged balls and the damaged cones…to the bottom of the ocean…it'll be some time before anyone can get to them. By the time that happens, the warheads will be completely useless as well."

Ota sighed. "So stop running your mouth and do it."

Gagan smiled. "Yes, Sir."

After the flatbeds were emptied and eight disarmed nuclear warheads were sinking to the bottom of the ocean, all of the personnel who were stealing food trucks went back to their work and the three "ship" Teams along with Team 7016, Jumped back to the flagship.

Dinshee sighed. "It's time to start wreaking havoc on this pack of warships and then go home. We might as well start with this one."

Soolchakan scratched his chin. "Are you sure that we want to start with the lead ship?"

Dinshee snickered. "We gotta get their attention…and maybe stop the whole bunch at one time while they're trying to rescue everyone off of this one. Yeah, I think that if we start with this one we'll make the biggest splash."

"So," said Eebahee, "to the bottom of the ship."

9

Side Commander Rasaktoo was sitting on the bridge of the convoy's flagship, totally bored. Ten days out of the port in Neopaure and twelve days to a port that they would probably have to invade, take over and conquer on the east coast of North Chilamte. He had been itching for a naval engagement where he could test his skills at invasion and conquest. Now he realized that there was a great deal of boredom involved in just getting to the destination.

The last few log entries had been completely mundane and he was wondering if he should go back and change them. No point in doing that. No one would believe it.

The Executive Officer, Second Commander Wyloth came running up to where Rasaktoo was sitting. "Sir, I've just received a report…from the aft ships in the convoy…"

Rasaktoo came up out of his seat. "What're you talking about? Everyone in this convoy was told to maintain complete radio silence. Who broke that silence?"

"No one broke the silence, Sir, the message was sent by the beacons."

He closed his eyes and flushed in embarrassment. "Of

course…the beacons. All right, what's so important that it has to come to my attention?"

"Sir, uh…ships…18, 19 20 and 21…they seem to have… lost their cargo…Sir." He smiled weakly with a look of concern on his face. "I…did a resend message…and…they confirmed… Sir."

Rasaktoo snarled in disgust. "How does a ship lose its cargo…in the middle of the ocean?"

"I…don't know, Sir, but…they're pulling forward…"

"What? What happened?"

"Sir, the Commander of number 101 noticed that…all of a sudden, number 18 was riding much higher in the water. He signaled 18 and they went down to the holds to check…and all of the trucks…are gone, Sir."

"That's impossible."

"Then, Sir, 18 looked at 19 and noticed that he was not sitting low in the water either. 19 noticed it on 20 and 20 noticed it on 21. All four of them have checked their holds and…there's not a single truck…on any of them…Sir."

Rasaktoo leaned back in his chair and crossed his legs. "All right, Wyloth…what's the joke?"

"Sir, it's not a joke. All four ships said that they're pulling up beside us…so you can see how high they are in the water."

"The only way that they could be riding high, is if they jettisoned their cargo. IF they jettisoned their cargo, I'm going to bust all four of those ship Commanders down to Leading Officer." He huffed. "If someone on the ship jettisoned the cargo…without the ship's Commander noticing it…I am going to bust them down Officer Trainee."

Wyloth sighed. "Sir, take a look. Number 19 is, right now, pulling up along our port side."

Rasaktoo huffed. He got up, giving Wyloth a very nasty glare, and went over to take a look. His disgust turned to surprise when he saw that indeed number 19 was riding way too high in the water. He turned back. "Tell the entire convoy to halt! I'm going over there to check their holds myself."

Wyloth cleared his throat. "Uh…Sir, should I transfer your flag?"

Rasaktoo was ready to punch his Executive Officer in the face. He turned back and smiled through clenched teeth. "I'm not transferring the flag, I'm inspecting another ship in the convoy."

The signals were sent out to the rest of the convoy that they were stopping and why they were stopping.

Once the convoy was stopped, a longboat was lowered and Side Commander Rasaktoo took the short trip from 17 to 19. The entire time he was on the smaller boat, he was thinking of all kinds of ways to reprimand and/or destroy the Commander of 19. When his boat was pulled up out of the water, up onto 19, he looked for Commander Soshkon. He noticed the man, standing at the greeting point, looking very nervous, ready to greet the Commander of the convoy.

They performed the normal rituals of greeting and boarding.

Rasaktoo got up very close to Soshkon and spoke softly. "I don't know what the joke is, but I don't like, or have time, for any silly jokes. Now what's going on?"

Soshkon shook his head. "Sir, it's not a joke. Somehow... all of the trucks...that you saw being loaded...are now gone."

Rasaktoo huffed. "Show me!"

Soshkon sighed. "Follow me, Sir."

They entered the hatch and started the descent into the lower decks of the ship that would eventually take them to the cargo hold. The entire trip was done in silence.

When Soshkon entered the hold he ordered the lights to be turned on. The lights came on in banks that started forward and went aft until the entire massive cargo hold was lit.

Soshkon turned to Rasaktoo. "As you can see, Sir...all of the trucks that were loaded...back in port...gone."

Rasaktoo did not move his head or where he was looking. "Why did you jettison?"

"Sir, we jettisoned nothing. IF we were going to jettison, I would've informed you, FIRST. If we're going to jettison, while underway, you know how many bells, whistles and klaxons would've been going off. You can't open the cargo bay doors... without the klaxons going off...and they'd wake the dead when they sound off."

"So…how was it done…without hearing any klaxons?"

"Sir, you've seen the report…from Headquarters. They said that the Owlams have some kind of teleportation capability. I didn't believe it when I read the reports - I believe it now."

Rasaktoo scoffed. "I still don't believe it."

"I believe it," said another man.

Rasaktoo looked to see who was speaking. "You…you're Commander Bindinton…aren't you?"

"Yes, Sir, Commander of ship number 18."

"And you are saying that you believe this *shybeelan thwod* about some…mythical teleportation capability?"

"I believe it, Sir, because my cargo holds have been cleaned out as well, Sir."

Rasaktoo's mouth went dry. "You…ship number 18…you have…650 brand new, class G, laser cannons. You're telling me that…all of those cannons…are…gone?"

"There's no sign of them on board the ship and I have no idea as to how they were removed."

"This is impossible!" spat Rasaktoo through his teeth. "I've got to check…ship number 20. They have…the nuclear weapons on that ship." He turned to head back to the main deck. "Make sure that my boat is ready to go. I need to get to 20…right now!"

It was decided that Soolchakan and Bonarain would be the ones to remove a large portion of the hull. They had received the training, at the gorge, in portioned moving of inanimate objects. It was also decided that they would remove them near the middle of the ship. No one was prepared for two large holes in the hull on opposite sides, below the water line and having all of the floodgates malfunction at the same time. Of course the gates were not malfunctioning, they were just not there. The gates were sitting in the sand dunes in Desert dimension as Soolchakan and Bonarain went into Spy dimension and manufactured two holes, large enough for them to go through while standing.

Most of the bridge personnel on 17 were making a pool to see how long it would be before Rasaktoo came back up on the main deck and fired Commander Soshkon from his position on the ship.

A warning light started blinking on the console. No one was paying attention to the console, so no one saw it. The light was a warning, telling them that bay seven was taking in water. Two more warning lights started blinking and were also ignored. There was now water flowing freely into bay six and eight. Two more lights started blinking for bay five and nine. Then a klaxon went off, now that the water was pouring into four and ten as well. Seven bays were flooding, and that was what set off the klaxon - finally.

Wyloth was the first back into the bridge, checking the console. All other personnel immediately went to their posts, looking a little guilty. After getting over the momentary shock of seeing most of the warning console lit up, Soshkon came back to reality.

"Close all of the bottom floodgates…NOW!"

Two men went to another console and hit all of the emergency "down" switches for the floodgates.

Soshkon looked over the blinking lights, determined which one was in the middle and turned to one of the other Officers. "Turn on the monitors for bay seven! Put the viewing on my console!"

The warning lights for three and eleven started blinking. The klaxon got louder.

Soshkon saw water gushing in bay seven. "What's the status on those floodgates?"

"They're all down, Sir, but none of them have locked!"

The warning lights for two and twelve started blinking.

Soshkon growled. "View the floodgate…between seven and eight!"

The screen changed.

The man handling the cameras sat there in shock. "Sir… the floodgate…it's not there!"

"It's not down…recycle it! NO…RECYCLE ALL OF THEM!"

"Yes, Sir!"

The warning lights for one and thirteen started blinking.

The camera man pointed. "SIR…LOOK…the frame that

holds the floodgate is moving. The frame is in place…the gate… it…is just gone!"

The warning light for bay fourteen started blinking.

Soshkon let out a grunt of dismay when he saw that the camera man was correct. "Check some of the other floodgates!"

There were several flips of the screen as different monitors were checked. "Sir, all of the floodgates…are gone! There're holes in the bottom of the ship…water is coming in…and we can't do a thing about it. We're sinking…fast!"

Soshkon grabbed the microphone and hit the "full ship" speaker. "All personnel…abandon ship…I say again…all personnel, abandon ship. This ship is sinking and we don't have time to look for any luggage. Get on the lifeboats and go to another ship in the convoy.

A young Officer came running down to the cargo hold, on ship 19, as fast as he could move. He got to the bottom and ran towards the Commanders. He tripped on something and went sprawling face first into the deck, tearing his shirt badly. He got up and continued his hasty trip to Rasaktoo.

He stopped, went to attention and saluted as best he could while panting. "Sir…your Executive…Officer has…transferred your flag…to this ship…Sir."

"What'd that *Fonsosk* do that for? I told him that this was just a visit…not a transfer!"

"Sir…your ship…number 17…is…sinking."

Rasaktoo did not respond. He just stood there with a look of astonishment on his face.

The young Officer saw his expression and simply nodded to tell him that it was not a joke.

Rasaktoo broke into a dead run for the stairs. He started taking them two and three at a time.

The young Officer *was* much younger and able to keep up with him all the way. "Sir, the personnel on that ship are already abandoning the ship and they're taking the lifeboats to other ships in the convoy."

Rasaktoo did not see just a ship sinking, he saw his command and career sinking. Four ships had reported losing their cargo - for no reason whatsoever. One ship had definitely lost all of the cargo, according to his personal eyewitness inspection. His flagship was sinking. What else could possibly go wrong?

He flew out of the hatch and headed to the starboard rail. He was totally sickened by what he saw. His flagship was sinking fast. The bow was almost to a point of going under.

The area around the sinking ship was filled with lifeboats. There were still some personnel on board that were trying to launch some more lifeboats that were full of troops. Soon, very soon, all that they would have to do was get in the lifeboat on the deck and just wait for the mother ship to sink out from under them.

Rasaktoo started thinking about the shouting match that he had won, back at port. He informed everyone there that he would not let the convoy shove off, until there were sufficient lifeboats for all personnel on any and all of the ships. He had won the argument by telling the harbormaster that it was mainly a question of morale for the ground troops that he would be transporting. If any of them were under the impression that there were insufficient lifeboats, then any act of abandoning any of the ships would break out into total mayhem. Because of the fact that he had made them put on additional lifeboats, the entire unfortunate situation was being accomplished without any signs of panic.

He turned away from the scene unfolding from the sinking ship.

Wyloth was standing there…with the command flag and a disc. "Sir, I recorded everything that happened…up until I transferred your flag. There'll be another Officer bringing the final recording…when he departs…17."

Rasaktoo nodded and accepted the disc. "Put my…flag up there where it belongs," he said unenthusiastically

"Yes, Sir."

The four Owlam Teams were standing on ship number 19, in Observation dimension, watching as 17 slowly went under.

Quoolz walked a little way towards the aft and urinated over the side. He came back zipping his pants back up. "When do you want to sink the next one?"

Dinshee shrugged. "We'll wait until they think that they've got everything under control. That's when the next one goes."

Eebahee looked at the Commander's flag waving high. "Is it gonna be this one…or do you want to massacre another one?"

Dinshee looked thoughtful. "Winmit, pick a number."

Winmit shrugged. "Uh…100?"

Dinshee checked her list. "Yes, there is a ship with that number. That's the next one to go."

Yobdool looked around at the ships that he could see from his vantage point. "Uh…which one is it?"

Dinshee pointed. It's the sixth one…going from left to right, in the second row."

Chyning stretched. "Should we go over there now…and get ready?"

"In a little while," said Dinshee.

Bekani opened up a pocket on the side of her cargo pants. "I got some of these things…from one of the food trucks…before they took off with it. It looks like some kind of energy bar. Does anyone want one?"

Dinshee scoffed. "Did you get enough for all of us?"

Bekani scoffed back. "The box holds twenty."

Dinshee giggled. "Okay, pass em out."

Everybody took one, unwrapped them and started eating.

Bonarain shook her head. "Not much for taste, but they're

sure chewy."

Fyning swallowed a mouthful. "It looks like they're about finished with that rescue operation. Should we go get number 100 now?"

Dinshee sighed. "Yeah. I really hate all of this killing and destruction, but...we gotta protect ourselves."

They all made the Jump to ship number 100.

Rasaktoo walked slowly to the bridge. He was getting a little suspicious about the situation, however, considering the fact that all four of the *special cargo* ships had been cleaned out, he was beginning to believe the teleportation story as well. He wanted to confirm, with his own eyes, that all four of the ships were emptied, however, they had lost enough time already. They had to continue on. Besides, if the Owlams did have some kind of teleportation capability and were able to clean out four ships that were out on the high seas...then maybe, just maybe Algothon was in deep trouble...no matter what they did.

One of the main problems was not the lost ship, it was all of that lost food. They had been looking at feeding over 100,000 personnel on an eight day forced march and now, they were going to have to live off of the land. He seriously doubted that they would be able to find enough for that purpose.

The order to get back underway was about to be given when the ship-to-ship intercom started blaring.

Rasaktoo clenched his teeth. "Did some fool forget about

the radio silence?"

Soshkon picked up the microphone. "We're supposed to be maintaining radio silence…this had better be important."

"This is Commander, Vill. I'm on ship number 100. We're…sinking!"

Rasaktoo just covered his face with his hands. "What next," he muttered bitterly? He looked up. "Get all of the troops on that ship rescued…and then get me the report on…how and why it sank…as soon as possible."

Soshkon nodded. "Yes, Sir."

Just as soon as all of the troops from ship 100 were rescued, ship 93 called in that they were sinking.

Just as soon as all of the troops from ship 93 were rescued, ship 313 called in that they were sinking.

Just as soon as all of the troops from ship 313 were rescued, ship 39 called in that they were sinking.

Rasaktoo was pacing on the bridge of ship number 19. "As soon as we get back…IF we get back…I'm going to talk to those shipwrights. I'm going to demand that they build a ship, unlike anything they've ever designed and built before." He looked at Soshkon. "Do you know what kind of ship I'm going to demand?"

Soshkon just shrugged.

Rasaktoo looked around the bridge. "I NEED A SHIP THAT IS CAPABLE OF *FLOATING*!!!"

Soshkon had taken the intercom off of speaker. He was listening to the chatter on headphones. He looked up at Rasaktoo sadly. "Ship number 102 reports that they're sinking."

Rasaktoo flopped down in his seat. "That...that's six ships. We can't afford this kind of loss. We haven't even faced any enemy and we're suffering...huge losses...in equipment." He glanced around desperately. "NAVIGATOR!"

The navigator, Officer First Class, Shinjatz jumped up. "Yes, Sir."

"Where's the closest land...to our current position?"

"I'll have to check to make sure, Sir...if you'll standby."

"We're not going anywhere right now," grumbled Rasaktoo.

After doing some measurements, Shinjatz walked over to Rasaktoo with a chart. "We're equal distances away from two points, Sir. We could head northwest and get to the northeastern peninsula of North Chilamte, or we could head southeast and get to the western peninsula of Neopaure."

"Really," said Rasaktoo. "What's the difference in distance between the two destinations?"

"It's less than one *hyzink*, Sir."

Soshkon groaned. "Sir, ship 183 reports that they're sinking."

Rasaktoo looked at the chart. "If we...go to North Chilamte...that'll mean probably...a fifteen to seventeen day forced march to Owlam…in a march where we have to live off of the land. If we head to Neopaure…we shouldn't have to fight… much of anyone and we can disperse the troops…have them make their way back to Algothon and…try again at a later date…once we have ships that we can trust." He hung his head. "Navigator, as soon as we can get this…floating *wreckage*…back underway… send a message to all ships…that're still floating…head to the coordinates…that you found…on Neopaure."

Shinjatz sighed. "Yes, Sir. It'll be done."

Bonarain looked at the next intended target. "Are we going to let them have a break…and head home…or are we gonna keep breaking their ships?"

Dinshee scoffed. "What do you think? I'm not giving these *h'oolyach* any breaks at all. I think that…pretty soon, we can have all of them in lifeboats. All rowing back to their home." She let loose an evil giggle. "They won't have any food or water and they'll have to row for…oh, I don't know…twelve to fourteen days. I wonder how many'll make it back alive."

Eebahee rubbed her stomach. "Are there any more of those energy bars around here? I could sure use something to eat."

Bekani checked her pockets. "I've…only got two left… but I know where I can get another box…real quick like."

Eebahee looked at Dinshee. "Well?"

Dinshee shrugged. "Yeah, I guess we could all use something to eat. Go get some more and we'll *chogo* the next ship after that."

Bekani smiled. "Be back real quick."

She came back with two boxes and each person got at least two of the bars. They were lounging as they chewed on the bars.

Moonta stood up looking concerned. "Oh…oh no…this ship is moving again." She held her stomach. "Oh no."

Voldom was looking around at all of the ships. "Hey… they're turning. They're…uh…are they turning *back*?"

"I don't care if they are," said Dinshee. "Before they get back home…they're all going to be in lifeboats…or dead." She looked at her crew. "Is everybody finished eating?"

Chyning sat there chewing. She looked around and noticed that she was the only one still chewing. She swallowed what was in her mouth and grinned at Dinshee.

Before Dinshee could order the Jump to the next ship, Yobdool interjected. "Hey, why do we have to go to a different one? The one we're on is floating…and moving under its own power. We can always sink that other one later."

Dinshee shrugged. "Okay, let's tear this thing up. Everybody to their stations…in this ship."

Soshkon hung his head. "Sir?"

Rasaktoo glared at him. "Don't you dare!"

Soshkon sighed. "Sir, ship number 88 is sinking."

Rasaktoo leaned back in his chair and sighed. "Commence rescue operations." He closed his eyes and shook his head.

Before they could attempt to get underway, ships 62, 306, 21 and 206 started sinking.

Rasaktoo had the intercom put back on speaker. "When we…IF we can ever get back underway, full speed…on all ships… back to Neopaure."

Ship number 299 started sinking.

While they were waiting for the rescue to be completed on 299, all of the log discs were brought to the flagship.

"They're all the same," said Vill. "Multiple hull breaches in bay seven, and those…*Fonsosks* at the shipyard…didn't install one single floodgate."

Rasaktoo was fuming. "Right now…all ships…RIGHT NOW…go to emergency. All ships lower all floodgates NOW. Let's see if there are any ships in this convoy…that have their floodgates. Inventory all of them and…from that, we can…hit someone…at that ship building facility for gross negligence. Thirteen ships…all sunk because not one of them had their floodgates installed."

The report that came back left Rasaktoo, almost, in a state of shock. All of the ships that sunk did not have floodgates. All of the ships that were still floating had all of their floodgates intact and working.

Dinshee stood there fuming. "These *Doovofts* figured it out! They closed all of the floodgates…and now, we're gonna try something else, in order to get our job done."

"Not necessarily," said Bonarain.

Eebahee gave her a dirty look. "You got something in mind?"

Bonarain smiled. "We go ahead and make the holes and for some inexplicable reason…the floodgates…just…fall out…of their frames. Now they're sinking…even with the floodgates… and…there's nothing that those *bimyocks* can do about it…because the floodgates…failed."

Voldom gave Bonarain a dirty look. "You…are so…evil. I mean that's such a…nasty thing to do…I really don't know what to say…other than…" He grinned. "…let's get to it."

The call came in on the intercom.

"Flagship, this is number 113. We're sinking!"

Soshkon picked up the microphone. "Ship 113, what happened to your floodgates? You reported that they were in place…down and locked."

"Flagship, this is number 113. The floodgates failed. They just…fell out of their frames…from the water pressure."

Rasaktoo was sitting slouched in his chair. "Fourteen ships down. That leaves…twenty…in questionable condition."

Soshkon walked up to Rasaktoo. "If we rescue very many more of the personnel from the sunk ships, we may end up sinking the rest of the ships…from the sheer weight of all those people."

Rasaktoo had a white knuckle grip on the arms of his chair. "How long will it take us…to get from our current position to… Neopaure?"

The navigator answered. "At flank speed, we can make it…because of some favorable currents…in about six days."

Rasaktoo was trying to think. "How long can the engines on those lifeboats last?"

"Until they run out of fuel," said Soshkon. "But, Sir, those boats weren't supposed to take anyone…more than…maybe twenty *hyzink*."

"How long would it take the lifeboats to get back to Neopaure?"

"It could take…anywhere from twelve to nineteen days… depending on where they hit the beach, Sir."

Rasaktoo bowed his head. "All ships, fill the fuel tanks on those little tanks on the lifeboats. All ships, put extra fuel in the boats as well. They'll need it…if the worst happens. The next ship that has any problems, you're on your own."

"*Flagship, this is ship number 101, we're sinking.*"

Wyloth went to Rasaktoo. "Sir…would you like to get some sleep?"

Rasaktoo scowled at him. "I'm not going to be caught

sleeping in a bed...if this bucket goes down. Is that where you'd want to be?"

Wyloth clenched his mouth shut and simply shook his head.

"I didn't think so."

"*Flagship, this is ship number 79, we're sinking.*"

Rasaktoo hung his head. "We've lost almost half the ships and we still haven't encountered any enemy...yet. All of our losses are flaws in the design...or materials that can't stand up to the punishment that they have to take."

Kiyalee looked at the last ship they damaged, then to the fleeing convoy. "Look at them. They aren't stopping to pick up anyone. They're leaving them out here to die."

Voldom laughed. "They probably can't afford to pick any more of them up. They don't have the room on all of those ships for all those people. I don't know whether they're worried about the body weight or the number of people."

"Or both," said Quoolz.

"I was up on the bridge of this ship," said Winmit. "I checked on what they're doing and I found out that they're running for the western peninsula shores of Neopaure. They think that they can make it in about six days."

Dinshee clicked her tongue. "They can make it...if we let them. When I think about it, I don't think that one single ship is going to make it. They might make it in lifeboats…but I guarantee you that none of the big ships are going to finish the journey."

Vingami folded her arms. "So why aren't we allowing any of the ships to finish the journey?"

Dinshee gave her a patronizing look. "Because that would allow them to try something against us…again…with the same ships."

Quoolz sighed. "Is there a rush?"

"No," said Dinshee. "We've got three days to finish all of them."

Bekani frowned. "But they said that it would take six days to get to Neopaure, why are we rushed into three days?"

Dinshee scratched her chin. "That'll give them plenty of time to think, while they're rowing that last bit…to home."

Soolchakan yawned. "Okay, who's next?"

Dinshee shrugged. "The one that we're standing on."

"Flagship, this is ship number 145, we're sinking."

Rasaktoo shut his eyes. "That makes half of the convoy. I wonder if…any of the ships will make it."

"We need to get at least one of them back, Sir," said Soshkon. "That way they'll be able to dry dock it and look at it and see what kind of design flaw is plaguing us."

Rasaktoo scoffed. "It might not be just a design flaw. Have you ever thought that…maybe they didn't use the right materials?"

Soshkon closed his eyes. "If they used inferior materials, that's criminal negligence. If any one man dies from a ship sinking, because of a flaw like that, I'd love to be the one who executes the…"

"*Flagship, this is ship number 44, we're sinking.*"

"I'm sick of hearing that," said Wyloth.

"Unfortunately you must remember it," said Rasaktoo. "That way, if there is a trial…for some negligent designer…you can show your anguish when giving testimony."

Soshkon looked at the tally of ships that were gone. "Should we call the High Command?"

"We're supposed to maintain radio silence," said Rasaktoo.

Soshkon laughed. "For WHAT? We're in full retreat! If we call them and tell them of the situation, maybe they can send some rescue ships out to help us."

Rasaktoo smiled. "Ships…designed by the same people… who designed the ones…that're sinking out here…right out from under us…now?"

Wyloth looked at the calendar. "They did last…this long. Some of them. If they can get to us, then we'd all have a better chance of getting back."

"Yes," said Rasaktoo. "We'd have a better chance of getting back. We'd also risk the chance of being detected by an enemy. If someone out there is listening, all that they're hearing is that some ships are sinking. They don't know who the ships belong to. If they find out that this is part of the Algothon Navy... that'll give some of those *Hongoths* the courage to resist and that'll make our job harder all the way around."

Soshkon sighed. "Sir, you must transfer your flag."

Rasaktoo frowned. "Why?"

Without looking around or doing anything else, he just spoke softly. "Bay seven is rapidly taking on water."

Rasaktoo clenched his fists. "Signal 229."

"Yes, Sir."

Ships 19 and 229 stopped long enough to transfer the task force commander to 229. As soon as the transfer was done, 229 took off at flank speed as 19 slowly disappeared under the waves.

Dinshee shook her head. "Now that was just plain rude. That Commander left a sinking ship...after leaving several sinking ships in his wake." She huffed. "Rude!"

"He's an Algothon," chuckled Yobdool. "What'd you expect?"

Am-Eesa stretched and yawned. "Should we take that one he got on next?"

Dinshee just shook her head. "I think I'll just let him stew and fret for a while...before sinking another one out from under him."

Yista looked down at her pad. "Nineteen down, fifteen to go. This is starting to get boring…and tiring."

"Repetitive work is always boring," said Eebahee. "The problem is that…it's still gotta get done."

Moonta still looked like she had not grown accustomed to the sea. "So, come on. Let's get this done. These stupid buckets aren't sinking themselves."

"That's a shame," yawned Winmit.

"If we do very many more of them today, I may have to stop and get a little sleep," said Bonarain. "This is using a lot of energy…and those bars of…whatever that stuff is…isn't helping much."

"We've been burning up a lot of energy," said Voldom. "A night of sleep might do us all some good. Yista did say that there's still fifteen to go and we still have about six days. Any time someone is just too tired, say the word and we'll discuss it then."

"Flagship, this is ship number 127, we're sinking."

Rasaktoo sat there motionless. He could not think about eating because he felt too sick, emotionally, to put anything in his mouth. 'Why me,' he thought? 'How did I inherit this…band of useless buckets? We thought we could build a navy…and now… all we've done is help defeat ourselves. I hope I can get back and find out whoever did this…and I'll…oh I don't know what I'll do right now.' He turned to the Commander of 229. "What was your name again?"

"Uldask, Sir,"

"Thank you. What's the tally now?"

"We still have fourteen ships floating…and going at flank speed for our shores."

'Our shores!' He grunted. 'We're heading for the northwestern part of the peninsula. There's still a lot of roving bands of renegades, confederates and those *Hongoths* who want to be free. There's even a few Elf races there that…haven't realized who's in charge.' He chuckled. 'In charge! Hah! Maybe in charge on the land…but definitely not on the sea.'

"Flagship, this is ship number 122, we're sinking."

Rasaktoo pounded his fist on the armrest. "I wish… that we'd all sink right now…or stop sinking altogether. This is torture! *Why* is this happening to us?" He leaned his head back and shut his eyes. 'Now we're down to thirteen.'

Uldask walked up to Rasaktoo. "The sun is going down, Sir."

Rasaktoo sighed. "Turn on all of the dim running lights and slow to one third. We don't want to be slamming into each other. We've lost enough ships to design flaw already." He closed his eyes and rubbed his head. He was not sure whether he had a headache from weariness or the frustration of losing all of those ships.

Soolchakan took Kiyalee off to the side. "Excuse me," he said. "It seems that the inventory of trucks that we took off of the ships and the trucks that arrived at Owlam and the gorge…are off…by one. Do you know anything about that?"

She looked at him with wide-eyed innocence. "What makes you think I did anything?"

"Because I know you." He scoffed. "You fought for a good truck. You fought for the newest truck. You've been keeping it in good working condition for over twenty-five years now. We don't seem to be aging…if you believe that stuff that Doctor Shurmook keeps talking about…but the truck *is* aging. It's aging and there isn't a thing that we can do about it. I know that you love that truck but you also know that a new one would be great. Those Algothon trucks are all new." He scratched his chin. "What would you do… for a new truck?"

"But our garage only has room for one truck. That Algothon truck…if I took it…where would I park it?"

"*That* is what I'm asking *you*."

"Good question…where *would* I park it?"

He sighed. "Look…we're on the same Team. We've been on the same Team…ever since the firestorm. Don't lie to me… where's the truck?"

Her shoulders sagged, she looked off to the side and flushed. She gave him a nasty look. "It's in our garage."

"The garage only has room for one truck...that large."

She gave him an enigmatic smile. "Yes, there's only room for one truck...in Home. There's only room for one truck...in Spy. There's only room for one truck...in Observation."

He chuckled. "So...you hid the Algothon truck..."

"In Observation. Our original truck is in Spy." She folded her arms and gave him a nasty look. "Are you gonna make me give it back?"

He chuckled again. "No. They decided that the Teams that were responsible for the larger Owlam trucks should get hold of the Algothon trucks...for maintenance and...possible replacement... if needed. We were going to get one of them anyway...the High Command just...preferred that they were the ones to distribute... rather than one of us...taking."

Bonarain came in from another room. "I heard what was said," she said admonishingly. She looked at Kiyalee and shook her head. "You naughty little thief."

Kiyalee wrinkled her nose. "Oh shut up. You aren't exactly the most innocent person in the world."

Soolchakan rolled his eyes. "What's that supposed to mean?"

Kiyalee waggled her finger at Bonarain. "Who swiped two boxes of those Algothon rations out of one of the other trucks?"

Bonarain looked back shocked. "How did you...but...I... how did you find out?"

"Oh, *please*! I just happened to Jump back home for a change of clothes and a bath." Kiyalee giggled. "I went upstairs and was quietly sitting in *my* private area on the fourth floor. You didn't see me when you brought that stuff up there."

Soolchakan huffed. "So the two of you...are stealing Algothon supplies...and storing them in our Headquarters."

Bonarain walked over and flopped down in a chair. "So did Chyning," she said dejectedly.

Soolchakan let out a pained groan. "Now what?"

Bonarain took in a deep breath. "No, Kiyalee, I didn't see you. You must have...Jumped out of there...before I noticed you...or before Chyning got there...with another box of those rations."

Soolchakan was now sitting as well. He had a blank look on his face and had a blank stare off at nothing. "Kiyalee...did that truck...that you grabbed...did it have anything...in the back?"

She flushed with a guilty smile. "I took a full one...full of food."

Bonarain looked a little concerned. "What's gonna happen now?"

Soolchakan shook his head. "Nothing really. Supreme Officer, Holla is a little upset over the...wide ranging and intense pilfering...that went on, but...as long as we were all stealing new stuff...that we got from Algothon, she's not going to do, or say, anything about it...yet."

Chyning walked in. "So…we don't have anything to worry about?"

Bonarain looked up startled. "You were listening too?"

Chyning gave her a coquettish smile.

Soolchakan got up and glared angrily at all three of them. "You don't have anything to worry about, IF you tell Headquarters exactly what you took. Hold back nothing! Confess it all and you…along with about a hundred others…will be forgiven."

All three women sighed with relief and started giggling.

"NOW," said Soolchakan. "We're being called for the next sinking."

Rasaktoo woke up startled. He noticed that the sun was in the east. He looked around the bridge. "Uldask…how long…was I asleep?"

Uldask smiled weakly. "All night, Sir."

"Were…there any more ships…that…?"

Uldask sighed. "20 and 90, Sir. We're down to eleven."

Rasaktoo got up, feeling a desperate need to find the head. "Let's hope that this new day…gives us only good news."

Uldask nodded. "Let's…hope."

After relieving himself and splashing water on his face - as well as a trip to his quarters to change his underwear, Rasaktoo returned to the bridge.

Uldask gave him a sad look. "Ten, Sir."

Rasaktoo groaned. "What?"

"Number 151 just called in…and…" He looked away to the northeast.

A member of the ships cook personnel came up to the bridge with some glasses of fruit juice. He gave each person there one of the small glasses to drink.

Rasaktoo looked at the *very* small glass before he drank. "That's a little meager isn't it?"

Uldask sighed. "With all of the *extra* personnel on board… we're all having to survive on…meager rations, Sir."

Rasaktoo sighed. "Why should I be any different?" He quickly drank the juice. It had that canned taste, however, his empty stomach seemed to be appreciative of anything that went in there and seemed to be begging for more.

While the rest of the bridge crew was keeping track of staying on course, Rasaktoo watched the clock. Every tick of the clock moved them closer to that Neopaure shoreline. He could not get the nagging feeling out of his mind about the teleportation. Could it be possible that those pesky Owlam had something to do with this? Were they capable of teleporting in, sabotaging the ship and then teleporting out? The thought was laughable. No, it had to be a design flaw. All of the reports were too consistent. All of them started with multiple or massive hull breaches in bay seven. It had to be a design flaw. They had to get at least one ship back to Neopaure intact.

"Commander, Uldask!"

"Yes, Sir."

"Have you sent anyone down to bay seven…to check on things?"

"Yes, Sir, after the fifth ship floundered, I've had several men down there inspecting the hull for any form of a…anything out of the ordinary."

"Are they still down there?"

"Yes, Sir. I've kept them down there in shifts…all day and all night. We've also tested the floodgates…several times."

"Thank you."

"*Flagship, this is ship number 74, we're sinking.*"

Rasaktoo, along with several other personnel on the bridge, sat there muttering a few curses.

Voldom looked over some of the refugee soldiers that were forced to sleep on the decks for lack of any place else that had any room. "Officer, Dinshee…are we going to step up the pace…and sink all of them today?"

She looked around the crowded deck. "No, we're gonna make them suffer a little longer. I figure that we'll take out…oh… maybe four more today. Tomorrow we'll leave them with…one or two. Those will be taken care of the last day that *we're* out of here."

Three days later, Rasaktoo stepped into the lifeboat. This ship, the third one that he had been on, 229, was the next to last ship. He commanded number 55 to continue on at flank speed. Stopping to pick up more personnel would only weigh that ship down unnecessarily. Keep moving and try to get at least one ship back to the mainland so that the hull could be inspected and find out why they kept failing. He hoped that when his lifeboat finally found the beach that he would be able to get back to Algothon and find out just exactly what had happened. He never got the report that number 55 never made it to land.

Back in Owlam, Team 7016 was at home, each one, enjoying a bath and their new Algothon cuisine.

10

The Staff was in the conference room.

Holla looked at a computer screen. "Can anyone give me a condensed version?"

Ahandi shrugged. "All of the ships were sunk…eventually. The reason it took as long as it did to sink them, it took all four Teams working together. They had to punch big holes in the bottom of the ship and remove these large steel doors that were called floodgates. If they hadn't been working together the Algothon would have known that it was some kind of sabotage. Since they don't have any ships from that convoy to examine…they have no conclusive evidence."

Holla nodded. "The ships were sunk and we got a treasure trove of new equipment…along with a lot of food. What happened to all of that huge army that they had with them?"

Wilfadge clicked his tongue. "By some kind of incredible quirk of fate…or maybe it was the discipline of the soldiers…the vast majority of them made it to shore. They were starving and weak. They landed in an area where the locals weren't friendly to anyone from Algothon." He chuckled. "That's not much of a surprise. They had to fight their way back to Algothon…weak and starving. When that bunch set out, they had exactly 101,954 people. The number of different ways that you can die at sea or on land, in hostile territory, it's difficult to tell how many died where or how. The number of personnel that finally made it back to Algothon...according to the reports that we've been able to..." He cleared his throat "...find...41,826."

Holla nodded. "They lost...just over 60,000."

Teelila looked at her fingernails. "They lost over 60,000 and they never, came in contact with us."

Holla bit her lower lip. "How is it going with that thing... messing with the codes of the high up security muckity-mucks?"

Chaza snickered. "In forty-six days, that Hallang guy changed his codes six times. Our spy, Wahamee was on hand to grab his codes. She also got the codes for the other three top security people and we're having fun with their codes as well. We think we overdid it...a LOT. We got the codes for the three top echelons of security and we used them all over the city. They've now instilled new security measures and we haven't figured out how to overcome that. They have it now...two people have to feed their codes in and they also have to show a facial recognition on camera, especially in the high security areas."

Holla huffed. "The 'on camera' is the problem."

Chaza looked up at the roof. "Exactly."

"How are we on finding this military archive and the backup?"

Hadathoo shook his head. "Stumped! They haven't had to

go fix anything yet. Until they do, we're at square one."

Holla hung her head and huffed. "All that trouble to find and grab the others and now we know we only got half the job done." She looked up. "Do we still have control over their outer space cameras?"

Dwalooa giggled. "Yes, we do. We've let them think that they're controlling them, but the cameras that they keep on trying to set up to watch Owlam and nothing else - for some reason they keep on turning and staring out into space."

Holla looked back at the report. "Were they able to follow that bunch of ships as they floundered their way back to Neopaure?"

"No," said Shyshee. "They didn't have an array…or even one camera watching the ocean. They didn't consider it important to just watch a bunch of waves, so they don't watch when they're over open seas."

Holla bit her lip trying to keep from laughing. "So they didn't see a thing and weren't aware of anything…until…when?"

Shyshee smiled. "They didn't know that there was anything that was amiss until they didn't find a landing on North Chilamte. They kept looking for the forced march. A convoy of trucks and a huge amount of soldiers walking…never found it. They didn't start worrying until they didn't see an attack on Owlam. Then they were completely baffled until some of the troops finally straggled back to Algothon. That was when they began hearing and investigating all kinds of things about their naval disaster."

Holla scoffed again. "It would've been nice if they had received absolutely no information at all. I understand that the Commander of that convoy had all kinds of discs made up, and copied, that told everybody what all of the individual ships went through."

"They never got it," said Wilfadge.

Holla looked at him in surprise. "They…never got a single one of the discs?"

"Not a one," said Wilfadge with a smile.

Holla chuckled. "You didn't have anything to do with that did you?"

Wilfadge looked affronted. "Me? You think I had something to do with the disappearance of those discs?"

Holla giggled at his mocking. "Yes, I absolutely think you did."

"Well it wasn't me," he said as he held his nose up in the air.

Holla giggled again. "But you know who did."

He looked back at her with mock anger. "Of course I do! It was two of my Team - Oolooa and Chani. They somehow used those outer space cameras, found the stragglers and purloined the discs."

"How did they know who had the discs?"

Wilfadge snickered. "The Algothon Naval Officers have

very garish and showy uniforms. The higher the rank, the more elaborate the sashes and shoulder boards and colors of the uniform. No problems spotting them at all."

Holla gave him a suspicious look. "How many of these Officers survived to get to land?"

"Twelve."

"How many of the twelve got back to Algothon?"

Wilfadge looked up at the ceiling while twiddling his thumbs. "If I remember correctly…none."

"So the only thing that the Algothon, back at home, can go by is the accounts of the people who went through it…without any audiovisual backup."

Wilfadge just grinned.

"How are we doing with our friends at the Turgon Wall?"

Hoynama shrugged. "We're still rotating some personnel to and from the wall. We try not to keep anyone there for too long a time."

"Has anyone conjured up the courage to try out those Algothon pulse cannons?"

"We've done a few things with them," said Hadathoo. "They don't seem to be booby trapped…like ours. They, of all things, have a blue beam. It is really *mean and nasty* at close range. It doesn't seem to have anything near the range of our 459's."

Holla scoffed. "*We* haven't figured out the range of those 459's."

"We have on the Class G." Hadathoo scoffed. "At two kilotaja, it makes a boulder...warm." He shook his head. "At fifty or less taja, it'll blow the *piddleeyanks* out of something. At one kilotaja, it can still chew something up...slowly." He scoffed again. "Between one and two kilotaja, it all depends on how much power is still in the power pack as to how much it can mess something up."

High Commander Krondon and Prominent Investigator Hallang were having a meeting with all of the members of the High Councils of the three districts of Algothon.

Krondon looked around the room with disdain. "All right, I'm here. What did you people want?"

One of the council members stood up. "We were won..."

"Hold on," said Krondon. "I have no idea who any of you are. You seem to know me, but I don't know you. If you want to say something to me, the least you can do is to have the courtesy of introducing yourself."

The man stood there looking like he was going to explode. He calmed himself and sniffed. "I am Ravanim. Senior member of the North District." He cleared his throat. "We were wondering what you intend to do about this Owlam problem."

Krondon scoffed. "Until I'm given sufficient *good* equipment that's in *good* and proper working order, I'll think about it."

A woman stood up. "You were supplied with…"

Krondon held nothing back. "WHO ARE YOU?"

She stood there with her eyes closed and red cheeks. "I am Vaheela. Senior member of the East District."

"Thank you."

She huffed. "As I was saying, you were supplied with thirty-four good strong cargo vessels. What have you to show for that? Nothing! Why shouldn't you be removed from your office because of gross incompetence?"

Krondon stared at her for a moment. "The incompetence was in the hands of the scammers who manufactured those ships. You're aware of the reports, are you not? Every man that survived from that fiasco, sailor or soldier…all said the same thing. Not one encounter with any enemy and yet every single one of them sank. There was nothing good or strong about those collapsible pieces of trash."

Another man stood up fuming. "I am Korots. Second member of the East District. I was the one who made sure that those ships were built rugged and sturdy. To make sure, we've been running the first three ships, just outside the harbor, long and hard. None of them have failed…at anything."

"Oh…yes, the prototypes," scoffed Krondon. "I'm sure that those three ships - numbered 1, 2 and 3 are more than sturdy. You were able to get your contract because of the handling of those three ships. After proving the capability of those three ships, which were probably built with material that was superior to the specifications, you sold the Algothon military a bunch of junk. Unfortunately none of the Commanders made it back here with the discs that recorded the failures, but as I said, every soldier and sailor that did survive, said the same things. The hull breaches all occurred in bay seven. The floodgates either collapsed under the weight of the water or were not even in there to begin with. Even more unfortunate, all of the evidence against you and your incompetence is all at the bottom of the ocean."

Another man stood up. "I am Mypich. Senior member of the Circle District. It is disgraceful what happened to the convoy. What *we* are here to discuss…what are your plans in regards to the Owlams? What are you planning on doing to take care of them and get them out of our hair before everything goes completely *kussking* crazy?"

Krondon laughed. "I'd like to be able to do something about the problem. First problem: All of the evidence against the Owlams is totally circumstantial. Second problem: The Owlams are on a different continent and we're having a hard enough time trying to control *this* continent. Third problem: We tried to launch an all-out attack against the Owlams…and our convoy didn't even get to the half-way point. I can't mount any form of an attack against someone that I can't get to. Until you have a way for us to get to North Chilamte…with an intact military unit…what am I supposed to do? How do you intend on assisting me or arming me?"

Another man stood up. "I am Porgoolt. Second member of the North District. We launched that nuclear strike to put fear in everyone's heart for us. You were supposed to get out there and take over those places before they got back on their feet. Why didn't you?"

"You launched that mass nuclear strike, hoping that it would cause everybody, everywhere to fear us beyond anything that has ever come along before. All it did was create over one hundred new races of Elf. We're still not sure which one is the meanest of them all. Several of them have tried to do their own conquering and several of them have been conquered…or destroyed. You wanted us to take over the world before those people could get back on their feet? How about that residual radiation that keeps plaguing us? What about that? I've lost a lot of my military force to…a weird disease that looks like they were burned to death. It all stems from them entering cities that got hit…and coming out… half dead, just from walking through the destroyed area. You want me to go in there and take over without giving me all the information that I need to take over and at the same time, protect my forces from something that none of us can see or fight. You hypocrites! We didn't injure them…we made them mad."

A woman stood up. "I'm Sasaheema. Third member of the North District. You, Sir, are evading the subject! What are you going to do to clean up the mess?"

Krondon sighed and shook his head. "I'm not evading the subject, you're not listening. I can't send the troops out there without some good intelligence data. I can't send them out there without sufficient personal protection. You want me to send them out there with neither. That's why I can't do anything. Your *special* scientists who designed that…weapon! They had no idea about the residual damage that still remains today. According to what they've been able to analyze, it may last for a good seventy to eighty years. We're only twenty-five years deep into that. We still got at least forty-five to go, where we need special protection against the residuals. Meanwhile, I can't send anyone inside one of those bombed out cities...*because* of the residuals. You want me to send troops to another continent, where an enemy that you haven't proven yet, is supposed to be the main problem behind all of our problems with the rockets. To do that...you give me... shoddy ships. Those things fell apart out there and we lost over 60,000 troops, sailors and soldiers, plus an extraordinary amount of equipment for nothing. How am I supposed to clean up anything, when all of the residuals, that you didn't know about, and faulty equipment, is causing more damage to our military than any enemy?"

Another man stood up. "I am Nazkest. Second member of the Circle District. What do you need? What will help in getting our goal of world domination accomplished...or at least headed in the right direction?"

Krondon shook his head. "For one thing: Ships that don't just fall apart. Another thing I need is *proof.* You keep on claiming that the Owlams are at fault. How? We haven't been able to get to North Chilamte and so far, we haven't seen any Owlams here...anywhere on Neopaure. You saw one...count it ONE of the Owlams on South Chilamte. Your evidence sounds strongly compelling...but...it's still conjecture...until you have some solid proof. Third, some kind of protective equipment where my troops don't have to die just walking through the streets of a bombed out city…from something that they can't see and is a residual effect… from something that *we* did."

Another woman stood up. "I'm Ambensik. Fourth member of the East District." She looked down and sighed. "I agree with you…the evidence against Owlam…mostly conjecture. It's conjecture, but, there are no other leads that go anywhere else. The ships? We're still looking into that one. I agree with you that… testing the three prototypes will be inconclusive. We'll start doing a torture test on some of the other ships. As far as the personal protective equipment, the only thing that has been designed so far, it weighs more than the man. Every one of the men who have tried to walk in that bulky mess are exhausted after less than 100 paces. We've considered what you have complained about. I guess that we were premature in blaming you for incompetence. We're all going to have to get together and figure it out…without a bunch of finger pointing."

"I can agree to that," said Krondon.

"So can I," said Hallang.

Ravanim stood up again. "Let's all go back to our prospective areas. Get with your Staffs and…do some brainstorming. We've got to work this out…before everything goes completely downhill."

The meeting adjourned.

Ota, Nachichi, Natsa and Blana were all sitting there after the Algothons had departed.

Ota shook her head. "That was useless."

Natsa scoffed. "The only thing that they decided on was to stop the finger pointing."

Blana sighed. "All of their compelling evidence…points directly at us. Is there any way that we can…invent something that points to…somebody else?"

Nachichi growled. "Like who…Teltermak?"

"Fat chance of that," said Blana.

"You heard them," said Ota. "They're off to do some brainstorming. I hope our people are listening in good."

"Maybe while they're brainstorming, we should start doing some more brain *damaging* on them," said Natsa. "That might be better all round for us."

Kloob walked in. He cleared his throat to get their attention. "Each one of those Council members has just grown a tail. Hopefully we'll learn more from them."

Nachichi scoffed. "Learn something positive? From a politician? That'll be the day."

Kloob snickered. "I said - hopefully. Who knows…if we do get something, it won't be the first time a politician has screwed the works by giving up information that they didn't consider important."

Natsa gave him a disgusted look. "You actually think that a politician would do that?"

Kloob shrugged. "I've heard some politicians who gave up classified information to prove how honest they are and to promote their agenda against their opponent. Politics helps espionage all the time."

Kiyalee was examining the engine compartment of her new huge acquisition. "They're telling us to avoid using these trucks until they figure out if something our spies heard is true."

Bonarain stood there confused. "Did the Algothons put some kind of booby trap in there like our three stage trigger for the pulse cannons?"

Kiyalee shook her head as she slowly continued her perusal of the engine. "There's…supposedly…some kind of device in here, when the engine is turned on, they can use their flying cameras… and find it…because it sends out a signal. They can track, not only where it is, but how fast it's going, what direction it's going…even how much fuel is in the tank and the oil pressure."

Bonarain looked skeptical now. "Is there some kind of manual on it?"

"It wasn't with the truck."

"How are you supposed to find it? I mean, some of the mechanical parts are probably different…so…how are you supposed to be able to tell what belongs and what doesn't?"

Kiyalee huffed. "There's certain things about the laws of physics. There's certain things about how these machines work as well. You can't violate them and expect something to work. An engine is an engine…and no matter who designs it…they'll still function the same way…or at least close enough to where you can find a…strange component…that doesn't fit…anywhere."

Soolchakan and Chyning had walked in to look at this new truck. They both heard the conversation that was going on.

Chyning snickered. "You're telling me that those flying cameras could find it? How?"

"I don't know," said Kiyalee. "All I know…Holla sent out a message that we don't start the trucks until this thing is found."

"We don't even know if the tracking system really exists," said Chyning.

"Yes, we do," said Soolchakan. "Do any of you read some of the updates that come out of Headquarters?"

Bonarain frowned. "What'd I miss?"

Soolchakan closed his eyes and shook his head. He gave all three women a disgusted look. "I should make each one of you read it out loud to make sure that you did see it." He sighed. "It seems that while looking at one of the monitors that was looking down through those flying cameras, one of them that moves that is, a signal came up out of the ocean. Then two, then three, then four…up until they had all eight signals. While the truck has to be running, in order for this signal to work, those firestorm weapons just do it. The Algothons know where all eight of their firestorm weapons, that we dumped in the water, are located. Fortunately, they're in water deep enough that even the Algothons can't get to them, but they do know exactly where they are. Because of the fact that they now know, for certain, that those weapons were jettisoned at sea, they still aren't looking past sabotage and espionage…as far as the sinking of those ships."

Bonarain shook her head while chuckling. "If that's the case, how're we supposed to find this…component…and deactivate it…without turning the silly thing on…to test it?"

Chyning slapped her fists on her hips. "You got any suggestions…or are you just going to criticize?"

Bonarain looked thoughtful for a moment. "You said that that flying camera couldn't pick up the signal…until it flew over the location of the firestorm bombs?"

Soolchakan simply nodded.

Bonarain closed her eyes.

"This is Officer Grade 6, Bonarain calling anyone in Algothon who is at a monitor, watching the flying cameras. Is there anyone doing that right now?" She sent the hail out three times before she got a response.

"This is Officer Grade 6, Zoona. I'm watching one right now. What'd you need?"

"Are any of those moving ones…flying over the city of Neksheth-Or…right now?"

"No, not at this time why?"

"Can you tell me when one of them will be there?"

"I can keep track of it…now WHY?"

"We need to conduct a little experiment with the Algothon tracking system. Neksheth-Or makes a good neutral place to do it."

Zoona looked off to the side and giggled. "Are you sure that you wanna do this?"

"How else are we going to find out about their tracking system···if we don't give them something to track···while you're monitoring it?"

Zoona snickered again. "Let me know when you're in position. I'll let you know when the thing flies in range of Neksheth—Or."

Bonarain gave Soolchakan a big smile. "Shall we go to Neksheth-Or and get ready?"

"Hold on," said Soolchakan. "We haven't had anyone there in a while. Let me do a quick reconnaissance and find a good place to do this…experiment…out of sight of any scavengers that just might be in the area."

Kiyalee chuckled. "And what're we supposed to do in the mean time?"

"Sit in the truck and wait," said Soolchakan flatly.

With that, he Jumped to a spot that he remembered, just outside of Neksheth-Or. He got there and was horrified at the destruction that had taken place. He was up on top of the wall, in the southern area of the city. Nothing was moving except a few pieces of fabric, in the wind, that had not burned up in the fires.

There were several enormous holes in the wall where a bomb had scored a direct hit on the wall. He remembered the destruction that had occurred in Owlam, however, it had not been as bad as this. Apparently the Neksheth-Or had sent their weaker bombs in the first mission. The big ones had been held back and were waiting for a hard strike - later.

He saw one place on top of the wall that would be perfect. It was isolated because two bombs had struck on either side of that section and the ramps going up to the top of the wall were on the other side of the breaches. They could sit up there for quite a while before some courageous (or idiotic) mountain climber found their way up there.

He Jumped to that section of the wall. He looked around for a while. It was perfect. The only ones who could see what they were doing up there, would be someone else who was on top of the wall. Since there was nothing on top of the wall that was usable, no one should be up there. If they Jumped the truck here and had a good long wait until the flying camera was overhead, they would be able to observe the other parts of the wall and see if anyone was watching them. He picked up several small pieces of damaged concrete, and laid them in a circle to make a specific landmark for this part of the wall and then Jumped back to the garage in Owlam.

Chyning was sitting in the cab of the truck looking very bored. "It took you long enough."

"Yes," said Soolchakan. "And while I was there, I got an idea."

"Oh, this ought to give us a good laugh," mocked Kiyalee.

Soolchakan gave them a disgusted look. "All three of you, right now, get up to your precious sewing machine."

The three women exchanged glances and then shrugs. They got out of the truck and headed for the elevator.

"Officer, Soolchakan calling Officer, Zoona. Can you hear me?"

"This is Zoona, are you ready to try our experiment?"

"Not yet. I'm just giving you a heads up that it's going to be a little while. We have some preparing to do before we start it. That might give you some leeway on timing their flying camera and give us the best time to start."

"Okay, I'll watch and be standing by."

"Thank you."

They walked out of the elevator and the three women turned and stood there with their arms crossed as if they were daring him to come up with something clever.

He stared into the sewing room in surprise. "There...*two* sewing machines, when did that happen?"

Bonarain gave him a patronizing look. "We've had a little bit more time to do some more scavenging."

"Okay," said Soolchakan. "Here's what I want you to do."

It took almost half the day, however, when they were finished they all headed back to the garage and got in the truck.

"Officer, Soolchakan calling Officer, Zoona. Can you hear me?"

"This is Zoona. It took you long enough. That thing has done a fly by over Neksheth–Or twice already. It's going to be there again⋯shortly."

Soolchakan smiled. "Great! We're going there now." He Jumped the truck to his spot on the Neksheth-Or wall. He looked at the three women. "Will one of you hop all of us, except Kiyalee, into Home dimension?"

Chyning scoffed. "Why, they'll see us!"

He glared at her. "We want them to see us. Why do you think I had you make these disguises?"

Kiyalee squawked. "Then why am I *not* wearing a disguise?"

"Because you're going to be in Spy, in the engine compartment and/or other parts of the truck, looking for something that is…anomalous. You're looking for something that doesn't help the truck, but is hooked onto it and just might be sending out a signal."

Bonarain nodded. "Good idea," she said flatly. She thought of the imagery and brought the truck, and all inhabitants, to Home. "We're in Home."

Soolchakan cleared his throat. "Kiyalee, hop to Observation and put that headlamp on."

Kiyalee grunted, put the helmet with the lamp on top and hopped to Observation.

"Officer, Zoona calling Officer, Soolchakan. The flying camera is going to be there⋯VERY soon. Are you ready?"

"**Just about.**" He could think faster than he could talk so he sent it to his Team, even though they were right there. "Kiyalee, into the engine compartment. Chyning, start the truck. Bonarain, you and I···outside the truck···NOW!"

Kiyalee watched the exterior parts start moving as the engine was fired up. It was a little unnerving at first, watching the fan blade start spinning, however, she calmed herself easily because she could not hear it and she reminded herself that nothing in Home could hurt her here in Observation. "**What am I looking for**?"

Soolchakan grimaced. "Anything···anything that doesn't look like a normal part of a functioning engine especially when Zoona tells us that that camera is watching us."

Chyning shook her head. "This engine···is LOUD!"

"Ain't no stealth technology here," thought Bonarain. "This truck can't sneak up on anybody."

"**Fine,**" sent Soolchakan. "Bonarain, Chyning, get out of the truck. We need to be seen walking around it."

"Whatever," chided Chyning.

"The satellite is coming into range now," sent Zoona. "It's picking up the signal···and it set off an alarm···here in this Intelligence Gathering facility. Everybody's going to the monitors. All of them are switching···to the one coming up on you guys."

Soolchakan was thrilled that his plan seemed to be working. "Kiyalee, look for anything that might have just started up···and again, it's something that doesn't look like it helps the engine run."

Bonarain and Chyning were walking around the truck looking for anything under the back that might be hooked to the frame. They tried to look like they were doing some kind of inspection - which they were.

Soolchakan got up on the front bumper and opened the hood of the truck. He started looking around at the different parts of the engine (not having the slightest clue what he was looking at, seeing as how he was not a mechanic).

"The signal is getting louder," sent Zoona. "It's all personnel to the monitors. They're VERY interested in this."

Soolchakan chuckled. "Good!"

Kiyalee was not paying much attention to mental chatter. She had noticed that a very tiny blue light, located on a box on the interior of the right fender well, had suddenly turned on. She was staring at it intently as the little blue light got brighter.

"A portion of the wall just came into view," sent Zoona. "There's a little of the destroyed city coming into view now. There's something in that···beacon that's giving them directions. One of the top supervisors, he's doing some adjustments. He's trying to aim the camera at you. There's the truck and···HOLD ON···who is that··· around the truck? It's the wrong truck!"

One of the Algothon supervisors looked around the room. "Who is that...around the truck? Who are they?"

One of the technicians shouted. "I have signal recognition on the truck. It's definitely truck number 55202."

"I confirm that signal," said another technician.

"I know that," shouted the supervisor. "Now, who are those *Hongoths* that are running around outside it? Does anyone recognize that uniform?"

"They look like...Galsino," said another technician.

"Yeah," said another technician. "That's what those Galsino Elf have been wearing...ever since the mass attack."

"Soolchakan, you've got to watch yourselves. There's some Galsino there and they've got a truck as well."

Soolchakan grunted in disgust. "That bunch of Galsino is us, you *Bimyock*. We're in disguise! WE did this so that the Algothons wouldn't know that we're Owlamites sitting here playing with the truck."

"Oh," thought Zoona timidly. "It worked."

Kiyalee was studying the blue light that had one wire coming out of it. The wire went directly to the battery. The box was receiving power from the battery, however, it was not in a position to give anything back and help with the proper running of the engine. She sighed and shook her head. She pulled out her wire snips. She hopped a portion of the wire into Observation and snipped the wire.

"The signal just died," sent Zoona. "All of the alarms just⋯stopped. Did you do something? What did you do?"

"I just cut a wire," sent Kiyalee. "The little blue light just went off. Do you think I got the right one?"

"You must've! Everyone here is in a panic now. They're trying to reestablish the connection with the truck. They had all of the stuff on it⋯a heartbeat ago. They had⋯location by longitude and latitude⋯whatever that is. They had oil pressure, how much fuel was in the tank⋯and that⋯a few heartbeats ago, there were four people in it and now there's only three."

Soolchakan's jaw dropped. "This *chokwad* thing knew how many people were in it?"

"That's what it was showing," sent Zoona. "Now, it's showing⋯nothing."

Kiyalee was still standing under the engine compartment in Observation. "Should I hop back yet?"

"No," sent Soolchakan. "You don't do anything else until we get the word from Zoona that the Algothons can't see us anymore."

Kiyalee grunted, folded her arms across her chest and stood there sulking.

Soolchakan continued looking down at the engine. "Zoona, I need an update on anything that those *doovofts* are doing."

"Okay, well⋯right now, they're still trying to

reestablish the link with the beacon and⋯EVERYBODY
THERE⋯FACE TOWARDS THE BACK OF THE TRUCK⋯or look
down⋯NOW!"

Bonarain and Chyning did both, they faced toward the rear
of the truck and bowed their heads. Soolchakan did not have to
move because he was already in that position.

Soolchakan was still a little curious. "Zoona, what's
going on?"

"Some *chogo* here got the idea of zooming in on your
faces. The satellite is moving on now and they wanted to
see, to make sure, that you're Galsino. So far, all three
of you have been looking down and they were trying to get
any of you while you might have⋯looked up⋯or looked
towards the camera."

Soolchakan snickered diabolically. "Wasn't there
something in that report from Algothon⋯they said that
they had only noticed Owlamites doing any invisibility
or teleporting?"

"Yes," sent Zoona. "Why?"

Soolchakan snickered again. "Ladies, since Kiyalee
is in Observation⋯and still standing in the engine
compartment⋯the two of you and I, are going to take
this truck and hop into Spy. The Algothons are going to
observe some Galsino people, either going invisible or
teleporting⋯depending on how they look at it."

Bonarain chuckled. "Which one of us is going to hop
the truck?"

"You may," sent Soolchakan.

Bonarain shook her head. "Give the signal⋯as to when."

Soolchakan gave the signal. "Zoona, did it work⋯in any way at all?"

"Oh it worked," sent Zoona. "Mercy! The foul language! I just learned at least seven new Algothon cuss words that I'd never heard before."

Holla was sitting at the head of the table in the conference room. She was red faced and madder than she had been in some time. Some of the Staff thought that they saw heat waves coming up off of the top of her head.

Wilfadge tried to quell his normal joviality and be serious, before he ended up as the target of her rage. "Sir, they did discover where those beacons are on the trucks. That led to another discovery on the cannons. The beacons on the cannons look the same except they're smaller. We've been able to remove all of the beacons from all of the cannons and trucks and the Algothons think that it was the Galsino that did the dirty work."

"I know all of that," said Holla in a sinister growl. "The problem I'm looking at - Team *Bimyock* never once contacted anyone in the upper echelon or the Staff before pulling off their little stunt. They have no respect for me or any of us for that matter. None at all!"

Hoynama scoffed. "How much respect have we shown them? You talk about how they should respect us while we make jokes about them and beat them down at every opportunity. What's the matter…are you that jealous?"

Holla looked like she was even madder now. "Jealous… OF WHAT?"

Hoynama shook her head. "Which Team came up with the only home, in all of Owlam, which other Teams tried to fight over and take away from them? A home that was used as the one and only model for all of the units that're being constructed in the gorge. Which Team discovered how to not leave tracks, while we're in Spy? Which Team discovered how to hop other items, even something as big as a house, into other dimensions? How many Teams have found more than one *useful* dimension? How many Teams have someone like Bonarain who can figure out almost anything and simplify it enough to teach it to others? Now, which Team had the courage to try to find out where and how to identify that silly beacon and in the process, mess up all of the intelligence data in Algothon that says that only Owlamites have teleport and invisibility capabilities? Who did this? It was done by Team 7016. Not Team *Bimyock*! Team 7016! When're you going to start showing them some respect? Respect is a two way street. When're you going to show them some respect for what they've done? If you want everyone to clear everything that they do, prior to them doing it, then what you need to do is either put out an order…or use the *Voice of Power* and make it an edict under that. They were using some initiative in trying to find those beacons. If you don't want anyone to use any initiative then give the *chokwad* command and stop complaining about it."

Holla closed her eyes and did some deep breathing. She

opened her eyes and appeared to be very much calmer. "I'm not complaining about the results that this Team has come up with. I'm talking about the example that they're setting. Do anything you want, anywhere, anytime, for any reason without letting anyone in the upper echelons know what you're doing. What they've accomplished and what they did accomplish is wonderful. I'm just tired of finding out about what they DID afterwards and not what they're planning on doing...before they do it."

Hoynama nodded. "Then why don't you go to them and ask them in a civilized manner? Talk to them. Sit down and chat with them for a while. Dine with them. Stop talking nasty ABOUT them and start being completely open WITH them.

Holla sighed. "You're right. They discovered Observation and Beasties. They *fixed*...a problem with Spy that none of us knew about...until they encountered that Teltermak patrol. At the same time, they figured out a way to do partial hops. All from one Team. I think I will go visit them. It'd be prudent to make sure that they're on my side."

Wilfadge cleared his throat. "If you weren't going to make friends with them, just think of the confusion that they could cause. Look at what they did to the Algothons with those Galsino disguises."

Holla nodded. "Did they do anything about the beacons on those firestorm weapons?"

Ahandi looked back at her shocked. "Those things have been disabled and are at the bottom of the ocean. Who cares?"

Everyone at the conference table had a good laugh.

11

Ota sat there with her teeth and eyes clenched. "You followed...*who*, in order to try to find the military archives?"

Hoyna stood there confused. "We...I had my Team following...that High Commander Krondon and...his Aide... Commander Bajaon...why?"

Ota opened her eyes and stared at Hoyna dull-eyed. "The only time that the chief *Bimyock* of the military is going to go to those archives is on an inspection tour. If you want to find the archives, you have to follow the military computer technicians. *They* go to the archives to check on them all the time. *They* go to the archives to perform necessary and preventive maintenance on the archives. Find *them* and follow *them*." She hung her head and huffed. "Get out of my sight!"

Hoyna walked out dejectedly. She found her Team lounging under a tree eating lunch.

Skog looked up at her and smiled. "I take it that the meeting didn't go very well."

She snarled at him. "Shut up." She huffed several times. "Okay, you were right! We need to find military computer repair technicians. They're the ones that we have to find and follow."

Skog smiled at the other two women on the Team. "She's so polite when she hides an apology," he said sarcastically.

Sangtee and Oonipi both looked at Skog with disdain.

"So," said Sangtee, "Since you're so smart…where should we go to find these technicians?"

Skog shrugged. "They're military. So we go to military headquarters and start looking for someone whose primary duty appears to be repairing a computer. They could be repairing computers anywhere in the headquarters. Any more stupid questions?"

Hoyna sighed. "Team 4241, as soon as you're finished eating, we move out…to…" She sighed again. "…the military headquarters."

Skog sat there snickering.

Prominent Investigator, Molheedrow was pacing in the interrogation room. "Superintendent, you say that you saw three Galsinos fooling around with one of our trucks?"

"Yes," said Superintendent Loohondo. "They were going around the truck and doing some kind of inspection. The stats originally showed that there were four but…we never saw the fourth individual. Maybe…he was under the truck the whole time…that they were in our view."

"Maybe it was the fourth individual who cut the signal off."

"I…really couldn't say…who cut it off. There was one of them standing on the front bumper and looking in the engine compartment. That could be the one who deactivated the remote."

"You said that you never got a good look at their faces…is that correct?"

"We never got *any* look at their faces. All three of them were looking down…at different parts of the vehicle the entire time that they were in view. Sir, why don't you just look at the video? We filmed it!"

"Yes, it was filmed. And then some *Hongoth* saved it to the archives. Oh…hold on…right now…we have NO ARCHIVES! So…tell me: Who saved it and where was the *fliggit* video saved?"

Loohondo clenched his eyes shut. "It was supposed to have been saved…on a hard drive…in the monitoring office."

"But it wasn't was it?"

Loohondo shook his head sadly. "No, Sir, it wasn't."

"Now you see why I'm asking these questions."

"Yes, Sir."

"Can you confirm, beyond any shadow of a doubt that the three individuals were Galsinos?"

"No, Sir…I can't confirm anything…other than the fact that there was a trio there, under direct observation, who were dressed like the Galsinos."

"You're certain that it was one of our trucks?"

"Yes, Sir, of that, we are certain. The signal came in very clearly that it was truck number 55202. That was confirmed by at least four of the people doing the monitoring."

"Was the cargo still in the truck?"

"I don't believe so. According to the information, the truck was sending us the empty weight, plus the weight of four people. Initially that's what we got. Then, something happened to one of them and it was sending us information about three people in close proximity. Then the signal went dead…moments later…the trio and the truck…just…vanished."

"Are you sure it vanished? When you consider what happened, you had to adjust the satellite in order to keep an eye on it. What's the chance that you jiggled the wrong control stick and now you were staring at some other part of the wall?"

"No, Sir. I remember seeing the truck vanish and…there was this little circle of rocks that were sitting there…and after the truck, with people, vanished, the circle of rocks was still there."

"Were you able to see that…circle…the next time the satellite went over that area?"

"Yes, and I also got a good look at that part of the wall. There was no way that truck could have been driven up there. None of the ramps, from ground to the top of the wall were connected to that section of the wall."

"Do you wish to amend any of your statement?"

"Sir, I have here affidavits from each and every individual who was in that room at the time. You can read them and see for yourself."

Molheedrow sat down. "Thank you," he said dully. "You can leave now."

Loohondo smiled. "Thank you, Sir." He glanced back down at the stack of affidavits before getting up and leaving the room.

Steenda walked in after Loohondo was gone. "Investigator Molheedrow, I think that you were too nice to that man."

He shrugged. "What good would torture have done? Until we find out exactly who did the save…to the archives, we don't know who to…rake over the hot coals."

"Yeah, we need to find out who did it…"

"WHY? It's not like it was an act of treason. It was an act of habit. It's a habit that…until we get some new archives…that we can keep our hands on…all of the saves will have to be to a mainframe…in the room."

"Why won't the military let us into their archives? I'm sure that it's in there."

Molheedrow laughed. "After losing nearly 300 of those memory poles, the military just doesn't trust us."

"They could put it on a disc. What's so hard about that?"

He sighed. "Make a suggestion to Hallang. Maybe he can talk them into it."

"I will," she grunted. "I just wish that since we're

now Prominents as well...they give us the same respect as... Prominents...just like one who was a Prominent a little longer than us."

Holla looked at the report. "We've been doing everything we can to repair our 459's. Still, we don't have anyone who has enough knowledge. Why did we have to lose all of our technicians? Is there any way that we can get someone trained...to do this kind of delicate work?"

Wilfadge shrugged. "Unfortunately, that kind of talent cannot be ordered on someone. You either have the passion to learn it...or not. You can order someone even using the *Voice of Power* but...if they don't have the skill...it just doesn't seem to work. They might try...but there has to be a certain...inborn talent."

"I hate to think that we're going to have to rely on those... Algothon class G...weaklings. None of them are anywhere as near powerful as the 459. I just...didn't think that they'd be breaking down...so fast."

"They are, so we have to come up with something that... either replaces them or we come up with a way to weaken our enemies."

She shook her head. "The Kalash have some people who can fix those things. The trouble is that they can fix their own. If we show them our 459's and what they're capable of, I still wonder if they could possibly fix them...because they're...very different than the Kalash weapons...and I just..."

"Keep on rambling," he said. "They break down. We knew that. What we may be left with is whatever we can steal or utilize our dimension hopping skills to an even greater extent."

She snarled. "That could possibly give away…our greatest weapon of all. That just doesn't help us remedy our situation or repair any 459...or any 456...or even any old 420."

He just shook his head.

"Have you heard anything about finding those military archives in Algothon yet?"

"No, not yet. Since they finally came up with the correct idea and started following some computer technicians, they still haven't come up with any positive results. They found a few ways to screw up some of the other minor systems, but until they can get one of the technicians to go to the actual archives, to repair or upgrade something, we're stuck in neutral."

"So we keep following technicians until we get some positive results."

"Yes. The only problem there is that they have more technicians than we have spies. What they're doing is picking someone who seems to be more capable and therefore utilized more often and follow that individual for…oh say sixty to ninety days. See if that brings out anything positive."

"Let's hope that it happens soon."

"Let's hope for positive results…no matter how long it takes."

She hung her head. "No matter how long it takes." She looked up. "It seems that...because of this crazy new situation that we find ourselves, because of those firestorm weapons...none of us will ever be able to retire...no matter what."

He grimaced. "That sounds like...death is our only way to retire."

She chuckled. "If what Doctor Shurmook says is true... and none of us are aging...I don't really see any problem about growing old and having to do a mandatory retirement...on anybody."

Officer Leader, Till was ignoring a lot of his responsibilities because of what he was finding in the archives of the Algothon. They had opened up a world of knowledge that no one else, in Owlam, had dreamed of. The Owlam were too busy killing their enemies and defending themselves from those same enemies. No one had made any headway in centuries. The battle lines were in the same place that they had been for over six hundred years - at least from the perspective of the people of Owlam.

Till was finding out incredible things from their section on astronomy, their local star system, constellations and a new phenomenon called: "UFO". He could not help himself with these things. He could not get enough of it. No matter how much he found he wanted more. He put everything he could find on his own computer in order to be able to read up on it any time he had the chance to read.

Time dragged on. The saboteurs in Algothon kept doing their usual job of frustrating the technicians even though it had become repetitive and extremely boring.

The saboteurs also kept doing their job of fouling up any form of transportation that the Algothon could find that could possibly get them from Neopaure to North Chilamte. In fact, the Algothon could not find any transportation that got them off of the shores of Neopaure at all. They would launch a ship full of troops and the survivors would end up swimming back. The Owlamites decided that sinking a ship was not enough - the lifeboats were suffering a great many number of leaks as well.

After four and a half years of getting absolutely nowhere, the High Commander, Krondon was relieved of duty. A Vice Commander became the new High Commander and for four years he did not achieve any results as well. He was relieved of duty and another Vice Commander was promoted to the exalted rank of High Commander of the Algothon Military. The High Council members hoped that this one could achieve...something. He did talk a great deal about what he would do. Now they were going to give him the opportunity to live up to his boasting. Unfortunately, in celebration of his promotion, he drowned in a drunken stupor in his own bathtub (aided of course by two Owlamites).

Also, during this time, two of the Prominent Investigators met with strange deaths (because it was assumed that they got too close to figuring out what was really going on) and had to be replaced. Hallang and Pasket both ended up dead and had to be replaced by the two ranking High Investigators, Bramiks and Torwhool. Now, Steenda was the ranking Prominent and she was being closely watched by certain Owlamites…just in case she got too nosy.

The next choice for High Commander had to prove that he was a bit more conservative in regards to the consumption of alcoholic beverages. Hopefully this would avoid another situation of a High Commander being in office for only two days.

The High Council was in full attendance at the promotion ceremony for the new High Commander, Indazhon. He marched up to the stage to receive the flashy medallion that was worn by the ranking military member. He stood there at attention as the chain was put around his neck by Dronjolok, the Dictator for Life of Algothon. He then gave a long winded speech about how he would lead the Algothon Empire to a new height (while several Owlamites were planning a new strategy on how to embarrass this pretentious snob).

While the promotion ceremony was going on for Indazhon, Ota and Nachichi were in the office planning a surprise for the new high muckity-muck. They were tired of the fruitless search for the military archives and were making a schedule, for one of the next few days, where this new High Commander would go and perform an inspection of the archives and the security surrounding them.

They had two different copies of the inspection order.

Ota was perusing the drafts. "Which one do you think did a better job of forging that Dronjolok's writing and signature?"

Nachichi shook her head. "They're both good. Eelok and Tetch have been working a long time to get his ostentatious scrawl done correctly."

Ota giggled. "Maybe we should have had a few more contestants try it. Someone else may have done a better job."

Nachichi grunted. "Don't you remember? We did have nine others who tried. Tetch and Eelok were voted better...by the other nine."

Ota sighed. "You're right. One way or another, we have to decide which one did the better job."

Nachichi looked at both of them closely. She raised her eyebrows and held up one of the drafts. "Tetch!"

Ota simply nodded.

Nachichi placed the phony orders under two other pieces of paper in the Commander's 'in' box.

The two of them departed the office. They were going to return the following day and find out when Indazhon was going to put the inspection on his calendar. He held off doing the inspection for six days. All four of the Officer Leaders that were in the area were ready to do all kinds of nasty things to him if he did not hurry up and inspect. They had been waiting eight and one half years to find the elusive military archives and the last six days were the most tedious.

Indazhon got in the back seat of his vehicle with his primary Aide, Commander, Fleem. They rode in silence from the Military Headquarters in the southern section, north to the gates that connected the two parts of the split city.

Ota clenched her fists. "They can't be going there! We've gone through and inventoried every single vault in all seventeen subterranean levels. There was…nothing like those archives that had those memory poles…inside those cabinets."

Blana hushed her. "We're not there yet. It could still be somewhere here in the southern section."

The vehicle was parked in a spot just before they got to the middle underground connector tunnel. Indazhon, Fleem and the driver all got out of the vehicle and walked into the connecting tunnel. Indazhon pulled a small remote out of his pocket and punched a button on the remote. The three of them looked up. A panel opened up above them and a small number pad came slowly down, on a pole, from the open panel. Indazhon entered a code on the keypad. A section of the wall opened up revealing a circular staircase. Indazhon and Fleem went down the stairs, while the driver just stood there waiting for their return.

Nachichi snickered. "We never looked in any of these tunnels, did we?"

"Nope," said Blana. "These sneaky *chokwad* seem to find all kinds of ways to hide things."

Ota snarled at them. "Shut up, both of you and let's see where we end up going."

Natsa huffed. "We may find a lot more subterranean vaults down here that are full of…who knows what."

They descended for what they guessed was the height of a two story building. At the bottom of the staircase was a hallway that extended a long way, both left and right.

"This is irritating," said Nachichi. "Here's a…whole

complex. A great big subterranean area that we didn't even know about. All the time we've been here and we never saw this *chogo* thing before."

"Shut up and keep following Commander Muckity-muck," said Ota.

Indazhon and Fleem had turned to the left. They passed four iron doors on the right before stopping at the fifth. Indazhon went to a number pad and entered a code. A small door, next to the big one opened up. A technician met them, wearing a special "clean suit". The two visitors walked in. Inside the smaller area, the two visitors were required to put on a clean suit as well.

The four Officer Leaders watched patiently as the cumbersome outfits were donned. They stood there getting a few giggles as they watched the clumsy attempts at putting the things on over their normal clothing.

Finally the dressing was accomplished and they were ready to enter the clean room. They walked through double doors where huge fans buffeted them with a strong wind as they moved through a small corridor. At the other end, another set of double doors opened and the fans shut off.

Indazhon was given a hearty welcome by several other personnel who were all dressed in the same clean outfits.

The four Officer Leaders found themselves in a vault that was larger than any other that they had seen. As they listened to the tour guide, they found out that the main archive and both backups were in this same vault. This information gave the four saboteurs a strong sense of relief as they now realized that they had found all of it in one strike after *eight and one half* years looking for this elusive vault.

Fifty of the cabinets were the main set, fifty more were the first backup section and the other fifty were the second backup. All of the memory had been put in one vault.

"So," said Nachichi. "How are we going to steal all of these?"

"We're not," said Ota. "There hasn't been that much added since we took the others…that we don't know about. We're just going to come down here with bags of chalk dust and throw it all into the cabinets. If a finger smudge is too thick for that area between the armature and the plate…I wonder what a fistful of chalk dust will do."

Blana giggled. "That's a lot of chalk dust."

Ota had an evil grin on her face. "I know. I also know where we can find that much chalk dust."

Natsa clicked her tongue. "Are we going to explore all of the other vaults in this area before or after the destruction?"

Ota shrugged. "Before. It'll be a lot quieter if we do it before. If we try to explore after the destruction, there could be a horrid amount of noise and I don't like that."

"Well," said Blana. "Shall we get the rest of our people down here and start the inventory?"

"No, we don't call everybody down here," said Ota. "Find the people who aren't busy following their current assignation and get them down here. We're going to inventory all of these vaults. No telling what the military is storing down here."

Blana huffed. "Whatever is down here, unless they've got another exit, that's a lot larger than that staircase…all the stuff has to be rather small. That staircase can't handle anything large."

Natsa looked at Blana in shock. "You're right! There has to be another exit. The cabinets that these memory poles are in are way too big to be brought down that circular staircase. They'd have to bring the things down, one piece at a time."

Ota sighed. "Okay, we're looking for whatever is down here, we're looking to destroy this memory archive and we're looking for a freight elevator. Now, whoever we bring down here, I want one of the computer Teams down here…just in case."

Nachichi pulled out the duty roster. "If that's the case - right now we can spare Computer Team 255 and we've got Teams 5051 and 5500 who were standing by for an assignment…just in case we found this place today."

"So…let's get them down here…and we'll start inventorying as well," said Ota.

Holla read the report. "They found the archives! It's about time!" She leaned forward on the desk. "I wonder why it took them so long."

"It was the location," said Niyniy.

Holla had a dull look on her face. "How many areas under

that *chokwad* city could they bury a vault?"

"It isn't under the city."

Holla looked at the map of Algothon. "Then…where…is it?"

"According to what Ota sent us, they had the audacity to hide the military stuff, in vaults, that aren't actually inside the city walls."

Holla looked even closer at the map. "WHERE?"

"They put the things close to being in the way of danger. They have those underground connecter tunnels that run between the north and the south sections of the city…"

"Which is completely dumb," scoffed Holla. "It lets any enemy have a corridor between the sections."

"Yes, Sir, but it's a very small corridor. Most of that area between the north and south walls, it's only twenty taja wide."

"Okay, I can see that. Twenty taja…you'd be hard pressed to get two vehicles…side-by-side in that corridor."

"And the Algothons could rain fire down on them from both sides."

"And the vaults are under this open area?"

"They haven't done a complete survey as to the exact location, but, that hallway is somewhere, either underneath the corridor or it's under the north wall."

"But, if someone accidentally broke in…to one of those

connecter tunnels…they could have easy access to either portion of the city."

"No, Sir, there are plenty of defense mechanisms in place."

"Have you read the entire report?"

"Yes, Sir."

Holla sat down smiling. "Good! Give me a condensed version."

Niyniy snickered. "If someone did get down in there, the Algothons have these airtight concrete and steel barriers at each end that they'd close. Then they'd blast this gas of some type in there that…somehow moves all of the oxygen out. Anybody in there would suffocate, or at least have a very difficult time breathing. Then, even if they do find that hidden staircase, it's a small circular staircase where the footing is a little treacherous and you have to go down single file. Very easy to defend."

"Yeah, very easy to defend, if you have enough weaponry down there."

"They do, Sir. That one hallway, the doors to the vault are all on the north side. The hallway wall on the south has several hidden panels on it, that'd probably be known to any defenders. They have easy access to all kinds of weaponry, power and conventional."

"Is that the only way in that hallway?"

"No, Sir. At each - east and west ends of the hallway - the hall turns and there's a freight elevator at each end. Those freight elevators go up into a couple of storage warehouses that are against the wall. Seeing anybody coming or going into those warehouses would *not* be suspicious, because they're clearly marked as storage facilities. They are storage facilities that we checked on but didn't know that the freight elevators had a special hidden button…for going down."

Holla had a disgusted look on her face. "Those sneaky *Chokwads*." She shook her head. "What's in the other vaults?"

"We don't know yet, Sir. This is only the preliminary report, saying that they have found the military archives."

"Good! Let me know when the full report comes in."

"Yes, Sir."

Niyniy headed back to her office while Holla opened up the yellow binder and started reading.

Nayna caught Niyniy as she was leaving Holla's office. "Why did you tell her that you read the report?"

Niyniy scoffed. "You read it too! Don't tell me that you weren't just about to die from curiosity!"

Nayna wrinkled her nose at Niyniy and went back to her office.

Ota yawned as she was walking through one of the huge military vaults. "These Algothon military sure like having an overabundance of extra parts for all of their equipment."

"It's a good idea," said Nachichi. "We probably have something like this back at Owlam. We just haven't needed to get into it…yet."

Blana giggled. "Yeah, we've been too busy acquiring things from all of those subterranean vaults at Axswain and Galsino and Teltermak and Zee-Altha…"

Natsa snickered as well. "…and now…Algothon and Neksheth-Or."

Ota shook her head. "We've been able to get quite an abundance of supplies without having to use up any of our own."

Nachichi suddenly got a look of surprise on her face. "I wonder…did anyone ever bother checking under Turgon and that destroyed city…what'd they call it…Hashkay?"

The other three women stared at her for a few moments.

"I don't know," said Ota as she frowned while pondering. "Why don't you put in an inquiry to the Command Staff and see what happens."

"I think I will," said Nachichi.

The four women walked out into the main hallway. They saw the other three Teams waiting for them.

Ota smiled at them. "Do you people have anything new to report?"

Yotonjo shook his head. "Nothing special to report at all… in ten of the vaults."

Ota raised her eyebrows. "In...*ten*...of the...*twelve*... vaults? What's in the other...*two*...vaults?"

Yotonjo chuckled. "First, the one. You know about the vault with the archives. Three banks of those memory poles - one is the main and the other two are the backups. Next, the ten: They also have a storage area in there for more of those memory poles. Ten of the vaults have, as we have all seen, an overabundance of extra parts for vehicles, weapons, communications systems, protective equipment, medical supplies, food as well as anything else that military needs to complete the mission of defense and/ or conquest. Now...the twelfth. In that vault, they have a large supply of captured or stolen enemy weapons. They can test them, disassemble them, reassemble them...find out anything of the accomplishments of the enemy and then probably redo and improve their own weaponry."

"I think that another shoe is about to drop," said Blana.

"You're right," he said with an enigmatic smile. "There are two very special enclosures in that vault. One contains a very small version of the *heelmashk* weapon. It's more than likely that it's just a mock up. The other...it contains...Owlam weaponry!" He paused to let that thought sink in. "They have a few of the old style pulse pistols as well as the new. They have old and new pulse rifles. They also have some old and new pulse cannons. There are those antique 379's, there are some 404's, there are some of the 420's, there are some 456's and...they have eighteen of our 459's. Now how did these *Chogos* ever get hold of those?"

Nachichi shook her head. "They probably had some spies

in Owlam prior to the firestorm attack. Those *Wathoot Fovoks* probably obtained those things…just before the attack and brought them here."

"Wait," said Ota. "You said…*special*…enclosures. What do you mean by 'special'?"

"The sign on the one with the *heelmashk* simply gives us the *indication* that it's a mock up. There's a video that shows what the capability of that thing is. The one where our goodies are stored - a very big warning. These *Chogos* got hold of some of our weaponry, but they don't know about the three-stage triggers. Apparently the Algothons have lost several technicians who tried to fire the things and/or disassemble them. The warning states that they need a lot more technical information before they can utilize *our* weapons."

Blana had a look of horror on her face. "Oh no! We were the ones who suggested that multi-stage trigger on the power weapons that the guards have at the Turgon Wall. These *Doovofts* could get that technology from those…"

"No, they won't," said Natsa. "That's a different system. Don't you remember? Nakalak pulled a different system out of our archives so that we didn't give the T'Mor any of the information on our pulse weapons. It's still a three-stage trigger, but different components and concept, altogether."

"It's still scary," said Blana. "Some creative technician might be able to figure it out…eventually."

Holla put the inquiry in front of the Staff. "Okay people, did we ever explore the cities of Hashkay and Turgon? Do we know if they have any subterranean vaults with all kinds of goodies that we can use? I don't want to take anything away from T'Mor... they might not like it. They may have maps to their underground and if we start taking that stuff, it could ruin our relations with them and all of the other allies in the area."

Wilfadge pondered. "We did check those cities."

Holla was a little surprised. "We...did?"

"Yes, we did," said Wilfadge emphatically. "We had several Teams go in there and find out if there were any subterranean levels and what was in them...after we rescued the T'Mor."

Holla felt a little silly. "Did we find anything there that could be used?"

"We found, and confiscated, any food items that were available in Hashkay," said Wilfadge. "We also found some supplies that were distributed to several Teams as well as some medical supplies that are now being stored here...by our Medical Staff. We didn't check on the city of Turgon yet. We were waiting until we could be absolutely certain that no Turgons were anywhere near there."

"Maybe it's time we checked Turgon," said Teelila.

Holla scoffed. "Maybe we should have done some more snooping in Algothon with our very experienced tunnel finder, Officer, Eeleeg. Maybe we should have sent him to Algothon, eight years ago and we might've already found and taken care of those military archives then."

Ahandi looked at the report. "I'd still like to find…whoever the Algothon spies were…who stole several pulse cannons that I hadn't even heard of until Nagasoom's attack against Axswain. They got those things out of our arsenal…before most of us knew that they existed…and that means that their spies waited until the last moment to get them out of here."

"They weren't as proficient as you are giving them credit for," said Teelila. "They got the cannons, but they didn't get any manuals. It's an irritant that they got the cannons…but satisfying that they didn't get the tutorial manuals."

"That just adds to the mystery," said Wilfadge.

Holla shook her head. "Let's go to something else. Wilfadge, what's the report from the gorge?"

He smiled. "The progress continues. Two days ago, they completed unit number 4,000. With each one that they complete, they're getting more and more proficient at it. The fact that we're sending all of that additional temporary help is aiding immensely in getting everyone proficient at purposely hopping rocks together… er…*joining* them…so they become stronger. We have all kinds of people who can *join*, build and repair. It does make the work go faster."

Holla nodded. "If these temporaries are becoming more proficient at hopping in order to purposely *join*, maybe each one of us should take a turn down there, learning and doing."

Ahandi nodded. "So, let's inform Team 3784 that we're

coming and get ready to learn something new."

Teelila hunched down in her seat. "Is it really necessary for us, the ones on the high Staff…to go rooting around in the dirt? Can't we just send our Teams to do it?"

Holla gave her a dirty look. "If you've read any history, you'd know that some of these people, who called themselves King or Queen or some other snobbish nobility title, they put themselves above that kind of work. Then, when it came down to defending themselves from the enemy or even knowing how to cook or clean for themselves they were helpless. I don't intend on being a helpless snob. If I can't do some cooking for myself, or I'm not even able to dress myself, who am I to tell someone else that they have to go to war and possibly get killed? No! Under my administration, there won't be any deadbeats. If you can't do it for yourself, you had better learn…or starve."

Teelila looked off despondently and then started looking at her long, decorated fingernails, as if she were saying goodbye to them.

Holla snickered. Officer, Teelila, you just made up my mind as to who is going first." She now had a huge smile on her face.

Teelila rolled her eyes, tried to cover her fingernails and moaned.

The three women of Team 113 were going through the medical supplies that had been found in the military vaults in

Algothon.

Ipti threw some boxes of gauze into a larger box. "Remind me, someone…why aren't we just killing off these *Doovoft* Algothons?"

"The reason hasn't changed," said Nelnee as she added more items to the big container. "We're learning things that we lost, when we got hit by the firestorm. All of the military personnel that we had left, the vast majority were just watchers. Now we're learning a few more things about coordination between sections, transportation, espionage, tactics, strategy and anything else that the Staff at Headquarters deems necessary."

"Can't we learn any of that from Kalash…or Rahanan-Sar…or T'Mor? Why do we have to learn it from these *Bimyocks*?"

"If we're seen watching or heard asking questions of those people, they might get suspicious. Since we're not telling the Algothon about anything that we're learning…or stealing from them, it still gets us some of the things we need and at the same time it messes up their ideology that we're so powerful at espionage and sabotage. If we're so good at those things, why haven't we attacked them…openly?"

Ipti threw another box inside the big one as hard as she could. "We haven't attacked them because they number over twenty million and we got less than thirty thousand."

"They don't know that. They're still trying to count us, but with all of the moving around that we do - they can't get an accurate figure."

Teeska walked over with some more stolen goods. "Ipti, why do we have to keep repeating this to you?"

"Because it still doesn't make sense to me and maybe one day, one of you will screw up and explain it in a way that does make sense."

Teeska sighed. "This box is full. Ipti, Jump this container to the medical staff back at Owlam. Then come right back."

Ipti huffed, grabbed the box and vanished.

Nelnee started preparing another box. "I can understand some of her frustration. We found that military archive, over a year ago…and we haven't done anything with it…but look at the information."

"Someone in the Staff…decided to take it slowly…so we can find out more."

"More about what?"

"What do they know about us?"

Ipti was back. "Haven't we found out everything that they know about us…at least five times over?"

The Team Leader, Officer, Ko walked over. "No, we have *not*! We're still learning about some of their methods of satellite espionage and some other covert things they've been doing. Our computer people are still learning some more things about their computer systems…such as updating and upgrading a computer system. We don't have the fully qualified technicians to do this and we're learning from watching them. You just have to be patient."

Ipti grunted. "We've been patient! For thirty-five years we've been patient. It's more fun being over at the missile silos, yanking wires and making components disappear. Why're we taking this stuff...and stockpiling it back at Owlam...and that gorge?"

Nelnee huffed at her. "Do you wanna end up on some assembly line where they make this stuff? These people are still manufacturing things that we need. The only way for us to get new products and equipment, we take it from the people who tried to kill us."

Ipti looked at the faces of her Team. "Yeah, we really need another box that contains a thousand clean tongue depressors." She lackadaisically dropped the box into the new big container.

Eeleeg stood there shaking his head. "These people must have really been desperate. I'm sure glad that I didn't have to fight this fight."

Noniaka looked around the abandoned vault. "It's no wonder...that when we rescued the T'Mor from this pit, they didn't take anything with them. They absolutely gutted their city supplies...of everything."

Moym picked up a piece of equipment that had been cannibalized for parts. "I can't even guess what this thing was originally. I see that it was something that was manufactured but...as what?"

Taskayee shrugged. "It probably had some use in its original state, but…with the Turgons snapping at your heels every day, you kind of forget any luxuries and go with anything that'll help you fight those animals off and help your survival."

Eeleeg closed his eyes. "Supreme Officer, Holla, this is Officer Grade 3, Eeleeg. Can you hear me?"

Holla squawked in frustration. "Why is it…whenever someone calls me…it's always when I'm in the bathtub, cleaning my neck?"

"Sorry, Sir…I just wanted to report back on our findings."

"Okay, which city are you in and what did you find?"

"Sir, we're in T'Mor and we…"

"T'MOR! What're you doing there? We know that they used up almost everything, defending themselves from the Turgons! What could you possibly expect to find – or learn – there?"

"Sir, we weren't sure until we got here. One thing we did find was that…many of the vaults have collapsed. This area is mainly tundra and that stuff is soft and flexible. If you don't take care of things…constantly, you start losing a few things here and there. Since the T'Mor didn't leave until we helped them, they were taking care of their vaults, all six subterranean levels. If there are any subterranean levels in Turgon, they've been neglected…a lot longer than anything in T'Mor…and I really don't hold much hope that there's anything in that city that's still usable."

Holla sighed and hung her head. "Go ahead and take a look anyway. You never know⋯what you might find that⋯ somehow, miraculously survived."

"Yes, Sir. We're moving on to Turgon."

Holla sighed and went back to washing the back of her neck.

12

Ota was standing in the conference room with the Staff. "I'm sorry, Sirs, but, we're all getting very tired of waiting! It's been over three years since we found the military archives and... you still haven't given the word on when we're supposed to destroy it. We've got enough chalk dust there. We could take out three times as many of those poles. I and everyone there... *please*...when?"

Holla pursed her lips. "I didn't want to tell you because it's classified. I can see how frenzied all of your people are getting. If you're an example of what's going on there, we're waiting for a shipment of prisoners to the Turgon Wall. We're hoping soon, that there'll be at least three Galsinos in one shipment. When that happens, we're going to do a crazy little rescue routine and bring the Galsinos here. Then we're going to turn the Galsinos over to you. That's when you let all of the chalk dust loose, destroy the poles and put the Galsinos in the vault. Make sure that they suffocate from all of the chalk dust in the air and the Algothons won't have a clue as to how they got there or when. They'll have to admit that the Galsinos do have the capability of teleporting and destroying their archives." She smiled. "Any questions?"

Ota fought hard to keep from chuckling, however, it was

a lost cause. Her laughing was infectious and soon everyone was laughing, or at least snickering a little.

"Sir...that's...absolutely...vicious. You're going to make the Algothons think...that the Galsinos...are like us?"

Wilfadge sat there with a smug look. "We're following up on a little scheme cooked up by Team 7016."

Ota stopped laughing and frowned in confusion. "What... scheme?"

Holla grunted. "Do you remember when we got the word out to everybody how to find those locater beacons on the Algothon trucks and cannons?"

"Yes, Sir."

"Team 7016 pulled this stunt. They disguised themselves as Galsinos and let the Algothons watch them looking over an Algothon truck. That's when they were able to find that *chokwad* beacon and disable it. They then hopped the truck into Observation...or maybe Spy...or whatever and made it look, to the Algothons, that the Galsinos were caught red-handed with an Algothon truck that they teleported."

Ota was standing there slack-jawed while listening. "That is so dirty...it..." She started chuckling again. "You should be ashamed of yourselves pulling a stunt like that," she said in a mocking way. "It should confuse the *piddleeyanks* out of those Algothons."

"That's the whole idea," said Holla with a big smile.

Ota blew air out through fluttering lips. "Sir, I hope it's soon."

"So do we," said Holla happily.

Ota suddenly got a worried look on her face. "Uh…what if the Galsinos don't suffocate? What happens then?"

Wilfadge shrugged. "I suppose that we could…hop some poison into their systems and make it look as if it were a suicide mission."

Ahandi scoffed. "Teleport in and not be able to teleport out? That doesn't make any sense."

Hadathoo chuckled. "It would…if the one with the teleport machine misses his spot and *joins* with the wall of the vault along with the teleport machine."

Holla nodded. "That might require a fourth Galsino."

"It's definitely worth looking at," said Wilfadge.

Holla sniffed. "Okay, that's tabled until later…when we have some Galsinos." She looked up at Nayna. "Who's next on the agenda?"

Nayna licked her lips. "We have a report from Officer Grade 3, Eeleeg on the revisiting of the vaults in Hashkay and Turgon.

"It's about time," said Shyshee.

There were a few other rumblings and snickering around the conference table.

Eeleeg walked in looking rather glum.

"I don't like the looks of this," said Ahandi. "You look like…"

Eeleeg shrugged. "There's nothing that we really want that was left there. Either in Hashkay or Turgon. I looked at T'Mor first, because those were cared for…up to a certain point. When the T'Mor had exhausted all supplies in any of their vaults, they then abandoned them to the elements. In Turgon, the vaults were never taken care of. The Turgon vaults couldn't really be called vaults. They had no doors. They were just rooms in a manufactured underground system. When the firestorm hit, almost all of the exits were blocked and there were several of the Turgons who were trapped in the underground area. They changed as well. They became the ravenous monsters that we know of and they devoured *all* of the food that had been stored down there. Once they finished all of that, they worked on eating each other. The last one to die, in the underground, died of starvation. We found only one complete skeleton. All of the supplies down there…they tore through all of them, probably looking for food. Nothing usable – everything destroyed. In Hashkay, there wasn't very much that was salvageable. There were a few of the citizens that were trapped down there, because the firestorm collapsed the top two levels of the underground. From what we could find, they tried to dig their way out…in several different places and were totally unsuccessful. They used up a lot of their supplies and possibly suffocated by using up all of the oxygen. We found evidence that some of their spare weapons, for some reason, detonated from… unknown causes. That made some huge dents in their supplies and oxygen. If you want to scavenge in there, again…go ahead. You might find something that you like, but I don't put much hope in there being anything…there."

Teelila frowned at him. "You said…only the top two levels caved in…what kept the other levels intact?"

Eeleeg sighed. "The top two levels were all in tundra. After that, they'd carved into bedrock. The ones in the rock held firm. The problem for them was that no matter where they tried to dig out, those new tunnels just collapsed under the weight of all of the rubble up on top. It seems that none of them were structural engineers and new how to build a proper support system."

Holla hung her head. "All these years after the firestorm weapons were used against all those cities…and just now…we're finding out about other casualties…that no one knew about…even though we scavenged there before." She looked up sadly. "Thank you for your report Officer, Eeleeg."

Officer Grade 6, Zhonsant was standing in the office, next to one of the ranking guardsmen who was of the Rahanan-Sar. Zhonsant was in Spy dimension. There had been two new shipments of prisoners bound for the Turgon Wall that had just arrived in port. This guard would not put the two manifests down and he would not hold them still. Zhonsant was having a terrible time attempting to garner any information from either one.

The guard, who had been awakened when the ships came in, put the rosters down and started stretching some of the sleep kinks out.

"Sorry," said Zhonsant. As the guard was stretching, Zhonsant took hold of the man's beard and hopped the mouth and nose into Stink dimension. When he saw the eyes bulge open in surprise, he hopped the face back. The guard ran into his bathroom and started heaving.

Zhonsant picked up the manifests and started reading through them quickly. The sounds coming from the bathroom made him a little sick so he hopped to Observation. He looked towards the bathroom. "Again, friend, I'm sorry."

He went back to reading. Forty-six prisoners on one ship and thirty-three on the other. He smiled triumphantly. Three Galsino on one ship and two on the other. Now they had five Galsino, all being moved to the Turgon Wall at the same time. The Staff had requested four, however, five might be even better. He had to get the Teams ready to snatch the Galsinos.

"Officer Grade 4, Siynooma, this is Officer Grade 6, Zhonsant. Can you hear me?"

The response came back with a bit of a surly attitude. "Yes, I can hear you. Now what is it···and it better be important!"

He tried to maintain his composure. "I've got the manifests from two ships that docked here at the same time. Between them, they have five Galsinos on them."

Siynooma perked up. "Five? There are five? Do they each have nice long terms to serve?"

He groaned in disgust. "What difference does that

make? We've got five Galsino prisoners···ready for us to transplant."

Siynooma snickered. "Just joking. I'll get everyone there, quick time."

"Thank you." He placed the manifests back on the desk in Home dimension…just in time.

The guard came out of the bathroom still looking a little queasy. He walked over to his mug, picked it up and sniffed the contents. He walked to the window and poured the contents outside. He went back to peruse the manifests.

"This is Officer, Siynooma, calling all members of Teams 6797, 6909 and 6938. Zhonsant found five Galsino for us in the central port. All personnel Jump to the central port and let's collect those *Bimyocks* and get out of here."

There were several very elated responses to Siynooma's hail.

All three Teams gathered near the processing area (in Spy), waiting to find out where their targets were going to be located.

"The manifests showed a total of seventy-nine new prisoners," said Zhonsant. "Hopefully, they'll put some of the five Galsinos together."

Officer Grade 7, Dozzell was a little upset. "We were told to find four of those *doovofts*. What are we gonna do with a fifth?"

"We have to take all five," said Siynooma. "That way… they'll think it's some kind of Galsino plot. Galsinos everywhere will get the blame. If we only take four…it'll leave too many *big* questions."

Officer Grade 6, Fiyakee was a little confused as well. "And what if Supreme Officer, Holla tells us that she only wants four?"

Officer Grade 5, Yaza shrugged. "There's always Jahong's Death. It won't hurt my feelings to dump one of those things in there."

Officer Grade 7, Lilata tried to change the subject. "If there's a total of seventy-nine prisoners and they usually put eight in each holding cell…we should see ten cells being used. We just might have to break into five of the cells in order to get our task accomplished."

Siynooma shrugged. "If we have to break into five - so be it. Before we do, however, I wanna know who else is in those cells with them. We may have to do some head-knocking. I just don't want to kill…unless we absolutely have to."

Officer Grade 7, Soobasoo giggled. She pointed near the end of the line of shackled prisoners. "There's a Teltermak! I wonder what they got him for."

Yaza shook her head. "How about that! We haven't seen one of those *things* for several years. It's sure nice to see one in shackles."

Officer Grade 7, Minwhen looked up apprehensively. "Are we gonna go ahead and kill that Teltermak?"

Siynooma shook her head. "Can't answer that question

yet. We'll see though." She gave Minwhen a dirty look. "Don't be so eager to kill. I know that the Teltermak are a pain. This one is caged…so don't worry about him so much."

Officer Grade 6, Teera sighed. "How are we gonna get split up…in order to bust into five cells?"

Officer Grade 7, Banakati sneered. "Maybe we'll get lucky and they'll put some of them together and then we only have to do two cells."

Officer Grade 5, Yinshosk shook his head. "Yeah…luck! Maybe we'll get *real* lucky and they'll put all five in the same cell."

Officer Grade 7, Fiywhee huffed. "I'm not gonna hold my breath waiting for that kind of luck."

The twelve Owlamites waited, hoping for the best, while the two superintendent guards - one Rahanan-Sar and one T'Mor - had a few discussions. They each did some annotations on their pads, compared notes and then gave the assignment sheet to the other jailers.

The supervisor jailers went down the line checking tags that were hanging off of the bellyband chains. They would remove each prisoner from the line as they found each one on the list that they were looking for and make a new line of eight. As each line of eight was fastened together, they would move the line to one of the holding cells with all of their chains jingling that melancholy tune of imprisonment.

The twelve conspirators watched as the first three lines did not include any of the Galsinos. The fourth line was started with the Teltermak. The supervisor went down the line and pulled a Galsino.

"All right," said Siynooma. "There's the first one…in the fourth holding cell."

The supervisor then pulled another Galsino.

Yinshosk snickered. "Good! Now we know that we won't have to break into five cells."

The supervisor then pulled another Galsino.

Soobasoo squawked with glee. "How good can our luck get?"

The supervisor then pulled a man that was under five taja. He had ebony skin and was wearing a large plastic mask over the bottom of his face.

"I wonder what race that guy is," said Fiywhee. "I also wonder why the mask."

Lilata grunted in disgust. "That mask is usually reserved for prisoners who have a nasty attitude and a tendency to spit on the guards."

Yaza huffed. "How childish!"

The supervisor then pulled another Galsino.

Yinshosk laughed. "Four of them! Are we gonna get lucky?"

The supervisor pulled a tan-skinned prisoner that made all

of the Owlamites look up gawking.

Siynooma shook her head. "He's…gotta be…over nine taja in height."

Lilata cocked her head as she looked at him. "Is it possible that he's an Elf? You remember that the Axswain were all pretty tall…but they also had fur. This guy…he's just…*tall*!"

"They'll have a list hanging on the door," said Dozzell. "We'll be able to find out then…if he's an Elf…or just a very tall Heyyah."

The supervisor then pulled the last Galsino.

"Oh, I don't believe this," said Siynooma with a big grin on her face. "We hit the jackpot. All five Galsino in the same cell."

Fiywhee snickered. "I didn't even have to hold my breath…and it happened. What're the odds?" She looked away. "Of course, I may have to hold my breath from the smell of all those prisoners."

Siynooma chuckled. "Maybe they're just being nice and letting some of the same races stay together."

Zhonsant shrugged. "Who cares why? I'm not complaining about having to only do one cell."

Minwhen pointed at the holding cells. "Maybe they are. All three of the first ones they filled, all of them were Heyyah."

"So…" said Siynooma. "Now, we wait for nightfall. Then we strike!"

Soobasoo looked up expectantly. "Still haven't decided what to do with the Teltermak?"

"No, I haven't," said Siynooma.

Yinshosk looked at the document box that was on the cell door. "I was thinking that we should read up on those other guys in there…with our Galsinos. There might be some interesting reading on them, depending on whether or not, they *are* Elf."

Siynooma nodded. "It wouldn't hurt to get all of the information on them that we can find. That big guy…he could be trouble…if he has a mind to do something to us."

Lilata pointed at cell number four. "Did you see that? They came out of the cell, after locking them down. None of the guards brought that spit mask out. They're gonna leave it on that guy…all night."

Teera shrugged. "Some people learn the hard way…some *bimyocks* never learn. They think that they're above the law. That's why they end up here."

After the guards departed cell number four, Yinshosk walked up to the box, reached into it, in Spy, hopped the papers into Spy and pulled them out. He walked back to the group reading the papers. "Okay, let's see what we've got. According to the description, that tall guy *is* an Elf. He's a…Ragal! Seems that being over nine taja…is normal for any of the Elf from Ragal. That darker skin is another marker of that race. He's in for life for what they've called: Habitual offender." He turned to the next page. That Teltermak is in for…" He looked up in disgust. "… openly practicing cannibalism! Yuck! That little dark-skinned guy is also an Elf...from Tendixive. He's another habitual offender who..." He frowned as he looked at the document. He looked up in shock. "That...spit guard...isn't there because of an attitude problem...the Tendixive Elf...they have poison glands in the back of their cheeks...and they can *spit*...venom! Seems he used his capabilities and blinded nine people. He's in for nine twenty-five years sentences...to be served, one after the other. They're also going to surgically remove his poison glands."

"Okay," said Siynooma. "We've learned new things about a couple of Elf races. Anything special about those Galsinos?"

"No, there's a list on each one of...several different crimes. One of them has received two life sentences. One has been given... one stretch of *thirteen hundred years*." He grunted in disgust. "Pedophile!" He shook his head. "Two habitual criminals and one who has a weakness for jewelry and tried to filch the jewels of all of the rich bigwigs...in some city in South Chilamte."

Siynooma looked at the colleagues. "Now we know what they're in for. It doesn't really matter. After we get through with them, none of that'll be of any consequence. Just make sure that we have a fifth dummy put together for the switch. Any questions?"

Dozzell grinned. "Are we gonna kill any of those other three or are we just gonna knock em in the head?"

Siynooma chuckled. "We'll take a look at how they're situated before we make that decision. Right now, as I said, all we have to finalize is that fifth dummy."

"I'll check how they're situated," said Zhonsant. "Be back in a moment." He headed to the cell and walked through the door.

The foul smelling cell was a normal situation for prisoners waiting to be moved to the Wall. All eight prisoners were lined up on a concrete shelf that ran the length of the room. The shelf was slightly slanted, so that any excrement, which someone might let loose, would flow downhill to a gutter, at the feet of the prisoners, and then could be washed out a small hole in the back of the room. All of these cells reeked of sweat, urine and feces. The door of the cell opened up to where there was a narrow aisle way for the guard to walk down the row to check on, or feed, each prisoner. Sixteen chains were imbedded in the concrete and had the shackles for both of the ankles of each prisoner. The prisoners would then be cuffed to each other by the wrists, when put down for the night.

The tall Ragal was the first one in the line, closest to the door. His right wrist was in a shackle that was connected to the wall. His left wrist was in a cuff that was connected to the right wrist of the Tendixive. The Tendixive was connected to the Teltermak on the other side. The Teltermak was connected to one of the Galsinos, who were all lined up just waiting to be snatched by the Owlamites.

"Couldn't be better," chuckled Zhonsant. "It almost looks like the guards are in on it and helping us."

Fiywhee and Minwhen headed for the tunnel system. To make it look like someone had prepared for the escape, for a long time, there was one main tunnel that ran, lengthwise, under all of the cells. There was a shaft that was dug up to, just under, the concrete foundation. All of them had stopped at the foundation, until they knew which cell would have the target escapees, and then finish the digging into the cell. The two women had to go and prepare that shaft under cell four.

Lilata and Banakati had become the seamstresses who put together a dummy that would replace a Galsino. They had prepared four, in anticipation of swiping four and now had to quickly make the fifth.

The remaining personnel rested up for what was going to be a night of performing several hops and Jumps.

Siynooma sat there impatiently checking the clock. Time was dragging on, now that all of the preparations were completed. She, like all of the Teams, was more than ready to execute the plan and get out with their unsuspecting victims. She frowned as she watched several guards going in and out of cell four. "What's all that noise in our target cell?"

"That Ragal is being a professional headache," said Teera. "You know the rule here for the prisoners. No talking while in the cells! That *bimyock* hasn't shut his mouth since he was put in there."

Siynooma clenched her teeth. "That could be a problem!"

At that moment, one of the Rahanan-Sar guards walked in cell four with a large club. The Owlamites heard a loud thump and a grunt of pain. The guard came walking out, wiping blood off of the club. He turned to another guard and chuckled. "The rules *will* be obeyed! I don't care who that *skofoyd* thinks he is."

Siynooma cocked her head to the side. "Then again... maybe not."

The sun was finally setting. The prisoners were all fed

their evening meal of gruel. The Owlamites got ready for the final steps of the plan. The guards did their regularly scheduled bed check and then went back to their posts.

"Let's go," said Siynooma.

Dozzell and Zhonsant went into the cell in Spy, each with a large bottle of some concoction that the medical staff had come up with. They knelt down, hopped the bottles into Home and poured the contents out on the floor.

Dozzell shook his head. "Are you sure that this stuff will have evaporated by morning?"

Zhonsant snickered. "This stuff will knock them out and evaporate before the next scheduled guard check."

"I hope you're right."

The two men turned their flashlights on and watched the prisoners in the room start nodding off from the fumes.

The Tendixive looked around. He started sniffing loudly with a confused look in his eyes.

"Uh-oh," said Zhonsant. "You don't think that guy is immune to this stuff do you?"

"Let's hope that it's just a stronger tolerance and it takes a little while longer to knock him out."

Zhonsant just grunted in agreement.

A few moments later the Tendixive did nod off, and both of the Owlamites sighed in relief.

Soobasoo had entered the cell and was watching. "They're all out," she called out merrily.

Fiywhee and Minwhen did some fancy hopping to make a hole in the floor at the end of the cell, farthest from the door. They had to make it look as if someone had dug through and not smoothly hopped the concrete out of the way. They then covered the hole with a cleverly painted piece of canvas.

They put a mask on each of the Galsinos. The masks were full of more of the knock-out liquid and were guaranteed to keep them unconscious for quite a while.

Zhonsant took his club and gave the three who were staying behind a very large lump on their heads. He swung harder when he lambasted the Teltermak.

Yaza, Teera, Dozzell, Fiyakee and Soobasoo each grabbed hold of a Galsino and Jumped them to a different place, just outside of the prison compound. Lilata and Banakati Jumped their dummies in and started replacing the Galsinos.

Siynooma squawked. "That last one…it's a mess…it doesn't look that good."

"So put that one on the far end," said Zhonsant. "It'll be harder to notice that way."

Siynooma nodded in agreement. "Not much we can do about it other than that."

Yinshosk and Zhonsant took bolt cutters and cut the chains to make it appear as if the prisoners had been cut free. All of the damaged links were hidden under the dummies. The ends of the chains were tied, with a small piece of string, to the shackles that were on the dummies to make it appear that everything was "situation normal".

Siynooma looked around. "Are we finished?"

"Yeah, we sure are," said Yinshosk.

Siynooma got a nasty look on her face. "Now, the part I hate."

All of the Owlamites that were still in the cell departed by way of the tunnel. This way the ground would look disturbed, as if several people had crawled through the long tunnel.

At the other end, they found five sleeping Galsinos that were bound and ready for transport.

Siynooma looked around. "Are we all ready?"

"One question," said Minwhen. "If we're supposed to make it look like these Galsino have teleport capabilities...by now, teleporting them out of here, why didn't we teleport them out of the cell without all of that...evidence that we left behind?"

Siynooma closed her eyes and shook her head. "I don't know." She opened her eyes. "This was the plan that the Staff came up with. We're just doing what they wanted...and if there's any flaws...it's on the Staff and not us, because we followed their instructions."

Zhonsant shrugged. "Maybe it'll make them think that the teleport equipment is too expensive or...too noisy...or too rare to waste here."

"Fine," said Yinshosk. "Let's get these *bimyocks* out of here."

All twelve of the conspirators Jumped to a carefully selected location in the ruins of the city of Galsino where Teams 82 and 7012 were waiting for the victims.

Natsa looked at the victims in shock as she tried to wave the stench of body odor away. "FIVE? There were only supposed to be four. What do we do with the fifth?"

Yinshosk smiled at her. "What's the difference between four Galsino corpses and five Galsino corpses?"

Natsa glared at him. "A mess!"

"No, one corpse," he said with a grin.

Natsa shook her head. "We've only got paperwork for four of them."

Siynooma shrugged. "So use your copier machine and make a fifth. You weren't going to finish them until you had the names of the four. Just make another one."

Natsa sighed. "Okay, fine, give the names to Eesteesee so she can finalize the documents."

Yinshosk pulled out his pad and gave it to Eesteesee. She took them, got on her keyboard and made the finishing touches.

Natsa was still a little troubled. "Supreme Officer, Holla, this is Officer Leader, Natsa. Can you hear me?"

The response was immediate. "This is Holla. I can

hear you. Did everything go according to the plan?"

"No," thought Natsa. "They came here with five Galsino instead of four."

Holla was momentarily surprised. "Why five···why didn't they leave one behind?"

Siynooma had been listening in. "Sir, this is Officer, Siynooma. We felt that if we left one of the Galsino behind, it'd raise more questions. By taking all five, we cut those questions out."

Wilfadge interrupted. "I don't see a problem. Five dead Galsino instead of four. Does anyone really want to object to that?"

Holla chuckled. "So make a fifth official Galsino document of pardon for the fifth one. Get rid of all five at the same time. It's not like it's a mammoth change of plans."

Natsa shrugged. "I see your point. So, when do you want them in Algothon?"

Holla grunted. "If we're going to convince the Algothons that the Galsino have teleport capability, I want that garbage in Algothon, no later than tomorrow. Do you understand?"

Natsa smiled. "Not a problem, Sir. The packages will be there before midday···Algothon time."

Holla smiled. "Good! Keep me informed."

"Yes, Sir."

Eesteesee stood there watching the printer as the documents came out. "We've got the pardons ready. Now all we have to do is make sure that we get the right one with the right *Bimyock*."

"We're going to triple check it," said Natsa. "It's not that I don't trust anybody, I just don't want *any* foul ups."

"We also need to give all five of them a bath," said Eesteesee. "No one'll believe they were sent to Algothon smelling like that."

Yinshosk snickered. "I understand."

Natsa, Siynooma and Yaza all checked the paperwork.

Yaza smiled. "All the paperwork is where it's supposed to be." She got a pouting look on her face. "Can I go home now?"

Natsa snickered. "Teams 6797, 6909 and 6938, thank you for what you did. We'll take it from here and you are all dismissed."

All members of the three Teams vanished.

Natsa scowled at the sleeping Galsinos. "Like the boss said...let's get this garbage to Algothon."

Teams 82 and 7012 got hold of everything that was needed and they all Jumped to the designated spot in Algothon.

Ota greeted them with mock enthusiasm. "So, we got the scapegoats for our wonderful little conspiracy. I heard that there are five instead of four. How's that going to affect us here?"

Natsa smiled. "All that it means, here, is that we just have to pose a fifth Galsino instead of just four."

Ota nodded. She turned to the group that had been waiting for the arrival of the Galsinos. "Okay, my conspirators…get what you need, get down there…and destroy!"

The computer Teams of 254, 255 and 256 Jumped to the military archives vault. Teams 84 and 108, dressed as Galsinos, took the Galsino prisoners and other paraphernalia that was going to be used.

The computer Teams readied themselves with the chalk dust. Blana, Yoyasa and Imast of Team 84 stood at the ready, near the cameras, with Galsino power pistols. Goloomo and Team 108 took the prisoners and got ready to pose them for the aftermath.

Blana looked around. "Call out…if you're ready!"

Nineteen affirmative responses came back.

Blana took a deep breath. "NOW!"

Blana, Yoyasa and Imast made short work of the surveillance cameras. Teams 254, 255 and 256 started hopping the bags of chalk dust into Home and throwing them into the hard drive cabinets. Kloob, Wanipi, Goloomo, Xakisi and Hathoya hopped the Galsinos into Home, poisoned four of them and posed them.

Intruder alarms were going off all over the place in the Military Headquarters and the military vault area. Several of the "clean room" personnel armed themselves and headed for the vault area. Several more military personnel, in the disguised storage facilities, headed for the freight elevators. High Commander

Indazhon called for his vehicle to be ready "yesterday".

The clean room personnel were met with a hail of deadly rays from power weapons. Fifteen Algothon technicians were all dead before any of them could even make the slightest assessment of what was going on. The other personnel arrived at the vault doors and had no way of getting inside because there was no one there (who was still alive) that was going to open the door for them from the inside.

High Commander Indazhon was headed for the archive area trying to get a situation report from anybody who was at the scene. He got very little information and as a result was extremely angry and frustrated when he did get there.

The Owlamites finished what they were doing and all hopped to Spy so that they were not choking from all of the chalk dust that filled the room, even though they were wearing filtered masks. They did a once over to make sure that they had demolished all of the archives. Another once over to make sure that the Galsino were posed properly.

Blana looked at her Team of saboteurs. "Mission accomplished...I hope. Let's get out of here."

Everyone Jumped back to where they had been making the preparations.

Ota looked at them with apprehension. "That didn't take very long...did you...?"

Blana folded her arms. "We got everything done that we could. It's your turn."

Nachichi called her people. "Teams 73, 113, 330 and 5051...let's go in there and watch and see what the Algothons find out."

All sixteen Owlamites Jumped to the destroyed archives.

Officer Grade 2, Ko looked around aghast. "They made a mess!"

Nachichi shook her head. "That's what they were supposed to do."

It took quite a long time before any Algothons were able to get into the vault to inspect the damage.

Indazhon arrived at the warehouse. His vehicle was driven to the entrance near the connector tunnel. He went through the ritual of getting the hidden door open and nearly slipped and fell three times as he rushed down the circular stairs. He ran into the hallway.

Indazhon saw all of the people standing around in the hallway. "What's going on here? Why are all of you just standing there? Is anyone inside giving us any report at all?"

A Chief Officer snapped to attention. "Sir, no one inside is responding. We haven't been able to get anyone's attention...or reaction from the other side of the door."

Indazhon growled. "Let me in there." He got to the keypad and entered his code. He stood there impatiently drumming his fingers against his legs as the keypad beeped and buzzed. The readout showed that a second emergency code was required. He entered that number as well. There were three more beeps and finally the door unlocked.

Everyone in the hallway started choking from all of the chalk dust that came wafting out of the door.

Indazhon turned to one of the Officers. "Just in case, get some other computer technicians down here. I don't like what I'm seeing…already."

The Officer walked over to an intercom and started punching in a number.

Indazhon put a handkerchief over his face and walked in trying to wave all of the flying dust away. "IS ANYONE IN HERE…ALIVE?"

No response.

He looked up at the ceiling. "Why aren't the exhaust fans on? Everybody, start looking for survivors and…why the fans are off."

After looking around in the area where the technicians worked and in the vault, everyone in the area was completely white with chalk dust.

Nachichi was sitting there in Spy trying to see through the cloud. "Do you think maybe…we used too much chalk?"

Ko snickered. "It does give the impression that this was done intentionally, doesn't it?"

Officer Grade 3, Wahada shook her head. "How soon do you think it'll be before they call one of the Prominents?"

Officer Grade 4, Tandani scoffed. "With his ego, this high muckity-muck commander will probably try to keep it a military issue. He might not even tell the Security forces what happened."

"He'll have to," said Nachichi. "When he has to admit that he has no archives any more. He'll have to tell them something."

Tandani leaned back and propped her feet up. "It's going to be some time before they can even start investigating. No one can see that much through this cloud."

They finally found someone who could come down to the vault and get the fans going…for a short time. There was so much dust in the air that the filters were clogged very quickly. Now they had to get someone from the maintenance area to come clean the filters out.

While they were waiting, someone finally came up with the idea of getting some industrial sized vacuum cleaners in there and try getting up some of the dust with those. It did not take very long to clog the three vacuums even though they had huge tubs for the debris.

Nachichi giggled. "Maybe we did go a bit overboard with the amount of dust that was used."

Wahada shook her head. "We did want to make sure…I think we did."

Finally, half way through the next day, they had the clouds of chalk dust under control. Then they started opening all of the cabinets and had to start the cleanup all over again.

Nachichi grunted. "We *did* use too much. This is really

getting monotonous."

A medical team of forensic pathologists was called in to examine all of the bodies. The doctors did not think that they would have any real problems. Then they saw the "very specially posed" body of one of the Galsinos. The entire right side of his body was *joined* inside a wall. The left side of his body was still in a position that looked as if he was standing and had some piece of equipment in his hand. Most of that piece of equipment was also inside the wall.

The other four Galsinos were all sitting near the standing one. They each had an empty vial, either laying next to them or in their hand.

Indazhon saw the Galsinos and was not sure what to make of it. He sighed in defeat as he called in the Security people to investigate and try to determine what happened.

Steenda showed up to cover it herself. When she saw how things looked and got the initial briefing from the first responders, she put fifteen investigators on it, full time, until such time as they got a solid answer for every question that anyone could think of at the time.

The pathologists were able to get the four bodies of the prone Galsinos out without any problem at all. The one that had over half of his body *joined* into the wall was something else. Not one of them wanted to make the decision on what to do or how to try it.

Indazhon and Steenda both were getting upset with the doctors.

Indazhon finally had enough. "What're you sitting here debating about? Why don't you take the body?"

"We can't," said one of the doctors. "If we try to take it, we have to cut it away from the wall...and..."

Steenda scoffed. "AND WHAT?"

The doctor was rather startled by her abruptness. "It'll make a tremendous mess."

Indazhon got in the doctors face. "So get a bucket and a mop, start cutting and make a mess. We need that body out of here! We need you to do your job."

"But...High Commander, we'll only get half of the body!"

"That's better than nothing," said Steenda harshly. "Until someone can figure out a way to get the other half, you're going to have to settle for what you can get...and examine that. Now...as the Commander said: Start cutting."

The doctor swallowed. "We can't even figure out what we should use to cut the...remains...away from the wall."

Indazhon groaned and hung his head.

Steenda shook her head. "What about a hacksaw?"

The doctor waved his hand at the thought. "That might cause too much damage."

Indazhon snapped. "TO WHAT? The man is DEAD! You can't kill him AGAIN! I'm pretty sure that the cause of death is some kind of trauma dealing with the shock of becoming part of the wall. He lost all use of the right side of his body and that created some kind of catastrophic shutdown of all of his other internal organs…including the brain! We're not looking for some weird mystery about how he died. The other four…that's a different question. Now…CUT HIM DOWN AND BE HAPPY WITH WHAT YOU GET!"

Again the four doctors started debating on what they should use to cut the exposed part of the body down.

Indazhon grabbed two of the doctors by their throats. "If you don't start cutting, before I count to ten, I'm going to have my men cut him down with a chainsaw. Now make a decision! One! Two! Three!"

One of the doctors held his hands up. "We'll use some scalpels…different sizes…at different parts of the body. That should do it."

Indazhon let go of the two doctors. All four pulled scalpels out of their kits…and started debating where they should start.

Steenda slapped one of the doctors in the back of the head. "Either you start cutting with the scalpel, or you start chewing with your teeth. Start SOMETHING…NOW!"

One of the pathologists started on the front, the other on the back. They first cut away all of the clothing. They then cut, starting at the top, the skin as close to the wall as possible. Once they were through the scalp they had no choice but to use a saw on the skull. They had to use the same method all the way down. Cut through the skin on the neck with scalpels and the neck bones, that were protruding from the wall, with the saw. There were all of the bones in the spine and the sternum that had to be sawed. The pelvic area gave them no end to trouble.

Finally the gruesome task was finished. There was still a lot of soft tissue and portions of bones that had not been removed. Indazhon gave the order to get in there with scrub brushes and sanders and get everything that was not inside the steel of the wall...off of the wall. The scrubbers and sanders needed several buckets to vomit in during that process.

Next they had to mop the floor for any other residue from the body that had dripped down onto the floor.

What was left was a picture, in the steel, of a cutaway portion of the Galsino anatomy.

Steenda shook her head as she looked at it. "What should we do with that part of the wall?"

Indazhon sighed. "There's nothing we can do with it. He seems to be an integral part of the wall now. The only thing that we can do is just smooth it off and...paint over it." He touched the place where the Galsino had been holding onto a mechanism. "Right here...right here was the prize that we needed. It has to be one of their teleportation devices."

Steenda got close and narrowed her eyes as she tried to make out any part of a technological device. "Is there any way to recover it?"

"No," he said sadly. "They used it to come in here. They did their job of sabotage and then realized, when they saw him imbedded in the wall, that they were stuck. Once they'd finished their job, the other four realized that there was no way out of here…so they committed suicide rather than be taken alive and have to explain their actions."

"All this time…we've been looking at the Owlam. The Galsino turned out to have…talents…just like the Owlam. Only the Galsino got caught in the act."

Indazhon grunted. "A catastrophic failure…or a planned piece of misdirection."

The Owlam High Command Staff were sitting in the conference room going over the initial report.

"So far, so good," said Ahandi. "They actually now think that it was the Galsinos all along that *chogoed* their stuff."

Teelila looked at one of the pages of the report, rather baffled. "Where did we get hold of a bunch of Galsino pulse pistols?"

"During that Galsino attack when they tried their *heelmashk* weapon against us," said Wilfadge. "There were a bunch of those *Fovoks* that were killed, by blast trauma, when that thing blew up. We got most of that weaponry intact. Plus, we actually did get several of them alive and got their weapons as well. We've got a whole bunch of those weapons in one of our underground vaults… in Observation dimension…of course."

"We got a bunch of Axswain, Teltermak and Zee-Altha weapons in that vault as well," said Hadathoo.

Chaza dropped all of the reports on the table. "I'm still a little confused about those flying cameras of theirs. When we stopped them from launching...anything...how did they get more of those *chokwad* things up there...when nothing else is getting launched?"

Holla sighed. "Each one of us is supposed to have a yellow binder on our desks. There are reports about that very subject in that binder. Haven't you been reading those reports?"

Chaza flushed. "I...must have missed that report...I don't remember anything about that."

"I don't remember seeing anything on that as well," said Dwalooa.

"Me neither," said Shyshee.

"Same here," said Hoynama.

Holla grunted in disgust. "NAYNA, GET IN HERE!"

Nayna came running into the conference room. "Yes, Sir. What can I do for you?"

Holla smiled. "It seems that several of our Staff didn't get the report on those camera satellites. Could you make a copy for them and give them a briefing, please?"

Nayna looked around the room with a bit of a guilty smile. "How many of you need that report?" When she saw the number of people who raised their hands, she grimaced. "Yes, Sir, right away." She retreated from the room.

Chaza smiled. "Can you give us the condensed version?"

Holla shrugged. "Why not. Directly after they launched the firestorm weapons and before we found Algothon, they also launched several of those camera satellites up there. Some of them have one camera, others have as many as eighty…that we know of. All of them were orbiting all around the globe, taking all kinds of pictures and invading everyone's privacy. It seems that they can, somehow, change the orbit of those things. They can put them in one place or they can have them flying all over the place. There's a lot of them up there, so they're able to move them around as they please…whenever they please."

Shyshee frowned. "From what I hear, they can now see anywhere on the planet…at any time. What happened that changed it from roving satellites to ones that can look everywhere all the time?"

Nayna walked in. "Sir, that's a new report…that just came out."

"So spill it," said Holla.

Nayna smiled. "It seems that if they want one of those things to change where it's going, they have to wait until it's within range of the antennae at Algothon. For some reason, the satellites can send messages to each other and eventually relay it to Algothon, but they can't receive instructional messages, from Algothon, unless they're close to the antennae at Algothon.

Dwalooa was sitting there slack-jawed.

Hoynama shook her head. "I understand…I think!"

Nayna smiled. "Would you like me to explain it again?"

"Please, no," said Shyshee. "If you understand it...fine... just give me the report and let me read it several times and maybe I'll get it."

Wilfadge looked back at the reports. "How soon do you think we'll find out what their final guesswork is on the incident?"

Holla shook her head. "I'm not going to expect it for some time. They've got a lot to look through and over...before they can understand any of it. I wouldn't be surprised if it takes six months or more."

Teelila snickered. "Meanwhile we keep messing up their rockets."

13

Six months later, the Owlam Staff was sitting in the conference room feeling a little embarrassed and guilty. They were reading a report about how some Galsinos had somehow been able to sneak into the Central Port Internment Area and steal away with five Galsino prisoners. The reason for the escape incident was unknown because there were already twenty-seven Galsinos imprisoned at the wall. Why had these five been so special?

They read on about an elaborate tunnel system that had been used to aid in the escape. A tunnel had been dug under all of the cells, however, only the cell where the Galsinos were temporarily placed, had been finished. The building where they found the other end of the tunnel had been thoroughly cleaned and therefore there was no evidence as to who or how many had taken a part in the escape.

There was a reward posted for the return of the five fugitives and anyone who had participated in the escape.

Holla sighed. "It's a headache…having to keep some secrets from the allies. I wish we didn't have to do it."

Wilfadge wadded up the paper. "We have a right to survive. If we have to keep secrets in order *to* survive…so be it!"

Ahandi scoffed. "So be it...*indeed*! If our allies ever find out...we're in big trouble."

Dwalooa shook her head sadly. "We may have dug ourselves in too deep already. We're having to go through all kinds of crazy mental exercises to remember what lies we're telling our allies...so we don't tell the wrong tale."

Holla yawned. "I know I may have asked this before, but...how are we doing at the gorge?"

"Fast approaching 5,000 units," said Wilfadge. "The more that are built, the more proficient they get and the faster they build them. Just in case you're interested, we've also started digging vaults. Each unit will have a vault attached to it, so we'll be able to store all kinds of things there."

Hadathoo clenched his eyes. "Wait a moment! You say that we're going to have almost 6,800 homes...and one of the large underground vaults...for each unit?"

"Yes," said Wilfadge. "Why not?"

"We seem to be hollowing out a lot of that area. I know that it's mountainous...and it's a lot of bedrock, but...that's a huge amount of holes in that gorge."

Teelila looked at the remnants of her fingernails sadly. "Have you ever been there?"

Hadathoo flushed. "No, why?"

Teelila gave Holla a nasty look. "Why did I have to go and it seems that very few others have had to go?"

Holla shrugged. "It sounds as if Officer, Hadathoo is long overdue for a term in the gorge." She gave Hadathoo a big warm smile.

"I guess I've been putting it off," said Hadathoo. He gave a guilty chuckle and shrugged. "I'll head that way tomorrow."

One and one half years later, Indazhon looked at a very large file on his desk.

Steenda had come in and placed it on his desk and then sat down.

Indazhon pointed at the file. "What…is this?"

Steenda scoffed. "Believe it or not, it's the report on that incident in your archives vault."

He shook his head. "Is there anything helpful in there?"

She sighed. "No. The archives were a complete loss. There was absolutely nothing that was salvageable. All of the plates - destroyed. All of the armatures - destroyed. All of the information, unless it was on a hard drive, somewhere else - lost forever."

"What about those Galsinos?"

"We have the one partial body…that was carved off of the wall and death was due to the shock and trauma of teleporting halfway into a wall. We also have four Galsinos who…after destroying the archives, found that they were trapped in that vault and committed suicide, using a powerful neural toxin…that came from a snake."

"What kind of…snake?"

"According to the information that we could glean from zoological archives…on hard drives, it was some kind of venomous snake that had green and brown bands going around its body and it was indigenous to the area around the city of Galsino."

"What kind of weapons were they using?"

"They were using weapons that they developed. They'd been modified because of the change in the hands of the Galsinos."

Indazhon frowned at her confused.

She huffed. "Look at the pictures of the Galsino bodies. They're in there. Someone took a close up photograph of the hands. They're hands turned into…claws."

He flipped through, over 1,100 pages until he saw some pictures start flipping by. He looked through the pictures until he found the autopsy reports on the Galsinos. He found the pictures one of the hands and just sat there staring at it. "It…looks more like…the talon of one of those extinct predatory birds."

"They could use their…*talons*…as a real nasty weapon if they wanted to."

He sighed. "Is there anything in here that says…Owlam?"

"No," she said sadly. "All indications are Galsino. All of those earlier clues pointed one way…to Owlam. Now, either both of them are causing us constant grief…or it was the Galsino all along…or the Owlam have victimized the Galsino and tried to make us believe that it was the Galsino alone."

"I remember something about a battle between Axswain and Owlam. The Owlams were using some powerful, long-range laser cannon. They also used that cannon to shoot one of our arrays out of the sky…from fifty-two *hyzink*. We can't dismiss them…from innocence yet."

"Our evidence is, unfortunately, still too inconclusive…to absolutely prove guilt."

He shook his head. "What a mess we got ourselves into. Thirty-nine years ago, we unleashed a hail storm of nuclear weapons. Our scientist said that it would make us so powerful that…no one would dare stand against us…ever again. Now… we're still trying to conquer this continent and…many of the people on the other continents are massing against us. All because we can't seem to get another rocket launched."

"Let's not forget how the scientists botched it…in regards to this pesky residual energy that keeps killing most of the plant and animal life. They're now saying…from some other kind of research that they're doing on what they call a half-life…that it should dissipate to safe levels after seventy-five years."

He chuckled and then growled. "Wonderful! That means that we only have thirty-six years left to put up with it…whatever IT really is. I'm already fifty-two. I'll be eighty-eight when it subsides…if I live that long."

"I'll be eighty-four…if I live that long."

"I wonder…how many species of plant, animals, birds and

bugs were…completely killed off by that energy."

"For centuries, we've been warring with each other. I don't remember if anyone ever sat down and…counted all of the species or even worried about cataloging them…let alone naming them."

He looked at the file. "Getting back to it - is there anything that you've read…where we can really learn something from it and figure out exactly what happened?"

She clicked her tongue. "Funny thing. One of our people, who is currently stationed at that Turgon Wall, happened to hear about five Galsinos who were…aided in a prison break. They broke out and disappeared without a trace. Our spy there obtained the information - easily because the T'Mor were trying to find out who helped the escapees and how it was all done." She leaned forward. "That information was brought here. Those pathologists compared the fingerprints and DNA to the five saboteurs. *Perfect* match!"

He closed his eyes trying to grasp the thought. "So, they escaped from prison, came here and destroyed…but…if they escaped from prison, why did they come here to commit such a… tremendous act of sabotage?" He opened his eyes and looked at her as if he was pleading.

"That's only part of the story. I looked at the date of their escape. It was only two days before they ambushed our archives."

He slouched down in his seat. "They escaped from that internment center…on the *west* coast of North Chilamte…and in only two days, they were here on Neopaure…over eight thousand *hyzink* distance from the prison and…committed that act?"

"What do you think about teleportation capabilities now?"

"If I didn't believe it before…what can I say?!"

She nodded. "AND…in the top pocket of their outfits… each one of them had a letter of full pardon, signed by someone who shows his Galsino rank as…"Grand Shadow of the Galsino Forces", a pardon that says that if they committed this act of sabotage - all sins would be forgiven…for the good of and by the Galsino people…dated the day after the escape."

"It didn't take long to convince them to cause us no end of grief."

"No, it didn't." She cocked her head to the side. "I heard some strange thing…about that wall in the vault…where half of the body is."

He nodded. "Had to cover it with a seal. Even though that part of the body was…permanently part of that wall, the tissues began to decompose and…the stench in there was intolerable."

She was shocked. "Even though…it had permanently become a part of that metal?"

He nodded. "It's still…organic…partially…somehow…I think. Either way, it still began to stink horribly…even through eight layers of paint."

"Getting back to it, do you believe that both the Galsinos *and* the Owlams are a problem to us?"

He nodded. "Absolutely. We can't stop or afford to put

our guard down from either one...until they're all dead...or we have absolute proof that exonerates one of them."

She nodded. "I agree."

Ota looked off to the side. *"H'oolyach!"*

Holla angrily threw the report across the room. "Those wretched Algothon still look at us as a threat! What's it gonna take to convince them that we're...not?"

Nayna was a little scared. She tried to smile. "Maybe if we stop killing them...or stop sabotaging them...or let them kill all of us."

Holla growled. "If we stop the sabotage, those *doovofts* would launch another attack against us. They were ready to bring eight of those warheads on a ship so that they could plant them here and make this entire area a charred, residual energy flatland." She slammed her fist down on her desk. "I'm so tired of fooling around with them...but...we're still learning all kinds of things from them...and we can't afford to destroy them all until we've learned all that we can from them."

"Sir, did you want me to get a copy of that report to all of the Commanders and Vice Commanders?"

"Yes. Get it out immediately."

Nayna chuckled nervously. "It's going to take quite a while to get that done."

Holla looked up confused. "Why?"

Nayna shrugged. "Because I have to pick up all of the papers and then get them back in the correct order...before I can make copies."

Holla looked at the mess and groaned. All of the papers had come out of the binder and were scattered widely throughout the office. She closed her eyes and sighed. "Okay, get it out...as soon as you can."

Niyniy came out of her office to help Nayna pick up all of the report.

Aktool came out of his office. "Sir, we've had an unusual request from...several Teams that got together and...well... they..."

Holla glared at him. "What?"

"Sir, they were wondering if they could...transplant some of the trees and other shrubbery...from Beasties and Forest dimensions...and see if they could survive here...yet. We're all aware of those Algothon scientists who said that it would take seventy-five years before that energy went completely away... and...they were wondering if we should try getting some new... greenery...here."

Holla stared at the ceiling and contemplated the idea. She looked back at Aktool. "Call the Staff together. It's a good idea, but, I want some more input from them before I okay it." She pursed her lips while doing some more thinking. "Call the medical personnel in on this as well. They might have a few ideas on what we should or should not do."

The entire Staff was in there rather quickly. The doctors showed up and were somewhat surprised that they were all called. After hearing the plan, they got together and did a little brainstorming of their own.

Doctor Shurmook stood before the Staff after the doctors had all talked it over. "We agree that this plan is worth trying. Where we disagree with what you want...the size of the trees that are transplanted. It would be nice to have...a lush forest... somewhere around here, if you bring in a large amount of *very* tall trees, those Algothon would probably notice it and...so much for them not thinking of us as the ones doing it. Our suggestion is to bring in a few saplings. We bring them here, scatter them, keep an eye on them and see if they can flourish. If they do, then we'll *slowly* add more and no one will be the wiser."

"Tell them about the other part," said Doctor Vonggon.

"Yes," said Shurmook. "I was getting to that. The trees in Forest. I see them as trees that are all in a four season area. That would be appropriate for our local area...the city of Owlam. The trees in Beasties are of a tropical variety. I noticed that it's very humid when I was in Beasties. Those trees would be more appropriate if we located them near the gorge. That part of South Chilamte is...near the equator and it's rather hot and humid...so... put them in their normal geographical area here...that matches where they are...there...in Beasties."

Holla nodded. "So...how many saplings do you suggest?"

"Make it totally manageable," said Doctor Voolatha. "No more than two dozen trees...in each area...and scatter them...so as to not arouse too much suspicion."

Wilfadge chuckled. "What happens if other people in the area notice them and decide to keep an eye on them as well?"

Doctor Saysay snickered. "Then we'll have to do our observation, *in* Observation."

Teelila leaned forward and turned to Holla. "If they want to have these restrictions and observations that they're talking about, I suggest that it be the doctors who do the transplanting and observation."

Doctor Aneensa shrugged. "Why not? Since we changed to Owlam Elf, we seem to be immune to virtually all diseases that we had problems with before. Now, all we have to do is take care of a few strained muscles or broken bones…if someone has had an accident. It'll help kill some time and who knows? It may just replenish this entire planet with foliage."

Holla smiled. "Does anybody disagree or have any arguments with any of that?" She looked around. "No? Okay, Doctors, any time you're ready to start it up…start it up."

Teelila perked up. "If we're going to be bringing in a bunch of plants…what about animals?"

"I don't know about that," said Doctor Shurmook. "If you take an animal out of its natural environment, it could cause more problems than any of us could imagine. It won't have any natural enemies…like that giant sand snake from Beasties. If we accidentally bring one of those things in here, they could end up procreating completely out of control and next thing you know…

we'd have to hunt down and kill all of them before they kill all of us."

Doctor Aneensa put her hand to her forehead. "We also have to think about microorganisms." She dropped her hand while shaking her head. "We could accidentally bring something here… that no Heyyah, Elf, beast, fish or plant has an immunity to. An entire species of Elf, beast, fish or plant could be wiped out…or it could kill 90% of everything that lives on Hardooth. We're going to have to look at any of the saplings very carefully before we do any mass migrations."

Hoynama scoffed. "So, we just bring plants that bear a close similarity to what was already here."

Doctor Kazkim waved his hands. "No, no, no, no, that's not good enough. *Close* does not mean *same*. Think about what we had here in Owlam. We had the *chawata* bush and the *skonik* bush. The berries of the *chawata* are edible…*were* edible…until the firestorm burned them all up. The berries of the *skonik* bush looked almost the same as the *chawata* berries, except for a tiny white mark, where the berry connected to the stem. We had to do a city wide eradication of the *skonik* bush, inside the city wall, because some children were eating the *skonik* berries and were dead before anyone knew what happened. *Chawata* and *skonik* are close, in appearance, but totally opposite as far as nourishing versus toxic."

There was a long silence as everyone pondered the statement.

Ahandi sighed. "Are we finished then?"

"No," said Holla. "I was wondering how many units are done at the gorge."

Wilfadge smiled. "We're just over 6,200 units completed."

Shyshee looked a little skeptical. "When you say finished - do you mean totally finished, or just the walls are done?"

Wilfadge grinned. "I mean ready to move in, furnish it and be comfortable."

Dwalooa smiled back. "So there's less than 600 units to be done and the entire project will be finished?"

"As far as homes are concerned, yes," said Wilfadge. "The next project would be...a hospital, a conference room, a conference auditorium and whatever else we can think of that we need."

Chaza sighed. "Are they...fit to live in?"

Wilfadge gave her a surly look. "We're doing everything we can to make them as comfortable as possible. Once you move in...you can decorate the place...whatever way you desire. THAT will make them totally fit to live in."

Holla looked at Wilfadge hopefully. "How soon will we be able to move in...as a whole...if necessary?"

He smiled. "Another year and a half and all of the problems will have been worked out totally. Electric, running water, windows to the outside...that no one can see from above...unless you're stupid enough to have a light on at night with the window open. A place for all of our vehicles, including the captured vehicles from Algothon, plenty of storage for our…" He cleared his throat. "…all of our *acquisitions* from Algothon, Axswain, Galsino, Teltermak and Zee-Altha…like the archives."

Hoynama snickered. "Will we ever be able to pull them back into Home dimension?"

Wilfadge gave her a sideways look. "Not while any Algothons are alive. They could track them…and then we'd have even more problems."

Teelila scoffed. "I don't see why we just don't get rid of the whole bunch. They caused all of the problems in the world today, so we should…"

Holla interrupted her. "…keep them around while we continue to learn from them. When we stop learning from them, then we'll get rid of that headache…forever."

Officer Leader, Till continued looking at the pictures of outer space anomalies. Many of the people who had seen these things could not prove whether or not they were some manufactured space craft or some unknown *thing* that occurs naturally in outer space. Many of the arguments, in favor of "Other Planetary Beings" actually existing were very convincing - to some. There were counter statements from skeptics that were equally compelling.

Till continued going through all of the information in the archives, in regards to outer space. He could not get enough of it. He was finding out many things about the solar system that just about boggled his mind. He wanted to share it with others, however, he could not find anyone who shared his interest, let alone share the obsession in what he was finding.

Sixteen months later, Officer Grade 4, Roosook reported to the Staff. He stood before them beaming with pride. "Sirs, I am pleased to tell you that we've completed all six thousand eight hundred units. All of Owlam can move in at any time. You can inspect them…and choose your specific unit…at your leisure."

Holla closed her eyes in confusion. "Sixty-eight… hundred?" She opened her eyes and looked around at the other members of the Staff. "Why…the extra twenty-four units?"

Now Roosook looked confused. "What…extra…twenty-four units, Sir?"

Holla looked at Ahandi in a dull normal manner.

Ahandi snickered. "Officer, Roosook, there are only six thousand, seven hundred…seventy-six…Teams. Partial or complete, you've made an extra twenty-four units. Why'd you make extras?"

Roosook chuckled nervously. "I…always heard the figure of…sixty-eight…hundred. I…thought that was…what was… needed."

Shyshee scoffed. "So we've got twenty-four extra units. It's not like they held us up making twenty-four *hundred* extra units. I don't really see a problem."

Chaza chuckled. "We could use the other twenty-four as a centralized meeting place…for smaller meetings…such as several Teams that have to go…wherever in order to take care of some business."

Holla looked around the table. "Sooo…who is going to be the one responsible for cleaning these extras?"

"Cross that bridge when we determine exactly which units are the *vacant* twenty-four," said Wilfadge with a shrug. "It could be eight or nine Teams who take turns with the upkeep."

Teelila frowned. "The thing that I'm wondering: How do we break it down? Here in the city, we have a north, south, east and west. There, it's all in one big line."

"Do it in sectors like the Sodle did at the wall," said Dwalooa. "That was a straight line, and they numbered it. We could do the same there."

Wilfadge looked at the architects. "How high…and how long…is this entire complex?"

Roosook smiled. "Sir, we stacked the units twelve high. There are the eight bottom rows that are five hundred sixty-seven units wide. The top four rows are five hundred sixty-six units wide."

Holla nodded. "Are they stocked…or furnished…with anything?"

Roosook shrugged. "Sir, that's up to you. You can furnish your unit with anything you want. There are refrigerators and stoves in each unit that you can use right now, so you can stock whatever food you want. Then you can decorate it to your taste."

Holla looked at her Staff smiling. "How do you want to do it…as far as breaking up the different commands?"

"Sector numbers," said Ahandi. "Start in the north and number them down to the south."

Holla nodded. "Master Officer, Ahandi, you're now the Commander of Sector 1. Senior Officer, Dwalooa, you're the Vice Commander for 1. Master Officer, Teelila, you're the Commander of Sector 2. Senior Officer, Hadathoo, you're the Vice Commander for 2. Master Officer, Wilfadge, you're the Commander of Sector 3. Senior Officer, Hoynama, you're the Vice Commander 3. Master Officer, Chaza, you're the Commander of Sector 4. Senior Officer, Shyshee, you're the Vice Commander of 4."

Chaza shrugged. "Who starts claiming a new home unit… and where do we start?"

Holla tapped her fingers on the table. "I'll start. I'll claim the unit in the center of the top row."

"It's a fair place," said Roosook. "You'll have to choose either 1-282 or 1-283."

Holla nodded. "1-282."

Ahandi did a little mental figuring. "That means…if I'm in the top row and center of Sector 1…that should be…1-71."

"I'll take 1-72," said Dwalooa.

"That gives me 1-211," said Teelila.

Hadathoo chuckled. "1-212."

Wilfadge looked up at the ceiling as he calculated. "1-352."

"So I get 1-353," said Hoynama.

Chaza sighed. "1-493."

Shyshee clicked her tongue. "1-494."

Holla turned to Niyniy. "Are you keeping track of this?"

Niyniy smiled. "Yes, Sir, and I'm sure that I'll be keeping track of a lot more, before all of this is done." She looked up a little confused. "How are you gonna allow the other Teams to choose?"

Holla shrugged. "The way we always do it - numerically… with one exception: Our Team of architects…they get the next selection."

Roosook smiled. "1-1. I like that area and it'll make it easier for all personnel to find us…in case there's a need for some changes."

Niyniy sighed. She had to assign 6,766 more, full and partial Teams to the different units in the gorge. There was no time like the present to start. Get everybody assigned to their new "emergency" location as soon as possible. She got ready for the long, long, *long* roll call. 'Ten down, six *thousand*…seven *hundred*…sixty-six…to go,' she thought. She started the roll call. Eleven days later when she had finished assigning units to Teams, she felt as if she was just about one heartbeat away from insanity...if she had not crossed that line already. She decided to go to the gorge, to Unit number 1-282 and pick out her private area in the new home.

The doctors took two dozen young saplings from Beasties and two dozen from Forest. They planted them in the area appropriate for that type of tree, considering the areas that they had come from.

The ones that they put in the tropical area showed no signs of any rapid growth or wilting. They just simply maintained, according to the type of tree that they were.

The ones that came from a four season area, around Owlam, did show something quickly. Most of them wilted, very quickly. They were in close proximity to a city that had been hit with one of the nuclear weapons. The trees that did not wilt were planted in the area where the Zee-Althan people had been massacred. They showed signs of new growth and height very rapidly.

The only thing that the doctors could determine was that the ones in tropical area were nowhere near a bombed city. The ones that wilted near Owlam, were in a very dried up, contaminated area...except for the ones that were planted in...Zee-Althan blood. The two saplings that were planted in the blood grew over one taja the first year and flourished even more the next year.

They were satisfied that the new trees could live here, multiply and flourish - as soon as the residual energy died down to something that was a little more tolerable to the plants.

Ten years later, all of the Owlam personnel had been to, claimed and decorated their new gorge homes as they saw fit. There were several of them that wanted to take up permanent residence in these new mansions, now. Holla stopped that one because the gorge was only supposed to be a backup and not a primary area of residence…yet.

During that ten years, there had been several Prominent Investigators who ended up having some very unusual (and fatal) accidents. The current list of Prominents was: Hashasee, Kladoothik, Tun and Beeshree. The current High Commander was named Sososkool. The Prominents and the High Commander of this era attempted to maintain a more friendly working relationship. They hoped that they could make things a lot smoother than what the people of the past had gone through.

Team 7016 was taking a turn in Algothon, as part of a rotating group of Teams. Everyone was going to get a chance to do it, while someone else was furnishing, decorating and stocking supplies in the gorge.

Hashasee sat there drumming her fingers on the table. "Are you sure that there's absolutely nothing on the Owlams? We've got more cameras and people watching that area and yet…we still can't get one piece of evidence on whoever it is that's fouling our systems."

Kladoothik shook his head. "The technicians troubleshoot the components. Put the components in where they belong.

Walk away from the rocket…and we have another failed launch, because the components aren't working. For fifty years, this same problem has occurred so many times that no one can count all of the incidents. Same thing though, all launches are fouled because one or more of the components fails…at launch time."

Hashasee growled through her teeth. "Aren't the cameras watching?"

Tun let his breath out slowly. "We watch…and watch…and watch. We've been watching…and we have been reviewing. We still don't know how or when the systems have been compromised. All we know is…as soon as the technician finishes the work and closes the panel…nothing works."

Beeshree looked at the other Prominents. She bit her lip. "Is there any way…that they could…possibly be…inside the rocket…and foul the systems in there?"

"Oh, get real!" Tun was disgusted. "There isn't enough room for an insect to get inside there. You think that a full sized adult could be crawling around in there, messing up the system, after the work's been done? If you're going to come up with a theory…try to come up with one that has, at least some form of feasibility."

Beeshree scoffed at him. "We have to look somewhere outside of that form of thinking. For fifty years, we haven't been able to launch anything successfully…unless the payload was fouled. We've had more eyes on all of those rockets…than we've got cameras. Still…the sabotage goes on. Feasibility? I think that we have to look at the UN-feasible. Reality has taken a nose dive into oblivion."

Kladoothik grunted. "Maybe some of those stories about… some of these Elf races having…magical abilities are true. I know it sounds ridiculous…but…after fifty years…somebody should've caught something…or somebody doing something…unless there *is* some magical ability going on."

Hashasee hung her head. "You're talking about legends… that are thousands of years old…and have no legitimate…"

"DID not have legitimacy…at first," shouted Kladoothik! "Now…we see all of these different races of Elf that have been… created…because of this residual energy from the bombs. Don't you think that there's a remote possibility of something happening to them…where they have special strange and…yes, possibly magical powers?"

Tun scoffed at him. "You mean, just because some of them developed wings…and body fur…and can spit venom, maybe some of them can perform spells? Why haven't they put on a bunch of special shows…as traveling performers? They could make a fortune showing off their special powers."

Kladoothik stood up and leaned closer to Tun, across the table. "Not if they want to keep it a secret from us, the ones who were trying to conquer them to begin with."

Tun squinted his eyes as he stared at Kladoothik. "Could… that be a reasonable answer? Do you actually think…?"

Kladoothik sat down. "What other answer is there? We've covered anything and everything that's within the realms of reality.

The problems persist. We have to think…outside of reality."

"Sounds like they want to get us," said Kiyalee.

Chyning scoffed. "Really? You think that's what that means?"

"One of them is grasping at flower petals in the clouds… and just might convince the others that he's right," said Bonarain.

Soolchakan shook his head. "You think that we're going to have to participate in another assassination?"

Bonarain sighed. "Unfortunately…yes."

"You heard what Holla said," said Kiyalee. "She doesn't want any more…taking out all four of these *chogos* unless…it's absolutely necessary. Too many times in the past…all four have been taken out at one time. That situation…has made these people more suspicious."

Chyning grunted. "Against us or the Galsino?"

"Both," said Bonarain. "They just haven't figured out a way to attack us…or the Galsinos."

Soolchakan snickered. "They can't get to us and the Galsinos are too spread out. They haven't figured out a way to get both of us without a major assault force…and that sinking of those ships…sure made them change their minds about that tactic."

Bonarain sighed. "These people are so…inconvenient!"

Hadathoo and Wilfadge were looking over some of the

information that they had obtained from Algothon. There was such a wealth of it, that neither man was sure where to begin looking.

Wilfadge heard Hadathoo clicking on several things, however, he could not be reading any of them thoroughly. "What exactly are you looking for, my friend?"

Hadathoo looked up from his screen. "I'm wondering about how we built some of the things that we did."

"We had manufacturing plants," said Wilfadge cynically.

"Yes, I know that...but...where did we get all of the raw materials from?"

"Raw materials...what are you talking about?"

Hadathoo let out an exasperated grunt. "I see in some of these things that there were trades going on between certain areas of Hardooth. People in one place had a lot of iron ore... which they traded for food or tin or copper. People would trade... skins of animals for food or some kind of processed ore. They'd trade their raw materials for someone else's raw materials. There isn't one area, anywhere on the planet, that could have been self-sustaining. Not one!"

Wilfadge began to see the problem. "So, if we needed steel, to make the frames of our vehicles, we had to trade something, that we had, in order to obtain that steel. If we wanted that special type of plastic...that goes into making the casing for the 459 cannons, we needed to trade with someone, with something...in order to obtain those materials..."

"Materials which are not obtained locally."

Wilfadge had a sinking feeling. "That was…what all of those freight trucks…and convoys of trucks…and all of that were. They were bringing certain goods in…and taking certain goods… out."

Hadathoo nodded. "From whom…and to whom?"

"So there actually was some kind of trade commerce going on."

"And as soon as the firestorm weapon blew away the central part of the city, we lost all of that information…who we're trading with…what we're trading for…and with."

Wilfadge sighed. "No wonder we don't have any more raw materials to repair the trucks and weapons and…whatever. We have no idea…all of that information…our connections in commerce…went up in flames."

"And ever since then, we've had to steal anything…and everything that we need…in order to maintain our existence."

"Should we…attempt to restart…some of those trading deals?"

"With whom?"

"We could start with the Kalash. We could add the Rahanan-Sar, the T'Mor…and any other allies that are dealing with the Turgon Wall. That'd be a good start."

Hadathoo stroked his chin. "I wonder why no one thought of this before."

Wilfadge scoffed. "Probably because we've been trying

to keep our mendacious and thieving ways a secret from all of our allies. We've stolen all of the things that we need and lied to everyone about it. We haven't really needed anything, except for truck parts and some electronic stuff to repair our pulse guns and cannons. We stole all of those trucks from that naval armada. We got a few pulse cannons from that incident as well."

"Yeah, we got that, but it didn't help us repair *our* equipment."

"I think that this is definitely something that we need to bring up at the next Staff Meeting."

"I agree."

Officer Leader, Till, the Team Leader for Team 31 had been able to get all of the computer equipment he needed in the new unit in the gorge. Here he was in Unit 1-31, still working on finding anything he could on anything about outer space, sightings of UFO's - faked or real - anything on the planets, rockets that could leave the atmosphere - and return. He still could not get enough. Every search that he tried came up with more information, however, a lot of it was redundant.

He got one of the computer experts to hook him up to one of the Algothon flying cameras and was able to turn it out to look into outer space. The magnification factors were sadly insignificant for what he was attempting, however, he did get some very good looks at the different planets in the solar system… and certain information about those planets that the Algothon were keeping a secret…until such time as they were able to achieve the capability of traveling to these other planets.

Even though most of the information was repetitive, he kept on digging. He was insatiable.

Holla called the Staff meeting to order. "Any new business?"

"Yes," said Wilfadge. "We were wondering if anyone knows what our commerce was."

Ahandi snickered. "What are you talking about?"

Hadathoo snarled at her. "What were we trading, to others, in order to obtain all of the necessary raw materials and parts that we needed in order to keep our city…well defended?"

Teelila looked at both men as if they were crazy. "What difference does that make now? We don't have it any more… whatever…*it*…was. Do you think that we can resurrect something from the ashes of the inner city?"

"We were trading something," said Wilfadge. "It was valuable enough to get someone to give us raw materials for our trucks and weapons. If we could somehow…yes, resurrect it, maybe we could get an upper hand on something again without any more lies…to our allies."

"I'm pretty sure it was pharmaceuticals," said Shyshee. She looked around the table with a bit of a guilty smile.

Holla chuckled. "What makes you say that?"

"Maybe you should talk to some of the doctors," said Shyshee with a shrug.

Holla made a mental call to all of the doctors in Owlam. Two responded to the inquiry about the pharmaceuticals: Kazkim of Medical Team 221 and Voolatha of Medical Team 222.

Holla smiled at the two doctors. "What do you know about this...trade and commerce...that we used to have?"

Kazkim looked at his colleague and smiled nervously. "We used to be part of the manufacturing process for *Tuzine*. It was, and if we could make it again, the most powerful antibiotic drug ever invented on this planet."

Voolatha cocked her head to the side. "If we could make it again, I know that it would help us...*immensely* in any trade agreements...with anybody on the planet."

Chaza glared at the doctors. "IF? IF? What did it take to make this drug?"

Kazkim smiled. "The primary ingredient was our biggest secret. It was made from the root of the *Shoonshook* plant."

"The other secret," said Voolatha, "was the process in which we turned the root into the antibiotic."

Kazkim shook his head sadly. "All of the *Shoonshook* plants...were burned up in the firestorm attack."

Dwalooa stood up looking very angry. "Are you telling me, that those foul smelling plants, that grew wild all over the city, were the main reason that we were able to buy truck parts and weapons parts?"

Voolatha shrugged and smiled. "That's the reason that we always let them grow…all over the city. They were what made us our fortune…and nobody but a select few, knew the ingredients or the process of making the drug. I haven't seen any of the plants… since the firestorm…so…what's the point of bringing it up?"

Chaza stood up with a very strange look on her face. "Uh…you say that the *Shoonshook* is the primary ingredient?"

"Yes," said Kazkim.

Chaza cleared her throat. "What…are the other ingredients?"

Kazkim scoffed. "What difference does it make if we don't have the *Shoonshook?* The other ingredients are easily obtainable and the process is easy, for us to make, because we know the process."

Chaza chuckled nervously. "I don't know if you were aware…but there is an area…in the southwest sector of Owlam where there are a few plants…still growing. Not every plant died from that residual energy. If there's at least one *Shoonshook* that's still growing there…could you take a few cuttings…or seeds… and start another grove of *Shoonshook?*"

Kazkim stood up, his eyes wide open with excitement. "If…there is so much as one of the plants still alive…yes, we could get seeds and…and start an entire plantation of the *Shoonshook.*"

Voolatha was standing as well. "We could be manufacturing the drug, as soon as we get at least ten plants going strong. The only problem is getting them to grow…quickly.”

Kazkim closed his eyes. He stood there silently, communicating telepathically with someone else. He opened his eyes. “We have to get to this…area in the southwest that you’re talking about. If we find any *Shoonshook* plants there, according to Doctor Saysay, we could plant it or…them…or some of them…in the Zee-Althan massacre field. According to Saysay, the trees that were planted there are blossoming beautifully. The *Shoonshook* should do the same.”

Shyshee looked at Chaza. “Are you talking about that…?”

Chaza was looking excited as well. “You know I am!”

Shyshee looked at Voolatha hopefully. “Do you know what the plant looks like?”

Dwalooa scoffed. “Look like? What look like? Just take a sniff! If you smell something that’s almost bad as Stink dimension, you’ve found that silly things.”

Holla gave Dwalooa a sweet smile. “Well Dearie, if you’re so sure that you can sniff that thing out, why don’t you join Chaza, Shyshee and Voolatha and go to this area in the southwest part of the city and see if you can find these…highly valuable plants?” Holla looked at Voolatha rather worried. “You did say that the other ingredients are easy to get a hold of, didn’t you?”

Voolatha smiled. “Right now, the one and only ingredient that we’re missing - the root of the *Shoonshook*.”

Holla stood up. “Chaza! Shyshee! Dwalooa! Voolatha! All of you to that garden in the southwest…NOW!”

Chaza and Shyshee vanished.

Dwalooa stood there looking worried. "I don't know exactly where it is."

"Neither do I," said Voolatha.

Chaza reappeared, grabbed Voolatha and both of them vanished.

Shyshee reappeared, grabbed Dwalooa and both of them vanished.

Holla looked around the table. "Wilfadge, Hadathoo, thank you for asking that question. This may be a turning point in our lives…if they can find that…*Shoonshook*."

14

Dwalooa called back to the conference room. "Dwalooa calling Holla, can you hear me?"

"This is Holla, what did you find?"

"It is with mixed emotions, I inform you···we found that smelly plant. This garden of weeds is full of that horrible smelly plant. We can start manufacturing our pride and joy – Tuzine – and maybe start profiting from it again."

"What is Voolatha doing? Why didn't she call?"

"She's too busy identifying which of these weeds is Shoonshook and which is···something else···that I can't even pronounce. She said that the seed pods are full and that we need to harvest them and start planting and growing them anywhere that we can."

"According to what was said, we need to get as many seeds and plant them in that Zee–Althan massacre field."

"That's a good start."

Holla had a huge grin on her face. "Wilfadge, Hadathoo, why didn't anyone ask this question before?"

Wilfadge shook his head sadly. "Because we were so ignorant of a lot of the things going on in the inner city…we didn't even know what questions to ask."

Hadathoo grunted. "We were just the 'watchers in the wall'. We knew our responsibility and virtually nothing else. No one in the city could have ever seen anything like the firestorm happening to us. An attack that destroyed almost everything…but the wall watchers."

Holla thought for a moment. "Chaza, this is Holla, do you hear me?"

"Yes I do, but I'm kinda busy gathering seed pods. Is this important?"

"Go get that···Officer, Bonarain from 7016. We may all need a class in botany. Maybe she can figure out a way for all of us to learn faster."

Chaza nodded to herself. "I can do that." She handed her pouch of seeds to Dwalooa. "I got something I gotta do." She closed her eyes. "Officer, Bonarain, this is Chaza, can you hear me?"

Bonarain was wringing out her washcloth. She looked up disgusted. "Yes, Sir, I can hear you."

"What are you doing right now?"

"Washing my neck."

"Hurry up and finish. We have a job to do. Tell the rest of your Team that they're getting involved as well."

"Right now, Soolchakan and Kiyalee are in a tub as well. Chyning is waiting until one of us is finished, then she's taking a bath. Then, we're all going to have lunch. I don't think that your chore is important enough for all of us to starve."

"It is important."

Bonarain angrily wiped more of the mucus off of the back of her neck. "HOW important?"

"Tuzine!"

She stopped scrubbing for a moment. "WHAT?!" She sat there in the tub letting loose with several noises of disgust.

"Did you hear me?"

"Yes, I heard you, I just don't get it···or care."

Chaza growled at no one in particular. "I'm Jumping over there. Make sure that I'm welcomed."

Bonarain sighed. "Chyning, we have a guest coming. Let her in when she gets here."

Chyning looked up from her lunch, chewing on a mouthful of food. She looked over at the door, waiting for someone to knock. "Okay."

Chaza called Bonarain again. "I'm here, where is your silly building?"

Bonarain closed her eyes and shook her head. "It's in Spy dimension where we left it for over twenty years, once we found out some of the capabilities of those wretched flying cameras."

Chaza contemplated that thought for a moment. She shrugged and hopped to Spy. The main doors to the building were a little to her right. She walked over and knocked.

Chyning opened the door looking a little apprehensive and wearing a bathrobe. She smiled nervously. "Hello...Sir. What can I do for you?"

Chaza walked in. "Didn't she tell you to get ready?"

Chyning looked up at the ceiling suspiciously. She was considering the fact that this building had three bathtubs and all three were currently occupied. "She said that someone was coming for a visit. She didn't say why and she didn't say to get ready for anything."

"Why aren't you dressed...for any duty? It's the middle of the day."

Chyning clenched her teeth. "I'm waiting for one of the others to finish their bath. Then I'm going to take a bath, because the nasty stuff is dripping down my back."

Chaza shuddered in disgust. "Okay. I'll...wait...until after you've taken a bath as well." She walked to one of the tables. "Got any kwatha?"

Chyning shrugged. "Just some of that third rate stuff."

Chaza sighed. "That'll do for now."

Kiyalee walked into the room, wearing a bathrobe and drying her hair. She saw Chaza and stopped in surprise. She let out a guilty chuckle. "Uh…what's the…occasion…Sir?"

Chaza shook her head. "The occasion is, I need for all of Team 7016 to get washed, dressed and fed…and get ready to go."

Looking a little confused, Kiyalee tried to think it through. "Uh…of course…Sir." She turned to Chyning. "There's a free tub."

Chyning grunted a response, grabbed something off of a plate and headed for the stairs while stuffing the food in her mouth.

Kiyalee was not sure what to do. Chyning had departed so abruptly without any instruction as to what needed to be done for the guest.

Chaza sighed. "Go ahead and eat. I'll finish this… substitute kwatha while…the rest of your Team gets fed."

Kiyalee smiled, still looking nervous. "Thank you…Sir." She headed for the kitchen. She came back into the dining area with a bowl full of something that was steaming. She sat down at a table and started eating, while still eyeing Chaza nervously.

Bonarain came down the stairs next. She just nodded to the two people in the dining area and went straight to the kitchen. She came back out moments later with a steaming bowl of her own and sat down at the same table with Kiyalee.

Chaza sighed. "Look, the last time I was here, yes, I know that things happened…that shouldn't have happened. Now, we need to work together and put all of those…unnecessary…silly mistakes behind us."

Bonarain and Kiyalee stilled eyed her suspiciously as they ate.

Soolchakan came down the stairs and stopped. He stared blankly at Chaza for a moment. He, like his Team, was wearing a bathrobe. He sniffed and headed for the kitchen. He came back out with a steaming bowl, sat down with Bonarain and Kiyalee and started eating.

Chaza smiled and sighed. "Okay, you've all made it clear that you don't like me. I…understand. I'm here because Holla ordered it. I'm here because…you, Officer, Bonarain…have a wonderful talent for teaching. You can take some of the strangest categories and figure out a way to teach others - who are having a hard time understanding - to understand and excel. We…all of the Owlamites…need your skill…for a better future for all of us."

Soolchakan and Kiyalee both stopped chewing and were both looking back and forth from Bonarain to Chaza, very confused.

Soolchakan swallowed. "What'd I miss?"

Chaza smiled. "I had a discussion with Bonarain earlier. Let's wait until Chyning is finished bathing and then we'll all be here and no one will have to repeat themselves."

After everyone in Team 7016 had bathed, eaten and dressed, Chaza explained the entire situation to them. All of them were Jumped to the area in southwest Owlam to see the "garden".

Kiyalee looked around disgusted. "That stinky *weed* that

grew all over the city…is our financial *salvation*?"

Voolatha smiled. "That stinky weed is the primary ingredient in the manufacturing of *Tuzine*."

"But we don't need it anymore," whined Chyning. "According to Doctor Shurmook, we're all showing that we're immune to bacteria and viruses and several different poisons. Why do we need that drug?"

Dwalooa got directly in the face of Chyning. "This drug IS needed by the rest of the world. We found out that there's a lot of people who are trying to take…what little they have left…albeit fifty years old, and try to figure out how to make it again. We're the only ones with the secret and we can make it…and sell it…for all kinds of profit, in order to obtain all kinds of goodies to help out our future."

Kiyalee still looked confused. "So, how come, all of a sudden, we know the secret to that drug…when it was lost in the firestorm?"

Voolatha snickered. "We were always the ones who manufactured the *Tuzine*. What was lost was the fact that, people like me, who cooked it up, didn't know that there was still a lot of *Shoonshook* plants that were still alive. I thought that all of them had been burned up in the firestorm. I didn't know that this area was just out of range of the firestorm. If I had known about this… patch…I would've been out here harvesting seed and planting it anywhere I could in order to start up our export commodity…of *Tuzine*."

Bonarain looked around…and then up. "I don't think that

we're doing the right thing."

Dwalooa scoffed. "Why not?"

While still looking up, Bonarain explained. "If the Algothons are looking at us, right now, they're going to wonder why, all of a sudden, a bunch of us are in this patch, harvesting seed from a bunch of weeds."

Chaza had a look of horror on her face. "Oh...*h'oolyach*!" She looked around. "You're right!"

"Right now, there's only eight of us here," said Bonarain. "If we bring anyone else here, I suggest that it's in Spy or Observation."

"Okay," said Chaza. "No one panic! I'm going to contact Holla and see if we're being noticed." She clenched her eyes tight and pursed her lips. Moments later she opened her eyes and took a deep breath. "Holla is going to check with our spies in Algothon. She's checking to see if anyone is watching us...specifically."

Kiyalee chuckled. "So...what do we do...in the mean time?"

"Walk around aimlessly," said Soolchakan. "Just walk around and look around...and don't touch anything."

They all followed his advice. They wandered through the weeds, not doing anything but walking slowly. After, what seemed an eternity, Chaza froze. She put her fist up to her mouth and concentrated as she was mentally communicating with Holla. She finally let out a loud sigh of relief. "Okay, according to Holla and the spies, no one in Algothon is looking at this area...at this time. We're safe!"

Bonarain smiled. "Everybody hop to Spy. We'll continue gathering seeds and then we'll get out of here…in Spy and the Algothons won't even know we were here or why."

All of them hopped to Spy and started aggressively gathering the seed pods of the *Shoonshook* plants. After they were satisfied that all of the seed pods were harvested, it was time to go.

"I'm gonna need another bath," whined Kiyalee. "I stink like that nasty *Shoonshook* weed."

Voolatha snarled at Kiyalee. "Right now, that smell is better than the smell of any precious metal…to us."

Kiyalee growled back. "I'm still gonna take a bath and get this wonderful…*golden* smell off of *me*."

Voolatha was giggling with delight as she looked at all of the seed pods that had been gathered.

"I'm sure glad that you're happy," said Holla. "Now, is there any way that you can get those foul smelling things out of my conference room?"

Voolatha looked up at Holla, still grinning widely. "We can hop them into Spy. That'll keep the smell away."

Teelila was holding her nose. "DO IT!"

Voolatha pulled the tablecloth up and wrapped it around all of the pods. She wadded it into a bundle and then hopped the bundle into Spy. "I'll get your tablecloth back to you as soon..."

Holla waved at her. "Keep the foul smelling thing! I'll find another one...somewhere...that doesn't stink...so badly."

Ahandi was still waving the smell away. "It's lingering." She looked at Voolatha. "Okay, so what do we do now?"

Voolatha looked around at the Staff. She was still elated at the find. "I'm going to need two other doctors - Kolokoko and Lokondon. They were part of the Team that helped cook up the *Tuzine*. They were relatively new, as far as being in the laboratory, but they do have *some* experience, which is a lot more than anyone else."

Holla nodded with her eyes closed. "Whatever you need! It's gonna be done."

Hoynama frowned. "When should we get our first batch?"

"It might be about at least a year," said Voolatha. "All I have here is the seeds. We've still got to go out there and harvest some plants. It's the roots that give us what we need. This first batch is gonna be small, because I won't have the abundance of roots that I had...fifty years ago."

Holla nodded. "That makes sense. Do you need anything else?"

Voolatha flushed and chuckled. "I need to have a conference with all of the...*men*...of Owlam."

Holla looked as if she had been slapped. "What's wrong with the women?"

Voolatha chuckled nervously again. "There's...uh... nothing wrong with the women...it's just that...well..." She bit her lip. "I'll tell you what, Supreme Officer - you can sit in on the briefing...and you'll understand why I need...just the men."

Holla looked at Wilfadge. "Can you take care of that?"

He snickered. "You can take care of that a lot easier than I can. You can call them all here and they'll respond...without questioning it or any belly-aching about it. I just ask you to give them a day to respond. Some of them may be taking a bath right now and if you tell them to come here now...it might get a little embarrassing."

Holla sat there staring blankly at Wilfadge. "You're right." She turned only her eyes to Voolatha. "Should that include all of the men who are currently on other assignments at other places in the world?"

Voolatha clasped her hands in front of her. She smiled and cocked her head to the side. "The more men we have, the faster it'll go and the sooner we can put the drug out...by the gross."

Holla shrugged in resignation. She took a deep breath. "To all of the men of Owlam, I am calling out to you. I am calling out, even to the ones who are overseas, at this time. We have need of all men to report to your designated parking spot at the parking lot of the old conference auditorium on the north side. You'll be briefed, at that time, as to why. The report time will be midday, Owlam time, tomorrow. This way, if you're doing something important, it can be finished up and you can be there. This includes any regularly scheduled neck-cleanings. You will be there. To the women of Owlam, if there is a problem with them being there...at that time, let me know as soon as possible. This meeting is critical to the future of Owlam. All men be there, unless excused for some other drastically important mission." She looked at the two men on the Staff.

Wilfadge shook his head. "I...think...that'll do."

Hadathoo simply nodded. "Uh-huh!"

Ahandi had a sour look on her face. "You mind if I'm there?"

Holla smiled. "No. As a matter of fact, I think that the entire Staff should be there."

The next day, all of the Staff were standing just inside the main entrance, along with Team 7016. They were holding a sign that they would flash at all of the men as they arrived. The sign simply said: Hop to Spy. Most of the men Jumped to the parking lot around the same time. There were a few that were early and a few that arrived late. Each one arrived, saw the sign and hopped to Spy.

After seeing no more arrivals, Holla made another call. "If there are any men of Owlam who have not arrived at the parking lot, respond now and let me know why you're not here."

There was no response.

Holla smirked. "All 6756 Owlam men are here. Let's get

on with the meeting."

The Staff hopped to Spy. They were now standing behind Doctor Voolatha, who was behind a podium.

Voolatha got close to the microphone. She motioned for all of the men to come closer. "I'd like to thank you for all coming today. I realize that you didn't have much choice, but I'm going to thank you anyway. Now, the reason that you're here. I don't know how many of you remember, but, there was a drug, an antibiotic that was widely used...before the firestorm. It was called *Tuzine*. I don't know if you knew or not, but that drug was manufactured here in Owlam. I thought that because of the firestorm, we'd lost the main ingredient in the making of the drug. Yesterday, we found a place in Owlam, where it still exists and so, we can restart manufacturing the drug." She saw the looks on many of their faces. "I know what some of you may be thinking... yes, according to our doctors, we're immune to all of the known diseases...so why do we need this drug? The reason we need it... one of the main reasons that we needed it, before the firestorm... trade! We're going to manufacture it and use it as an export...so we can trade with others...and get certain items, from them, that we need."

Many of the men were loudly asking the question: "What's that got to do with us?"

Voolatha held up her hands to quiet them. "I understand that you're confused...but...one of the secrets...that was kept... for many years, was a certain idiosyncrasy of plant itself...the plant that is our main ingredient. The plant that we use is called the

Shoonshook plant. It's a very bad smelling weed…that grew wild all over the city. We allowed it to grow wild…and prevalent…in order to make sure that we had plenty." She sighed. "I'm trying to think of the best way of saying this."

One man up front scoffed. "Open your mouth and communicate!"

There was a lot of laughter from that comment.

She smiled. "Yes, but it's somewhat…indelicate." She cleared her throat. "One thing that was discovered was that the plants were flourishing the most…in a certain area where a lot of…taverns and alcoholics were…very common. It was discovered that…many of the men…would come out of the taverns…intoxicated…and…they would relieve themselves…on the plants."

Again a great deal of laughter rose up from the congregated men.

"What we discovered…the *Shoonshook* plant…thrives on…urine."

Now the laughter was almost thundering - and drawn out.

Wilfadge could not help himself. He got up near the microphone. "If it thrives on urine, why're you talking only to the men? If I remember my anatomy classes, women are capable of conjuring up urine as well."

More thunderous laughter.

Voolatha hung her head and put her hands on both side of

her head until the laughter subsided. "Yes, women can urinate as well."

Wilfadge scoffed. "So is it because men have a better way of aiming at the target?"

More thunderous laughter.

Holla had heard enough derision. "Everybody shut your mouths until she's finished talking!"

The only noise that was heard was a slight wind.

Voolatha looked at Holla. "Thank you, Sir," she said timidly. She turned back to the men. "The strange thing about this plant...is that it grows...faster and better when it's...fertilized... with *male* urine. Female urine can be used to...fertilize it, however, it doesn't grow as fast...as when male urine is used. What we're going to do...we've gathered a lot of seeds. We're going to pass out these seeds...as far as they go. The men who receive a seed, plant it...somewhere and...begin *nurturing* it. As soon as it...buds, blossoms and the blossoms turn to seed pods... gather the seed pods...and we'll pass out more seed to other men as well. Once you all have at least five plants, then we'll be able to start harvesting the plant for the roots...and we'll be able to start manufacturing the pills...by the thousands."

Hadathoo walked up to Voolatha. "You're serious? Male urine...is a better...fertilizer...than female urine?"

Voolatha huffed in exasperation. "If there's any of you who don't believe me...once you have several plants...put one or two off to the side and let the women pee on those. Then compare which plants grow and blossom up and out faster."

Hadathoo looked at Wilfadge. "I will!"

Soolchakan felt rather confused. "Uh...Sir...normally... you do all of this stuff...or anything like this...in numerical order. I'm on Team 7016...so that means I'll be last...in getting any seeds."

Holla smiled. "Not in this case. Seeing as how Officer, Bonarain is on your Team and she has that uncanny knack of being able to teach all of the subjects that we've put in front of her... you're going to be first on the list. You get a seed and she's able to observe what happens to the plant. Then, if there is something that she can teach others...she'll have the necessary, *first-hand*, experience in tending one of the plants."

Bonarain let out a disgusted squawk. "I have to...watch him...*pee*...on the plant?"

"No," said Holla with her eyes closed in exasperation. "You watch the daily growth of the plant. You don't have to be there when he...fertilizes it. You just observe the plant...daily." She smiled.

Bonarain looked off to the side and sighed despondently. "Yes, Sir."

Holla handed Soolchakan a seed with a big smile on her face. "You have your seed, Officer, Soolchakan. You know what to do with it. Team 7016, you're dismissed."

Soolchakan looked at the seed in his hand. He smiled at Holla. "Thank you, Sir," he said halfheartedly. He vanished.

The rest of Team 7016 vanished as well.

Wilfadge and Hadathoo received their seeds and vanished.

Niyniy started calling the roll, by the numbers, in passing out the remaining five hundred fifty-four seeds they currently had. Once they finished passing those seed out, Holla informed the others that they would be called as soon as there were more seeds available. The meeting was over.

Teelila stood there looking sickened. "I want one of those seeds...for myself. I wanna see...*first hand*...this rotten little seed...that prefers *male* urine to female urine."

Voolatha shrugged. "Sir, according to all of the books I read...and still have...it was consistent. The plant grows...faster and larger...with the stuff from males." She shrugged again. "I can't explain it."

Teelila blew a raspberry. "I still feel slighted...by a *chokwad* plant."

One year later, all of the men had several plants in different stages of growth. They had planted them in areas near the gorge, as well as Owlam, Axswain, Galsino, Teltermak and the Zee-Althan massacre field. Any area where the plant could get plenty of sunlight and the men could Jump to, each time they had to relieve themselves.

"I feel even more slighted," said Teelila. "After the man on my Team, Officer, Sorn, planted some new seeds, I got a seed and the other two women on my Team got seeds. Sorn peed on his seeds…and they grew like mad. I peed on my seed. Amafee peed on hers. Noyafa peed on hers. None of them grew as fast as…any of Sorn's plants. So, I traded one of the plants with Sorn." She sighed. "My new plant…that used to be his…stopped growing… rapidly. The one that used to be mine…now his…started shooting up and budding…so quickly." She slammed her fist on the table. "I'm being insulted…by a plant! Because of my gender!"

Wilfadge and Hadathoo were trying desperately not to laugh…and failing miserably at it.

Most of the women looked at the two men with disdain.

"It's something strange in the chemistry," said Shyshee. "It's just a plant…not capable of…love or hate…or any sentient thought. It's just the nature of the plant…and the chemistry."

"I still don't like it," said Teelila as she folded her arms and hunched down in her chair.

Holla shook her head. "Like it or not, we're getting a good crop and Voolatha has finally started harvesting some of the roots…in order to start cooking the stuff up so we can sell it."

Dwalooa frowned. "Where should we test it first, to see if the stuff still works? Since we don't get any diseases any more… we can't test it on ourselves."

Ahandi shrugged. "Prisoners at the Turgon Wall. Find some prisoner that has some disease and try it out. I can't think of anyone else that we can use as a lab rodent."

"Good idea," said Holla.

"I don't know," said Hoynama. "Those Algothons have spies at the Turgon Wall. If we show up…with some fresh *Tuzine*…right in front of them…we may be asking for trouble."

Teelila chuckled. "So we use it as a two-fold operation."

Holla looked confused. "How do you two-fold something like that?"

"Simple," said Teelila with a devious smile. "We drive up in one of the Algothon trucks…loaded with *Tuzine*. We tell the T'Mor that we have finally rediscovered the way to manufacture the drug. We make sure that we do it right in front of the Algothon spies. We make sure that the truck looks so nice and clean…and when someone asks us where we got a new truck…we simply tell them that there was an attempted raid…by some Galsinos…and we stopped the raid…killing the Galsinos in the process. We have no idea where the Galsinos got the truck…but since they're dead and they don't need the truck anymore…we're using it."

"That's a dirty trick," said Chaza.

"Yes, it is," said Teelila with a smirk.

Holla chuckled. "We keep the rumor alive that it's the Galsino who are the ones causing all of that grief to Algothon. I like it."

"We may have to come up with some more dead Galsinos," said Hadathoo. "I mean…if the Algothons are watching us, we have to display the capture of the truck to them."

Holla looked thoughtful. "All we really have to do is find out where the Algothons are *not* watching. Claim that the attempted theft took place in that location. We got the truck, the Galsinos got dead…and here we are."

Shyshee shook her head. "We won't steal Galsinos from the Turgon Wall or any of the other facilities associated with it."

Ahandi sighed. "It's gonna make the Galsinos hate us even more, if they ever find out who did it to them."

Wilfadge scoffed. "It's gonna make *everybody* hate us, if any of the truth about what we've been doing gets out."

Holla nodded. "We have to tread very carefully… everywhere we go and with everything that we do."

Three months later, Team 7016 had the privilege of driving their new Algothon truck up to the main headquarters at the Turgon Wall. They had with them four hundred bottles, each holding fifty tablets of *Tuzine*, and two doctors - Hoonsi and Initaya - who were going to administer the drug to any experimental patient at the Wall.

Soolchakan looked around as they drove up and parked. "Officer Grade 7, Dozzell, are you here, can you hear me?"

"I'm here. You already did one of the things that you wanted to do. Two of the Algothon spies saw the truck coming in, contacted four of their cronies and now all six of them are gawking at you⋯with great interest."

Soolchakan snickered. "So we definitely have to make sure that they hear where we⋯ahem⋯got it from."

"Amen."

Kiyalee had been listening to the conversation and was looking around the area. "Over to the left of the building, you said that there's six of them. I see six men who are looking rather shocked at what they see."

Dozzell smiled. "That's the ones. That's the bunch that you need to put the show on for."

Team 7016 got out of the truck and positioned themselves at the four corners of the truck…armed with pulse rifles.

Four men came out of the building. The two Owlam doctors got out of the truck and smiled at the administrators of the Wall as they approached.

The T'Mor man bowed his head slightly to the newcomers. Since he had a beak instead of a mouth, it was difficult to tell whether or not there was a friendly smile there.

"I am Commander, Chocho Sah, T'mor Commander of the Turgon Wall." He introduced the other personnel who accompanied him. "This is Lead Officer, Milthiy of the Great River, Chief Representative of the Kalash here at the Wall. This is Tyhond, Thon Velgogin, Chief Representative of the Rahanan-Sar, here at the Wall. This is Administrator, Toyobachi Zizzin, Chief Representative of the Argaman-Or here at the Wall."

Hoonsi smiled as she shook hands with each one. "I am Doctor Hoonsi of the Owlam. This is my colleague, Doctor Initaya. The others are Team 7016 of the Owlam, who are here as our escorts. Initaya and I are here to ask for your permission to test an antibiotic that we recently rediscovered. We thought that it was lost forever, but, during some clean up, we came across some documents that…somehow survived the firestorm attack. It gave us the ingredients and formula for preparing the drug - *Tuzine*, and we would like to see if we got it right. I understand from some of our representatives, here at the Wall, that there have been a few outbreaks of…certain diseases. If this *Tuzine* was made correctly, we may be able to assist in getting rid of those diseases."

Chocho was standing there with his eyes wide open in shock. "You've found…rediscovered…*Tuzine*? That'd be a wonderful thing…if it *is* true!" He turned to the other Leaders, who had the same expression of shock and hope. "I think that they should be escorted to the hospital…at once!"

"I quite agree," said Toyobachi. "If we can get that mess under control…or eradicated…it'd be best for the health of everyone…guard or prisoner."

Milthiy looked thrilled. "I have some news from home… that we've had a bit of a nasty outbreak in the City of Kalash. This would be…" He choked as he nearly broke out in tears. "If this is truly *Tuzine* and it works…we could destroy that pestilence and…I need to watch the tests myself." He pulled out a handkerchief and wiped his nose.

Toyobachi smiled. "Please, let's not get ahead of ourselves. Let's go inside, work out a few details and get the tests started immediately."

The two Owlam doctors smiled and chatted as they went inside with the administrators.

Dozzell had been watching the Algothon spies (from Spy dimension). "Officer, Soolchakan, get ready. There's two of those Algothons working their way over to you."

Soolchakan tried to keep a straight face. "I see them now. I've got the story all ready for them."

Dozzell called out again. "Officer, Chyning, I think that one or two of them are headed for you as well."

Chyning was a little startled. "Are you sure···oh wait, I see them. Nosey *chokwads*!"

The two Algothons casually walked up to Soolchakan.

The taller one of the two men smiled at Soolchakan. "Nice truck you've got here."

"Thank you," said Soolchakan in a cordial manner.

"It looks rather new. I wasn't aware that anyone was… doing any new manufacturing of vehicles. Where'd you get it from?"

Soolchakan shrugged. "As to how new it is, I can only guess. The way we got it…we confiscated it after an attack on a village…that was totally unsuccessful…by the renegades."

The Algothon looked confused. "What…happened…if you don't mind telling me?"

Soolchakan smiled. 'Here goes the line of *h'oolyach*,' he thought. "I and some of my colleagues were in a village near Owlam. We were there seeing if there was anything they had worth trading for and we had a few things that we thought they might be interested in. While we were there, a bunch of Galsinos drove in...in this truck and started...shooting indiscriminately. They didn't say anything, they just opened fire." Soolchakan shrugged and smiled. "We hadn't gone there to defend the village...but we had to defend ourselves." He held his pulse rifle a little higher for a moment. "After a few bursts with this thing...along with my colleagues...the enemy was destroyed...and the villagers had no aversion to us keeping the truck." He smiled.

The two Algothons looked at each other. "What'd the Galsinos say? Where did they get the truck?"

"They didn't say," said Soolchakan with a grin.

"What...they refused to talk?"

Soolchakan snickered. "It seems that they did *not* like the idea of being taken alive. The last two, on the ground, critically injured, and they were still trying to shoot at us. The only way that we could survive the attack...uninjured...was to..." He sighed. "...shoot to kill."

The Algothon snickered. "That's why...they didn't say."

Soolchakan simply smiled.

The other Algothon finally spoke up. "I wonder if that's the same thing that happened to us."

Soolchakan frowned. "What do you mean?"

The shorter one shrugged. "About fifteen years ago, when I was a lot younger, some...renegades...came into our village. They didn't say anything, they just started shooting, burning and looting. They didn't have a truck though. By the time they were finished, there wasn't one single house that was...*not*...burning. Those of us that escaped the attack...we wandered for quite a while...until we got here at the wall and...obtained employment here. We don't have any place else to go...so here we are!"

Soolchakan smiled. "At least you've got something."

The two Algothons chuckled.

"Yes, we do," said the tall one. "Looks like this is going to be a life career here...but again...it's something."

"Nice talking to you," said the short one.

Soolchakan smiled back and the two men casually walked back the way they had come from. He glanced back behind him. "Bonarain, are those two *chokwads* still talking to Chyning?"

"Yes, they are. I think that they're trying to sweet talk her as well."

"Into what?"

"They're MEN! What do you think?"

"She knows her duty."

"Looks like they're finished. They're headed back to the others."

Chyning broke into the conversation. "Would it be all right if I exterminate those two *chogos*···right now?"

Bonarain chuckled. "We don't want to arouse any

suspicions. Maybe later!"

Soolchakan watched the other two headed back to the group. "Okay, quiet! Dozzell, what're they saying now?"

"I'll relay the conversation," thought Dozzell.

The six Algothons got together to compare notes.

The short one that had been talking to Soolchakan looked around. "Let's get around the corner of the building. Don't want to be seen talking about this."

"Oh, by all means," thought Dozzell.

They moved out of sight.

"All right," said the short one. "Report!"

One of the men that had talked to Chyning started talking. "That *Ninyit* in the back corner, she told us how they got the truck by killing a bunch of Galsino raiders, in some unnamed village near Owlam."

Chyning mentally snarled. "*Ninyit*, indeed···uh···what's a *ninyit*?"

Soolchakan snarled back at her. "Quiet"

"That's the same story that we got from that *Thwod* up front."

"Should we try talking to the other two women?"

"No," said the leader. "The one on the other side of the front...she looks too determined to do her job. The other woman in the back is too homely. She'd be suspicious just from any man asking her for a date."

"They're DEAD," snarled Bonarain.

Kiyalee and Chyning were having a hard time maintaining composure.

"Shut up and stay calm," thought Soolchakan.

"Their leader is gonna be DEAD," snarled Bonarain.

One of the two that had remained behind started talking. "We heard those two Owlam women say that they're doctors."

The leader frowned. "Doctors? What does a doctor want here?"

The other man spoke. "They said something about a drug they called - *Tuzine*."

The leader was startled. "Are you sure…she said… *Tuzine*?"

"That's what it sounded like."

The leader paced around with his hand on his forehead. "We've got to contact Sector Five…as soon as possible."

One of the other men was flabbergasted. "And tell them what? We found a truck…in the hands of the Owlam…and some…drug?"

The leader got in the man's face. "Did you ever study anything in school? *Tuzine* was a wonder drug that disappeared after our all-out attack. It cures just about anything bacterial.

If these *Hongoths* have found the formula…that's just…too important to *not* report. Let's not forget the fact that…we now have some information to report…on one of our missing trucks."

"Okay," said one of the other men. "So this drug is important. That still doesn't give any credibility to the story about that Galsino attack where the Owlams got their hands on one of our trucks."

"Yeah," said one of the others. "A total attack, where they refuse to be taken alive?"

The leader huffed. "It could've been a planned suicide attack. The Galsinos surrender *one* of the trucks…to the hands of the Owlams. Now, we see *ONE* truck! One truck in the hands of the Owlams. That could get some of the suspicions off of the Galsinos, now couldn't it?"

"If it's true."

The leader nodded. "That's why we need to get this information back home. We have to risk it. Tell Shonkton to get the radio ready."

"**They bit on something**," thought Dozzell.

Hoonsi and Initaya came out of the headquarters building with the Argaman-Or representative.

Hoonsi smiled. "Officer, Soolchakan, I would like you to meet Administrator, Toyobachi Zizzin. He's going to go with us to…" She gave Toyobachi a side glance. "…hospital number…5?"

Toyobachi smiled. "Yes, Doctor."

"It seems that they have a rather large outbreak of sexually transmitted diseases there. They haven't been able to cure anyone, so that sounds like an excellent area to test the *Tuzine*."

Soolchakan smiled. "Yes, Doctor." He turned to Toyobachi. "Pleased to meet you, Sir." He turned to his Team. "Ladies, let's mount up, we've got another destination."

Soolchakan, Bonarain and Chyning climbed into the back of the truck. Kiyalee headed for the driver's seat. Hoonsi, Initaya and Toyobachi all climbed into the large cab of the truck.

Toyobachi leaned close to Kiyalee. "Just follow that road going north, my Dear. I'll tell you when we get there."

Kiyalee smiled at him. "Thank you, Sir."

Hoonsi smiled. "So, what's the story about this outbreak of STD's?"

Toyobachi grunted. "It seems that there was a prisoner brought here from an Elf race called…Moplytak. They're extremely short people. I believe that your measurement is… taja…and these people are usually less than four and a half taja in height. They're also…very family oriented. The family is everything. When he was sentenced to eighty years at the Wall, his wife came with him. Since he is of very short stature and not very strong, it's possible that he may not last eighty years. He's been through five Turgon attacks, so far, and because of the fact that his wife will give up…sex…to anyone who helps him stay alive, she has contracted an STD and is passing it along to anyone who helps her husband stay alive."

Kiyalee squawked in horror. "That...is disgusting! Why would anyone go back to her for seconds? If she infected them... why go back?"

Toyobachi cleared his throat. "My Dear, if you've already been IN-fected with an incurable disease it's difficult to be RE-infected with the same disease. They already have it...so what difference does it make?"

Kiyalee still looked nauseous. "It's still disgusting!"

Toyobachi smiled. "I agree, however, I'm not a part of that circle, thank the Great Maker. The people who're infected, they should be an excellent group of candidates to try this drug. From what I understand, this disease flares up...in a rather painful manner...every now and then. You'll have to discuss all of the symptoms and problems with the doctors at number 5, when we get there."

Initaya shook her head. "How many people are we talking about...being infected in this circle...I mean?"

"I think that there are about thirty."

Kiyalee again let out a squawk.

"Just DRIVE," said Hoonsi. "Don't worry about our medical conversation."

"Yes, Sir," said Kiyalee, still looking sick.

Initaya looked a little sick herself. "Thirty? You said thirty? She is a busy little...whatever you want to call it."

Toyobachi smiled. "Yes, that's what we call it."

Kiyalee drove on maintaining silence, however, she could not hide her repugnance over the issue.

Hoonsi, Initaya and Toyobachi continued talking about medical, maladies, procedures and cures.

The drive was quite long, even though Kiyalee was driving as fast as she could so that she would not have to listen to their conversations any longer than she had to. She was the one who was the most relieved when Toyobachi finally pointed at a building and indicated that this was their destination. After parking the truck, she was the first one out. She looked up at her Team members who had been riding in the back. "If those people are going to discuss more medical *h'oolyach* on the way back···someone else is driving."

15

A T'Mor man came running out of the hospital to greet them. "I was told...I heard...is it true...do you have...have you rediscovered how...?"

Initaya scoffed. "YES...to all of it! WE have rediscovered and manufactured some fresh *Tuzine*. We're here to test it and make sure that we did it correctly."

The T'Mor man started shaking Initaya's hand, would not let go, would not stop shaking her hand and would not shut up. "Wonderful! So wonderful! I'm Doctor Tynong Fathk. I've gathered as many of the people that are here...that are infected with a plethora of different maladies. I'm so glad that you found this drug again and..."

Initaya yanked her hand away. "Yes, Doctor Fathk, we're here to try to cure all ailments, but we're not going to get anything done if all we do is stand here talking."

Team 7016 was unloading the drugs and other equipment from the truck. They had two two-wheel hand trucks loaded with several cases. Kiyalee and Chyning were handling the trucks while Soolchakan and Bonarain kept vigilance with their pulse rifles.

Tynong looked at the weapons. "Is that…really… necessary?"

Hoonsi smiled. "We are talking about a drug that is possibly…of very great value."

Tynong sighed. "Oh well, all right." He motioned for them to follow. "Let's go start treating patients."

The Owlamites followed the T'Mor doctor into the hospital. All of the familiar scents that go with any hospital were all present. There were numerous people who were watching the procession move along with the precious cargo. Numerous people all stared at the boxes with hope and wonder in their eyes and were whispering to others that were next to them.

"We seem to be quite popular," thought Soolchakan. "I hope this stuff works. Otherwise there's gonna be a lot of very upset people···doctors and patients."

Hoonsi responded. "I wish Voolatha were here. She knows more about this stuff than I do, and···I wish she were here."

Initaya chuckled. "Just have a little faith. She followed the formula that we used in the past. I don't think that we're going to have any problems."

They continued to the ward where Tynong Fathk had set up everything for the experiment. He turned and looked back at the procession with wide eyes. "On my right, this is where the female patients are and the males are on the left. I was told that you were informed about…our epidemic…of STD's. That is just one of several bacteriological problems. I have a list of all of the different diseases and we have taken all of the necessary precautions for the ones that can spread by air. We have two patients with…airborne problems."

Hoonsi smiled. "From what we understood, the STD is the biggest problem. Why don't we look at that one first?"

Soolchakan looked around in disgust. "Is it a real necessity for us to stay here? We brought the stuff. Do we still need to guard it?"

"You're here until we say you can go," thought Hoonsi emphatically.

"Again, let's take care of the ones that can show positive results in the fastest manner," said Initaya.

Kiyalee grumbled. "In other words - where's the walking epidemic?"

Hoonsi and Initaya both glared at Kiyalee.

"It is not your place to judge," thought Hoonsi.

Kiyalee just wrinkled her nose at Hoonsi and looked away disgusted.

The doctors were taken to the female side, with Chyning pushing the cart full of pills and other equipment. There were only six patients in this section of the ward. One of the women had one of the airborne diseases and she was staring in a dull manner at the doctors through the glass barrier. The other five were in beds that were in a row, on the other side of the room.

Tynong took them to the first bed. "This one is our promiscuous Moplytak Elf. Her name is Pibber Tooktookoo. From the tests that we've taken, she is currently infected with three different STD's that we know of. One can be cured with the antibiotics that we have on hand. The other two, hopefully the *Tuzine* will do something…nothing else has."

Pibber was sitting in the very middle of the bed with her knees up against her chest and a blanket wrapped around her. The only part of her that could be seen was a small portion of her face which showed some rather angry eyes.

Hoonsi and Initaya looked at her chart.

"I don't see her weight annotated in here," said Hoonsi.

Tynong pointed to a place on the chart. "Right there."

Hoonsi shook her head. "That won't do. The drug is administered according to body weight. I don't know your weight measurement. We're going to have to weigh her on our scale." She turned to Chyning. "Get the scales out."

Chyning scoffed at her. "I'm not a nurse and I'm not your servant. If you want a piece of equipment, you get it yourself. I don't know what half the stuff in these boxes is and if something gets mishandled, it's gonna be your fault. I'm not gonna get blamed for anything that gets busted." She continued staring at the doctors defiantly.

Hoonsi sighed. "She's right. Maybe we should've brought a nurse or two." She smiled at Chyning. "Next time, we'll remember." She pulled two boxes off the top and took the third. She opened the box, pulled the scales out and set it on the floor. She turned to Pibber and smiled. "I need you to stand on the scales so that we can get an accurate weight. That'll determine the proper dosage."

Pibber did not move - other than her angry eyes that looked from one doctor to another.

Tynong leaned closer. "The sooner you cooperate, the sooner you can be cured."

Pibber hung her head. From the movement of the blanket, it was obvious that she had cocooned herself in it and was now having a difficult time getting out of it. Hoonsi was ready to tell Chyning, however, remembered the defiant confrontation and decided to just wait until Pibber got herself out of the predicament. After finally getting out of the blanket, the tiny Elf woman hung her legs over the side of the bed. Tynong hit a lever that was hooked to the bed and the bed lowered. Now, Pibber could get off the bed without having to hop down.

The Moplytak Elf woman was indeed just short of four and a half taja in height. She had a very petite build. Her skin was a uniform dark tan color. Her eyes were darker than her thin hair. Her forehead protruded out much further than would be normal for any Heyyah. Hoonsi had thought, at first, that she had a lot of hair, however, it was actually the size of her head. The portions of her arms and legs that could be seen outside of the hospital gown, had several large sores on them.

Initaya looked at the sores. "That is usually a sign of... later stages of *Soginan*. Is that what she's been diagnosed with?"

Tynong nodded. "*Soginan, Fellstug* and *Byleeshium.*"

"Don't worry, my Dear," said Initaya. "We're going to take good care of you."

Pibber just hung her head.

Hoonsi was doing some figuring on a calculator. "Pibber, how old are you?"

Pibber shrugged. "I was twenty-eight when the flashfire attack hit our city." Her voice sounded high and squeaky.

Initaya frowned. "You don't look much older than that... now."

Tynong chuckled. "It seems that when those Heyyah in Algothon launched that attack, they never dreamed that they'd give most us an incredible longevity. I was sixty-four when the attack hit. Now, I'm well over one hundred and ten...and I feel better than when I was thirty. Considering that, I don't think that age is going to be that important - among the Elf races."

"That attack did come up with some...extraordinary results," said Hoonsi with a smile.

Chyning did a few mental calculations about her age and nearly gagged. She had not thought about it much, however, she realized that she was currently over seventy years old.

Hoonsi and Initaya put their heads together and came up with the dosage that was necessary for Pibber.

Hoonsi opened one of the boxes of pills and checked each bottle for the different unit measurement of each pill. She found the one that she was looking for and pulled it out. "This is for her. Four times a day, she gets two pills. She is to take all of them, no matter what. We'll check her progress every two days."

Initaya smiled at Tynong. "Who's next?"

Team 7016 spent the next "very boring" six days watching the pills they were guarding, dwindle in number as they were being administered to the different patients. Only once during that time did anyone attempt to steal any supplies off of the truck. That was when they found out about another race of Elf that they were not familiar with: Opoteeve. These people were just over seven taja in height, had a very nasty attitude and opinion of other races and had bright green skin. They did not glow like the Zee-Althans had, however the skin color seemed the same. The Opoteeve Elf was given some rather harsh punishment by the Turgon Wall Guard. The Opoteeve tried to blame Team 7016 for his suffering, however, none of the Team felt any guilt about his loud ravings or how he was suffering from the pain of his punishment.

Three days later, Doctors Kolokoko and Lokondon showed up…with four professional nurses. Their truck had a much larger payload of pills, personnel and equipment in it. Chyning got a good giggle about seeing the nurses.

Teams 3406 and 4348 were the guard contingency in this truck.

An Owlam woman walked up to Soolchakan. "Officer

Grade 4, Sondeea, Team Leader for Team 3406."

"Officer Grade 5, Soolchakan, Team Leader for Team 7016. Welcome to the Turgon Wall."

Sondeea snickered. "I've been here before. Remember when we fought the Sodle?"

"Yes, but now…it's a little more tolerable. The only attacks are the Turgons…and that's rather random."

"Have you heard…or seen any of these attacks?"

He chuckled. "I heard an alarm south of here, four days ago. Our mission is to protect the drugs from getting into the wrong hands. We don't worry about the Turgons."

She smiled. "That's true. I understand that…someone did try something…a few days ago…an Elf called an…Opo…uh…"

"Opoteeve!"

"Yeah, that's it. What happened?"

"He tried to sneak up here and steal anything he could off of the truck. In all this time, Kiyalee still remembers and feels very strongly about protecting her truck…and its contents."

"What happened to the Opoteeve?"

"He has large bruises on his stomach, groin and the entire left side of his face. Kiyalee can kick…very hard."

She snickered. "I've heard. I also heard from Dozzell that the attempted theft was something arranged by the Algothon spies."

Soolchakan huffed and closed his eyes. "Why does that NOT surprise me?" He looked at her and shook his head. "So, are we going to be needed…to assist you in guarding this new shipment, or are there some more reinforcements coming up?"

"The other reinforcements should be here…shortly after midday. As soon as they get here…Team 7016 is relieved…and you can go home."

He sighed. "Thank you…*very* much."

"Before you leave, check with Ota…in Algothon."

He looked at her confused. "Uh…why?"

"She'll check the monitors at Algothon. If no one there is looking, you can go ahead and Jump back to Owlam…instead of having to make that long, boring drive."

He smiled. "I will definitely check with Ota. Question is though, why should anyone in Algothon be looking at us…when we're leaving the Wall…headed home?"

"According to Ota, some of the Algothons want their trucks back."

"How rude!" He rolled his eyes. "That's just being… selfish."

"Oh…I was meaning to ask…have you heard anything about how the *Tuzine* is working?"

"I can't tell from the beaks on those bird faces, but everyone else is all smiles. Apparently it's working just fine. I don't think they would've asked for a second batch…if it wasn't doing its job." He pointed to the doctors as they were conversing. "Look at Hoonsi and Initaya. "They're giving all kinds of smiling reports to Kolokoko and Lokondon. Those nurses seem to be smiling real big as well."

Sondeea nodded. "Have you come across many other Elf races?"

He shrugged. "We have to keep our eyes on the truck. We're not to go up there to help any fighting on the wall, because some inmate might get frisky and try to steal the truck. We did get a look at that walking epidemic though. There's this Moplytak woman who would have sex with anyone…as long as they help protect her husband in any Turgon attack."

"What do they look like?"

"Somewhat dark skin, dark hair, about four and a half taja high…"

"Only four…and a half?"

"Yup! They also have…an oversized forehead…er…the whole head really."

"Any others?"

"Well there was that Opoteeve. Just over seven taja and green skin. Then there's this bunch that they have here, helping the guards and administration at the wall. They're called Shan-Kawdar. They're about seven taja in height, they've got very dark skin. Not as dark as the Sodle were, and…they have no lips. They have…a mouth like…those shelled reptiles that you've probably seen pictures of. They don't chew, they just bite the food off…and swallow it whole. Those…carapace lips…look like they could cut through bone.”

“What are they like?”

He growled. “Picky, picky, picky, picky, picky! Whenever you’re around them, you MUST adhere to ALL rules, to the letter! I’d like to slap them…hard…several times. I doubt that they have a clue as to what ‘having fun’ is all about.”

“They’re really that strict?”

“I wouldn’t be surprised if they have specific rules on how, when, where and why you can get sick…or pick your nose.”

Sondeea sighed. “It takes all kinds.”

He grunted.

The next truck showed up. Another doctor, two more nurses and two more Teams that would be guarding the drugs. Team 7016 was informed that they could go home.

Team 7016 climbed up in the truck. “Officer Leader, Ota, this is Officer, Soolchakan, can you hear me?”

The response was surprisingly quick. “Officer, Soolchakan, this is Ota. I hear you. I’m also warning you about an ambush that the Algothons have planned for you.”

“Really? Well, I wish a nasty pox on the rotten soulless *bimyocks*.”

"Just head on out and I'll let you know when you have to get ready for the ambush. It's not close to the Wall. You're going to have to go a little ways before you get there."

"But you will keep us informed."

"Oh absolutely. I'm sitting here in one of the control centers and I can hardly wait to see their reaction···when we foul their plans up."

"Okay, Team 7016 is heading out···and standing by for···any helpful information."

With a full tank of gas and some rations in the truck for the trip, Team 7016 headed south, back to Owlam. They did drive for quite some time. The sun started going down.

Bonarain looked around. "She wasn't joking when she said that it wasn't close."

Chyning huffed. "They probably wanted it this way so that no one'll hear any shooting."

"I don't know about that," said Soolchakan. "We did pass a small village…just a few moments ago."

"Team 7016, this Ota···SLOW DOWN!"

Kiyalee was startled at first, however, she did let off the accelerator. "I'm listening."

"Good! All personnel, Team Algothon, Special Ambush Team and Team 7016···get ready for 'Operation: Mayhem'. Is there anyone who is not ready?"

A single response came back from a female. "WILL YOU PLEASE HURRY UP···THIS···GYAAACH···SNAKE···IT···IT WON'T STOP SLITHERING! Oh how I hate these nasty things!"

Ota sat there somewhat shocked. "Who is this?"

"This is···Officer Grade 7, Tangga! I'm the one stuck with this···oh you nasty little···the snake! Will you please hurry···so I can get rid of this HORRIBLE···thing?"

"Who assigned you to handle the snake?"

"This is Officer Grade 4, Tandani, Team Leader of Team 5051. I'm the one who made her handle the snake. She messed up an assignment and I told her that if she messes this up, the snake would be the least of her problems."

Ota tried desperately to NOT give the impression that she was laughing. "All right. Position the snake! Team 7016, hop to Spy···NOW!" She did a quick three count. "Drop the snake, NOW!"

"THANK YOU!"

Soolchakan held his hand up to the women. He did the hop for the truck and everyone in it. "Done, Sir. Team 7016 is in Spy!"

Ota sat there looking up at the lights. She heard a rather loud bang and the lights, plus everything else electrical in the room, went dark. She heard several shouts of surprise and a few nasty curses. "Special Ambush Team···hit 'em···now!"

"Done, Sir."

"Team 7016, stop when you get a signal from Zhanzhee, of Team 7013."

"How am I supposed to···oh···I think that's her. Yes···it is her···okay, Sir, we've stopped."

Ota let her breath out quickly and smiled. "Officer, Zhanzhee, how did it go?"

"This is Zhanzhee. There were twelve of them and twelve of us. It took less than a heartbeat and the situation is completely under control."

"Okay, good! Officers, Onggot and Tolosk, how is it going there?"

"This is Officer, Onggot. We can keep these *Bimyocks* dancing with problems as long as you like."

"Good! Wait until you get a call from Zhanzhee. They've got to position the bodies and then we can allow them to turn the power back on."

"Yes, Sir, not a problem."

Kiyalee stopped the truck. They were on a road that had been cut through a large hill. "We got walls on each side that're higher than the truck. This'd be a perfect chokepoint for an ambush."

"I think that's what the Algothons had in mind," said Soolchakan. He looked up. "You could attack someone and shoot down from both sides and not have any of your people in danger of being hit."

Zhanzhee walked up to the truck. "Hello, Officer Grade 5, Zhanzhee, Team Leader, Team 7013. I was the one leading my Team along with Teams 7014 and 7015. We ambushed the ambushers. Now, they want us to position the bodies, so that it looks like they screwed up badly in trying to ambush you."

"How, nice," said Soolchakan in a droll manner.

Zhanzhee smiled. "They told us to kill eleven of them. The last one…once they turn the power back on and they're able to see you…from the flying cameras, they'll see your Team dispatching the last one. I've got a little script for you…that I'll send to you… and you can put on a show for them."

"Huh," said Chyning. "Why should we need some silly script?"

Zhanzhee cleared her throat in an admonishing manner. "These people have some…special communication devices. They're in direct communication with someone back in Algothon. We've killed them, but not the devices. The script is so that we can cause some more confusion for the Algothons…as far as who is stealing all of their equipment."

Chyning sighed. "Yes, Sir."

"Zhanzhee, this is Ota, are you ready yet?"

"This is Zhanzhee, you can turn the power back on when you're ready."

Ota smiled. "Onggot, help them start that thing."

"This is Onggot⋯done!"

"Team 7016, hop back to Home and get ready to put on a show."

"This is Soolchakan, we're ready."

MEANWHILE: While all of that coordinating was going on, the Algothons were having some very different conversations.

Prominent Investigator Hashasee was watching the main wall monitor. They had one of the satellites aimed directly at the ambush team that was going to retake one of the missing trucks. The ambush team had reported that they heard the truck approaching. Then there was a loud bang and all power in the room went off. They were sitting there, in a very dark room, staring at blank monitors. The only light was from an emergency light on the wall. As soon as the main power was cut off, the emergency lights would come on automatically.

Hashasee growled. "Where's my power? I need to see what's going on...get the power back on...NOW!"

One of the supervisor technicians, in the room, shook his head. "The back-up generator...it should've...kicked in... already!"

She snarled back at him. "Well it looks like it didn't. Somebody get down there, with a handheld radio and find out what the holdup is...I need to find out what's going on in North Chilamte."

Two men got up. One grabbed a handheld radio the other grabbed a flashlight and they headed out of the room.

Hashasee sat there fuming as she waited...very impatiently.

A voice came through the handheld. *"The emergency generator is out of fuel. The tank is completely dry."*

Hashasee glared at the supervisor with pure hate in her eyes. "OUT OF FUEL?"

The supervisor just stood there sputtering, making some rather unintelligible noises, not sure what to say or how.

Hashasee picked up her handheld. "Don't just sit there… fill it up!"

"Yes, Sir."

She sat there stewing for a few more moments. She keyed the handheld again. "What's taking so long down there?"

"Sir, we have to prime it before we can start it. The thing was completely dry."

She growled in a rather loud (and unladylike manner). "DO IT!" She sat there snarling and thinking very nasty thoughts. The power started to come back on, there was a flutter and it went dead again. "NOW WHAT?"

"Uh…Sir…the fuel line…broke. There's a mechanic here. He said that he can get the thing working again…very quickly, but he's going to have to watch it very closely, in order to keep it running."

Hashasee keyed the handheld. "I don't care if he has to wet-nurse the *fliggit* thing. Get it working…and KEEP it working."

"Yes, Sir."

She huffed and leaned back in her chair.

Several moments later the lights fluttered again and then came on. The monitors started coming back up as well. Technicians started rapidly making the necessary entries on their keypads to reestablish the link with the satellite.

The main monitor came on and was focused on the ambush site. The shoulders of everyone in the room sagged simultaneously as they all saw what was on the screen. None of the ambush team were where they were supposed to be. Eleven of them appeared to be dead or wounded so badly that they weren't moving. The twelfth was being kicked savagely by one of the female Owlams. She pulled her power pistol out and fired at the downed man six times.

Chyning stood there with her pistol still aimed at the man. "Are you finally dead, you *chokwad*?"

Soolchakan walked over to her with his pistol ready. "What's the matter?"

"He wouldn't die," shouted Chyning!

Soolchakan looked at the other two women. "Are any of the others still alive?"

"I don't think so," said Bonarain. "I've given them all a hard kick to the throat…just to make sure."

Kiyalee huffed. "Who are these people?"

"I don't know," said Soolchakan. "At first, I thought it might be some Galsinos, trying to take the truck back. Now that

I can see them…none of them are Galsinos. They all look like regular Heyyah."

"So they're not Galsinos," said Bonarain. "So…who are they? Who else would want the truck?"

Chyning shrugged. "They're probably just a bunch of thieves. They didn't know what we had and they just wanted to steal…whatever they could get their hands on."

Kiyalee clicked her tongue. "Should we collect the bodies and report this…to…somebody?"

"Collect their ammunition…but not the bodies," said Soolchakan. "We'll leave the bodies here. If someone wants to… look at the bodies, they can come out here and see for themselves. I'm not ready to haul a bunch of dead bleeding bodies in the truck. No telling what it would take to clean the truck…or how it'd smell…after a hot day." He sighed. "Let's just get the guns, look for any identification…and report it…whenever we find someone who might be interested."

Hashasee shut the monitor off. She got up and slowly walked out of the room, mumbling a few obscenities on the way out.

Ota sighed. `"Mission accomplished."`

One year later, Hashasee was to receive a completed report on all of the findings, from all of the investigators, concerning the disastrous failure of the attempted taking of the truck and the simultaneous failure of all of the equipment. She called the other

Prominents in for the briefing.

"Give us all the bad news," said Hashasee. "All of us at one time, so none of us have to repeat this disaster."

There were several Owlamites at the briefing...in Spy.

High Investigator Kilmix cleared his throat. "Where the problem started...was of course with the power failure at the Junjon relay station. It seems, from some organic material that was found on a destroyed transformer, a snake, somehow, crawled up the power pole to a transformer. It got up on top of the transformer...and...apparently its head hit one connection... the tail hit another...it formed a completed circuit...and caused a catastrophic overload in the transformer. The snake was fried in the process and the transformer exploded. The resulting shrapnel took out ten of the other eleven transformers at the relay station."

Tun sat there with his mouth wide open. "A...*SNAKE*?!"

Kilmix smiled weakly. "Yes, a snake. Since that incident, the power company has put some bands around the lower section of all of the poles...to prevent any kind of incident like this repeating itself."

Tangga was sitting in the briefing. "Oh that...oh that horrible little beast." Her entire body shuddered with revulsion and she sat there rubbing her arms all over herself, while other sounds of complete disgust were coming out of her mouth. "HATE those things!"

"Shut up," snapped Ota!

Kilmix continued. "As you know, a reptile will go to the

warmest place that it can find. The transformers are usually very warm…so…it did a slither climb up the pole and tried to find the best place on the transformer to…keep itself warm."

Hashasee snarled. "That explains the relay station mess that shut off the power. Go on."

"Yes, Sir," said Kilmix. "Now the emergency generator. The four personnel who were supposed to make sure that ALL of the generators were ready to start, at a moment's notice, have been fired. Why the fuel tank, on that specific generator, was empty, none of them could give any credible answer. All of the logs were checked off at the proper intervals, however, when it was needed, the fuel tank on that one was completely empty as well as the fuel lines. After they got some fuel in the tank, to start it, they had to prime the fuel lines. As soon as they did that, the connection from the fuel pump…broke…from metal fatigue."

Ota looked at Onggot. "Good job!"

Onggot smiled at her. "Thank you, Sir."

Kladoothik shook his head. "How does…a fuel pump break…from metal fatigue?"

Kilmix shrugged. "Sir, it seems that…where the hose is connected to it with the clamp…it somehow just…broke off and sent fuel spewing all over the place."

Ota looked at Onggot. "How did you do that?"

Onggot snickered. "You just take a small portion of the thing into Observation…and move it. Then you hop it back."

Hashasee shook her head. "So why didn't they just switch us to another generator? There are ten of those things down there."

Kilmix cleared his throat and shook his head. "It seems that…when the technician went over to do…just that…he tripped over a cable…and disconnected…all of them."

Beeshree scoffed. "Those connections are supposed to be strong enough to take something like that, aren't they?"

Kilmix shrugged. "They're supposed to be able to take that kind of punishment….but…for some reason…this one didn't."

Tolosk haughtily shook his head back and forth. "They're supposed to be able to take it, but I disconnected them, you *Bimyock*!"

Ota chuckled. "Quiet! I want to hear this."

Hashasee hung her head. "All of them…disconnected."

"Yes, Sir," said Kilmix sadly. "It took them…longer than expected to reconnect…because it was such a mess…when he tripped and pulled them loose."

Hashasee sat there with her teeth clenched. "So all that time we were electronically dead, and blind, waiting for the power to come back on…it was because of an empty fuel tank, metal fatigue, negligence…and an adventurous snake?"

Tun shook his head. "So that explains the problems here. What about that ambush? What went wrong there?"

Kilmix let out a growl of his own. "THAT…is something completely different. Unfortunately, because we were not able to observe what happened…we can only guess. Before the power went off, we saw all twelve of our specialists, exactly where they were supposed to be. Then the power went out. When the power came back on…the twelve were…NOT where they were supposed to be…eleven of them were dead and we were able to witness the death of the twelfth." He shook his head. "What happened that got them out of position? We haven't been able to come up with any feasible theory. How did the Owlams kill all twelve, without suffering any injury? That one is a complete, mind-boggling mystery? Since we don't have the bodies…we can't do any autopsies…and again…we can only guess."

Tun clenched his fists. "And no one has come up with any acceptable guess?"

"Everything borders on insanity or complete violations of the laws of physics," said Kilmix. "The only thing that we're sure of…whatever they did…they did the wrong thing…all of them."

Hashasee sighed despondently. "What about that conversation afterwards…what have you gleaned from that?"

Kilmix shook his head. "We're no closer than we were before. According to what the spies at the Turgon Wall got…the Owlams obtained the truck because of a failed raid by Galsinos. How did the Galsinos get the truck? Everything still says teleportation…but we *still* haven't seen how they do it. That…act of vandalism…in the archives…the only way that they could have possibly…infiltrated that room…without anyone seeing them, the act of teleportation is the only way…unless you believe in magic. We've never been able to register any form of power surge, or anomalous power fluctuation and there would have to be some kind of power…THING occur…that we could see or read with our instruments, *somewhere*. They're using teleportation…we just haven't been able to find out how. We also still haven't ruled out any innocence on the part of the Owlams."

Tun hung his head. "So we're still stuck in neutral. Is it the Galsinos or is it the Owlams?"

Kilmix cleared his throat. "Uh…Sirs, there was one of the Chief Investigators who came up with a theory…that it was…a completely different race of Elf who is doing all of this. This…unknown…culprit…is, or has been, constantly leading us astray, pointing us at both the Galsinos and Owlams." He cleared his throat again nervously. "This might be why we…haven't been able to nail it down to…one or the other…because there is a third party."

Tun closed his eyes. "Oh shut up."

Hashasee sighed. "Thank you for muddying the water even further. We wanted a briefing on what is known about that disaster with the truck and our power company. Please, unless you have some solid proof, keep that kind of theory to yourself."

"I'm sorry, Sirs," said Kilmix. "I thought…that you should be made aware…of any theory…and…well…I'm sorry."

"You're dismissed," said Hashasee.

Kilmix smiled and bowed slightly as he backed out of the room.

Beeshree slouched down in her chair. "I thought of that…

third party, some time ago. I just didn't have any proof of it, so… that's why I kept my mouth shut. We can't just…brush it off to the side because…there is a possibility. No matter how remote, the possibility exists. Diverting the attention of the enemy is…and always has been…a very effective tactic in defeating an enemy. We were focused on the Owlams. All of a sudden, when we got ready to go and…eradicate the Owlams…the Galsino pop up. Now, we have the Owlams…of which we've never been sure of their numbers. We have the Galsino…whom we cannot find any large collection of them in any one place. And the possibility of a third party that could be playing us, in two or three ways."

Tun opened his eyes and stared at her in a dull manner. "So…how do you prove any of it? Whoever is doing the playing… is very good at it."

"We have to get smarter than our enemy and the puppets of the enemy," said Hashasee.

Kladoothik chuckled. "If you get smarter than the puppeteer, you're automatically smarter than the puppets."

Hashasee smiled at Kladoothik. "Yes, but, the question still remains: Are we smarter than the puppets…yet?"

Ota sat there chuckling. "You're not smarter than the puppeteers, that's for sure. You can't even figure out who the puppeteers are."

"You're being very facetious," said Nachichi.

Ota chuckled even harder. "Yes, and I'm enjoying every moment of it. These people bombed us out. They wanted to conquer and enslave us. Instead, we have them running in circles. It feels good."

The Staff was called to the conference room.

Holla looked around confused. "Who called us here?"

"I don't know," said Ahandi.

Doctor Kazkim walked into the room. "I was the one who sent out the call. I thought that you might like a report on how we're doing with the *Tuzine*."

"Oh," said Holla. "Yes, that would be nice. Everybody have a seat and let's hear the report."

All eyes went to Kazkim.

Kazkim smiled. "The reports that we heard from the Turgon Wall are very encouraging. We stepped up production as soon as we heard the news. It's having a wonderful effect on *all* bacterium. There are several of our allies who are rather upset that it doesn't do anything with viruses, however, we did inform them that it is not an antiviral." He chuckled. "I have heard that several of them suggested that we go the route of trying to find an antiviral that's as powerful as the *Tuzine*. I wish I knew how to go about that…but…while I am a doctor, I'm not a chemist who dabbles in that form of experimentation and invention of pharmaceuticals." He sighed. "Wish I were."

Hadathoo leaned forward grinning. "Are we going to be able to export our treasure…to other continents…and get rich off of the trade?"

Kazkim shrugged. "I'm not a salesman. I'm also not a diplomat. It'll take someone who's good at bartering to get us all rich off the profits of export. Right now, our main problem will, of course, be trying to keep up with the demand. We've moved several plants to the gorge. The soil there is more to their liking and they are growing much faster there."

Shyshee squawked. "But, if we…if the Algothons see a bunch of plants…in neat rows…won't they be able to figure it out?"

Kazkim shook his head. "Oh no! We've taken the precaution of putting those plants, along with their soil, into Spy dimension. The sun still shines in Spy, so the plants are getting plenty of sunlight. We're having to move a lot of water into Spy in order to keep the soil wet…"

Teelila sat there with her nose out of joint. "Are the men doing their job…watering…the plants the *special* way?"

"Oh, yes," said Kazkim. "Some of them are consuming enormous amounts of water in order to do it, but they're doing their job…keeping the plants well fertilized."

Wilfadge snickered. "Let me know where I can be… *utilized*…the most…for the welfare of the plants that is."

Most of the women glared at the grinning Wilfadge. Hadathoo looked up at the ceiling trying not to laugh.

Hashasee stood up with fire in her eyes. "You're telling me...that the Owlams...have found out the secret formula for... *Tuzine*?"

High Investigator Skokom sighed. "Yes, Sir. According to the doctor here, the Owlams took the drug to the Turgon Wall, to test it on some of the inmates. The results have been, according to the people at the Wall, an overwhelming success."

Hashasee looked at the doctor that was standing next to Skokom. "Have you seen the reports?"

Doctor Klindybo stammered several times, cleared his throat several times and had to do several things in order to control his breathing."

"That was a yes/no question, doctor," said Hashasee through her teeth.

Klindybo swallowed hard. "Yuh...yes...yes, Sir...I've... read the reports...from the spies."

Hashasee sat down slowly. "And according to the reports... it could NOT be anything BUT...real *Tuzine*?"

Klindybo shook his head rapidly. "No...no, no, no, it couldn't be anything...but real...*Tuzine*...Sir. If these reports *are* accurate...only *Tuzine* could have affected...the diseases listed...so thoroughly. No other drug...ever cured *Byleeshium* completely. *Byleeshium*, when treated with other drugs...just goes dormant. The patient still has outbreaks of...some rather nasty looking sores on their skin. When the sores are there, the disease is contagious and must be treated again. With *Tuzine*, the

Byleeshium is completely destroyed."

Hashasee closed her eyes in confusion. "How could anyone tell if the disease...is either dormant or destroyed?"

Klindybo chuckled nervously. "Oh...by...blood tests... of course. You take a sample of blood...or saliva...subject it to three different chemicals...and then look at the sample under a microscope. If the bacteria is still present, it now glows a sort of neon blue...very easy to spot...under the microscope. If you don't see any of the bacteria...you know that the patient has been cured. I read the report and it does state that they repeated the test on several patients after treating them. All of them came up negative for *Byleeshium*. This IS *Tuzine!*"

Hashasee smiled. "Thank you for the report. You're both dismissed." After the two men departed, she picked the microphone up. "Did all of you hear that?"

Kladoothik, Tun and Beeshree walked into the office.

Beeshree shook her head. "How can those people be so lucky?"

Tun laughed out loud. "Don't you see? This is a wonderful opportunity for us!"

Beeshree slapped him on the back. "Have you gone crazy?"

He snarled back at her. "We now have a GOOD reason for sending an emissary to Owlam. We can send someone there, along with everyone else. We can set up an office...somewhere near Owlam and use it as a relay station for any information that we can find out, by having someone there, gleaning any information that they can obtain."

Beeshree looked startled as she thought about what he said. She finally just said: "Oh."

"Yes," said Kladoothik. "We set up a relay station. Who do we send to be *our* representative?"

"We send a High Investigator," said Hashasee. "Maybe two. This way we'll be able to establish a communication site there as well." She grinned. "And it'll all be legitimate. We'll have to come up with a special code - one that talks about that stupid drug...along with buying it. This is good."

"So," said Tun. "Who do we send?"

Hashasee smiled. "We don't *send* anybody. We get two volunteers. A person who goes there...voluntarily...usually does a better job."

"I'll go ask for volunteers," said Kladoothik.

16

Two High Investigators headed for North Chilamte. They were Eestya and Choya. The two women volunteered readily for the opportunity to go to the city of Owlam and try to obtain any information that would give Algothon definitive evidence about those Owlams.

While Eestya wanted to get out of Algothon because of a bad relationship, Choya just wanted to get to Owlam and find the truth. Is it the Owlams or is it the Galsino that are causing no end to the nightmares that are happening in Algothon? She had heard, all her life, that there was some sinister force that was moving against Algothon and no one was sure what the origin of this force was. The primary clues were Owlam and Galsino. Two cities that were very close to each other, geographically. She was going there to find *Tuzine* and any evidence that she could to get a final answer. If she could get a definitive answer, maybe she could get promoted ahead of her peers to Prominent Investigator. That thought always made her smile.

Eestya was the ranking one in the group. There were four Chief Investigators in the group: Awndool, Prok, Sarskatama and Jeedokt. They also had four Investigators and four Investigator Trainees.

They also had some sixty military personnel in the entourage going to Owlam. They were going to Owlam on the legitimate business of obtaining *Tuzine*. Any shipment of the drug had to be guarded as if it were gold. This powerful antibiotic was the cure for every bacterium that had been discovered so far and no one wanted to see it destroyed or stolen. They just wanted to get their hands on it, chemically analyze it and try to produce it themselves. So far no one had been successful at any reproduction.

The group had boarded a ship…manufactured by someone other than the Algothon shipwrights. They were all wearing an outfit of neutral gray. Choya had gone to a central library and researched the trade routes and activities of people in the past who had bartered for *Tuzine*, some fifty-three years in the past. The Algothon people had only themselves to blame for the disappearance of the drug, seeing as how the manufacturing of the drug ceased on the very same day of the mass launch of the nuclear weapons.

Eestya looked out over the ocean from the deck of the ship and stretched. She had heard all kinds of rumors about how romantic it was on the high seas. All she could see, so far, was that she was bored to tears and many of the military personnel were spending most of their time turning green and carrying a bucket around with them wherever they went.

Choya came out on the deck to stretch as well. She was carrying one of the several books that she had brought with them.

Eestya looked back out over the endless ocean and sighed. "What're you doing up here? Seeing as how the sun is going down, there's not enough light to read. Better lighting in the cabin."

Choya chuckled. "I didn't even remember bringing it with me. I've been reading so much on the trade routes and what was being used for barter that…it just seems a part of me now."

Eestya frowned. "How many books can there possibly be on one trade route?"

Choya laughed. "It's not that they're instructional books. They're diaries of the people who participated in the trading business."

"The people in charge made daily log entries…so what. How could that be interesting at all?"

"It's not just the people in charge. Yes, the group leaders had log books. There were also people in the group that kept their own diary and that's what I've been reading. They were much more observant of the surrounding area and people than the group leaders. The leaders were only interested in making annotations of the business…and any troublemakers in their specific group. Yes, that's boring. The observations, hopes and dreams of the other people in the group…much more enlightening."

Eestya scoffed. "Maybe I should read a couple of those."

"According to the Commander of this floating city, it's going to be another twenty-five days before we get to that port on North Chilamte. It's going to take another six days to drive to Owlam. I think that you might have plenty of time to read…at least two or three."

"Got any recommendations…as far as who gives the best

information?"

Choya giggled. "You'll have to steal that one from Chief Investigator Prok. My first suggestion, however, is to go ahead and read one of the log books from one of the expeditions."

"I already have," snarled Eestya. "I didn't learn anything that I couldn't have figured out on my own."

Choya sighed. "All right, let's go take a look at some of the others. At least on the pages of a book...the words change from page to page and that gives a change of...something." She pointed out to sea. "That scenery...hasn't changed for three days."

Natsa watched the two Algothon women go back inside. She turned to her colleagues. "Team 82, what do you think so far?"

Osskood shook his head. "I think that they're on a mission of trade. They're also on a mission of espionage. They want, and need, the drug. They also desperately want to answer the question about who is fouling things in Algothon."

"I agree," said Siy. She snickered. "So many military personnel is an indication that they want to buy some of the drug... and *keep* it. The Investigators...they're going to stay, acting like they're bartering, and try to beg, borrow, steal or kill for any information that they can find."

Eesteesee grunted in disgust. She looked out over the ocean. "I don't trust them at all. Maybe they're trading honestly, but they're still spies. You don't send a spy to do the trading, you send a trader. No, their primary...is espionage."

Investigator Shiganeea was in her bunk trying to read one of the diaries that Choya had supplied. She was trying to do anything that might get her mind off of how seasick she was. When she had boarded this thing back at the port, she had thrown up twice before the ship left the dock. She had memorized the path from her cabin to the aft portion of the ship where she had to dump her "catch bucket". She had thrown up so many times that she could make the trip in the dark.

Chief Investigator Prok walked in the cabin without knocking. He had that smug smile on his face. "I can help you with your problem on this ship. I can really get your mind off of being seasick…with a different kind of…" His smile got bigger. "…rocking."

She shook her head. "You were disgusting back at the port, before I got on this big tin monster and you're even more revolting now."

He chuckled. "Come on, there's got to be something I can do for you…to make you feel better."

She swung her legs over the side of the bunk, quickly grabbed the "catch bucket" and smacked him in the side of the head. He fell to the floor groaning. She held the bucket up high, ready to strike again. "If you don't get out of here, I'm going to report you to Sarskatama…or Eestya or Choya. I don't have any reason to get…*close*…to you." She snickered. "I have to admit though, I do feel better, now that I've clobbered you with a puke bucket."

He got back to his feet, feeling the painful bump on the left side of his head. He pulled his hand back from the bump and saw blood in his palm. "You're gonna be sorry for that."

"Oh...SHUT UP...before I give you a matching bump on the other side." She held the bucket up a little higher.

Prok backed out, watching to make sure that he was ready if she did swing. He closed the door and turned to his left...to see Zogits and Toywhall standing there chortling at him.

Zogits shook his head. "When're you going to learn?"

"We all know why you're here," said Toywhall. "You caught...or gave that *Byleeshium* to Meesa and Banayeet. You're going there to get a bottle of *Tuzine* for yourself. Do you actually think that any woman is going to get cuddly with you...before you get dosed?"

The two men passed by Prok and went on their way, still chuckling over the situation.

After they disappeared around a corner, Prok stood there still seething with anger. "I'm gonna make all of you sorry...for the way you're treating me," he whispered. "You're all gonna be sorry." He staggered back to his cabin to nurse his wound.

Officer Grade 6, Brosk, of Team 6863, stood there (in Spy) watching Prok. "I wonder what he means by that." He clicked his tongue. "Do you have some other sinister plan in mind at our new...Trading Outpost? Yeah, I wonder."

Holla was walking along (in Spy) looking around at the area where a new thriving village was sprouting up, just northeast of the walls of Owlam. This was THE trading village. All trading was going to be done here and no one was going to be allowed inside the walls of the city - unless you were a citizen of Owlam.

The number of new races that had been created by the genetic bombs (as they were being called now) was intriguing. The Hospaltik were seven and a half taja tall with ebony skin and incredibly long arms. They could almost drag their knuckles without leaning over. The Pok-To were four and a half taja in height, had pale green skin and were all hunchbacks. The Yathar-Sar had dark brown skin, stood just over seven taja and had long thin body fur that appeared to be all over. Niyniy was cataloging all of the different races, if for no other reason, find out the "who, what, how and where" of these other survivors of the nuclear holocaust.

Many of these traders had not paid full attention to the pamphlets that had gone out from Owlam, in regards to trading for the *Tuzine*. Gold, silver and trinkets were not what Owlam was interested in. Seed! Seed for grains, seed for fruits, seed for vegetables - SEED! Seeds were more precious than any shiny metals or pretty trinkets and baubles. At the stations where the trading took place, there was a large sign. On it, was the list of things that would not be traded for or had very little value. Also on the sign was the fact that seed was more important than anything else as far as trade value. Holla knew that with the dimension hopping capability, they could have any and all seeds that they wanted. Better to trade for them. This would raise a lot fewer questions, once they started growing crops of their own.

She headed for the lines where traders had come to barter for the drug. She walked slowly along the lines and stopped in horror. In line number fourteen, she saw two Galsino men standing there.

She Jumped to the booth at the head of line fourteen. She quickly checked the roster to see who was on duty at that booth. "Officer Leader, Tadesha, this is Supreme Officer, Holla. Have you looked down the line? You have two Galsinos standing there in line."

Tadesha giggled. "If you'd been here earlier, you would've seen two Teltermak as well. Yes, we're trading with anyone, until you say otherwise. We did make the Teltermak pay dearly···and we're going to make those Galsino pay dearly as well. Do you have any objections?"

Holla pondered for a moment. "No, that'd make us look like···I don't even want to think it. Go ahead and trade··· hard···with them."

Tadesha smiled.

Officer Leader, Till was livid. Here he was bartering for seeds with someone from a place called Kawder-Ayin. The people were seven taja in height, very dark brown skin and their eyeballs were completely black. It was almost as infuriating as talking to the Sodle and wondering if they were looking directly at you. They did have some very good grain and fruit seed so the negotiations were short and very rewarding. He still wanted to get back to reading all of the information on the possibility of extraterrestrial life. He could not, because here he was stuck at station seventeen, involved in trade talks with…others.

Eestya wanted to start shooting all of the people in line ahead of her. She was a High Investigator, seventh in line of rank for the next promotion. She should not have to be waiting in line for anyone. She looked up at that infuriating sign that showed that seeds were more important than any gold or silver bars, trinkets, baubles or partial machinery. She frowned. *Partial* machinery? Then she understood. 'Today, I'll trade for a crankshaft. Tomorrow, I'll trade for a piston.' Either bring the entire piece of equipment or forget it. She sighed. She had twenty heavy bags of different types of grain seed along with several bags for melon vines and some fruit trees.

The line moved slowly. Eestya had to have relief from Sarskatama for a while, Choya for a while and Shiganeea for a while. She had an aversion to trusting any of the men with holding the place in line. She only needed them to move the heavy bags… if or when they were able to move forward.

Finally she was behind only one trading group. They called themselves: Raffa. They were nearly nine taja in height. Their skin was an unusual shade of light tan. Otherwise, they would have passed for normal Heyyah. The Raffa had several bags of seeds that they had tagged. The Raffa man read off the names of the seeds in the bags. The Owlam woman did not seem very interested…until the Raffa mentioned kwatha. She saw that the Owlam woman was *very* interested in kwatha. Eestya made sure that her bag of kwatha seed was brought up first.

Holla checked the roster. Booth number eight was currently being handled by Officer Leader, Yamananee. "Officer, Yamananee, this is Holla. Did you know that, behind these Raffa, there is a group from Algothon?"

Yamananee showed no emotion as she weighed the bag of seed that she was currently bartering for. "I'm aware of those *Bimyocks*. Did you have something special in mind?"

"Trade very hard with them. Don't give up much to these *Doovofts*. I wish that we could turn them down, but···that might raise some suspicions."

"I'll do what I can."

"Thank you."

The Raffa finally left with eight cases of the *Tuzine*, along with the instruction pamphlet, and smiles on their faces.

Eestya faced the Owlam woman with a smile. "I heard, while you were talking to that last bunch…you have a keen interest in kwatha."

Yamananee looked up and smiled weakly. "Oh *h'oolyach*! What do I do now?"

Holla sighed. "Get us some kwatha."

"Yes," said Yamananee politely. "We've been looking for kwatha, among other things."

Eestya signaled Investigator Trainee Bossix. He picked

the heavy bag up and nearly dropped it on the table. The wood cracked slightly beneath the weight of the bag.

Yamananee's eyes got wide when she saw the size of the bag. She looked back at her Team member, Oreesk. He sighed and walked up to the table to assist in weighing the bag.

Oreesk and Bossix wrestled the bag onto the scales and everyone watched until the needle finally stopped moving.

Holla grunted. "Oh, *h'oolyach*! That bag is worth four cases of Tuzine, by itself."

Yamananee smiled as she made the annotation. "We'll take that bag of kwatha for four cases of *Tuzine*."

Eestya shrugged and nodded. 'Decent start,' she thought.

Yamananee looked at the collection of bags. "What else do you have for trade?"

Eestya looked at the first tag. "I've got some grain seed here, for *Joolila*."

Yamananee typed in the name on her computer. "Oh, I'm afraid that we can't use that one."

"Uh…why not?"

"According to this information…you can't grow *Joolila* this far north. We'd have to go at least seven hundred kilotaja south of here, in order to be able to plant a crop of that."

Eestya was momentarily stunned by this information. Algothon was on a different parallel than Owlam. It was much further south and certain crops needed certain climactic conditions in order to grow. This might be a problem. "I have..." She checked the next tag as Bossix removed the *Joolila* bag. "... *Maktag Beans*."

Yamananee shook her head again. "That's another southern crop."

Eestya clenched her teeth. "Okay, I have some...*Pilkati*."

Yamananee grimaced. "That's a crop for even further south than the *Maktag Beans*."

Eestya went to the next bag. She looked up hopefully. "*Kushkani* Melons?"

Yamananee's jaw dropped. "*Kushkani* Melons?" She went to her computer. She typed it in. The information came up and she smiled. "That one is acceptable."

Bossix heaved the bag up on the table. Again it took both Bossix and Oreesk moving it to get it centered on the scale.

"I want six cases of drugs for that bag," said Eestya.

Yamananee smiled. "I'll have to check the quality of the seed, before I can authorize six cases." She looked back behind her. "Shondana, quality check!"

Officer Grade 5, Shondana came up to the table with a sharp knife. She slit the bag open near the center. She pulled two seeds out and quickly dissected them with the knife. She placed some of the pieces under a microscope and looked them over. She looked up from the microscope. "Good seed. Five cases...but not six."

Eestya wanted to spit. "You said the seed was good!"

"Good, not perfect."

Eestya closed her eyes and clenched her teeth. "All right, five cases."

The bartering continued. The Algothons departed with twenty-seven cases of *Tuzine* and a list of seeds that were acceptable and those that were not acceptable.

Sarskatama looked at the list. "Kwatha, *Kushkani* Melons, *Shoovaline* Melons, *Axcom* grain, *Mazikoti* grain, *Temvist* grain, *Bobon* beans, *Telikyte* tubers, and *Makiki* fruit…all good. The rest of them were turned down…completely?"

"Because none of them can possibly grow this far north," said Eestya dejectedly. "Plus, two of them are grown ONLY to make liquor. We should have thought of that, before we wasted our time dragging the wretched things here."

"Are there others…back at home that we could bring… next time?"

"There definitely are more. Before I waste my time with any of those, I want some botanist to give us some assurance on what will and will not grow, this far north."

Yamananee looked at the bags of seeds. "Sir, we did get a good variety of seeds."

Holla sighed. "We got nine, but I wish we had obtained them from another source. Those people will be back with more."

"FRESH kwatha? I think I can suffer through that one."

Holla snickered. "You're right!"

Holla Jumped back to the top of the city wall. She looked down at what the doctors, and a few other people who had actually been farmers, had been doing. They were going to Beasties and Forest dimensions and bringing back rather large amounts of top soil, mulch and fertilizer. This was being liberally distributed around the city, while the radioactive rubble was being dumped in Stink dimension.

Some of the crops were already starting to sprout from the rich soil that was being brought in. They found that before they could really grow a crop, of any kind, they had to remove all of the rubble first. The plants that were on the edge, near a radioactive area that had not been cleared yet, would not grow very large or just wither after coming up out of the soil.

The intelligence from Algothon had stated that the residual radiation would linger for at least seventy-five years. So far it had only been fifty-three. Twenty-two more years to go before they could call the area totally clean, however, they still had to survive.

The four Prominent Investigators were reading the report from Eestya.

Hashasee looked up. "Yes, that's very embarrassing. We should've checked on…certain geographical idiosyncrasies of certain plants before we…wasted that much time on them." She chuckled. "Who would've known that a plant can be picky?"

"A botanist," said Tun flatly.

Beeshree frowned at a certain part of the report. "What's this about Chief Investigator, Prok? You're saying that he couldn't keep his pants on?"

Eestya let out a disgusted growl. "The only reason he kept his pants on…on the way there - he did have *Byleeshium* and *Fellstug*. He did a private little barter…*somehow*…and obtained a bottle of *Tuzine* for himself. Once he was cured, he wouldn't leave Sarskatama and Shiganeea alone. He also tried a few things with some of the other female passengers on the ship." She took several loud, long, controlled breaths. "I don't want him on the next expedition!"

Hashasee gave Eestya a devious grin. "He *will* be on the next expedition. He will, however, not be a Chief Investigator. On the next trip, he will be, either a Senior or a Second Investigator. Maybe *that* will make him get rid of some of that promiscuity."

Eestya was ready to make a loud protest.

Hashasee stood up and gave Eestya a stern look. "We need to keep that team together! You know the way, you know each other…and the Owlams have seen you." She sat back down. "I will grant all of the High and Chief Investigators the authority to degrade Prok's rank even further down…if he pulls any more stunts."

"He still outranks Shiganeea," said Eestya angrily.

Hashasee shook her head. "Not if he keeps bothering her...or any of the other women in the expedition." She leaned forward. "Is there anything else?"

Eestya shook her head.

"Dismissed." After Eestya had departed, Hashasee looked at the other Prominents. "We *really* need to talk to a botanist... find out what grows where."

"I'll take care of that," said Beeshree.

Hashasee stormed over to Beeshree. "What do you mean... that botanist...is TOO busy to talk to ME...NOW?"

Beeshree was backing away with her hands up. "She's busy...on a project...that *you* assigned...to our scientists."

Hashasee stopped moving and was taken totally aback. "Uh...my project...uh...WHAT?"

Beeshree huffed. "You're the one who gave them a bottle of the *Tuzine* and told them to chemically break it down to figure out the ingredients."

Hashasee stomped her right foot. "The CHEMISTS! I didn't assign it to the BOTANISTS!"

Beeshree leaned forward and spoke very deliberately. "The chemists found that *all* parts of the pills were primarily chlorophyll. Once they established that, they needed the botanists, in order to determine which plants are in the ingredients. They found virtually no chemicals, just plant matter. So, yes, our top botanists are involved in YOUR project."

Hashasee stood there with a blank look on her face. "Plant matter. This whole time, we thought…chemicals. It turns out as…plant matter."

Beeshree smiled. "Yes."

Hashasee went to her chair and flopped down in it. She sat there pondering. She looked around and sniffed. She licked her lips and looked up. "Okay," she said quietly. "We'll…go to her… and see if she can take some time out…from her tests…see if we can get some other answers about what we can trade for."

Kladoothik shook his head. "Is it really that necessary?"

Hashasee hung her head. "We had that team DRAG twenty-three HEAVY bags of seeds…that turned out to be absolutely useless. They only had nine bags of seeds that could be traded. We got twenty-seven cases of *Tuzine*. The doctors, here in Algothon, dispensed all 324 bottles of the drug IN ONE DAY! It was a very expensive operation. If we can get there, with grains and fruits and melons and beans and…whatever else the Owlams want…we get more *Tuzine* with less wasted dead weight of grains that they don't want or can't use."

Kladoothik nodded. "Makes sense."

Tun stood up. "I'll see if we can make an appointment with her. See if we can interrupt her without fouling the process."

Hashasee nodded. "Thank you."

Beeshree scoffed. "We might need to talk to her, quickly.

It seems like every time something good is happening, certain key personnel just...disappear...without any trace of evidence of how...or why."

Tun scoffed. "Really! We have, on the books, over thirty-five thousand unexplained disappearances and...all of them are...prominent military, scientists..."

"...and upper ranking Investigators," said Hashasee angrily. "Get the appointment...quickly."

The top botanist, in the city of Algothon, Professor Nanzana, looked up from her microscope at Hashasee. "Now, is the *only* time that I have for you. This specific test turned out...a waste of time."

"Test for what?"

"Trying to isolate the specific ingredients in *Tuzine*." She picked up a book and made an annotation. "Test number 296... inconclusive."

Hashasee nearly gagged. "296 tests...and...you..."

"...haven't got one step closer than we were with test number 1. Whatever the ingredients are, they're all plant...and the mix...or process is doing a wonderful job of disguising the prime ingredients."

Hashasee nodded. "Understood. What I'm here for now, we need to know what crops...grain, fruit, melon or vine...will grow in the area of Owlam. We need to take seeds there...and we can't waste any more effort on…seeds that will only grow…near the equator."

Nanzana's shoulders sagged. "*You*…bothered *me*…for *that*? Any one of my students or colleagues could've…uh… CAN…give you that information. It doesn't take an expert at my level to find that information." She shook her head and snickered. "As it turns out, though, I do have a list handy. When we found out that the entire pill is plant matter, we made a list of all of the plants that are common to that area." She opened a binder and pulled out a list. "Make yourself a copy of that and go from there."

"I also needed to find out how you're doing…with the *Tuzine*."

Nanzana pointed to the microscope. "Nowhere. Other than the fact that…all the ingredients are…vegetable…not chemical… we're still stuck at square one."

"Okay, thank you. Keep working."

"I will."

Hashasee departed.

Ota called out to Holla. "Supreme Officer, Holla, this is Officer Leader, Ota. Can you hear me?"

Holla responded. "Must you always call me when I'm in the bathtub?"

"We all have to go through that ritual. As often as we're all in the bathtub…it happens to me as well."

"Yeah, yeah, yeah. What'd you need?"

"The Algothons have isolated the ingredients in Tuzine to plant···only! They're trying to break it down··· as to which plants now. Should we···butt in on the tests and foul them?"

Holla sighed as she wiped the back of her neck. "I'll get with the doctors and get back with you."

"Thank you, Sir."

Doctor Kolokoko laughed. She finally regained her composure and wiped tears from her eyes. "Supreme Officer, there's nothing to worry about…yet. According to our archives, which we have very carefully hidden in Spy dimension, it took 847 tries before the original Owlam scientists came up with the perfect formula for *Tuzine*. Also, according to the archives, they had most of the formula done, by the time they got to test number 153. All they had to do was make very slight alterations until they got what we have today. If what you say is true, they have almost 300 tests accomplished and are still baffled. I wouldn't worry. If they're able to isolate the *Shoonshook* and the *Idimberry* as two of the prime ingredients…then we *might* start worrying."

"Might?"

"The *part* of the *Shoonshook* is one of the best kept secrets of the ingredients. In most cases, when you use a plant, you use the leaves." She chuckled. "If I find that you've swallowed some toxin and I need to force you regurgitate, I'd grind up the leaves of the *Shoonshook* and make you eat that. If I want to cure a bacteriological infection, I don't use the leaves, I use the *deep* roots."

"What do you mean...deep?"

"I can't explain why, but, with *Shoonshook*, the leaves, the stalk and the shallow part of the roots are worthless in making *Tuzine*. We have to dig down, past a full taja in order to get the good root that we need. Anything less than digging down that far...no good."

"So, we keep that part a secret."

"That and the *Idimberry*."

"What's so special about that?"

"With the *Idimberry*, we use only the outer peeling of the berries. We have to make sure that we clean all of the inner flesh of the berry off, before we start the process. Any inner flesh - the whole batch is contaminated. These two parts of the process, make it incredibly difficult for anyone to copy the process. Maybe you should let Ota know this and then she won't panic...even if they do identify *Shoonshook* or *Idimberry*."

Late in the day. Doctor Kazkim called Holla. "Supreme Officer, Holla, this is Doctor Kazkim. Can you hear me?"

"Yes, Doctor, I can. What can I do for you?"

"I was just thinking. The Tuzine is not really safe here in Owlam, at this time. I was wondering if we could move the entire manufacturing process, along with all personnel doing it···to the gorge. This way, no one knows the formula or where it's being done. Do you think this is feasible?"

Holla sat there in joyful shock. She grabbed a kerchief, wiped her eyes and blew her nose. "Doctor, I think that that is a wonderful idea. Nowhere on the planet could it possibly be safer."

"I was also thinking that once we're there, we do the entire operation in either Spy or Observation. Again, this'll add to the security."

Holla giggled. "Doctor, anything that you can do that will ensure the safety of the formula···DO IT!" She leaned back in her chair smiling. No wonder the doctors had been so picky. There were some people who had grown the *Shoonshook* on top of their roofs in order for the plant to get sufficient sunlight. Those up there were in shallow soil and the only thing the doctors wanted from them was seed. The plants that were growing in the ground had the precious deep root. She chuckled about the *Idimberry*. Numerous times in her life she had found the berries growing wild. She had picked them and peeled that inedible outer skin off…and thrown it away. Now, she was finding out that the tough skin was a major part of the renewed wealth of Owlam.

Hashasee gave Eestya the list. "Here's some seeds that weren't taken to Owlam the last time. This time they will and maybe we'll get more of the drug…a *lot* more of the drug this time."

Eestya started looking it over. She shook her head in

disgust. "This list includes…ten…vegetables. We didn't take any vegetables with us the last time. Who's the dumb *Ninyit* that made that last list?"

Hashasee cleared her throat. "I am."

Eestya swallowed hard, flushed and chuckled nervously.

"That was just a preliminary…so to speak. We found out, from your first trip, that we should've consulted the botanists… first. Anyway you have your list."

"Not really, Prominent Investigator."

"What's the matter with it?"

"Are you familiar with gardening…or raising crops at all?"

"I am and have been an Investigator…all my adult life. I trained for it when I was young. What's the problem?"

"You have…uh…*Bembulla*…on the list."

"Yes, it's on the list, because the botanists say that it can grow in that climate."

"But…*Bembulla*…is a crop…that's very harsh. I mean, it does a great deal of damage to the ground."

"How can a vegetable harm the ground?"

"*Bembulla* completely saps the nutrients in the ground when you grow a crop there."

"So use more fertilizer!"

"It's not that simple. When you have a farm that raises *Bembulla*, they have to section off the land in four equal parts. This year, you raise a crop in section 1 only, leaving 2, 3 and 4 alone. The next year, you plant in section 2, leaving 1, 3 and 4 alone."

"Why can't you plant in all four at the same time?"

"Because *Bembulla* leaves nothing behind. It takes all of the nutrients and you have to leave the land fallow for three years in order for it to recover."

Hashasee sat there confused. "You...follow what...for three years?"

"Not *follow...fallow*! To leave the land fallow - it means that you don't plant anything there. You let the land rest. The next year, you can fertilize and plant your crop again. Unless it's *Bembulla*...and then you have to wait for three years."

"You're saying that you let the land...take a vacation?"

"You could say that. Or you could say that the land desperately needs a break to recuperate. With any crop, you have to stop every six or seven years. With *Bembulla*, you have to let the land recuperate for three years, because the *Bembulla* is so greedy in what it takes from the land. Haven't you noticed, at some of the restaurants here in the city? Only the finest restaurants serve *Bembulla*...and then...it's *very* expensive."

"Because...it saps the ground?"

"Because you can never grow a large crop of the stuff... every year."

Hashasee put her hands to her face. "Look, the more you tell me, the more confused I'm getting." She lowered her hands. "Just...go ahead and take the *Bembulla* to Owlam. Maybe...they like the stuff and...if it's...as expensive as you say...maybe it'll be worth a few more cases of *Tuzine*."

Eestya sighed. "Yes, Sir."

Eestya and Choya were sitting with the three Chief Investigators.

Eestya chuckled. "What do you think of the inventory?"

Sarskatama shook her head. "That's a lot of seed. I hope that this time...it's worth the trip."

Awndool huffed. "Yeah, the last time we went, we only got 324 bottles of that stuff...and the doctors used it all up in one day."

"That's why we've got a lot more bags of seeds and we made sure that these crops that can grow in the Owlam area," said Choya.

"Maybe someone has finally figured out how to deal with others peacefully, instead of blasting them into submission," said Jeedokt.

Awndool shook his head. "You're right. Our final solution...solved nothing. According to the history books, we've got more problems now, than we had before that mass launch."

"That must have been something," said Choya. "All those

bombs hitting all those cities…almost all at the same time."

Eestya scoffed. "I was five years old when it happened. I don't remember much about how the area outside Algothon looked…before the attack. I do remember it being much greener." She shook her head. "I've heard stories…all my life about what it looked like prior to the attack, but…I don't really remember it myself."

Choya chuckled. "It happened two years before I was born."

Awndool snickered. "You two are aging yourselves. I was born twelve years after the attack."

Sarskatama just stared off into space. "Fifty-three years ago and the world still hasn't recovered. According to those brilliant souls who made those devices…it's gonna be another twenty-two years before the residual radiation goes…neutral enough for plants to start growing again. I'll be sixty-two…at that time."

Eestya had her people place the twenty bags of kwatha on the tables. She observed the reaction of the Owlamites as they quickly examined the contents and all grinned as they offered seven cases of *Tuzine* for each huge bag of kwatha seeds.

Eestya leaned close to Choya. "I think we found the primary ingredient in the drug."

Choya smiled back and wiggled her eyebrows. "Let's check their reaction to the other stuff."

Eestya looked up and puckered her lips. "Do you think that we should hit them with the *Bembulla*...now?"

"Yeah, let's see their reaction to it."

None of the Owlamites had ever heard of it. Eestya had to explain all of the particulars of this vegetable. She was met with confused and skeptical glares.

Officer Leader, Mippa was the one taking care of number nine that day. She shrugged. "I don't know if...we could use a crop...that..." She looked up horrified. "You have to leave the land...fallow...for THREE years...after growing this stuff?"

"Yes," said Eestya, trying to hide her disappointment.

Mippa looked at her Team member, Pella. "Go find... Ahandi. Let's see what she says about this."

Ahandi allowed no bottles of *Tuzine* for one fistful of *Bembulla* seed. "We'll have to experiment with this...before we decide whether or not it's worth our time."

Choya snarled. "Definitely NOT part of the ingredients."

They brought all of the other seeds up for bartering. After it was over, the Algothons departed feeling a lot better about the trades that they had made.

Awndool looked at the list. "Last time, we came here with 32 different seeds and went back with 23 of them. This time we came with 28...and the only one they didn't go crazy over...was the *Bembulla*."

Sarskatama looked at their haul. "Five hundred and thirty-two cases with twelve bottles in each. Hopefully that amount will last a little longer."

"Hopefully those 'oh-so-brilliant' people back in Algothon have been able to figure out what the makeup of the *Tuzine* is and we won't have to keep coming back here...begging," said Jeedokt.

"If or when we come back," said Eestya. "We bring as much of that kwatha that we can get our hands on."

Holla gave the instructions. "I'm not sure what this stuff is, but...I think that maybe we should try it. I checked with some of the people in the farming section...and they said...why not?"

Officer Grade 4, Yonzhok, Team Leader of Team 195 looked at the seeds with a little disdain. "I don't like the idea of... raising something...if I don't even know what the finished product should be...or look like."

Holla was getting a little impatient. "I know and I understand. I don't know anything about this stuff either, but there is information on it in the Algothon archives. You have a civilian...who worked on a farm, before the firestorm. Team 196 has two farmers. Because of this, I'm assigning the growing of this...*Bembulla*...to your two Teams. We'll go ahead and make... try it...and see if it comes to something that we like."

One of the civilians from Team 196, Fromkolo shook his head. "I understand taking a chance at something...but...I've looked it up on those archives and according to the information that I've found so far...one crop is a four year risk. You raise one crop of this stuff and you have to let the ground go fallow...for *three* full years. That's not an experiment, that's a commitment."

The other civilian from Team 196 snickered. "I hope that you're willing to put up with the sacrifice...if it's a failure."

Holla nodded. "We took a chance with the Kalash. So far, so good. We took a chance with the Rahanan-Sar...same thing. We helped the T'Mor and...now we have a powerful alliance. This...*Bembulla*...it's a vegetable. If it fails...we don't have to make friends or honor a pact. If we don't like it, then we've lost the use of...a small parcel of land...for a few years...and we move on."

Neenela, the civilian from Team 195 looked at the seeds. "Come on, it's not like we're using up the same amount of land... like it takes for those long, long vines of the *Kushkani* Melons. One of those vines can go for over three kilotaja. This...just one section...at first. If we like it then we can go from there."

Officer Grade 7, Vovazee of Team 195 sat there with a sour look on her face. "I knew that having a farmer on our Team... sooner or later, we'd end up as sodbusters."

Yonzhok turned to the two Teams. "So far, all I've heard is talk. Let's start putting some action to it. We won't be able to start the planting of this stuff until the next Spring thaw. Let's go mark the area and follow all of the instructions for preparing the soil."

The two Teams departed.

Teelila scoffed. "Are you sure you want to devote land and

personnel to an experiment like that...at this time?"

Holla shrugged. "It's only two Teams...and a quarter of a section of land. We could do worse."

Teelila nodded. "It's in my area so, I'll keep an eye on it as well." She snickered. "Just out of curiosity."

Eestya, Choya, Awndool, Sarskatama and Jeedokt all sat in judgment.

Eestya glared at Prok. "You still haven't learned, have you? I don't know how many times you've been told, but you just...don't know how to listen. As a result of your last...silly promiscuous escapade, we find out that...once again you've been infected with *Byleeshium*. Now, we have to waste another bottle of *Tuzine* on you."

Choya leaned forward. "Not to mention the fact that you tried to infect Investigator Shiganeea as well."

"Yes," said Eestya. "So, as a result of this...stupidity and total irresponsibility, you are AGAIN demoted. You are now a Second Investigator. If you persist in this reckless lifestyle, we might just have to drop you all the way...if not altogether."

Sarskatama had a smug look on her face. "One thing that I'm glad to be able to tell you...the demotion is the unanimous decision of the five of us. No one had a second thought of demoting you."

Eestya looked at the other four people that sat in judgment

on Prok. She looked back up at him. "Normally, at this time, the guilty party is asked if they have something to say. I'm not going to do that, because I don't want to hear any more of your vain prattling. Dismissed!"

Prok spun on his heels and left the room. He wanted to leave without any fanfare or allowing them to give him any more rebukes. The bottle of *Tuzine* in his pocket started rattling and that noise seemed to mock him as well. He placed his hand over the bottle in an attempt at silencing the clinking sounds, however, he quickly realized that it was the contents and not the bottle that was making all that noise.

"Soon," said Prok through his teeth that were clenched so tight that it hurt. "Soon, they'll see. I'll have every one of them... kneeling at my feet. Then...I'll show that proud little tart... Shiganeea...she should've been...willing...all along. I'll treat her like...she treated me...and she'll...willingly come back for more. Hashasee, Tun, Kladoothik, Beeshree...and all the others... on down...I'll have all of them...bowing at my feet. They'll see. Soon, I'll execute my plan...and...they'll see!"

17

"*Kwatha*?" Hashasee looked at the list. Those stupid Owlams go crazy over this…*kwatha*?"

"Yes, Sir," said Eestya. "We get the most *Tuzine* for the *kwatha*. Those silly Owlams can't get enough of it."

Hashasee shook her head. "So, you think, from their reaction that this *kwatha* just might be a prime ingredient in the *Tuzine*?"

Choya snickered. "Either that or they're addicted to the nasty stuff."

Tun shrugged. "It's not so nasty. A good steaming hot mug of kwatha just before you go to bed…it's good."

Choya looked confused. "Hot? Steaming hot?"

Tun leaned back in his chair. "Haven't you ever tried it hot?"

Choya flushed. "No, I…was told that…it's best…cool."

Beeshree looked at Tun horrified. "You're serious? Hot?"

Tun looked around at the confused faces. "YES! You serve *kwatha* hot! If you let it cool down, it gets rather…or very disgusting."

Hashasee shrugged. "So, let's all get a...*steaming* hot... mug of this stuff and see if it IS better...hot." She shook her head. "Okay, now, these other things, did they have any reaction negative or positive to the other seed?"

Eestya wrinkled her nose. "They'd never heard of *Bembulla*."

Hashasee's jaw dropped.

"Don't be surprised," said Kladoothik. That tuber – *Kroshka,* for some reason, the only place in the world that it grows, or is eaten, is in the northern part of Neopaure. There are some edible plants that are very limited in their geographical range or location."

Hashasee shook her head. "Okay, that aside...did they have any strong reactions to any of the others?"

Eestya shrugged. "Nothing that stands out...like the *kwatha*."

Hashasee grunted in frustration. "Any of them could be a primary or secondary ingredient in the *Tuzine*."

Eestya shrugged.

"Get the list to our botanists and see what they can find out," said Beeshree.

After Choya departed, Hashasee looked around the room. "Has anyone heard *any* positive results about the satellite array over Owlam? Are we able to see anything there...at all?"

Tun shook his head. "Same old *fliggit*. Nothing but excuses. I've heard a few of them throwing temper tantrums at their computer screen. They feed all of the information in, doing everything they can to realign it and...all they get are 'error' messages or 'cannot find' messages."

"Another satellite," said Beeshree. "Can they move another one to that location over Owlam?"

"They tried that," said Tun. "For some strange reason the orbit suddenly decayed to a fatal level. The satellite burned up on reentry and if there was anything left of it, those chunks fell... somewhere...into the North Talanka Ocean."

Hashasee thought for a moment. "What about the city of Galsino? Can we get a satellite over that one...and see if anything is going on there?"

Kladoothik shook his head. "While our team was by Owlam doing their trading, two men went to Galsino. Nuthin'! There's no sign of any life there at all. The Galsinos left...and have NOT returned."

Beeshree sighed. "Speaking of return...when's the next trip to Owlam?"

"Next year," said Hashasee.

Beeshree frowned. "What about the seed?"

"We're going to double all of it...except for *kwatha*," said Tun. "That's going to be tripled."

Hashasee groaned. "Which means that we're going to

have to send more people as well. The load of seed is going to be tremendous and the return drugs…equally tremendous."

Ota leaned back. "Holla, this is Ota. Are you in your bathtub again?"

Holla responded. "How did you guess?"

"Just thought you'd like to know⋯the Algothons are going to try to double their take of Tuzine next year. Will we be able to handle it?"

Holla chuckled. "Easily! The doctors are putting out so much of the stuff, we're having to use some of the unassigned units at the gorge in order to store it."

Ota sat there nodding. "Thank you."

The next day, the Prominents were having another meeting.

Hashasee gave Tun a dirty look. "I see what you mean… about the *kwatha* being better…when it's hot. It's MUCH better."

Kladoothik looked off to the side. "That being the case, it seems that our thinking on *kwatha* being the primary ingredient in *Tuzine*, was horribly premature. It may not be part of it at all. It was just a case of those Owlams knowing that *kwatha* is better hot."

Beeshree scowled. "One thing I'll tell you about hot *kwatha*…it'll *absolutely* keep you regular. I've never been reamed out like that by anything else. I had a mug of that…*stuff*…and spent most of the night on the toilet."

The Staff sat in the conference room.

"Ten years of this trading…is getting boring," said Teelila. "If we gathered our own seed from the crops we raise, we wouldn't have to trade for seed."

"Then we wouldn't have everyone in the world coming to our home, begging for *Tuzine*," said Wilfadge.

Teelila grunted. "You're right."

Dwalooa wrinkled her nose. "Are the Algothons still trying to palm off that…*booboola* or *bumbumla*…or whatever that rancid thing is called"

"No," said Holla as she chuckled. "We got the message across to them that no one here in Owlam likes that…*thing*." She giggled a little harder. "One thing though, they come up with excellent seed for growing *kwatha*. I don't know if we ever had any that good from our seed."

Eestya sat there glaring at Prok. "I'm getting ready to retire. You don't know how happy I am that the last act, before my retirement, is to demote you…*again*! You are now busted down to Investigator Trainee. You're now the lowest ranking Investigator in all of Algothon. You outrank no one! Keep going the way that you are and the next class of Trainees that come out of the Academy will be ranked ahead of you…as well. Again, at this time, I'm supposed to ask you if you have anything to say. Again, I'm not going to ask you that, because I can't think of one thing that you could say that I want to, or care to hear. Investigator

Trainee…Prok…DISMISSED!"

Prok walked away ready to kill…something…anything. He started muttering to himself through his teeth. "As soon as all of the small details are worked out…I *will* order the strike. Those *Hongoths* have no idea who they're fooling around with."

Officer, Brosk shook his head as he followed Prok (in Spy). "Who're you working with? I've seen you doing some communications…I just don't know…who with. What is this… master plan? I wish that you'd give…something away…so I know…what to do. You're *so* irritating in these secret…*things*… that you're doing."

Hashasee left the funeral of Prominent Investigator Tun. She walked over to the new Prominent Investigator Metchkit. "Are you sure that the autopsy has been doubly confirmed?"

"Yes, Sir, I'm sure," said Metchkit. "He died from a cerebral hemorrhage that could *not* have been caused by any outside source."

She nodded. "Welcome to the level of Prominent. And in the future, remember, we don't 'Sir' each other."

He smiled. "That'll be a nice change."

"We have to get you settled in on the top floor. We'll have a meeting with Kladoothik and Beeshree as soon as possible." Hashasee looked back at the funeral pyre. "It's upsetting to lose a good Investigator like that. The main difference here, I at least know what killed *him*…unlike some 35,000 odd disappearances."

She blew her breath out. "There's not much information to update you on. We've been keeping all of the High Investigators fully briefed on everything. The only difference now…you have more authority and power to act on things."

"Again, that's a nice change. I wish that I had obtained the job in a different manner, but, that's part of life."

"Let's get back to Headquarters and see if any new information has come to light."

"I heard that Eestya retired a few days ago. Who's going to replace her on the *Tuzine* expeditions?"

"She's requested Jajoya."

Metchkit smiled. "I know her. She's a good choice…for any job."

"Do you think that she'll keep that *Fonsosk* Prok in line?"

He laughed. "She'll keep him on a short leash and pound him into dust if he tries anything with her." He scoffed. "Why do we keep him in the service?"

Hashasee stopped. She closed her eyes and sighed. "We think that he's up to something. So far, we can't figure out what. We keep him in the service in order to keep an eye on him. If we can figure out those secret communications of his, as to who he's communicating with…if it's a hostile group…we'll have him in jail…if not the gallows."

"Why don't you just ask him what's going on?"

"Because then he'd know that we've been watching him."

"It's pretty bad when one of your own is a key suspect in something covert and even the top echelon doesn't know what." He frowned. "Have you tried that mind control drug on him?"

"We haven't had a good batch of that stuff for some time. It doesn't seem to be as effective as before."

"Oh."

"He's been doing something, it seems for a while. He started it and hasn't had a face-to-face meeting with his...buddies...for quite a while. He's got something cooking and we're still baffled as to how he did it without us knowing about it."

"So he started something with someone else and has been operating covertly ever since."

Hashasee simply nodded.

Hadathoo snarled. "So those *Bimyocks* in Algothon are just as much in the dark as we are...about this...Prok?"

Teelila sighed sadly. "None of our people started watching him, until it was too late. All of his setup has been done and he's just doing some fine tuning on whatever his plot is. He seems to be certain that it'll shoot him straight to the top. Either the Investigators or maybe even the absolute autocratic ruler of Algothon altogether."

Dwalooa frowned. "Are we sure that it's not just some kind of silly delusional thing?"

Holla shook her head. "*Someone* is responding to his

covert communications. If it were just a delusion, we wouldn't hear anyone responding to him."

Shyshee snarled. "Can't we…triangulate…on his communications?"

"They're always too short," said Wilfadge. "Quick little blurts…both to and from. No involved conversations. He keeps on talking about the final *little changes* so that all areas are covered and nothing goes wrong. Not to mention the fact that this has been going on for several years."

Shyshee shook her head. "And those *Doovofts* are allowing him to…get away with it?"

Ahandi looked angry. "They're just as mystified as we are…and they're trying to figure it out as well."

"SO irritating," said Holla.

Wilfadge shrugged. "They've been watching him longer than we have and they still haven't figured out what he's doing… or with whom."

Hoynama looked around the table. "When are they due back?"

"They usually show up the later part of Spring," said Ahandi. "That, of course, is when you get the best *kwatha* seed."

Holla grunted. "I hate to say it, but the stuff that they've come up with…is so superior to what we usually had."

Wilfadge snickered. "I think that it's more satisfying because they're coming to us…begging for *Tuzine*. That's what makes it taste better."

Everyone got a good laugh out of that statement.

Two more years went by. Algothon and Owlam alike still were looking at the renegade Prok, still not being able to figure out what he was doing or with whom. The communications indicated that someone was on the other end of his com-line, however, nothing that anyone did led to any clues as to who he was on the other end. If he was somehow dropping papers covertly for his unknown operatives, he was doing it in such a manner that no one had seen it…yet.

Dwalooa looked around the table. "I don't believe that those Algothons are as innocent as they put up. I think that they're purposely steering our attention to this…Prok. If you remember, we told the world that we could bypass the Sodle jamming systems with that made up word. I think that they're trying to see if we use it to find out who he's talking with, when in reality, it's just another Algothon on the other end of that conversation."

"If that's true," said Ahandi. "Then they're putting on a *very* good show. None of our spies have been able to get anything."

"He keeps on getting demoted, yet they keep him in the investigative services," said Shyshee. "Why would they keep him there, if they weren't in on his charade?"

Holla growled. "The speculation could drive you insane. I'm of a mind to send just about everyone to the gorge. Keep only the barest minimum of personnel here in Owlam until we figure out what that Prok is doing."

Chaza looked a little puzzled. "The minimum? With all of the crops that we're raising inside the walls - the minimum number of people is still a very large number."

"I'm painfully aware of that," said Holla. "We may have to have the farmers here on short trips, just to check on the condition of their specific field."

"We always have Spy dimension," said Teelila. "If that *Doovoft* pulls something…strange…we all go to Spy. I don't really see that much of a problem."

Holla sighed. "Meanwhile, we keep the production - all aspects of it - at the gorge. No one lets anyone else know where the manufacturing is going on."

Hoynama looked at all of the other people. "Has he ever given any sort of time table, as to when…SOMETHING is going to happen?"

Wilfadge shook his head. "He's only said that once all of the small details are figured out, then IT will happen."

"I still think it's a ruse," said Shyshee.

Holla shook her head. "Until something happens, we keep selling *Tuzine*…and keep making everyone come to us. As Shyshee says, it could be just a ruse. We keep a close watch on him…and continue…the standard operating procedures."

Hadathoo bit his lip. "How many are currently keeping eyes on him?"

Holla sighed. "Team 6863 has been assigned the full time job of watching every move of this Prok! He never gets one single moment of privacy, anywhere."

The next year nothing new happened. The Algothon contingency showed up with another massive load of *kwatha* and several other crops that could be grown in Owlam. The Owlamites no longer had to steal any of their food from Algothon or any others. The crops were growing in abundance inside the great wall of the city of Owlam.

In Algothon, they did not realize that all of their emergency rations were completely gone from the lower sections of their underground vaults. They had not done any inspection or inventory in quite a while. They were very sure that no enemy could possibly get to the lower levels...in spite of the fact that they were missing their archives...they could not picture anyone getting to the lower levels for the food.

In the forty-sixth year of the tenure of Holla as "*The Voice of Power*", the Algothon contingency returned for another round of trading for the precious *Tuzine*. Prok was with them as usual.

Inside the walls of Owlam, in Home dimension, Bonarain and Kiyalee were slowly walking through the rows of the fresh growing *kwatha* plants. They were looking for the ones that were ready to be picked. All of the big leaves were the ripe dark green. They were looking for the ones where the edges were turning red. These were the ones that would supply the most flavorful brew of hot *kwatha*.

In Spy dimension, Chyning and Soolchakan were walking through the field of *Shoonshook* plants. He was looking for his blue marker stick that he had placed, the last time that he had "watered" the plants. He knew that he should have obtained a longer stick, because now the plants were tall enough to hide the stick. He knew that the stick was somewhere in the eighth row of the plants. His bladder was about to burst and he knew that he was supposed to get these things watered "equally". It was very necessary to find the marker before he "watered" the next plant… or his pants.

Chyning was not particular which plant she did her business on. She had been told that she had a way of killing the plants by tending them, so the only thing that she was allowed to do was water them. *Shoonshook* plants were regarded as weeds and it was deemed impossible to kill weeds, so that was why she was here with them instead of the *kwatha*. These plants grew faster from the male urine, so she would stop and water which ever plant looked the smallest to her. She was wearing a loose fitting shift dress with no underwear. This way, she did not have to stop and remove anything in order perform her watering services. Just stand over the plant with her legs slightly spread and relieve herself with a satisfied smile on her face.

The line, that the Algothon group was in, finally got them to the table to do business. Officer Leader, Yoobyool, Team Leader of Team 79 looked up and sighed. He did not want to be the one to handle the Algothons, however, now he had no choice.

The Algothons started placing the big bags of *kwatha* on the table. While Yoobyool carefully noted the weight of each bag, his Team member, Officer Grade 6, Zoyanima was cutting each one open to make sure that the entire bag was absolutely *kwatha* and not filled with some useless weed leaves.

The other two members of Team 79, Raztasa and Oypaypa would take the damaged bag, place it inside a box and take it to one of the many wagons that were there to hold all of the incoming seed bags.

Once the counting and weighing of all the *kwatha* bags was done, Raztasa went to a small warehouse building behind all of the trade stations and bring out all of the cases of *Tuzine* that were being used in that specific trade.

What none of the non-Owlamites knew was that there was nothing in this warehouse. As soon as, whoever was picking up the drug, entered the warehouse, they would establish a mental communication with someone in the manufacturing plant in the gorge. They would inform them of the number of cases that were to be Jumped to the warehouse and wait until they were all there. Once that was done, they would wheel the cases out to the customer. There was never any supply of the drug kept in the warehouse, just in case of, who knows what.

Prok was standing off to the side, with the *Tuzine* that had been traded for the *kwatha*. The Algothons were now putting the other types of trade seed up for bid. Prok simply smiled as he put a communicator up to his mouth. "Now," he said quietly. He looked up and off to the east. He just stood there smiling. 'The time has come,' he thought. 'Now, I will be the one passing out the demotions.'

Officer Grade 6, Brosk called in. "Officer, Nishka, that Algothon that I've been watching, he just called in a start signal. I don't know what's going to happen yet, but, something might happen very soon."

"Thank you for that information, Brosk. Keep your eyes open."

"Yes, Sir."

There were currently fifteen stations where the bartering was taking place. It gave the Owlamites a good feeling of power, making all of their customers wait in long lines for the precious drug. Sometimes they would see a contingency from the same city, in five or more lines. The secret little mental messages that went back and forth between the Owlamites would frustrate any plan of these people to say that "someone else from their city got a better deal for this seed than you gave us".

Most people coming in for trades usually tried to go to stations where it was a female doing the bartering. Many of them figured that they could get a better deal from a female than a male. Currently there were only four of the stations where a male was the main trader for Owlam. Holla had wanted to make all of them female, so that the beggars would think that they were getting the best deal, however, there were some races that would only come to the tables where the men were. People who were very sexually bigoted, like the Galsino, so she still had to put a few men on the stations. She had them positioned so that nothing appeared to be symmetrical. The four men were at stations two, three, eight and ten.

Everything was going along with the usual monotony of salutations, inventorying, weighing, bartering and each one putting their new wares in their vehicles and then bows, handshakes and farewell until next time.

At station number five, Officer Leader, Onga signaled Officer Grade 5, Rafagol to take some bags of *Milbenberry* seeds back to the wagon. He picked up one of the boxes that held the cut bag, hefted it up to his left shoulder and just happened to look up as he was getting ready to turn around. He froze in shock and dropped the box of seed. Onga and the customer were ready to both start admonishments when they noticed his horrified stare and where he was looking. They looked up to see what had him transfixed.

Coming in from the east they saw thousands of the Teltermak kites being flown in. To most of the non-Owlamite customers, these kites were something completely new. To the Owlamites, they were aware of what it meant and they also noted that these kites seemed much larger than what the Teltermak had used before.

"I think it's starting," said Brosk mentally.

Officer Leader, Afa-Ee, at station eleven, was currently the ranking individual at the trading area. When she saw the kites, she called out mentally: "All Owlamite personnel, the Teltermak are back. They're coming in on their kites from the east.

They're coming in, in great numbers. All personnel, to your battle stations!"

Holla heard the call, dropped her washrag, jumped out of the bathtub and headed for her weapon (and some clothing). "All Owlamites, this is Supreme Officer, Holla. We're under attack again. Get to your weapons and this time, let's finish off these miserable Teltermak – permanently!"

A new call came in: "Officer, Holla, this is Officer Leader, Ota. I'm in Algothon and there's an attack going on here as well. Those kites···they just suddenly appeared overhead···and···it is NOT the Teltermak! I don't know who these people are···but they are NOT Teltermak···and they seem to···uh···they can communicate telepathically! They're attacking the Algothon people mentally and I don't exactly know what's going on."

Holla sat there in shock for a moment. "Are you sure they're not Teltermak?"

"They are NOT Teltermak···unless those nasty Teltermak have changed radically since the last time that we saw them. These people···they're about the same height we are. They have the same color skin···they're all··· bald···even the women. They're bald except for a partial ring of thin hair that goes around the back of their head from ear to ear. They're very thin and···they have a TAIL! It looks···like···from the way they're attacking some of the Algothon military, that there's a poisonous stinger on the end of their tail. They···strike with that tail with what appears to be some very deadly results. No, Sir! I don't think for one heartbeat that these people are Teltermak." Ota continued watching. Some of the Algothons were able to shoot these invaders. It appeared that the invaders were easily killed by bullets or power weapons. The problem for the Algothons was that many of them would suddenly stop what they were doing and just stand there in a stupor. An invader would walk up with an evil grin and that whip-like tail would rapidly come around one side or the other, stab the Algothon and the victim would fall to the ground, convulse for a short time…then die.

Back at the trading center, Prok stood there with a grin watching all of the kites coming in. He stripped his shirt off and proudly displayed a rather gaudy vest that was striped with neon colors of orange and green. He held his arms out and slowly turned around several times, displaying this vest to all with great zeal.

High Investigator, Jajoya looked at Prok, completely baffled. "What're you doing, Trainee, Prok? Get your weapon out and get ready…for who knows what!"

Prok chuckled. He pulled his gun out, aimed it at Jajoya and fired, hitting her in the chest. "Shut up, slave! I'll tell you and everyone else when they're allowed to talk in my presence!"

There were numerous invaders that were now landing their kites near the bartering area. They were wearing the exact same showy vest that Prok was so proudly displaying. Several of them smiled and saluted him. Investigator Probik noticed Prok's familiarity with the invaders. He aimed his gun at Prok and suddenly froze, standing there slack-jawed. Prok noticed Probik, aimed his gun and put a bullet through the forehead of Probik. Probik slumped down dead.

Many of the people who were there for trading were now cowering behind their bags of seed, or anywhere they could come up with any form of cover. They were all now witnessing the strange attack by these unknown invaders. Those that were not hiding their eyes, at least.

One of the invaders walked up to Prok.

Prok smiled at him. "I can never remember those ranks of yours, my friend, Susugam."

He smiled. "I am *Bone Breaker*, Susugam. That's equivalent to what you call a Commander."

Prok nodded. "Yes, of course. Anyway, I've been watching these silly Owlams. They keep the drug stored in that small warehouse over there. As soon as your people showed themselves, they all ran to the warehouse. They're all cowering inside there. Have fun with them."

Susugam smiled. He closed his eyes and placed his index fingers against his temples. Several of the other Cacktash smiled and started slowly walking towards the warehouse with weapons at the ready.

A few of them holstered their weapons and placed their index fingers against their temples. Suddenly all of the Cacktash that were headed for the warehouse all stopped simultaneously.

One of them looked back at Susugam. "Sir, I can't find anyone in that warehouse."

Susugam lost his grin and scowled. He headed for the warehouse, doing the fingers-to-temples ritual. He slowed his pace as he closed his eyes and clenched his teeth. He dropped his arms and opened his eyes. "Throat Cutter, Shawshakt! Get someone in there and check it out!"

Shawshakt signaled two of the others to enter the warehouse.

A man and a woman both scowled at Shawshakt and carefully went to the door of the warehouse. Both of them had their weapons out and one hand to their foreheads as they got closer. They looked at each other with nasty looking frowns. The woman reached out and yanked the door open. The male ran in. He came out a few moments later, showing none of the caution that he had used going in.

Shawshakt frowned. "Report!"

The man scoffed. "Sir, Third Reaper, Woftonk reporting! Nothing in there but some tire prints from hand carts and a few footprints. Other than that…NOTHING!"

The woman was looking inside. She turned around. "Sir, Second Worker, Blonbelsa confirms…nothing."

Prok was standing there in shock. "Susugam, my friend…I swear to you, they always went in there to get the product…and they…when you showed up…they all…ran in there." He scowled. "Go back in there and look for a TUNNEL!"

Susugam turned to the personnel that were surrounding the warehouse. A simple nod of his head and all of them went in through any entrance they could find. He turned to Prok. "You'd better not be deceiving me!"

Prok scoffed. "How could I possibly deceive you?"

Susugam scowled.

"If you don't believe me, why don't you check with some of these other…*customers*…that you see cowering around here?"

Susugam grinned. He signaled other personnel with a nod and the other Cacktash started brutalizing all of the customers in the area. If a customer had already finished trading and had some cases of *Tuzine*, if they attempted to keep their drugs, they were either shot or stabbed with that whip-like tail. Each one that was stabbed, fell to the ground and convulsed for several moments… and then they were absolutely still. The Cacktash took their stolen loot and placed the small cases inside special pouches that were hooked to their kites.

A Cacktash woman walked up to Susugam. "Sir, Throat Cutter, Nyshlest reports. All of the other…*traders*…in the area report the same thing. All of the Owlams, they ran into that warehouse. There has to be a tunnel in there…somewhere."

Susugam snarled. He turned back to Prok. "We are the Cacktash! We do NOT go crawling underground like some cowardly hiding rodent. When we find the tunnel you pick someone to do the underground crawling."

Several other Cacktash personnel started congregating around Prok and the other Algothons (who were looking at what was unfolding in front of them with total horror and anger).

Prok smiled. "I think that the underground *rodent* crawling would best be done by the slaves: Awndool and Jeedokt.

Awndool stood up. "That's HIGH INVESTIGATOR, Awndool, you impertinent traitor!"

Susugam turned towards Awndool and clenched his eyes shut. Awndool screamed in agony, grabbed his head with both hands and fell to his knees moaning in pain.

Susugam scoffed. "When the Algothon King…Prok gives a command, you slaves OBEY! Any questions?"

"He's not a king," snarled Choya. Then she grabbed the sides of her head and was screaming in pain as Susugam stared at her.

Prok snickered. "Looks like they're going to need a little disciplining. They still don't realize who the masters are."

Susugam signaled to several other Cacktash. "Get over here and start the mental processes on all of these Algothon slaves."

A group of Cacktash walked up to the Algothon contingency and within moments, all of the Algothons were writhing on the ground in agony as the Cacktash stood in a circle around them, with fingers to their temples.

Prok pointed at Sarskatama and Shiganeea. "Do the… *special*…on them. They belong to me!"

Susugam chuckled. "We have a *special* gift for you. It's for any of your *special* toys." He looked around. "Second Reaper, Borefoosk! Bring out that gray box."

A Cacktash man ran back to his kite. He pulled a gray

box, that was about the same size as the *Tuzine* cartons, out of the cargo pouch and ran up to Prok with the box. "Here, Sir, these were designed for your pleasure. Use them as you will, for your pleasure."

Prok frowned as he accepted the box. "Thank you, Second Reaper." He walked over to the bartering tables to examine the contents. He opened the box and pulled an instruction pamphlet out. He laughed with delight as he read the instructions.

One of the other Cacktash shouted. "I found…something! I found…a…I think…one of the Owlams!" He was standing near the warehouse with his eyes closed. He was turning randomly, with his arms out as if he were trying to touch something. "Yes I found…an Owlam! She…she's trying to hide…a cloaking…uh… invisibility, something strange…I…need help controlling her!"

Two other Cacktash came up close to him. All three of them were now turning their heads with their eyes shut. They each made a few strange noises from their throats as they concentrated on the task. Then Officer Leader, Afa-Ee appeared. She was on her knees, holding her head and screaming in pain.

Susugam stood there grinning. "They *can* become invisible. That's something we definitely want." He looked at Prok triumphantly. "I can hardly wait to be able to do that!"

Afa-Ee suddenly stood up screaming with a wild look in her eyes. She grabbed two of the Cacktash that were torturing her and all three of them disappeared.

The third Cacktash slumped to the ground as if he had been sucker-punched. He looked up in surprise. "She…she's…GONE!

I can't find her! I can't find…Forgitch…or Polwhanggon! She went somewhere…she took them…with her and I can't find…*any* of them!"

"That's impossible!" screamed Susugam. "There's no way! She can't hide them…or herself. You had her thoughts… and lost them? The only way that can happen is…" He suddenly stopped in shock. "…if they're…dead," he whispered. "How… could she…?" He looked at Prok. "Did you know…of this?"

Prok shook his head. "That mental stuff? I can't do it. If something happened, that's telepathic…I don't know anything. You're going to have to be the ones who figure that out. I can't do everything for you."

Officer Grade 5, Entizi (a member of Afa-Ee's Team) suddenly appeared. She had a look of anguish on her face and tears in her eyes. She grabbed the third Cacktash that had been torturing Afa-Ee. The Cacktash disappeared, then so did Entizi.

Susugam was horrified. "They're…stealing my people! Find them! Find them and…stop this nonsense! People, get your minds working and find these Owlams and let's get them under our control!"

The other two members of Team 27 appeared. Officer Grade 4, Norsh and Officer Grade 6, Anofa. Both of them grabbed two Cacktash each. All four of the invaders disappeared and then so did Norsh and Anofa.

Susugam screamed. He pulled out his weapon. He was not sure what he was going to do with it, however, he wanted to kill someone…preferably someone Owlamite.

Officer Leader, Feentama, of Team 80 appeared. She was, however, somewhat transparent. She grabbed two of the Cacktash. Her arms and the upper half of the bodies of the Cacktash disappeared. Susugam aimed his pulse pistol at her and fired at Feentama. The beam went straight through her. She smiled. He fired at her several times as he advanced toward her. The two Cacktash reappeared whole again, however, as soon as she let go of them, they were both down on their hands and knees, vomiting. Feentama smiled again and disappeared.

Several other Cacktash came running up to Susugam. They reported that the strange occurrence that had happened with Afa-Ee, was happening all over the area. Each time, they had lost some Cacktash as well. The disappearances were piling up and no one could figure out what was going on. Susugam wanted to get some answers from Prok, however, Prok could do nothing but shrug, since he was not a telepath and had no idea what or how the Owlamites were doing…what they were doing.

Bonarain looked up from the field when she heard some of the panic that was going on. She saw the giant kites flying overhead, coming over the wall and descending inside the city. She immediately went to Spy dimension. She saw Kiyalee do the same thing.

Five of the kites went into the fields that were west of the *kwatha* field that 7016 was responsible for. Team 3503 was growing *Kushkani* melons in another field. For some reason, none of the Team members of 3503 were paying attention to anything and when the Cacktash swooped down on them, all four were felled by gunfire before they knew what was going on.

Bonarain stared in horror as she saw the Cacktash start butchering the bodies of Team 3503. She was not even sure that the four of them were dead yet, however, that did not stop the invaders from immediately starting the horrid task of harvesting organs.

A kite landed frighteningly close to Bonarain, she instantaneously started running towards two of the standing buildings that were in this area. She looked back and saw that one of the Cacktash was chasing her and seemed to be looking at her as if he could see her. Three other kites landed in the field and those Cacktash followed the original one. She kept running as hard as she could. She felt as if there was something invading her mind, however, she was too intent on getting to the buildings to think about it.

Five more kites landed in the field just north of the *kwatha* field. Team 6216 was growing *Voskeel* in that field. Team 6216 got the same treatment that Team 3503 had received. Now Bonarain was nearly in a state of total panic, just running because she could not think of anything better to do at the time.

The Cacktash man caught up with Bonarain and was matching her stride for stride as she ran. He was concentrating on invading and controlling her mind. He was having a difficult time with it because she had adrenalin pumping through her system and was not fully listening to his commands. All she could do was run.

Through his commands, Bonarain was receiving some

kind of imagery that she could not make sense of. Of course, at this time, she was not trying to concentrate on anything at all... just run.

She was in Spy dimension and the buildings were in Home dimension. She reached the first building and ran through the wall. The pesky commands that were coming from the Cacktash man instantly stopped and she fell to the floor with her chest heaving as she panted from the running. Her heart felt as if it were going to pound its way out of her chest. She rolled over on her back and looked back the way she had come from and it suddenly dawned on her. She had run through the wall in Spy - The Cacktash was in Home, as was the building. She slowly got up and walked back to the wall.

For some reason she could not hear Cacktash men outside...laughing. She slowly moved her face through the wall to see what was going on. The man who had been running with her had slammed, face first, into the wall as she went through it. He was now on the ground, on his back, with his knees up to his chest. He had a grimace of pain on his face and his hands were on his forehead, with blood oozing between his fingers. The other three Cacktash were laughing hysterically at the predicament of their fallen comrade.

A fifth Cacktash landed his kite near the building and started walking up to the scene. Bonarain saw his lips move, however, she could not hear him say anything. She could hear the three who were enjoying the spectacle...but not the newcomer.

One of the laughers stood up and pointed at Bonarain's

victim. She read his mind.

"That stupid *Moongfop* ran face first into the wall."

The newcomer stopped moving his lips and now Bonarain could hear him. "What kind of *Vongfop* reason did he have for that?"

One of the laughers gained a little control of himself. "He said that he was chasing some Owlam woman. He was mentally concentrating and running as fast as he could."

Another laugher shook his head. "He chased her right into the wall. He was running as fast as he could and...POW...the *Stumfop* hit the wall."

The injured man looked up at the newcomer. "I...saw her...mentally and...I was chasing her...and...somehow...her path...I had my eyes closed and...she led me into the wall."

The newcomer started laughing. "You were following an old trail, you *Woostfop*! It was someone who went into that building, where a door used to be, a long time ago."

She stood there mystified as to why the injured man had been able to find her mind in Spy dimension, however, none of them knew where she was now. She was even more puzzled by the fact that she could not see them moving their lips, however, she could hear them clearly. Yes, she could hear them clearly, in her mind. She was reading their minds. These people were capable of telepathy as well. They had a different talent though. They could read the minds of other peoples. She wondered how far it went. She started thinking of the imagery that was going through her mind as the Cacktash had been trying to control her. It had to be some kind of way to get into the mind of someone else…involuntarily. She carefully went through it…slowly and meticulously. It was some kind of way to read the minds of others - even if they were not capable of telepathy.

Another Cacktash landed her kite and walked up to the five that were next to the building. She was saying something and Bonarain could not hear her. Bonarain considered it and for some reason, after regaining control of her own mind, she had hopped into Observation dimension. She did not know why, however, she was there now. She took a deep breath and let it out. She hopped to Spy dimension. All five of the standing Cacktash stopped what they were doing and saying and all simultaneously turned and looked where she was standing. She hopped back to Observation. All five of them now looked confused.

All five of them put their index fingers up to their temples and closed their eyes.

The female Cacktash spoke up. "Someone, was there a moment ago, standing against the wall."

"I know," said one of the men. "I felt her too."

Another man shook his head. "How could she…come and go…so quickly?"

Bonarain walked up to the nearest Cacktash man. She reached out, grabbed him and hopped him into Jahong's Death. The other Cacktash stopped what they were doing and looked around confused.

The female walked over to where the victim had been standing. "Where...did Plooguth go?"

"I don't know," said one of the men. "He was there...a moment ago."

Bonarain reached out and hopped another one into the Water dimension.

The female started looking around with fear on her face. "Where did Chichkotho go?"

Bonarain hopped the other two men into Jahong's Death. The female Cacktash was hopped there rather quickly as well. She walked over to the fallen Cacktash. He had tried to get up, however, the attempt was pointless. He had fallen back down and was now laying there breathing erratically. Bonarain simply raised her foot and stomped, as hard as she could, on his larynx. His breathing stopped rather quickly, after some gurgling sounds were heard.

Another Cacktash landed near Bonarain. This newcomer looked around confused. He saw all of the kites and was looking for the pilots. Bonarain momentarily hopped to Spy. The Cacktash turned his surprised gaze directly at her. She hopped back to Observation. He started walking towards her, mentally trying to find her. As soon as he got close enough, she hopped him into Jahong's Death.

She looked back at the building that had been her refuge. She Jumped to the top of the building. She started looking around at all of the fields that surrounded this building and was horrified as she saw numerous Cacktash as they were hacking numerous

Owlamites to pieces with some kind of crescent shaped knife.

She fell to her knees. "This is Officer Grade 6, Bonarain! I'm calling all Owlamites! Get out of Home or Spy dimensions. These Cacktash invaders can't read us in Observation dimension. Everybody go to Observation dimension⋯NOW! They can't read our minds in Observation dimension! Go to Observation⋯now!"

She stood up and looked out over the fields again. There were two Cacktash who were chopping up someone...in her *kwatha* field. She could not see who the victims were. She had no idea where Soolchakan, Kiyalee or Chyning were.

She slumped down, started crying and sending the same message over and over. "Everybody go to Observation dimension⋯now."